The Bootneck

Quentin Black

An Outlaw's Reprieve – A Connor Reed Novella – For **FREE**

Click here for Free E-Book

CONTENTS

DEDICATION

To Colin and Peggy Lewis

PROLOGUE

'Bootneck' is a term used for a British Royal Marine. The origin is believed to derive from Marines—in the days of old—cutting the top from a leather boot and wearing it around their necks to prevent sailors cutting their throats.

In modern times, the title 'Bootneck' is one of respect and endearment used within the Royal Marine Corps. It describes a Marine with a reputation of a high level of soldiering ability, combined with an adherence to its Ethos.

"There are Marines…and there are Bootnecks."

ACKNOWLEDGEMENTS

Thanks to Lee Barret, Dean Robertson, Jon Knowles, Jason Gardiner and Holly Mew for supporting myself and this project.

To Dave Kenyon for your beta reading.

To Jessica Delaney for your proofreading.

To Andy Screen for the cover design.

AUTHOR'S NOTE

Any specific terms and phrases have been highlighted in italics and can be found in the glossary.

1

He lay motionless on an insulated foam mat. He was invisible to the naked eye, within a hide on the edge of the wood. The crisp winter darkness had descended over the woodland and meadow before him. The midnight frost on the grass gave notice to the cold attempting to bite him through his layers of clothing. The butt of the sniper rifle nestled into the crease of his shoulder, with the barrel resting on the lip of a sandbag.

He had spent the night just seventy-two hours prior digging in and constructing the hide. The plastic bottle of urine and a securely tied bag of his human waste lay in the rear left corner. His rations and a can of petrol—an unfortunate necessity—were entrenched in a hole covered with a steel panel, in the rear right corner.

Per his laser range finder binoculars, he lay 189 metres away from the target house. His gaze concentrated on the entrance of the old English manor.

Part of the upper floors on the side of the house that he could see were made of a white stone wall, separated with chestnut oak. There was a huge extension built onto the side which he knew extended the dining hall and kitchen. It also housed a spare bedroom with an en-suite bathroom. This brought the bedroom total to five. The driveway resembled a small pub's gravel car-park. Around and beyond the house lay an expanse of open countryside enclosed by tall, winter sparse trees.

When he first set eyes on the abode, a feeling washed over him akin to seeing an old red telephone box in an English village—a sense of nostalgia of a time before he was alive.

The sniper was now in his mid-twenties, and a couple of inches shy of six feet. The dark blond hair was cut into a 'one back and sides', and a foreign sun had bleached the tips.

He looked down at the house from a thirty-degree angle—it was always an advantage to be on the high ground in any type of firefight. His sharpened senses assessed every noise and movement around him—as ancient men had, before they became civilised. Indeed, the hair growth, made his symmetrical features appear more feral than usual.

In the three days of reconnoitring the target from his observation post, he had identified four bodyguards working a rotation. They took turns to cover the night shift with the other three dividing the rest of the day.

Tonight, they were all present.

He ascertained by their well-fitting suits that three were not armed. Close protection advisors wore loose suits if armed, to help hide any tell-tale bulges of weapons or body-armour. Judging by the way the fourth bodyguard's suit swelled under the armpit, he was wearing a chest rig with a pistol.

The wind whipped the light rain into a curve, and it collected on the leaves of the trees surrounding the hide. The droplets fell from them percolating through the ghillie camouflage, and the poncho underneath that formed the roof of the hide. This resulted in an irregular but cold drip down the collar of his black Rab Neutrino jacket. His trapezius muscle contracted involuntarily with every drop.

"For fuck sake," he murmured, realising he had not checked the poncho lining thoroughly enough when packing it.

He had read that in the past, the Chinese would chain a detainee under an irregular cold drip, for however long it took, until the prisoner 'broke' and confessed. He could well believe in the effectiveness of the technique.

He could not afford to take his eyes off the house now. A simple Google search revealed that the politician would be soon leaving for a meeting.

A suited Stephen Hardcastle preened himself in the mirror of his room, using a comb to sweep his professionally dyed black hair to one side. He was thankful that it had receded only an inch or two from his youth. The collar of his suit had been loosened as to not over-emphasise his double chin. The rest of the suit did its best to hide the bulges of fat spread over his body, particularly the portly hips at which the trouser belt pinched.

Hardcastle tried not to let his obesity bother him; Winston Churchill and Napoleon were both big men, and like them, he felt his bulk added a sense of power to his presence.

He was about to meet with a consortium of investors. They needed his influence to push through a piece of profitable legislation. This bill would allow for the building of private housing, which would cut into the 'green zone' of the London Borough of Merton.

Hardcastle's backing came at a major fee as he would have to pull in a few favours. Expansion in this world was inevitable and he may as well be the one to benefit from it.

A smile danced on his lips as he thought of this payment—and the young East European girl who would be sharing his bed tonight, courtesy of a discreet contact.

A high-ranking Met police officer put him in touch with this 'provider' almost ten years ago.

This provider had never let the politician down with his taste.

The Right Honourable Stephen Hardcastle liked them young—too young to be deemed legal by the sovereign judicial system but acceptable in other parts of the world. If he had been born in Angola, he mused, the law would have accommodated his sexual tastes—most of them, at least. Even the authorities in Thailand and Cambodia would turn a blind eye.

Besides, if it was not him, then it would only be someone else taking pleasure from them. At least he did not hurt them as much as some did.

He had also indulged himself in many what he termed 'strays' in his fifty-three years, all of which had been deliciously unexpected and the allure too irresistible. Strays, although exciting, were dangerous, as there was no knowing if one would tell tales.

This provider had always ensured a sense of discretion which was an obvious necessity.

As the sniper looked over his optical sight and shifted a little to get some blood flow into his well-muscled physique, he thought of the 'interrogation' he would put Hardcastle through.

He felt a small wave of pleasure course through him. It was a pleasure comparable to the moment immediately before deciding to hit a bully.

This time, it was magnified tenfold. Acting purely of his own accord, he could be caught and sent to spend the rest of his life in prison. Still, he could not let this go. He would never forgive himself—*nor should I.*

The country house lay isolated two miles from its nearest neighbour. He had confidence that the sound of any weapon's report would not be an issue. He originally thought of ways to bypass the harming of the bodyguards.

However, after learning that they had protected this monster for three years, the desire left him. They must have been aware of Hardcastle's insidious nature he knew, besides, living witnesses would only complicate the issue.

Boredom gnawed at him, but he resisted the urge to switch on his phone; he had not looked at it since his arrival. In the far distance, he could see a road running along a hill that formed the backdrop to the house and valley floor. His eyes picked out the lone headlights of a car, and he smiled, indulging in his 'soldier's illusion'. The fantasy often occurred on sentry during cold, wet nights like these. The soldier sought comforting thoughts to distract himself from the damp boredom of his surroundings. On this occasion, the sniper imagined the occupant of this car was heading home to his stunning wife, who would hand him his slippers. She would serve him a sumptuous meal by a coal fire—then follow this with great sex.

Ordinarily, he would have swapped places with the driver in an instant. Many a Marine fantasised about resigning from the military—putting *his chit in*—at these times. It did not matter that these firefly-like headlights moved through the dead of night, and the driver was likely to be a nightshift worker—dog tired—about to creep into bed to avoid waking a nagging wife.

Hardcastle was in his wine cellar looking for the Moet & Chandon Dom Perignon Oenotheque Rose, and the Chateauneuf du-Pape. These bottles were to be gifts for the provider. It was these little personal touches that made all the difference.

He cast his mind back to the last stray he had indulged in a couple of months previous—she had been a cherubic looking, blonde eleven-year-old from West Yorkshire.

Hers was the last school in several he had visited in that uncouth area of the city. The media had been in tow for the first few he had visited but now were absent after having their fill. Hardcastle and the girl's path had crossed in the corridor as he left the toilet. She had passed him, squeezing her bleeding finger en route to the *'staff room for a plaster'* she had said. He had told her he had some in his car and directed her there. After a coded message to his head bodyguard standing by, he had followed her. Once they were both in the car, he put the plaster on himself.

He asked for a kiss.

After a moment, the girl leant to peck him on the cheek. The sound of the central locking being activated shook an expression of incomprehension onto her face.

He had enjoyed exploring her immensely, but he had had to restrain himself from going further at the sight of her tears.

Usually they just froze.

Her absence might have been noticed if she was away for much longer and the sight of a tear-stained face may have led a member of the school staff to ask questions. He told her that this was their secret and girls who told tales upset their families forever.

When confident she had got the message and her face was dry, he disengaged the central locking. Watching her walk back in an obvious daze, he had admonished himself with how reckless he had been.

Then again, it was fate that had put this delicious, unexpected opportunity in front of him; it was not as if he had actively sought it out.

That had been nearly two months ago.

Now he climbed the stairs and saw his bodyguards in the hallway waiting to depart.

"Excuse me, I have to visit the little boy's room," he said.

He spent a few minutes in one of the house's four bathrooms, before emerging a little red faced to greet his security team.

Hardcastle recognised the prudence in having bodyguards, given the dealings he was involved in. However, he did not really think anyone would be foolish enough to get physical with him. Hardcastle had risen through the political world to attain power. Having four no-necked lackeys was a testament to the stature he had achieved. All men of power, from emperors and kings through to music moguls and film stars, had always had minions. It had been this way since time immemorial. They were chosen more for their discretion to his lifestyle rather than their professional quality in protecting him. They carried out all manner of errands and money kept their compliance.

It was evident to the MP that he had to be politically astute. Politics was not about what you did, but what you appeared to do and relationships cultivated with the correct people. To obtain true power one had to forgo his moral compass somewhat and understand that money was power.

So, when offered £1.9 million in exchange for the addresses of four high-ranking MI5 staffers, he had accepted. The offer came from a barrister. Who could prove that he himself knew the barrister to be corrupt? Who was to say what the addresses were for anyway?

He mused that he was born in the wrong era. If he had existed in Roman times, he would have been an emperor. In those times, the pursuit of power or pleasure had been considered the right of the elite.

That must have been a grand age of civilisation.

The sniper jerked out of his daydream as the door opened. He began to test and adjust his position. He watched two of the burly minders make their way to separate black Audis and drive away—*maybe they have gone ahead to survey the meeting site*. Sometimes a close protection advisor would park in a pre-selected space thus preserving it for the client's vehicle.

He would be surprised if these *mongs* did that.

After five minutes elapsed, the third bodyguard stepped out with an obligatory cursory glance. Hardcastle followed, tailed by the last guard.

Connor Reed waited for the natural pause at the end of his breath while lining up the crosshairs of the sight.

He began to squeeze the trigger evenly.

2

Nick Flint let out a quiet yawn. He had run surveillance on Hardcastle for twelve days now. Most of that time, he had sat in a monitoring truck staring at a multitude of screens.

At thirty years of age, his once bright ginger hair had mellowed into a rustic brown. The teenage acne had mercifully left only a few pock marks on an otherwise clean-cut face

He leant back from the monitor and pinched his stomach—*Not bad but not as ripped as I once was.*

Back in his Army career he had been a Physical Training Instructor. He often wondered if those were the best years of his life. At least he had got to exercise every day, and there was no fat on his five-feet-nine-inch frame. Hopefully, it would not be long until he was back in his hometown of Salford with his wife.

He commanded a surveillance team of nine men with three on rotation in the truck parked two miles away from the stately home. The other six were split into two cars and a van parked in different points ready for mobile reconnaissance.

Drumming his fingers on the table, he blinked several times. The civilian perception of his job often contrasted with the reality of it. He remembered speaking to a paramedic who told him the same thing—that the majority of his call outs were dealing with the elderly falling over, not major road traffic accidents as depicted on television.

Nick might have been used to fighting the monotony of staying alert for details during hours of surveillance, but he had never liked it.

Nonetheless, observation formed a large part of what he did in this black ops unit. There had been a dip in his enthusiasm for this work for a while now—a steady ebb over the past year or so. It strained his family life, the hours were long and could be very monotonous. The danger and thrills were few and far between.

Nevertheless, he was a patriot and stuck with it in the hope his keenness would return.

Secret cameras and audio bugs captured the surveillance footage and conversations. The two ex-Special Reconnaissance Regiment operators on the team had installed these into Hardcastle's home. The video from the cameras overlooking the grounds to the manor was grainy but could be cleared up after recording.

The installation had involved a sizable risk. Hardcastle employed bodyguards whose CVs stated they were well versed in anti-surveillance measures. However, upon considering their backgrounds, it was clear to Nick they were employed more as a visual deterrent rather than for their professionalism in protecting Hardcastle—'*All show and no go.*'

There was a difference between close protection advisors and bodyguards. The former pre-empted and avoided situations that would put the client in danger of any kind. The latter were simply reactive to it.

Nick thought of his friends in the Royalty and Specialist Protection team; they did not look particularly intimidating, but their effectiveness spoke for itself. Too often people could be over or underestimated depending on their size alone. These assumptions were naïve and could be grave in the wrong circumstances.

Cameras now hid in every room of the house as well as overlooking the immediate grounds to the property.

Hardcastle's indiscretions had come to the attention of Nick's employer a few months back. They included fraud, corruption and blackmail on a grand scale.

Also, he had a penchant for very young girls. Some not older than ten years.

Nick was not so naïve as to expect an order to assassinate the paedophile immediately. He knew the next year or two was going to be tedious. He had seen this before—the idea would be to track Hardcastle so that they could ascertain just how deep his corruption went and who else was involved. Then 'higher-ups' would have probably used Hardcastle for their purposes rather than to truly punish him for his crimes. However, this time Nick was part of a unit overseen by a man who would seek retribution.

He adjusted his posture. Their planted microphones made him aware Hardcastle was about to leave.

"All call signs, the target is preparing to leave", he radioed through to the rest of the team, who all replied back.

"Roger."

"Roger."

"Roger that."

He watched the heavy oak door open from the surveillance captured by the overhead camera viewing the grounds. He alerted his colleagues to prepare the revolving tail.

No sooner had he finished the transmission, he observed the surreal vision of the rear bodyguard jerking and the back of his head exploding to a distorted crack.

Connor felt the kick of the recoil against his shoulder.

He maintained a follow-through pressure on the trigger. The rear bodyguard's face vacuumed inwards before distorting into a pink explosion.

The cross hairs adjusted onto the bodyguard to Hardcastle's front. Two pops of blood burst from the minder's back, billowing him backwards as if hooked by a giant invisible angler. The bodyguard had managed to draw his pistol to retaliate before the pair of .338 rounds tore through him. Connor shook his head—*you should have been moving into cover, you fucking 'tard.*

Hardcastle had only just freed himself from resembling a monument of a frightened cat.

He attempted to run.

He made it three paces before collapsing forward as his left kneecap exploded. His scream pierced the night while his right leg kicked out as another round marmalized his ankle.

That is weird—the first one should have taken his leg off.

The politician's shock masked his pain. His hands hovered above the volcanic pulp that had previously been his knee. His fear amplified as he saw a masked figure jogging down in his direction, silhouetted ominously by a blaze.

3

Indecision momentarily rooted Nick as he saw Hardcastle collapse. He watched Hardcastle begin to drag his fat carcass to his car, the inert leg dragging behind like a slug's oily trail.

His focus swiftly switched to another monitor—a sinister figure in a black puffer style jacket and balaclava had come into view, making its way towards Hardcastle.

He fought the intense urge *to flap*. This was completely unexpected and not covered in the *actions on*. He could order his team to the scene, but he was oblivious to how many other gunmen were out there, or their capabilities.

His decision was made—he would simply wait with baited breath to see what would happen next.

Connor suppressed a smirk as he approached, slowly and deliberately. He listened to the politician hyperventilate and watched his eyes dance wildly.

Hardcastle's suit jacket was torn with the effort of heaving himself towards his car.

The sniper thought it best to go 'Clint Eastwood' and show no emotion. He would let Hardcastle's terrified imagination build him into a monster; such was an average person's undisciplined psychology. Connor had set the hide on fire with the petrol to get rid of any DNA evidence. He knew being silhouetted against the backdrop of the blaze would add to the effect.

The discipline of not showing any emotion was natural to him now.

When he had first joined the Royal Marines, it was not uncommon for a soldier to take a 'reefing' as an 'in-house' punishment for various infractions. Reefing involved being struck across the bare arse with a flip-flop for a pre-determined number of times. The aim was to take the reefing without showing emotion—to be *non-emotional*. If the recipient showed his distress, another reefing would be administered.

He smiled to himself as he withdrew the hypodermic needle. He stepped on Hardcastle's shattered knee cap, being a little surprised at the politician passing out—*you are lucky I don't have my flip flops*.

He returned the needle back to its case. It was no longer necessary. He fished the car keys out of Hardcastle's jacket pocket and began to drag his dead weight towards the Jaguar. His arms hooked under his bloody legs so that his head dragged along the gravel floor. This reminded him how much more of an effort heaving a dead weight was compared to a live body; particularly given the MP's obesity.

He scanned his surroundings once more and was satisfied to see the fire dying out.

Once at the car, he removed the plastic handcuffs—*plasticuffs*—from his day sack. He opened the boot and lifted Hardcastle inside, keeping his back straight as per deadlifting form. Connor hog-tied him with the plasticuffs. He stowed the sniper rifle in with Hardcastle after he had removed the magazine and thoroughly checked inside the chamber to make sure there was not a round still in there.

He had concerns about Hardcastle waking and screaming on the way, so he had purchased a heavy-duty stapler—*more exciting than adhesive tape*. Connor grinned at

23

the pinched duck-like face Hardcastle made as the clicks stapled his lips together—*like an Instagram chick, you fat cunt.*

He closed the boot, got into the cloud-feeling front seat and gunned the engine. It was a relief to take off the balaclava, and he nodded as the sound of a BBC Radio Two debate filled the interior—*Hardcastle wasn't all bad.*

Nick composed himself. As far as he could tell, the sniper was acting alone. He had deduced that as the man in the balaclava was carrying the sniper rifle, if there had been more men, another would have kept the weapon to provide over watch.

He was impressed by the rapidity of the shots that dispatched the two bodyguards and took down the MP.

"All call signs, prepare to initiate a polar bear. I say again, prepare to initiate a polar bear."

"Roger."

"Roger."

"Roger that."

The original plan called for a revolving tail of three vehicles keeping a visual on the target Jaguar—a 'grizzly bear' being its code term. However, Nick did not want to risk the unknown killer, whose skill set was not known to him, spotting the tail.

The team who had previously planted the surveillance devices in the manor, had also fixed the Jaguar with a GPS tracker so it could be followed at a distance—a 'polar bear'. Having that distance gave up an eyes-on reading of the situation, but Nick decided it was the lesser of the two evils.

Connor forced himself to focus through the elation of catching Hardcastle. He recognised his body experiencing an adrenal come-down and reminded himself of the old Samurai adage, *'When the battle is over, tighten your helmet straps'*.

He fought the urge to drive at speed, and the fleeting thought came that a cigarette would be a delight. Ironically, he always craved a cigarette when breathing in cold, crisp air. It reminded him how unpolluted his lungs now were and how one cigarette, mixed with the adrenaline coursing through his veins, would be a triumphant pleasure. A smoker on and off since fifteen years old, he was envious of the 'odd-one brigade' knowing he could not be part of it—that he would just get hooked again. After watching the ultra-clean-living forty-six-year-old Bernard Hopkins rip away the WBC Light Heavyweight boxing title from a twenty-eight-year-old, he had begun to think about his health more.

He wanted to age well. He wanted to be a guy that could handle himself in violent confrontations into his forties and fifties—an 'old lion' as he had heard it described. Attracting younger women as an older man would be a bonus too, although he was still firmly entrenched in his more mature woman phase now.

He realised any pleasure from smoking was illusionary. It just fed a nicotine addiction while he convinced himself he smoked for other reasons.

He smiled. Hardcastle's decision to drink, smoke and eat avariciously had been the right one—*living into old age would not be an option for the fucking endomorph now.*

Connor lamented on how and why he had now become a murderer and kidnapper.

His best friend had been Liam Scott. It had been the local boxing club where they had met, and Liam had come to his club after training for a year at a rival gym. He remembered the first sparring session he had as a twelve-year-old with the same-aged, dark-haired, tall and skinny Liam. They went at it hammer and tongs despite the coach's exertions to *'Calm the fuck down!'* Eventually, they were told to go *'work the bags until you both learn to behave,'* and they had become friends. After their boxing sessions, they would watch mixed martial arts and big-time boxing matches before practicing the skills they watched in Liam's garage. They were inseparable: joining a Muay Thai gym, a Judo dojo, playing snooker and chasing girls.

Liam's dad had been in the Royal Green Jackets—an infantry regiment—back in the eighties. After they had found the old man's photo albums depicting sun, sea, boxing, girls and war games, Connor and Liam had decided they wanted to be soldiers too.

Connor joined the Royal Marines just before his nineteenth birthday with Liam joining six months later. They reunited at 45 (pronounced 'four-five') Commando, a Unit based in the small sea-fishing town of Arbroath, Scotland.

'Four-Five is the most notorious Unit in the Corps. There are those Bootnecks who have and those Bootnecks who have not served there.' Connor had been stood with forty-one other recruits in the induction block at the Commando Training Centre as the Drill Leader Sergeant announced this. He had been nineteen-years-old, at the beginning of the eight-month basic training course designed to forge him into a Royal Marine Commando. He discovered that the Sergeant had spent almost all his career up at 'the mighty forty-fifth' as he called it. *Perhaps he was a little biased?*— Connor had thought. Yet he heard the claim repeated by others when joining the unit himself.

He liked to think *four-five's* notoriety was correlated to the greater proportion of Northerners and Jocks based there. He believed them to have a drier wit, harsher character, but often a warmer disposition. The truth was that the unit was away from the naval hierarchy down in the south-west of England, and sometimes the lads' behaviour was a little less reined in as a result. Its continuing commitment to a high professional standard, particularly to mountain and arctic warfare, had diluted its reputation of being the home of reprobate Marines.

After an intense period of pre-deployment training, he and Liam went on the same summer tour of Afghanistan together. They were in different fighting companies and therefore different forward-operating bases. Five and a half months into the tour with only three weeks until the unit returned home for good, Liam was killed by a suicide bomber. The youngster had held a piece of paper and was gesturing for a colouring pencil. He exploded as Liam had been handing one to him.

Connor thought back to his best friend's military funeral a few years before. Liam's eight-year-old blonde angelic sister Rayella had walked up and asked, *'Can I sit with you Connor?'*

He had raised his arm, and she snuggled underneath it. She had wrapped her arms tightly around him, not letting go throughout the entire service as she wept. His urge to cry had been blanketed by his numbness until he had a sense of her anguish.

He had had to hold it in.

Ever since then, Connor had always thought of her as his own sister. He visited the Scott family every leave period, and any weekend back in his native Leeds.

Rayella was always such a sweet girl. Always complimenting people or telling jokes, and so attuned to the moods of anyone around her. Her face always lit up when he visited.

The memories steeled his resolve as he pulled the car onto a vacated industrial estate and headed towards the empty warehouse.

The last of the tail vehicles stopped where Nick stood, and he got in. The black Astra sped away to catch the other two as Nick produced a phone from his pocket and dialled.

"Send," said the Scotsman on the other end.

"We have a situation. His bodyguards were shot and killed while escorting 'Foxtrot One' to his vehicle. He appeared to have been shot in his legs to prevent escape, clear so far?" Nick spoke rapidly but succinctly.

"Clear."

"After a period elapsing of one minute, an unidentified individual, wearing a balaclava and black puffer style jacket, came into view complete with day-sack and a sniper rifle. He appeared to cause Foxtrot One to faint by stepping on his injured knee. Then he dragged him to Foxtrot One's car before putting the sniper rifle and day-sack into the boot. He lifted Foxtrot One in with them. He had his back to the outside cameras, so all I could make out was him being as follows: Caucasian—he wasn't wearing gloves—compact build, wearing jeans, black jacket and looked around five-feet-ten. Looked like he was tying Foxtrot One up but I couldn't be sure. Then he closed the boot of the vehicle and drove away. I've initiated a 'Polar Bear'."

The response was immediate.

"Recovering Foxtrot One is the priority but do not take any action until the vehicle stops. We need Foxtrot One alive if possible."

"Roger."

"Try and keep the kidnapper alive too…unless he poses an immediate danger to you or your team."

"Got it."

Hardcastle awoke in his bed as if having barely escaped drowning. Then the dawn of realisation descended.

I am not in bed.

The first thing that made him aware of this was his inability to breathe through his mouth. He tried, but it only amplified the throbbing pain that bolted around his lips. He ran his tongue over the sharp metallic seal—they had been stapled together.

He rattled his wrists and ankles against their restraints like a bolt of electricity was shooting through him.

Fear washed over him like a bitter breeze.

He tried focusing his eyes on making out the ceiling but he could not see it. The standing lamp on his left blinded him. He turned his head away and began to hyperventilate. The icy, hard eyes behind the balaclava burned into him. The warm, wet sensation of urine spread over his right thigh and the smell wafted into his nostrils.

"I almost hope that you either refuse to answer my questions or attempt to be untruthful, then I'll have an excuse to disfigure you, Stephen," a menacing voice pierced the cold atmosphere.

Hardcastle's heart was beating so hard, he thought it was audible to the masked man. He flinched as the figure stepped toward him. He felt a blade rest on his cheek. The sharp point pricked his lower eyelid and the flesh opened like a flower in bloom as the blood tear danced down his face.

Nick stood in front of his team who formed a tight semi-circle. They were less than a hundred metres from the warehouse, on a grass verge, shielded by a small outhouse.

He issued them their QBOs—Quick Battle Orders. Nine minutes had elapsed since the Jaguar had halted. The team had been mindful of stealth as they alighted from their vehicles before silently shuffling into this position.

He and another had carried out a swift reconnaissance of the building. Nick had employed a snake camera through the warehouse's sole window. The image emerged, of a balaclava-clad figure leaning over the restrained Hardcastle—like a sinister surgeon.

There was a front and rear entrance and the Jaguar was the only vehicle near the warehouse other than the teams'.

"We'll use the dead ground to the left to stack up on the entrance. There are no windows on that side but there is on the right of the entrance, so we can't roll on the door. I'll go *point*, Mitch you'll be second, so have the *flash bang* ready. Toby, have the *Enforcer* ready if need be."

Both men nodded.

"Dan and Kev, peel off and cover the rear exit." Those men nodded.

"Remember, if he points a weapon anywhere near us then drop him. Otherwise, we're taking him in. Understand?"

All the men nodded.

"Prepare to move," Nick ordered, and the team checked their weapons and ammunition pouches.

"Move."

The team followed him as he cut a path to the building. He pushed any doubts regarding his plan to one side. In war, more was lost by indecision than wrong decision.

The left eye seemed to be trying to escape the blood pool of its socket—the eyelid was gone. Hardcastle's muffled sobs and screams echoed around the cavernous warehouse.

The pliers had bit into the lid, stretching it away from the eyeball. He had realised that he could not move his head lest it cause his eyelid to tear off. Pain had sliced across the fleshy hood switching his vision in that eye to a lens of red. He tried to blink the blood away but there was not a lid to close over the raw socket.

He thrashed wildly against his restraints. A low, sniggering laugh swirled around the monster that had done this to him. Hardcastle's stifled roars had prized loose the staples with an iron-tasting wet pain. A cloth had been stuffed into his mouth almost gagging him.

A strong, coarse hand forced his face to the side, and he felt a blunt cutting of his left ear.

He fainted.

Connor crouched over Hardcastle's prostrate figure with pliers and surgical scalpel in hand.

The doors crashed open.

The metallic clang alerted him to the cylindrical black tube that was bouncing within six feet of him. He tightly closed his eyes, dropped the implements and pressed his fingers into his ears. The percussion of sound fired into his body, and within seconds a pair of rough hands dragged him to the floor. For a split-second, he considered going for the commando dagger sheathed to his wrist. Instead he complied and accepted his fate.

He was disappointed not to have had longer with Stephen Hardcastle. He had planned on making it last hours. Still, Hardcastle's muted howls reminded him in addition to a shot out kneecap, ankle and sliced off ear, that only one of the MP's eyelids remained.

Connor smiled—*no surgeon was reattaching that fucker now.*

4

Bruce McQuillan was tired in a way that could neither be remedied by a good night's sleep nor an extended holiday. He doubted even a sabbatical could assuage this fatigue. He clasped the back of his neck and exhaled.

Tall and fit, the black hair greyed around the edges framing the hawkish features and alert eyes. His once thick Glaswegian accent had simmered to a lighter brogue and a more 'correct' pronunciation—except when his temper flared or when he was back 'home'. Today he wore a well-fitting light grey suit.

He was the head of the most operationally effective unit within the UK's security services. 'The Chameleon Project' was deniable with only a select few in the upper echelons knowing of its existence. Created in 1999, the unit's original remit was to deal with domestic threats born from the arrival of international organised crime syndicates. Many of these overseas crime lords settled in the UK to escape the harsher judicial system of their homelands.

Several private studies demonstrated that if the courts were to deal with the punishment and deterrence of every criminal and terrorist organisation, the backlog would go on for over a decade. Meanwhile the financial damage perpetrated by these miscreants would have severely hampered the UK economically.

That is where McQuillan's unit came in.

The missions they carried out were highly sensitive: blackmail, extradition, enhanced interrogation and assassinations were among the methods used.

The Scotsman was observing the seated kidnapper through the one-way glass of the interview room. Hardcastle's abductor seemed to be wearing an expression of mild boredom.

Bruce had half of Nick Flint's team transfer the sniper to this converted farmhouse in the rural quiet of Hampshire. He had developed several of these safe houses over the years. Nick Flint and the remainder of his team had taken Stephen Hardcastle to a similar one in the countryside of Shropshire. Money covertly seized from the offshore accounts of criminal kingpins had footed the bills over the years—McQuillan's take on the police's proceeds of crime initiative.

The man in the chair had been compliant as they processed him but refused to give his name. His photo was taken and forwarded to Bruce's computer tech guy, who found a match within ten minutes. The hit had come through a MOD database which, amongst other things, had the captive's Royal Marine military ID card on it. Bruce never asked how his guy gained access to these systems. He had read Connor Reed's service record which included the citations from his two operational tours. He was impressed.

Something did not compute in Bruce's mind.

Royal Marines were elite soldiers, but they were not Special Forces. They were given tasks within their fighting companies in a structured way. The eight-man Marine sections were not given nearly as much autonomy that a four-man Special Forces patrol would be. Although he was a sniper within the Marines—which was reputed to be one of the most difficult sniper courses in the world—it still did not rest well with McQuillan that the young Marine had the confidence to snatch Hardcastle alone. There had to be something else in his background that instilled in him such nerve. Bruce thought that the audacity to seize a high-ranking MP, assassinate the bodyguards and begin a violent interrogation alone was remarkable.

Connor sat in the sparse eight-foot square room and focused. His hands were bound separately with handcuffs to the armrests of the chair. He did not bother attempting a Houdini-like escape. Thoughts drifted back to the day that had set him down this path.

Nearly two months ago, he had visited the Scott family home in his native Leeds. At the time, Rayella was about to sit her 'Eleven Plus' exam, a prerequisite for entry into the local Grammar School. He had sat on the living room sofa opposite Mr Scott, who was reading a newspaper. Mrs Scott had set a cup of tea and a biscuit beside them both before perching on the armrest of Mr Scott's chair.

"Do you want to sit down, Ann?" Connor had asked, shifting to one side despite there being plenty of room on the settee.

"It's alright duck. I am going to get the tea on in a bit anyway."

"Where's Rayella?"

"In her room," she had huffed, and with her Yorkshire brogue raising a few octaves, "Really, the chuffing pressure they put these kids under to pass a flipping exam. She hasn't come out of her room for weeks now and hardly talks when she does. I've told her it's not the end of the world if she doesn't pass."

"If tha had mah way she wouldn't be going there anyway," piped up Mr Scott, snapping his newspaper on the sports page. "Bloody toffs up there."

"She's going there for a better education, so she doesn't have to work her fingers to the bone, alright Paul?" she said irately.

Mr Scott just studied his paper more intently, and Connor hid a smile.

"I'll go and have a word with her Ann."

"Bless you, Connor, thank you."

On arrival to her room Connor had knocked gently on the door, to be met by a shell of the usually vivacious Rayella. With her eyes red and puffed, he had instinctively known this was more than exam pressure.

"What's up with you?" he asked in a gentle voice. He stepped into her room and closed the door.

She had just shrugged her shoulders. He had reached out to coax her to look at him and had felt a jolt go through him as she flinched.

"Rayella, what's wrong?" The concern had coursed through his voice. She had looked at him with tears filling her eyes and shook her head.

"You can tell me anything, and I mean anything Rayella and no one has to know but me. Not if you don't want to, though." He was desperate to find out what was causing her this pain. After a few moments, she nodded her head and sat on the edge of her bed. Connor sat on the other end giving her space and waited.

"A man…," she paused, and he had felt his stomach lurch, "…under my…my knickers and my top…a man touched meh," and the tears had gushed down her face.

Connor had heard his heartbeat pounding in his ears, and the room seemed to spin. He took a few moments to compose himself.

"Can I give you a cuddle?" he croaked.

Rayella had silently nodded her head, and he wrapped an arm around her. He held her for a while

36

waiting for the numbness he felt to wear off. When it did, his concern for her kept switching to a cold rage towards the perpetrator and back again. He felt her arms haltingly thread around his torso, and he waited until she had calmed.

"Who is he?" he had asked softly.

Her voice continually wavered and stuttered throughout her answer, "...he were from... the Government.... a member of Parliame-me-ment.... he were visiting the school... I... I cut my finger, and he said he had plasters in the car..." She began to cry again.

Connor had breathed deeply. "What was his name?"

"Mr Hardcastle"

"What's the plan with him by there, Boss?" Kevin Anderson asked Bruce, referring to Connor. They stood in a small office-like room within the safe house. Kevin's strong welsh accent was still evident when not around strangers—although he refrained from calling Bruce 'Bud'. Bruce found his own accent coming through when around Kevin, who had worked with Bruce for six years now.

"I am going to speak with him," he answered, "we've nae time to wait for a full intel report to be worked up."

"Who do you think he works for?"

"That's the thing. I don't believe he works for anyone."

"OK...Do we know anything about him, Boss?"

"Only this. It's from his military administration login," answered Bruce, holding up the thin folder—it contained no more than twelve pages, "Royal Marine. Two tours of Afghanistan. Impressive citations from both. Service record marred by discipline issues. He's from Leeds, his Maw's name is Rebecca Reed, and her address is listed as his home address. Nothing has come back yet with regards to his Dad. That is pretty much it."

"Not tidy darts is it?" said Kevin, using the Welsh colloquialism for *'not good'*.

Bruce shook his head while looking at the bulging intelligence folder on Hardcastle. It did not have any markings on the cover as per his unit's standard procedure.

"Kevin, there's a label maker in the bottom of the filing cabinet behind you. Get it out for me please."

"You have a plan?"

"Aye," said Bruce, "just because we don't know much about him yet, he doesn't have to know that."

Connor thought of the girl he had arranged to see. He had rescheduled their date for after his encounter with Stephen Hardcastle. He found himself wishing that he had brought the date forward in light of his now uncertain future. *One last shag would have been good*—he thought—*especially as I now expect to spend at least a significant portion of my life behind bars.*

He thought of the mistakes he had made in executing his plan. It led to him playing what he called the *'What-if?'* game. He quickly put a stop to it; he would not let his mind wander into fear or a sense of hopelessness, particularly when he was in such a precarious situation. The mind, he knew, was the most powerful thing he owned, and was the only thing that could not be taken from him while he was still alive.

He knew these people were not any type of law enforcement agency—no rights had been read out, and he had been hooded almost immediately after being grabbed.

If he had to guess, he would have surmised it was MI5 and that they had had Hardcastle under surveillance. They would have followed him when he took the politician. The other possibilities were that it was a criminal or extremist group. Connor thought he knew what the lesser of the two evils would be.

He switched his focus back to pussy.

Bruce opened the door and met Connor Reed's impassive expression. He noted the symmetrical features emphasising a masculine face. The eyes were shark-like with no anger, fear or challenge; not dull, nor were they particularly enquiring, but they stared at him with a blunt candour.

Bruce placed the full file labelled with Reed's name and date of birth on the table in front of him. He caught the flick of the eyes to it. Stepping around the table he took off both the handcuffs that were anchoring Reed's wrists.

Then he sat across from him and met his eyes.

"Why did you do it?" McQuillan asked. He watched Reed intently.

After a few moments, the marine spoke, "He's a paedophile. He abused someone close to me."

"You have proof of this?" Bruce asked inquiringly.

"I didn't need any, but I am sure you have."

Bruce suppressed a look of surprise—*How would he know if I have evidence of Hardcastle's paedophilia or not?*

"The sniper rifle did you steal it from the armourer or did you pay him?"

"I am not saying anything else until I know who you are and what organisation you belong to."

39

The Scotsman sighed, "Without wishing to sound cliché, I am either your best friend or your worst enemy lad. I already know all about you, Connor. That you're a Royal Marine on leave. That your mother Rebecca lives in a lovely semi-detached house in the upmarket Roundhay area of Leeds. The amount of evidence we possess of your double murder with the kidnap and torture of an MP makes the extraction of a confession barely worth the bother. So please, just answer the questions."

There was a barely noticeable twitch in the Yorkshireman's face, and after a few moments, he replied, "He was gobbing off about it in the pub, so I stole it from the boot of his car. Didn't even have to jimmy the lock, just took the div's keys from his jacket when he went to the heads. Security isn't a dirty word you know."

'Heads', Bruce knew, was the Navy slang for toilets.

Bruce knew he was not lying—he had no reason to. The older man stopped himself from asking how he knew they had evidence of Hardcastle's misdeeds. He must have worked out they had the MP under surveillance.

"What about the two bodyguards? Why did they need to be killed?" McQuillan's tone was inquisitive rather than accusatory.

"Those cretins had been protecting him day and night for three years. No way he could have hid what he was from 'em, and that made them a party to it," Connor said, "and not that it matters now, but they would have been witnesses."

It was in that moment that Bruce made his decision. He wanted to know more. The low hum of the extractor fan prevented silence for a few moments.

"So, you orchestrated this entirely alone?" asked Bruce.

"Yes, at what point would I have needed other people?"

Bruce nodded, and asked, "Why torture him? Surely it would have been less risky just to kill him from the off."

Connor looked at him before answering, "Look, people die all the fucking time whether they are good or bad. They get hit by buses, and kids get Leukaemia. Why did that cunt deserve a quick death? It was worth the risk to bring justice to him."

"Did you enjoy it?" he asked watching the Marine carefully.

"Yeah," Connor answered laconically with a shrug of his shoulders.

"You ever heard of the notion that this is a reciprocal universe?"

"Is this the part where you tell me that violence begets violence, and if you live by the sword you'll die by the sword? That sort of thing?"

"Something like that, aye."

"I'll be sure to swap notes on that theory with Martin Luther King and Gandhi if I get the chance."

McQuillan paused and thought better of getting into a debate.

He took a calculated risk and held up the folder. "Sometimes your temper might have bled into other areas?"

After a few moments, Connor nodded slightly in what looked to be mild admittance.

"You're right, though, he was an abuser of young girls, probably for decades. You're also correct to assume that his wee security detail was party to it. They enabled it to happen, in fact, and that's why we've dealt with the other two." He shook his head perceptibly before continuing "Stephen Hardcastle is corrupt, with millions embezzled in off-shore accounts from selling sensitive information. We had him under surveillance to see how far his corruption went. We wanted to know who his contacts and co-conspirators were. Then you came along and threw a spanner in the works—still, no plan survives contact. We'll just have to improvise."

"We'll?" Connor said, sounding surprised.

"Yes, you'll work for me. Your other option is to refuse, in which case your future looks bleak, given that you have murdered two men and mutilated a high-ranking politician."

"I am not ashamed of what I have done," said Connor looking him in the eye, "If there's a trial, then so be it."

"You already know there wouldn't be a trial."

The words, tinged with the Glaswegian dialect, hung in the air. He studied Reed's reaction intently.

"How long would this arrangement go on for?" Connor asked.

"Indefinitely."

"Help you cut deals with beasts for the greater good?" came the derision-laced reply, "I mean, it's the sale of information that you people are bothered about, not the fact these girls he's molested will be traumatised and affected their entire lives?"

"Hold that thought until Monday. See if you feel the same way."

A spell of silence passed before Connor asked, "Do I get paid?"

"No lad, you'll have to steal your food and report to the Salvation Army between jobs," Bruce replied.

Connor's lips started to curve upwards before straightening, "You almost had your first *career laugh* off me."

"Career laugh?"

"Never mind. How much do I get paid?"

"You'll get paid well."

Connor did not say anything.

"Are you in or are you out?" asked Bruce.

"In."

Nick finally climbed into the passenger seat of the van, his brain screaming for sleep. The capturing of Hardcastle, and the kidnapper, alive without any harm coming to his men had shot elation through his insides. This euphoria and the left over adrenaline had kept him sharp throughout the sanitizing of evidence at both the warehouse and the manor.

The bodies and any significant parts were stuffed into body bags and piled in the van. The surveillance devices were removed, and the blood stains doused with cola taken from the kitchen. It was the best he could have done under the circumstances, he thought. McQuillan would send a fully equipped clean-up team in the morning.

"Where to Boss?" asked the driver.

"We're gonna have to use Hackworth Hall Dan, can't use the regulars to get rid of these," answered Nick in his Salford drawl, referring to the bodies.

Hackworth Hall was a disused farming estate that McQuillan had profiteered for a safe house in Shropshire. It was nearest of two that had an incinerator installed.

"I am gun'neh to get my head down, or I'll be scrikin'." said Nick

"No dramas."

He leant his folded arms on the dashboard and rested his head on them. The thrum of the engine sent him off to slumber immediately.

5

Thames House stood regally on the north bank of the River Thames. The paleness of the grey stonework made the seven-floor structure appear white at a distance. The windows, large enough to fit bears through, were crisscrossed with white bars. The two statues of St. George and a Britannia figure, stood either side of the grand archway entrance. Viewing the structure in its entirety, gave the building the appearance of being undecided whether to be a Cathedral or a prison. It was neither. It was the headquarters of MI5 and had been since 1994.

Within one of the soundproofed offices on the seventh floor, two men were in discussion.

"Absolutely not, that's a preposterous thing to even suggest," exclaimed Roger Stanton, across his desk to Bruce, his public-school accent emphasising his disapproval.

The Director General of MI5 was of medium height, with his black hair beginning to crown. His expensive dark suit contoured his frame well. Still reasonably trim given his fifty-four years and the sedentary nature of his profession. A large pointed nose sat on his round face—Bruce thought he had a look of The Penguin from the 1989 Batman film.

The office was sparse, with the mahogany desk as the centrepiece. A few expensive-looking paintings of ships and woodland adorned the walls. They almost compensated for the lack of a window. There were no personal photographs of family.

"There would be far too many loose ends to tie up with his current unit and his family," Stanton muttered, "and how did he get hold of a damn sniper rifle in the first place?"

"The serial number matches that of an L115A3 sniper rifle, allegedly stolen from an Army vehicle as they were transporting it down to Warminster for repairs. Report states it to be stolen at a service station en route."

Bruce did not see the need to tell Stanton what had actually occurred.

"You said he's a Royal Marine. I take it you meant he's Poole?"

Poole, the coastal town in the South West of England, was the home of the Special Boat Service. The SBS formed one half of the UK's Special Forces; with the other half being the SAS, the Special Air Service, based in Hereford. Although the SBS was now open to all UK armed services, traditionally it recruited solely from the Royal Marines, and they still made up the vast majority of its membership.

"No. He's sniper trained, but apart from that he's a regular Royal Marine," answered Bruce.

The space between Stanton's eyebrows compressed. "And you say he was working alone?"

"Yes," said Bruce, "we can train him off the books. Bringing him into the fold from his unit won't be too difficult. Royal Marines get drafted to different places all the time."

"This is a hell of a mess he's caused", Stanton said, pointing at Bruce with all eight fingers "two dead, with a Member of Parliament minus an ear, eyelid and the ability to walk. Questions are going to be asked. And you want me to sign off on training the man responsible for all this before we know more about him?"

Bruce remained calm throughout this.

In this instance, he could not insist Stanton permit Connor Reed's training. Despite the autonomy of his unit, he needed access to training instructors that only Stanton could sign off on.

Bruce had more latitude within the UK security services than any outsider would have thought possible. Still, running a training programme completely independent from the country's intelligence agencies was not feasible.

Bruce knew Stanton was a bureaucrat and he needed reassurances.

"Look, I haven't asked you for anything in years, have I? I can fabricate his background so that his inclusion won't raise eyebrows. Nothing I have done has ever blown back on the wider service. If the worst does come to the worst, I will fall on my sword."

Bruce's gaze was unflinching as he let Stanton consider this. Finally, Roger Stanton gave a resigned nod of acceptance.

Nick stood looking through the one-way glass at the shell-shocked Stephen Hardcastle. Bandages now covered the mutilated eye and ear. The 'shock of capture' still apparent in his body language—the hunched shoulders, and odd flicks of direction with his visible eye.

Nick heard Bruce's footsteps as he joined him. The older man towered over him by almost half a foot. Nick's fur-lined hoodie and jeans contrasted with Bruce's sharp suit.

"How was your drive?" Nick asked.

"Not too bad, two and a half hours."

"What's the plan regarding this tub of shit now?"

"Ye have forty-eight hours before the working week begins to extract everything ye can out of him," Bruce said, "by any means necessary."

"And then?"

"Well," McQuillan replied, "he's committed treason hasn't he."

Roger Stanton sat in his office thinking of his meeting with Bruce McQuillan. If anyone else had made the request to train a 'rogue', it would have been unceremoniously dismissed. His predecessor as head of MI5 had been one of three who had helped facilitate the existence of The Chameleon Project. The other two were the Chief of the Secret Intelligence Service, Miles Parker—MI6—and Henry Costner, a personal advisor to the Prime Minister.

Initially, financed to the tune of £13.7 million siphoned from various sources. Two years after its inception in 1999, two planes struck the World Trade Centre, and the clandestine unit's funding tripled.

Walter Morris, his predecessor, briefed Stanton in his handover of MI5 to him in 2004. Stanton remembered the lined face of the sixty-four-year-old Morris staring at him from where he now sat. The man's posture had begun to stoop, and the grey highlighted the sides of a full head of brown hair. His voice had been as authoritative as ever.

"The Project has been perhaps the service's best asset for protecting the UK's economy and citizens, Roger. They have been a necessity in this day and age, unfortunately."

"Desperate times call for desperate measures."

"Yes quite," Morris had said, "but there always comes a time when a dangerous dog, no matter how loyal, needs to be put down."

Stanton had said nothing.

"The thing you should grasp in your new position Roger is that sometimes the finger has to be sacrificed to save the arm. Making tough decisions is what makes a leader."

"You must clarify on this particular point, Sir."

Morris studied Stanton for a moment before answering.

"The Project by its very nature works outside the judicial system. One day this 'War on Terror' will calm, and public perception will change. That's when the media will resemble vultures looking for a feed. You've been in this game long enough to know. That'll be when this service needs your protection. You understand this, do you not?"

"I'll take your counsel under advisement," Stanton had answered, and Morris had pursed his lips.

A week after that conversation, Stanton had sat in a briefing room in the MI6 Headquarters of Vauxhall Cross with two of the most powerful men in the country across from Bruce McQuillan.

It was in this meeting that Bruce McQuillan revealed just how far he would go to protect himself and his unit.

The types Nick usually interrogated needed a cerebral approach; men used to and prepared for physical pain. In ordinary circumstances, he would have first attempted to enhance the detainee's suggestibility. Techniques that helped achieve this included sleep deprivation, white noise exposure or as a last resort, drugs. After completing this 'softening-up' process, a series of questions would be asked, of which the answers would already be known to him. He would begin with these, punishing any lies the detainee told, giving them the sense that he knew everything anyway.

Meanwhile, he would observe the detainee's body language for any shifts, however subtle, in posture and/or eye position that indicated any falsehood. If the detainee spontaneously corrected themselves during their answers, it normally indicated truth telling—a liar would 'stick' to a story.

Slowly, a relationship of sorts would be engineered, eliciting the necessary information.

In this case, Nick did not have the luxury of time. He would have to be blunt in his approach. Luckily, he knew Hardcastle, who having been privately educated and now a career politician, was unlikely to have had a fight in years—if ever. With the politician used to a position of power for decades, having it stripped away would be alien and frightening. Nick did not normally enjoy administering pain but might here. He had confidence his approach would get a result. First, he needed to get Hardcastle's attention—his injuries and the isolation had kept the politician in a state of shock.

Hardcastle took a deep breath as Nick entered the room, and let loose a sudden burst of indignation.

"You'd better pray to one's Lord—" the MP started but was cut short as a fist rifled onto his already swollen nose.

The crack was audible.

He grabbed Hardcastle by the throat, squeezing on the Adam's apple until the exposed eye bulged.

"You'd better pray that the information you give me is valuable enough to spare your life," Nick said, as he stared into the terrified eye.

Three hours later, Bruce and Nick stood outside the interrogation room. Hardcastle lay inside, curled into the foetal position.

"Well?" Bruce asked as they listened to the gentle sobbing.

"He gave me everything: dates, times, codes, account numbers. Couldn't get him to shut his face in the end," replied Nick.

"Any hint of deception on his part?"

"Nah, I had a couple of the accounts verified already. He never lied to the control questions. You can go over the transcripts to see if I've missed anything."

"Why thank you," replied Bruce with a small smile.

Nick accepted admonishment, replying, "What now?"

"I'll handle it from here. I get the feeling someone will be interested in seeing what happens to Mr Hardcastle."

6

Connor lay on a bed of a small B&B on the outskirts of Hampshire. The day before last, after his meeting with Bruce McQuillan, he had received a Chinese dish of beef and black bean sauce, a fresh set of well-fitting clothes, and took a shower. He was then driven to the B&B and told to wait. The room and any subsequent meals were already paid for. They had even given him his commando dagger back.

He sipped an instant black coffee while reading author Brian Tracey's 'The Power of Self-Discipline'. He had loved reading since being a young teenager and could not understand why more of the lads back at work did not. That said, proportionally more of the blokes in the Corps read than the guys he knew in 'civvy street'. He remembered a lot of the lads skimming through the pickup artist book 'The Game', before heading into town and employing the techniques absorbed. Great and exciting people would compress a backlog of lessons into a book which, in some cases, took only a week for him to read. He appreciated that one could do too much reading and not enough living; like someone who voraciously read books such as 'Teach Yourself How To Box' yet would never have the courage to set foot in a boxing gym. Information was only useful if put into practice.

He liked hotels and B&Bs. It was the feeling of being looked after in a place that was not familiar. Though the feeling of home was nice to come back to, moving around and travelling came naturally to him.

This stay had the added bonus in that he was not paying for it—they were.

That they released him so quickly surprised him. He was expecting a lengthy debrief at the least.

Still, Reed could not quite believe his luck.

The room phone began to sound, and he picked it up on the second ring.

"Meet me downstairs in five," said a voice Connor recognised to be Bruce's.

The phone went dead.

He pulled on a white polo shirt, fur-lined boots and made his way downstairs. He found Bruce in a light grey suit chatting to the receptionist as she laughed.

"Here he is finally," Bruce called, like he had known him for years. "Thought I was going to have to have another shave then."

The attractive forty-something-year-old brunette smiled at him as if she and Bruce were sharing an inside joke.

"Let's take a walk," he said. "Look after yourself, Janette."

Connor saw Janette flash Bruce a fabulous smile.

Once outside, Connor fell into step beside him as they walked along the quiet residential street. It was the kind of weather he liked—hot but with a gentle breeze.

"You're going on a course."

It was an order.

"To turn me into James Bond?"

"Yeah, you'll be just like him, with you being a working class lad of average height with a Yorkshire accent."

"Tha' accent adds to tha' character. Besides, Daniel Craig is my height."

Bruce did not acknowledge the attempt at humour.

"Your accent, your real accent, is distinctive and something you'll have to learn to drop if the situation requires it. We'll get into that later." Bruce stopped at a Blue BMW M3. "This is us."

"You drive this?"

"Yes, why shouldn't I?"

"Bit flashy isn't it? Besides, aren't you technically a Civil Servant?"

"Why? Are you a Communist?—not a believer in capitalistic enterprise?" Bruce said with a laugh.

"A little random and deep, comrade," Connor answered. "Anyway, where are we going?"

"To show you something I think you'll like."

They got into the car.

After a couple of hours, Connor began to recognise where they were heading as they approached the road he had initially taken to Stephen Hardcastle's home. He felt a sense of unease as he mentally examined the reasons why Bruce might have brought him here—*Maybe they are going to kill both Hardcastle and I. Maybe make it look like a burglary gone wrong. Surely they would not let me stay at a bed and breakfast if that was the case? Or are they going to show me how I fucked up?*

He stopped himself; all he could do was wait it out.

Bruce had been quiet for the journey as they listened to a political discussion on the radio. The M3 was a pleasant drive.

As the car turned into Stephen Hardcastle's long driveway, Connor saw the Jaguar back in its usual parking place. Three sturdy looking men surrounded the open boot.

"Let's go," ordered Bruce, as he switched off the ignition.

Connor walked a pace behind Bruce, heartened that he let him do so. Though if the men were planning to take him, it would be doubtful he could physically restrain the tall, broad, Scotsman in a way that would make the others back off.

Connor's eyes picked out the unconscious Hardcastle in the boot. The smell of petrol taunted his nostrils.

"What's this?" asked Connor.

"Mr Hardcastle, so overcome by the guilt of giving up civil servants to a terrorist cell, decided to commit suicide by dousing himself in petrol and setting himself alight inside his boot. At least, that's what the letter on his dressing table will say."

Reed hid his surprise. He had seen many things a lot of other people had not, both before and during his military career.

This was unexpected, though.

"Isn't there a risk of the closed boot preventing the amount of oxygen needed to feed the flames?" he asked.

The other men looked at Connor.

"Maybe, but the fumes from the petrol can he has in there will take care of the rest," Bruce replied.

"How did you convince him to write the letter out?"

"I told him we needed some insurance if he ever decided to turn on us—he went for it. These types always do. Predictable really. Now, would you like to do the honours?"

Bruce held out a box of matches.

Reed hesitated, surprising himself, considering what he had already done and been prepared to do to Hardcastle. Perhaps it was because all he saw was a helpless body now and not a monster. However, the face of Rayella came to him, and he smiled.

He took the box, his reluctance all but disappeared.

"Throw the box in after you've lit him up," said Bruce.

Reed struck a match. The body went up in a burst of flames, and began to thrash as the siren of screams sounded. The smell of burning pork assaulted Connor's nose, and a moment or two later the boot was closed, muffling the bawling.

"What about the reciprocal universe?" asked Connor as they retreated.

"Well that's it there in action, isn't it?" Bruce replied as the thudding Jaguar smoked.

Pierre Gaultier strode along the bustling streets of Paris wearing a wry smile. The sun lit his side of the sidewalk, relieved by a breeze. He was wearing navy blue suit trousers offset by a cream shirt rolled up at the sleeves, revealing his tanned forearms and a Berguet watch. It was the smile of contentment a man unconsciously wears when his stars metaphorically align.

He remembered when he was around twelve years old telling his Uncle Jean of his wish to one day be famous. When his Uncle Jean asked why, he replied, *'For the girls, for the Ferraris and to be able go anywhere I want to'.*

His uncle responded, *'Your wish should be to be wealthy rather than famous. Being famous is to be forever in a golden cage where you won't be free to wander among the people.'*

At times like this it gladdened Pierre that he had heeded his uncle's advice. He thought Paris to be a beautiful city, its greenery interspersed with magnificent architecture which suited his love affair with decadence. He walked along the street with a view of the Seine river, admiring the bustling multiculturalism of the city.

Gaultier had a thin but wiry frame. He sported stylish blond curls on the top of his head that was shaved at the back and sides. His mouth was a little thin and his nose a touch large, but the Frenchman carried himself with an easy confidence that attracted women. *That and my dress sense*—he thought.

The former French Commando had made his first arms deal fifteen years ago while working as a security advisor in the Congo; he had supplied a local militia group with a pallet of re-conditioned AKMs and 47s from a Middle-Eastern source. Now the arms dealer's business had grown to make him a multi- millionaire.

Pierre did not have any serious moral dilemmas regarding what he did for a living. He reasoned every organisation primarily backed their own interests. One's beliefs were essentially pre-determined by the environment surrounding them—*if you grew up in a village in Afghanistan, you were unlikely to become a Rabbi.*

Civilians had, at times, been killed in the crossfire with weapons he knew he had supplied. This had once given him pause for thought. Over the years however, these feelings had receded; just because they were civilians did not mean they were righteous people.

He had stopped supplying explosives after the 2007 Marriot Hotel bombing in Pakistan. The images of civilians burnt alive were too much even for him. More so, the realisation certain governments' agencies would hunt him more aggressively if the explosives he sold killed the civilians of their country.

Still, his power base had grown stronger as time passed and his most ardent clients had an anti-West agenda. Hezbollah, IRA and some upper-level Somali pirates had all been customers at some point.

After the attacks of September 11th, Pierre came to a crossroads. The West was under a genuine threat from these despotic fundamentalists. However, these zealots were potentially his most lucrative customer base. Saudi money was as good as anyone else's in his eyes. Besides, western contracts had all been secured by the big players.

He would be targeted by some of the world's largest and best-funded intelligence agencies if known to supply them. The feared Israeli Intelligence service of Mossad was particularly ruthless in dealing with the suppliers of their enemies. The death of former Hamas military commander Al-Mabouth had still been fresh in the memory, and had reminded everyone that Israel was never above flouting international law to deal with their enemies.

He refused selling to these anti-West organisations purely out of strategy—at least initially.

He watched the meteoric rise of his contemporaries, followed by the inevitable crash as their businesses were torn up by these western agencies. Pierre knew if he made ill-thought-out choices, it would result in his organisation being placed under surveillance. If he were to sell to more politically correct groups, his business would gain a reputation that would shield him in the future. Even if it meant he lost profits in the meantime.

All the while, he developed secret back-channels to these radicals who were becoming desperate and willing to pay more as their options dwindled.

Their desperation equalled financial gain for Pierre's business. When Pierre began to arm these terrorists in early 2005, his power and prosperity snowballed.

Ironically, the London bombing that summer had for a while lessened the scrutiny on his organisation. Those attacks had been carried out with homemade organic peroxide-based devices. Still, the stakes of selling to these anti-west groups became higher than ever. His patience and guile had begun to pay dividends in the shape of Saudi

Arabian oil money. He soon became one of the most powerful and wealthy arms dealers in the world.

The dojo hall echoed with the exertions of the two men grappling on blue mats; the sounds of one more predominant than the other. Posters and pictures of legendary mixed martial artists, boxers and Thai boxers adorned the walls in between windows that showed only sky. There was an octagon cage in the corner.

Connor Reed was pinned onto his back by the chest-to-chest pressure of the man positioned at a ninety-degree angle to him. It felt like being trapped under a fallen oak tree. The 'Americana' lock cranked his arm and his taps on the man's back to signal surrender threatened to become slaps. The arm was mercifully released. He felt the cobwebs of his elbows crack.

He had had sixty-six amateur boxing wins in seventy-one bouts. He had boxed extensively as a civilian and had won the Combined Services Open class light-middle weight Championship for the Navy. Eighteen months before joining the Corps, he had trained at his local Muay Thai club and won eight of his nine matches. While in the Corps, he had taken up Judo and got himself a place on the Navy team. He won several bouts and earned a bronze medal at the Navy Championship.

However, in the seventeen minutes of *rolling* with his new instructor, he had been befuddled a little and punished a lot.

The instructor whipped around him and levered him into untenable positions, before amplifying the discomfort with his body pressure. Connor felt a feeling akin to mild suffocation when ground into the mat. It bemused him that the instructor—the lighter man at around twelve-stone by ten pounds—felt like a sixteen-stone man. Because there was a time limit for when Judo matches went into *Ne-waza*—ground techniques—Connor had not felt this type of compression when grappling on the ground before.

This instructor had made Connor suffer in position before applying an armlock or stranglehold. Connor would tap out and enjoy a few moments of respite before it began again. This lesson was the first of the unarmed combat sessions, which he had been told would feature regularly not only in his training but throughout his entire career.

Connor was not surprised he was losing. He had recognised who his new instructor was upon meeting him.

A British mixed martial arts legend; George Follet was a pioneer of the sport back in the late nineties and early 2000s. He had fought at lightweight in the Japanese promotion of Pancrase. He had been only one of a handful of Europeans to do so. Pancrase had been a precursor to today's MMA, the main exception being the rules did not allow for closed fist striking, forcing the participants to use palm strikes instead. He did remarkably well, winning more than he lost.

He had been contracted to compete in the illustrious Pride Fighting Championships, the Japanese MMA event that had been considered the largest in the world at that time. The promotion routinely pulled in crowds of 80,000 with the record of over 91,000.

Pride FC had been hugely theatrical with massive pyrotechnic displays lighting up the fighters' entrances, similar to the scenes of America's professional wrestling. The female announcer's voice reverberated around the arena, whipping the Japanese crowd into a fervour.

Considered by many to be more brutal than America's counterpart, the UFC; the rules had permitted stamping and kicking to the head of a downed opponent.

George never became champion in Pride but he did defeat two future champions and had always been respected.

The younger man had been a fan of George Follet for a long time for many reasons: his willingness to test himself in an entirely unfamiliar environment, his balletic athleticism, heart and technical skill in all aspects of MMA. He remembered Liam being even more of a fan—*if only he could see me now.*

A thud echoed as Connor was catherine-wheeled to the mat by a hip throw.

Despite the judo training he had, the gap in the grappling prowess was pronounced. The dense physique reflected George's physical strength, with the legs, forearms and back laden with thick, striated muscle. It was also Follett's technical skill; the constant subtle shifts of position, manoeuvring Connor into place.

"Your stance is slightly too high, that's one of the reasons I can take you down. When we clinch, I want you to widen your stance and bend your knees. You're not shifting into a wrestling stance deep enough when we clinch. Your hips should be lower than mine," Follet instructed as they clinched. "OK. Wider. Plant into the ground. Bend your legs more. Now, switch your legs and drop to your knees while pulling my arm into you, like this."

George executed the move throwing Connor onto his back. He lay there and felt honoured to be his pupil. He did not kid himself it was not going to be painful. They had not even touched on striking yet.

7

The American watched the Frenchman through the busy vibrancy of the Parisian street. He was about to surprise this potential client in his inimitable way—his standard operating procedure with potential customers who insisted on meeting face to face.

Usually, his intermediary made the arrangements. In his experience, clients who wished to meet face to face had one of two agendas. Either they wanted to be as certain as possible that there would be no leaks, or they were control-freaks who hated 'middlemen'. In any case, these were the clients he deemed to be the most dangerous. Upon completion of the assignment, their need for control might extend to trying to eliminate him, to tie loose ends.

The American always sought to unbalance them from their very first meeting and maintain the upper hand. Surprising them before the designated meeting place gave credence to his skill level of which they were hopefully already aware. It also gave them a fleeting glimpse of their last moment should they ever double cross him. He had done this several times, and it had always produced the desired effect.

The American appeared almost slender in clothes. His tremendously sinewy musculature had grooves of definition throughout it. His blond hair and blue eyes were visual magnets to an otherwise unremarkable face. With the short beard he now wore, he resembled a Nordic Viking. Today, he dressed in a thin brown leather jacket with a light blue hoodie underneath.

He crossed the street, now approximately twenty metres behind the businessman, letting the snub-nosed Walther PPQ 45 pistol fall into his palm. He would press the gun into the Frenchman's back as they stood at the crossing lights. He would order him to an outside table at the coffee shop where they were to meet. With taking a seat behind the prospective client, he would preserve his anonymity.

He was now a mere ten feet from the man known to be Pierre Gaultier.

Shock rippled through his body like a brick thrown into a still pond, as a muzzle pressed into his own lower back. Simultaneously a right hand gripped his sleeve and forced his Walther to point to the ground.

"Libérez votre arme ou vous mourrez dans la rue," the voice growled—*Release your weapon, or you will die in the street*.

This disconcerted him; not only had the figure managed to ambush him but also spoke fluent French—meaning he knew he did too.

After a quick assessment, he allowed the hand to slide down and take the Walther away from him.

"Marchez vers le café et asseyez-vous," said the man, —*walk to the Café and sit down*— and Carl began to walk across the street. After thirty yards he took a seat in front of a seated Pierre Gaultier, outside the café.

"Well, Monsieur Wright—Monsieur Carl Wright, that was not how you thought this would turn out, no?" said Pierre smiling. His French-inflected English superb if a little text-book.

A vanilla latte sat in front of Carl—his coffee of choice when away from home. The man with the gun sat at an angle so the three of them formed a triangle around the table.

Pierre Gaultier sat casually, still looking the part of the flamboyant French businessman, while Carl remained the tourist. He mused that the Frenchman could be mistaken for a relation; his hair sported a comparable colour of blond, and his lean physique was not dissimilar to his own.

The gunman, with his hand now empty, looked more like a lawyer—suited and professional. The glasses offset the man's compact build, and his eyes were alert.

"I wish to congratulate you with your style. Your plan would have worked had we not already seen it in action, *mon ami*," continued Pierre. Wright remained silent and fought the impulse to tense his jaw.

"OK, to business," said Pierre with a dramatic clap and a triumphant smile.

"Who says I want to do business with you now? My anonymity is gone."

"Your anonymity is gone with us. It does not however have to go any further than this."

Carl silently cursed; they had him over a barrel, and he did not know how. He took a sip of his coffee with it being the only good thing in his immediate vicinity.

"Took a time to track you, we set up three assignments for you before this," grinned Pierre.

Carl recalled the jobs he had taken in Switzerland, Italy and Nigeria.

"So why the insistence of a face to face now?" he asked, locking eyes with the Frenchman.

"Because this assignment is rather delicate. I wanted to measure your professionalism before giving it to you," Pierre replied evenly.

"Meaning that it's so delicate that you wanted something to hold over me as a semblance of control?"

"I would word it more, let us say, precaution than control, Mr Wright, but you are quite correct. However, this assignment does not have to be any different than any you have done before."

The attractive young waitress approached to check if the cups were empty. She seemed to sense the atmosphere and backed away.

Carl weighed up his options. He could just tell them to go to hell. *For sure this Frenchman wouldn't have me shot right outside a café in daytime Paris?* However, they had his identity now. That meant he would be looking over his shoulder which didn't bode well in his line of work.

"The trick is to blend in, to be forgettable by your normality. This doesn't simply mean dressing in black like some fiction writers would have you believe. It means regular clothes with no loud or unusual motifs. No bizarre haircuts or eye-catching accessories unless the situation calls for it," said the instructor to Connor.

He was at a facility in the suburbs of Cambridge.

This began his first lesson in urban and counter surveillance. The curly-haired instructor was a member of the Special Reconnaissance Regiment that had formed the eyes and ears of the UK's Special Forces since 2005. Connor had been led to believe that the SAS, and to a degree the SBS, resented SRR's formation at first as they had handled the role themselves for many years. However, the SRR's worth had been proven over the years albeit with some teething along the way. Such was the nature of the unit that their successes did not often get highlighted.

"It's mainly a person's demeanour that allows him to blend into a setting," continued the instructor. "You need to have a plausible reason to be there, which will masquerade your real purpose. Continually remind yourself of that. The best lies are the ones believed by the liar. If you duck into an alleyway to wait for a target to pass you, you're going for a piss, understand?"

Connor nodded and the instructor continued.

"Then, if the worst comes to the worst and you're challenged, you are more likely to respond how your 'alter ego' would; saying, 'What the fuck are you staring at?' It may not seem wise at the time, but it may be more like the response you would give if someone were watching you taking a piss."

Connor was sure he had read that already in a former SAS soldier-turned-writer's book. It pleasantly surprised him that his first lesson had revolved around the human aspect of surveillance and not the use of technical devices.

He supposed that would come.

"The most important thing I can impart to you is this: if you think you're in danger of being spotted, discontinue. We can almost always pick up the target's trail again, but if they know that they've been compromised, they will go to ground. I have lost count of the times that's happened. What it leads to is thousands of man-hours going up in smoke, never mind the enemy strengthening their security protocols, you understand?"

Connor did understand. He too had come across that before, but not in his life as a Royal Marine.

Stanton sat in his office and observed the Prime Minister's advisor's attempt to mask just how upset he was. The breaths were a little more pronounced and the speech a little more enunciated.

Costner was fifty-one years of age, silvery-brown hair swept into a neat side parting and blue eyes framed by black rimmed glasses. He wore a smart but not-too-expensive suit as most politicians were required to do—smart enough to appear professional, not too costly to alienate the electorate.

As a politician, he had learnt to mask his emotions. Stanton could see it in the eyes though—Henry Costner was furious.

"Suicide by burning himself alive? Not pills, not throwing himself off a bridge, not hanging himself—no—apparently, he doused himself in petrol, climbed into the boot of his car, closed it—I mean, shut it from the inside and set himself on fire Roger?!"

"You'll also know that a suicide note was written, and this is substantiated, by his own hand."

"Save it, we both know that Stephen Hardcastle would never kill himself, and certainly not in that manner. I want to know whether it was the Scotsman's doing."

Stanton stared at Henry Costner for a few moments. He sympathised with his frustration. The Prime Minister would have been putting Henry under pressure in anticipation of the media fall out.

Nevertheless, Stanton knew that to give in to any strong-arming would set a dangerous precedent.

Stanton had used his influence to prevent the fact Hardcastle had been shot twice from spilling out. It was obvious that this was unknown to Henry. The fire had burnt away the evidence of the other injuries the MP sustained.

"You could always ask McQuillan yourself, Henry."

Costner shifted in the seat before saying, "I am asking you."

"And I am telling you, I will never confirm or deny operations undertaken by an unofficial unit to anyone, not even the Prime Minister."

The politician exhaled, "I hope you know what you're doing, Roger. You can only shield him so much. One day he's going to crash…and he's going to take you along with him."

"Duly noted," said the MI5 chief. "You can leave now."

"Hi stranger, how are you?" the redhead asked Connor. They stood on the doorstep of her warm, neat home.

"I'm all right, I have just been—"

"—busy with work, I know," Grace interrupted, in her light North-East of England accent.

Her closed-mouth kiss on the lips made him tingle a little. He stepped inside and handed her the bottle of red wine.

"Well, I was going to tell you that I have been busy with another woman, but whatever makes you feel better."

"We both know I've ruined you for other women. This will help ease my guilt," she said, holding up the bottle of wine.

"That's the other woman's wine. She gave it to me as a thank you."

"For leaving?"

Connor laughed.

Her wit often surprised him. She was the only girl who could make him laugh consistently—apart from Rayella.

"Now do you want a cup of tea before or after the sex?" she asked.

As he watched her brilliant smile reveal straight white teeth, he suddenly felt lucky to have met her. Her soft auburn hair fell just below her defined jaw. The hair colour accentuated large green eyes, framing high cheekbones and full-bowed lips.

Connor's childhood household consisted of his mother and his aunt, both of whom were considered beautiful. Attractive women did not overawe him. He thought this one of the reasons he seemed to be successful with them, despite looks he reckoned were good but hardly head-turning.

She never put pressure on him which he greatly appreciated. He never wanted to be put into a position of lying and knew that would happen if he got into a serious relationship. He enjoyed the chase of sex with different women too much. Walking into a bedroom with a game girl he had not yet fucked, remained one of his favourite feelings.

He loved visiting Grace, she had this combination of being warm, yet outrageously sexy. She was intelligent and funny, had a high-powered career but was still down to earth. Better still, she was deliciously quirky without being weird.

These characteristics kept him interested.

As she walked to the kitchen he admired her. She was a little taller than average, with D-cup breasts, a toned stomach, and shapely legs supporting a tight bum. She had a figure born of natural athleticism without the hardness of an obsessive dieter.

At first, Connor was nervous she would get into a relationship, and these fly-by visits would have to end. As time had gone on, he could see she was both intensely focused on her career as well as free spirited. For those reasons, he hoped she would not go for a long-term relationship for a while.

Stanton had not let it show to Costner, but he had shared his fury. He could not fathom why Bruce had chosen to kill Hardcastle in the manner he had either. The MI5 chief—already having to defend McQuillan—had received no prior warning.

He knew why Costner came to him directly. The PM's adviser did not want to ever interact directly with Bruce McQuillan.

Stanton recalled his first meeting with Bruce McQuillan. It had been the week after his appointment to the head of MI5, and the meeting took place at MI6 Headquarters, Vauxhall Cross. He and Costner flanked Miles Parker, the head of MI6 at one side of a huge oak table. Parker cut a towering tall and statuesque figure mirroring the fortress-like Vauxhall Cross itself. Bald with a commanding voice, Parker cast an intimidating presence to most.

The inimitable Scotsman had walked in with two brown folders under his arm. He had extended his hand over the table at Stanton.

"Good to meet you Mr Stanton," Bruce had said.

Stanton had felt the strong grip.

"You too Mr McQuillan"

Bruce had taken his seat in front of the trio.

"Apologies for being late here," he had said, skimming a folder to Parker and one to Costner, "these are for you two. The contents are for your eyes only."

Parker had stared at Bruce for a few moments before picking up and perusing the folder. Costner had followed his lead. The seconds passed, Stanton felt a change in the atmosphere without knowing why.

Parker spoke quietly with a quiet edge to his voice, "Where did you get this from?"

"I had my unit work it up."

The temperature in the room seemed to cool.

"Are you fucking insane?" Parker had asked.

Bruce's eyes had not wavered from Parker's. "I think it's the smartest thing I have ever done. My unit and I have always been expendable to this…committee. As soon as the risk outgrows the reward, we'll be thrown onto the fire Miles. And don't insult my intelligence by claiming any different…or you Mr Costner."

Stanton's mouth opened a little.

Whatever was in those folders somehow had the potential to damage the two men he sat beside. This Glaswegian had just threatened two of the most powerful men in the country.

The tension had been surreal.

With his meeting with Morris still fresh in the mind, Stanton had not been sure in that moment whether McQuillan had been smart or insane.

"What do you want?" Parker growled.

"I will now report to one man, that man will be Mr Stanton here. Other than that, I don't want anything. Just know that if there's any attempt to expose my unit from Vauxhall Cross, Westminster, or an unknown source in the media, the content of those folders will leak. Or if there's an attempt of blackmail on your part or even heaven forbid, an attempt on my life originating from any man in here, the contents of those folders will be released to all and sundry," Bruce announced, his voice clear and confident.

The words hung in the air.

When Henry Costner finally spoke, the shock was evident in his voice.

"You expect us to continue to fund The Chameleon Project without even reporting to us? That, excuse me for saying, is absurd."

"You can cancel the funding now. In fact, I suggest you do. I will fund my unit myself," answered Bruce, while displaying a shit-eating grin. "See, it's not all bad, you can tell the treasury to expect more money. Maybe the NHS will profit."

No one spoke.

When Bruce McQuillan had stood up, Parker and Costner had moved back an inch.

"A pleasure, gentlemen. Mr Stanton, I will be in touch shortly," Bruce had said before turning and leaving the room.

"Don't take the tea bag out too quick, it tasted like bats' piss last time. I will trade you in if you keep missing the required standard," said Connor with the ghost of a smile.

Grace turned as not to let him see her smiling. She thought back to how they first met as she made the tea.

After five years of medical school she had earned a first-class honours degree in medicine; two years of foundation training and another couple of years of core surgical training followed.

Back when she met Connor, she had just begun her six years of paediatric specialisation training to finally become fully qualified.

He had been seconded to Leeds General Infirmary for ten weeks. The Ministry of Defence initiated a short-lived scheme to send Royal Marine team-medics to hospitals for hands-on training. There was something about him that she loved. He was a paradox in many ways. His being a Royal Marine had piqued her interest but no more than that. His manner attracted her first; men could be intimidated by her, but this was not the case with him. He had no airs or graces, a razor-sharp dry wit and a unique way of observing things. He seemed so confident in himself too, and was by far the smartest of the thirty or so Marines that had passed through.

One day, he came into the common room and found her reading 'Emma' by Jane Austen and quoted one of her favourite lines, verbatim—*'Silly things do cease to be silly if they are done by sensible people in an impudent way.'* That he had read it surprised her, although he had told her to keep it a secret, with a wink.

On another routine Saturday night at the hospital, an irate Muslim male had been gesticulating to a lady, presumably his wife but only spoke Punjabi with bits of broken English. The man's speech had reached an angry climax when Connor appeared, talking to him rapidly in the man's native tongue.

More surprising was the way he had the man laughing within seconds. This allowed the nursing staff to deal with the lady, who had been suffering from gallstones. She had a sharp insight into another side of him whilst on the shift commonly known as 'Mad Friday'—the last working Friday before Christmas. This night was always notoriously busy on the A&E ward, and Grace had been on shift.

Her adrenaline had spiked upon hearing male voices shouting, swearing and berating one of the staff nurses outside her workroom. It was not in her nature to simply wait for security to arrive as one of her colleagues was being bullied. Besides, she had seen the two security guards on shift tonight bottle it on more than one occasion—*Were there any real men anymore?*

Grace came to the aid of the staff nurse trying to calm three drunken and agitated males who looked to be around their early twenties. One of the men held his torn T-shirt to his head. All three had muscular chests, biceps and shoulders. Their ape-like hunch suggested a lack of attention to the training of their back muscles.

However, they were all big strong men, particularly the ginger who stood tall and had been easily fifteen-stone in weight. Of the cronies flanking him, the one on the left had his lip permanently curled in a Neanderthal show of aggression. The blood from his scalp soaked his T-shirt. The last of the trio was relatively short but had huge, almost cartoon-like, steroid-inflated muscles. The plunging, U-shaped neckline of his T-shirt exposed the deep line of his pectorals. This image went hand in hand with his gelled blond hair, and the ear stud glimmering against his unnaturally tanned face. His whole manner reminded Grace of an angry strutting peacock.

Her professional demeanour and lack of openly displayed fear were usually enough to calm situations like these. However, the trio's concoction of drink, drugs, and insecurity mixed into a dangerous combination.

The three men crowded both women quickly, issuing saliva spraying taunts and threats, most of which were sexually themed. Before Grace—no stranger to violence—could react, it happened.

Connor appeared from seemingly nowhere to the ginger's flank, punching him with a combination of such speed and ferocity that the big man spun and reeled back as if on skates. The fury of the onslaught left his two companions stunned for a moment. The big man collapsed to his knees facing away from Connor. A knee smashed into his temple, sprawling him unconscious, like a puppet with its strings cut. Connor turned, wearing an

74

expression of focus as the bare-chested man rushed flailing at him. Connor's head shot in the protagonist's face like a cannon. The impact toppled the thug as the steroid abuser reached up to restrain Connor. Just as the balloon-like arm wrapped around the neck, Connor gripped the wrist with both of his hands.

Repeated head-butts slammed into the pocket Hercules's face, smearing pain and panic across it. Connor took the gripped wrist behind his opponent's back, wrenching his arm in a hammer lock between his shoulder blades.

Screams followed the dislocation of the shoulder.

The man's feet were whipped from beneath him by a foot sweep. The stamp to the head cut off the wails. The shaven headed assailant had managed to stand shakily. He ran away, blood streaming from his shattered nose.

The massacre had not been pretty or well-choreographed, but it had been awesome to Grace in its ruthless vehemence. Connor's eyes made contact with hers as he began to control his breathing, and she felt a jolt through her body.

He said, "I am sorry. I let the dark side take hold of me."

Grace had sneered, "Don't be silly. They deserved it."

He shook his head. "No…you don't understand," looking into her eyes, "I have never read Jane Austen in my life. I just noticed you reading it and googled a quote from it…"

He gave her a great smile, and she could not help but laugh.

She had become aware of the murmurings from shocked patients and staff. They were surveying the wreckage of two bloodied, comatose men and so she began to usher them away. She watched Connor rifle through the pair's pockets and remove the wallets. He looked at their driver's licenses before slipping them back.

As the ginger began to regain consciousness, Connor gripped his hair, cranking his neck and whispered into his ear. She saw the man's eyes get wider and he began to nod.

The hospital security was now on the scene and seemingly confident enough to take charge of the docile men. The bloodied pair reminded Grace of a black and white picture she had seen of shell-shocked victims of the London Blitz.

When questioned, Grace told the Police that the men attacked Connor first. The staff nurse who witnessed the attack followed her strong, confident lead. She was startled to learn that the two men never denied it. *Just what had he whispered in that man's ear?* she wondered. Charges from either side never came.

After that long night, Grace fell into her bed, wired. She stroked her pussy to the most intense orgasm she had had in years thinking of Connor Reed.

8

"How's he doing so far?" Bruce asked Jon Pepper.

Pepper was the chief instructor of the training programme Connor Reed was undertaking.

They sat in Pepper's office in London; Jon on a leather swivel chair behind his desk with two unmarked files on it, and Bruce across from him on the plush, black sofa. It was a medium sized room with a filing cabinet on the side. The computer stood on the desk and a couple of photos were set at an angle so only Pepper could see them. The great bay windows held a picturesque and hypnotic view of urban London; the congested traffic on the roads, hurried people and large, dominating buildings all on display.

Pepper, a few inches shorter than Bruce, had been until recently, a rail-thin man. Middle-age had filled out his frame more as the years passed. Flecks of grey permeated throughout his black hair, and he wore horn-rimmed glasses.

"Good so far. He's picking up the finer technical points of each subject well, and his weapons handling is of the level you'd expect from an experienced Royal Marine," answered Jon.

"Can you give me an approximate timescale for when the lad can go operational under supervision?"

"You know a lot of this training is continuous, but I estimate, given the pace he's learning at, he'll be ready in a couple of months, not including any operational specific training."

Bruce did not know why the young apprentice so fascinated him. He had seen so many recruits with more impressive credentials. There had been experienced soldiers from the SAS and SBS, expert MI5 or MI6 field agents, but none had intrigued him like the young Yorkshireman. He realised then the reason was that the Marine had worked completely alone in kidnapping Hardcastle. The level of audacity had been impressive, especially from one who seemingly had no formal experience of that sort of venture. His capture had been down to a twist of fate too. He could not have anticipated Hardcastle would be under surveillance.

Bruce knew the level of daring had to do with something in his background and that was also a worry— he did not yet know what it was. Connor might be the type to go off the reservation—he already had once. However, Bruce was not a shrinking violet himself.

Jon Pepper had also overseen the intelligence workups on Connor, and Bruce was hoping he could flesh out his background.

"What about this lassie he's been seeing?" asked Bruce.

"Grace Templeton: a trainee surgeon at the Leeds Royal and General. Adopted at seven after being rescued by social services from her abusive mother who was a drug addict. Father unknown. She was adopted by an Andrew and Rebecca Templeton, who lived in the affluent area of North West Ajax of Durham. He was an architectural engineer who was away working in the Middle East a lot. Her mother was a hair dresser who owned shops in and around Newcastle, three of which she owned before she met Templeton."

"You said her dad worked in the Middle East. Could he have been swayed by an anti-West ideal, when working there?"

"Nothing is impossible. But there's nothing to suggest that, other than he worked there. Besides, she worked at Leeds Royal and General well before the short-lived MOD scheme sending Marines there had been contemplated. I could dig deeper, but there isn't anything in the initial assessments that indicate anything untoward," replied Pepper.

"Dig anyway."

Pepper continued, "Grace has a record of various misdemeanours throughout her teenage years but managed to achieve consistently good grades. These misdemeanours include stealing a car, and apparently coercing a boy to be the passenger," Jon looked at Bruce as he said this, who could not help but to raise his eyebrows, "there's also a caution for common assault, and a couple for truancy issues."

"This wild child is now a trainee surgeon?" asked Bruce.

"Apparently so, and she is highly regarded by her superiors and peers," Pepper handed Bruce the file, "it's all in there."

"Now what about him?"

"An unusual background. His parents were never married nor did they live together but had an excellent rapport from what I have been able to glean. Connor took his mother's surname but his father, if you didn't already know, was a Greg Ryder, former head of the infamous Ryder family based in Leeds. Greg Ryder spent two years in prison over attacks made in a feud with local criminals who attacked his father Frank. Strangely no charges let alone convictions after his release, although it was an open secret he was in charge, not only in Leeds but he had at least an influence in other Yorkshire cities. Murdered in mysterious circumstances three years ago. Connor's Uncle Derek heads the family now."

Bruce stiffened at the news of the identity of Connor's father. He knew all about Greg Ryder. Ryder had been undoubtedly the most dominant Caucasian crime figure in the Yorkshire area; his name featuring heavily in northern England organised crime circles and beyond. He already knew the story behind the Ryder crime dynasty but allowed the Chief Instructor to carry on, despite Pepper being mistaken as to why Ryder had gone to prison—it had been due to the possession of a firearm.

Bruce felt a piece of the puzzle regarding Connor finally slot into place.

"The Ryder family initially dealt in protection rackets, although a vast majority of their money was made from imported cigarettes and stolen cars. Initially, there didn't appear to be any direct involvement in drug dealing. They taxed the dealers who distributed inside the clubs at the management's discretion. That changed over the years, and now they control the drug trafficking in Leeds as well as other areas of West Yorkshire."

Bruce also knew Greg Ryder had given large sums of money back to drug rehabilitation programmes and youth support centres. He was aware this knowledge was not widespread, though. It was not in the best interest of law enforcement agencies to let Greg Ryder be known as a quasi-Robin Hood character.

"Here's where it gets unusual. Connor's mother, Rebecca Reed, is a veterinarian living in an upmarket suburb of Leeds. As a child, Connor stayed mostly with his mother but visited his father regularly. He experienced both sides of the track, so to speak. A disruptive child, but he too maintained good grades. He began boxing at around nine years of age reaching the Junior ABA Finals at fifteen."

Jon Pepper looked at Bruce before continuing, "However, a violent incident at the age of sixteen in a local Fish and Chip shop resulted in him being sent to Borstal for eleven months. For some mysterious reason, he was still accepted into the Marines at the age of nineteen years despite his record. I am looking into that now. His service record is all in here."

John handed the file to Bruce.

"All in all, he has an excellent service record, with two tours of Afghanistan with forty-five Commando—four-five rather. Another strange thing; apparently, he's proficient in Punjabi, per his troop commander's citation—although it's a rare Afghan that speaks that language, so I am unsure how that came to light," he said thoughtfully, and continued. "He passed the notoriously difficult sniper course and had a stint on the Navy boxing team, where he became a Combined Services Champion. He also competed for the Navy's Judo team. There was a quick promotion to Lance Corporal, but a slower one to Corporal due to some discipline issues. His record shows he has a couple of violent incidents as well as some frankly ridiculous ones. Some would say he has been lucky to stay in the military."

Bruce did not say anything.

He already guessed Connor's father's hand in him circumventing the system to allow him in the Marines so soon after a custodial sentence. Adopting his mother's maiden name would have aided him too. Now Bruce knew why Connor had been capable of the Hardcastle kidnap. Raised into a life of crime, it was likely Connor had not been caught doing anything major since he was fifteen years old.

What he might have been involved in, only the Lord knew.

Connor and George moved around one another on the blue matting. The younger man kept his guard tight, concentrating on not over-reaching with his punches and kicks.

Whenever he fought in sparring or competition, he focused on no more than three things. He hated watching well-meaning coaches bombard young fighters with a myriad of advice just prior to their walk to the ring or cage. The chance of retaining the information was nearly nil once the bell rang. It surprised him to be doing this sort of fight training. He thought a discipline like Krav Maga, the brutally efficient self-defence system originally developed for the Israeli military, would be more appropriate to the situations he might find himself in.

That said, Connor had seen many of his Royal Marine colleagues victorious in drunken brawls with the standard 'wind-milling' technique—intent and aggression could go a long way even when the skills were lacking.

However, he had been looking forward to learning how to disarm a gun-pointing or knife-wielding adversary. Or how to dispatch multiple attackers within seconds, in cinematic style. Instead, he would have to face this complete fighting machine in front of him, regularly now.

Connor never liked playing the patience game when it came to fighting—not in the gym or the street. He felt it close to cheating; the unwillingness to take risks to the detriment of the fight's excitement. That was why he loved fighters like Roberto Duran, Mike Tyson, Dutch Muay Thai legend Raymond Dekker and Russian MMA icon Fedor Emelianenko.

Connor would employ feints to take the opponent out of position before using short attacks. Or to aggressively draw a lead and counter.

George was one step ahead of him though. While not dominated as he had been grappling, Connor had caught a couple of kicks to the thighs, and instantly knew he could not take a lot more of them. They were delivered with tremendous power and frightening speed. Connor scored with a *teep* to the mid-section, spun on his foot as it landed to execute a roundhouse kick. George pistol-squatted and scythed his shin into Connor's grounded leg. Astonished at George's anticipation, he fell as if suddenly pushed into a pool. Winded, the rigid matting felt little better than concrete. His legs shot up to prevent the mounting of his hips. Two kicks thundered into his legs and pain pulsed through them.

Frantic scraping sounds emanated as he began to shrimp his body away to stop George passing his legs. Cartwheeling to land at the side of Connor, George jammed his knee into his abdomen with immense pressure—*fucksake, could he break my stomach lining doing this?*

Blows from mercifully padded elbows and fists rained down. Connor kept moving his hips and arms to thwart the strikes bouncing his head off the floor. He reached down with one hand to push the anvil-like knee off.

George snatched his arm up, clamped it between his legs like a vice and Connor felt a steel-like arm trap his.

He grasped his own wrists to foil the arm bar, as the back of George's thighs pinned his face and torso down.

He anticipated the moment when George would try to wrench his grip apart. When the pull came, he would slip his elbow past the groin to escape.

The calloused palm struck his nose with a loud thwack.

Instantly releasing his clasped hands, he felt his nostrils burst with a metallic smelling gush. His arm hyperextended in a way that a break was millimetres away.

He tapped.

Connor realised as he lay on his back that many of these sessions were going to involve pain.

I don't care.

"Good in there, isn't it?" grinned Bruce, as he noticed Connor's swollen nose.

They were in the car park of the dojo. Bruce leant against the bonnet of his M3 eating a bought sandwich. He was dressed in a white polo shirt, dark jeans and brown loafers. Connor wore blue jeans, brown ankle boots and a thin green cotton sweater with the white t-shirt visible at the neckline.

"Can I ask you why you have me learning mixed martial arts anyway? I thought Krav Maga or something like that would be more appropriate?" asked Connor.

Bruce scratched his chin. "Because to anyone observing you fight, Krav Maga screams out that you have had formal training by some sort of military or law enforcement organisation. Whereas there's some form of MMA club in every major town and city in the UK."

Connor nodded before asking, "What's up anyway? I was under the impression we weren't seeing one another again 'til I'd finished the entire training package?"

"Aye, I like the 'learn on the job' approach where possible, and I have something I think we could handle," replied Bruce, as he threw the scrunched sandwich wrapper into a bin six feet away.

"You think that we could handle?"

"Yes, we. Think you're ready to be Bond now?"

"I've worked alone before as well, you know."

"Aye, and you got caught."

"On a technicality but point taken," Connor shrugged.

"Let's go for a drive," said Bruce.

Connor had arrived at the dojo by foot. Bruce gunned the powerful purring engine and pulled into the urban traffic.

"We're going to process out a broker we've been keeping tabs on for the past few years."

"Why is it that we are only getting around to 'processing him out' now? Nice term by the way," Connor inquired.

"Our unit doesn't officially exist thus any evidence amassed cannot be produced for any judicial process, you see, therefore it's always preferable to build an intelligence picture on these types of people first. We are in the business of undermining, hurting or destroying entire networks, not individuals who can be quickly and easily replaced. Sometimes it's a case of 'the better the devil you know'. Our methods aren't legal, and we can't bring individuals to trial, even if we wanted to. There comes the point where their deeds cannot be tolerated, and something more finite has to come to pass, you understand?"

"Yes," Connor answered, "what did he do?"

"Does it matter?" asked Bruce, looking at the younger man.

"Of course it does. If I wanted to kill just anyone I'd go work for a dictator. That or a gang boss."

Bruce allowed himself a smile to what he took to be a veiled reference to Connor's father—or his uncle.

"Good, I'm glad you question these things. You must always, for the rest of your career, ask why. Ask for evidence. None of your superiors will be perfect, not even me. Even if you don't believe in karma—and you should—these things can come back to haunt you if you get them wrong," stated the black ops commander. "Abeeb Zahid has laundered money for crime bosses and arms dealers of international repute. This irked me but what stuck in my craw was when he branched out into laundering for Abdul Uddra, a Saudi Arabian multi-millionaire who helps fund Al-Qaeda. Now that has to come to an end."

"What stops Uddra simply having his money laundered with someone else?" asked Connor.

"Nothing, but Uddra is a busy man and he trusts Zahid and he put a lot of eggs in his basket. When Zahid dies the majority of Uddra's liquid funds will disappear. The tech guys have located the accounts and will drain them when I say. Here's a folder with the various documentation and evidence," said Bruce, passing Connor a folder from behind his seat.

"It's OK, I'll trust you."

"Like people trusted Stephen Hardcastle? I suggest you get out of that mind-set."

Connor began to read the file.

"You want me to kidnap one of the most feared men in this business?" asked Carl, staring at the Frenchman's impassive face.

They sat across from one another in the back of the luxury vehicle as it slid through the traffic of the city. He had picked him up in the morning from his hotel, and he had dressed in a blue pin-striped suit.

"So, you have heard of him, yes?" smiled Pierre.

"Most people in my profession have heard of him."

"The contract does not involve you personally kidnapping him. You will simply help to…facilitate, mon ami."

"I am sure he will be fine with that detail should he escape," he replied. "And how do you plan on doing this?"

"This will be explained to you by another party."

"So, there are other parties riding shotgun now?" Carl asked, with an accusatory edge to his voice.

"I understand your reluctance Mr Wright, however as you are aware, this is a very dangerous man, and we need experts in this endeavour. If widening the net regarding this troubles you, I would suggest you take comfort in the fact that you do not have a choice."

The American looked at the near-aristocratic sounding Frenchman—*motherfucker is not even trying to pretend that I am nothing more than a mere pawn.*

Carl said "Lookit, killing him is one thing, no man is invulnerable to an assassin's bullet. I can tell you though even that wouldn't be a walk in the park. What you're talking about is kidnapping him, which will be doubly difficult."

"Yes," replied Pierre.

"So, what's my role? And who will I be working with?"

"I will answer the last question. You will be taking your direction from an important man inside the Russian Bratva," Pierre paused and smoothed his lapels, "as I am sure you can understand, I cannot give you his name. Rest assured that he is a very professional man. As to what your role will be, he will be the one to tell you."

Carl sat there feeling off balance and vulnerable. The last organisation that he wanted knowing his identity was one with the international reach and professional ruthlessness of the Russian Bratva.

Up until a couple of years ago Carl, like many, doubted they even existed in an internationally organised form. In his line of work, he became privy to how powerful the shadowy organisation was. He had been outmanoeuvred and was now at this Frenchman's mercy. He fought to resist any immature American-French World War Two references.

Pierre was successful judging by the car alone, and apparently smart, or else Carl would not be in this predicament. He had not even known of the man before today, but Pierre knew a lot about him.

He tried to reflect on the positive, and that was the money he would receive for the job. It worried him that this had got so complicated. He just hoped that it was not in Pierre's interest to fuck him over, or worse, have him killed after the job was complete. He knew that it would not be in the Russian Bratva's interest to keep him alive.

Pierre dropped him off at the hotel.

Pierre watched the assassin walk in the entrance and mused on his disgruntlement. In truth, it had been difficult to identify who Carl was; the arms dealer had to hire him for no fewer than five different contracts, not the three he had said. Impressed by the American, he hoped that he would simply accept the predicament he was in and execute the task at hand. Pierre was in a predicament himself, though. He had to keep Carl unbalanced but at the same time, not push him to the point that the

American would turn on him—*soon he will not be exclusively my trouble.*

The *Solntsevskaya Bratva* had sought Pierre out three years ago to supply them, although they never identified themselves as such. Pierre had learned through his contacts their identity. Over the years, the Bratva had grown infinitely more organised and powerful due to the struggles for supremacy within their organisation reaching their bloody conclusions. With this, a structure had been formed and rules were laid down to prevent the gratuitous bloodshed that had ultimately cost them all money.

Pierre knew the Bratva would take over organised crime in the West in the coming years. There were several reasons for this. One was that the organisation had begun to recruit ex-military and in some cases ex-*KGB*—or the modern equivalent—personnel. These backgrounds now provided the Bratva with a high level of professionalism. Traditionally, the Bratva had heavily recruited from the Russian penal system.

The group was also ruthless and cunning. As the USSR had collapsed, the value of life on the streets of Russia and the rest of the former Eastern Bloc countries remained low. Only the ruthless and resourceful survived.

Unlike the Triads, Turks, and a plethora of other gangs and organisations, the Bratva members were almost exclusively Caucasian men. This, with the now established procedure of elocution lessons among its higher echelons, had given them a greater freedom of movement in Western capitals.

Pierre had tentatively reached out to them for help not thinking his plea would be accepted. However, they had sent an emissary over to Paris to discuss the plan.

The man had been immaculately groomed and impeccably dressed, with no hint of a regional accent in his well-clipped voice. Pierre had seen enough dangerous people to see the darkness that shone from the man's eyes.

When the dark-haired, subtly imposing Russian introduced himself as 'Makar Gorokhov,' Pierre had felt the hair on his forearms stand on end.

This was the Russian that all other Russian criminals feared.

9

"OK, this is us," Bruce murmured, as they pulled into the pub car park in Cheshire. They sat in a nondescript black Astra they had switched into at a supermarket carpark along the way. It had been left there for them. It was the night after Connor's session with George.

The moon lit up the cloud it was trying to escape from to join the bright stars. The pub named 'The Cabbage Hall' was dark and empty at this hour of 2.15 A.M. The side road was quiet, miles from the M6 motorway. Bruce killed the engine.

Both he and Connor were now wearing lightweight, deep brown leather jackets. The tough hide cut down on leaving any fibres behind. Bruce turned to Connor.

"The house he lives in is around a half a mile up the road. It's set back from the road by a long drive, and high hedges obscure it."

"What about this car?"

"Someone will collect it soon after we leave and collect us when it's done," said Bruce as he pulled on his thin, black leather gloves.

"Right, talk me through everything. Start with the security measures the house has?"

Connor replied, "Standard alarm and two cameras overlooking the doors. We'll spray off the cameras, boot the door in, rip the alarm box off and cut the wires before the forty-five second timer finishes its countdown."

"Why does it have to be so... shall we say, agricultural?"

"That's the point—ransacked by burglars and killed in the struggle will be the initial assumption," answered

Connor pulling on his matching gloves, "then you'll leave a subtle trail of evidence to some drugs tsar."

"Yes, Victor Lonsdale in Manchester has some accounts that he handles, so we kill two birds with one stone."

"Bit like Fred West," said Connor.

They got out of the Astra and cut through a gap in the hedgerow running along the car park. They began walking across the fields, skirting the woodland towards the grand house in the near distance. The damp night was quiet, except for the wave-like sounds of isolated cars travelling along the obscured road nearby. The clouds mercifully kept the moon hidden—bright moonlight was as bad as daylight when stealth was required. They crept along the broad hedgerow to the side of the target house, being careful not to unduly disturb the vegetation.

"Here," whispered Bruce, handing a heavy Maglite torch to Connor, who weighed it in his hand. A heavy Maglite torch was a favourite of any UK motorist who felt the need to keep a weapon in their car. It was small enough to bring to bear easily but heavy enough to fracture a skull. Importantly, it could be easily explained to a policeman.

They conducted a *stop-short* at the hedgerow. After two minutes, Bruce turned to Connor, "Put this on."

He handed Connor a ski mask and, after donning his own, he took out a pair of secateurs from his jacket. He began to cut through the thin branches and foliage that obscured the side of the house while Connor kept watch.

"Avoid being on camera as much as possible, even with the mask. Going in from the side will allow us to obscure the security cameras front and back without being in sight of them," he explained, as his breath condensed in the air. Connor nodded—this was not his first time breaking into an occupied building.

Besides, it had been covered in the brief beforehand, but he understood the need to be thorough. Bruce cut through after a few minutes, and he and Connor formed up on the side of the house.

Abeeb Zahid was sat in his private study, finishing the last of his business emails.

The study was bare of any personal effects and the shelves filled with books he had never read. They were more for show for the guests of the lavish dinner parties he and his wife threw regularly.

He knew that the elite of the Cheshire area had never truly embraced him—he was a Muslim after all. They smiled and laughed at his jokes, and it was preferable to pretend their attendance at these parties was because of his wealth, rather than the fact that they were enraptured with his beautiful wife's charms.

Zahid's wife was out of town. He did not know if she was naïve and genuinely was not aware of his criminality, or if she simply did not care. It was probably like the attitude he adopted regarding her infidelity. She could pretend all she liked, but they both knew she was with her boss, not a spa retreat with 'the girls'—and he could not care less. Their marriage was what it was—a show. Still, her absence meant he could work without risk of intrusion.

It had taken him a while to trust the process of sending encrypted emails. Five years ago he would never have dared. He had to accept that times were changing or else lose business. Customers both nationally and internationally wanted to be kept constantly up to speed and that meant electronically. He was entirely comfortable with it now though.

His most profitable customer had funded both the installation of a hi-tech computer suite, and his tuition in IT encryption methods. His name was Abdul Uddra, a Saudi financier who funded various Islamic fundamentalist groups.

Abeeb was not as strong a sympathiser as he liked to appear in front of his more fundamentalist custom base. His God was money, and the status it brought. He did not care how these people spent their money, with the exception that he was paid promptly and well. He had been smart—so smart he had never been caught in the seven years that he had been handling seven-figure or more accounts and transfers.

In the beginning, he imagined government agencies being all knowing and powerful. With time, and as his wealth grew, this fear became relegated to the background.

Now, standing in his silk pyjamas he watched himself brush his teeth. Ten seconds at twelve different angles. He mused that if he was going to be caught it would have been back when he was nervous and inexperienced. Not now that he was a seasoned professional in the international money laundering game.

'Mr Negative', as Connor called him, tried to inject doubt into his thought process—*you are about to murder an unarmed man in his home who is not posing any immediate threat.* This notion surprised him given what he had done to Stephen Hardcastle. That had been intensely personal though and he alone had planned it. He quickly quashed this line of thinking with the countering affirmation that Zahid had funded many terrorists over the years to line his own pockets.

This was a necessary measure.

Connor reminded himself of the time, a few years earlier, that he had given first aid to a screaming little Afghan girl. The right side of her head had received severe burns in a vehicle-borne suicide bomb in Helmand Province. The glimpse of this memory hardened his resolve. He knew that every murderer, child rapist and corrupt banker could not all serve actual life sentences. There just was not the money to keep that many prisons running. Capital punishment was not returning to the UK any time soon either, as much as the working classes repeated it should when setting the world to rights in the pub.

Still, this did not mean he could not feel angry. Now he had an outlet for that anger. In fact, he could now strike a blow for justice himself.

Bruce crouched five feet away from the rear camera and beckoned him over. Connor felt like a young version of himself as he climbed onto the taller man's shoulders with the can of black spray paint at the ready. He remembered his Grandad carrying him on his shoulders in the same manner.

As Bruce stood and took his first step, Connor covered the Scotsman's eyes and stifled a belly laugh. Bruce shook his head violently to rid the obscuring hand and stared at Connor incredulously.

"Fucking *eejit*," Bruce muttered under his breath.

Bruce walked Connor just under the security camera and Connor took out the black spray can and blacked it out. Still carrying him, Bruce started towards the front of the house.

"Don't cover my eyes again, you wee fucker."

Connor did the same to the security camera at the front, and Bruce let him down. The Scot tried the handle to the front door and found it was locked.

"OK, keep watch while I open this lock," said Bruce, removing a lock-picking gun from the inside of his jacket. After a few moments, he unlocked the front door.

Connor felt the adrenaline shoot around his veins.

"Now, I'll rip the alarm off and cut the wires, and you take care of Zahid."

Connor took a breath—*this was it*—there was no turning back now. He had been shown diagrams from which he had memorised the layout of the house. He smashed the handle down, and his pounding feet raced up the stairs.

The bedroom door crashed through under his boot, and he found the wild-eyed Zahid scrambling from his bed. The duvet was wrapped around him like it was alive.

As Connor approached, he heard the horrific screams of the little girl in Afghanistan adjoined with the image of her pain-seared eyes and the smell of burnt flesh. Euphoria shot through him as he smashed the hammer into Zahid's skull with a thunking crack. The cranium caved in, and an expression of terror froze onto the launderer's face. Connor felt a primal thrill as he hammered the skull to a pulp.

The lifeless body slid to the floor with an inordinately large pool of blood emanating from the smashed head. A thought occurred to Connor as clear as day—he was not James Bond and never would be. Bond was meant to have a cold detachment when killing baddies.

But Connor loved it.

The sound of commercial pop music played through the medium of the wall-mounted televisions permeated throughout the Manchester gym. The treadmills and static bikes whirred as people zoned out to the images on the screens. Young men populated the free weights area dressed in tank tops and wearing snapback baseball caps, extolling one another with catchphrases such as, "It's all you!", "Push, push, push!" and "Lightweight."

Four Asian youths, with upper bodies disproportionately large in comparison to their legs, took turns on the bench press.

Some of Nick Flint's friends would ridicule gyms like this, but he liked coming now and then. From the spit and sawdust weightlifting gyms he usually went to it was a change of ambience. There were women here too. He could also bank on the squat rack being free. He stood in the rack breathing deeply after his second set with his palms resting on the barbell. He was amid a six-week hypertrophy phase, designed to increase muscle size.

The high protein/high carbohydrate diet consisting of six to eight meals spread over the course of the day could be tedious in both the preparation and the consuming. The heavy barbell squats performed for sets of ten could be brutal. However, the additional muscle mass could be very handy in his line of work, and he liked being a muscular guy anyway.

He remembered how lean he was after selection to become a badged member of the SAS. *Perhaps this sort of training was not so 'brutal' in comparison*, he thought.

He gripped the barbell tightly and ducked under it pinching his shoulder blades together. He rested it on the shelf of muscle underneath the base of his neck.

Nick squeezed his core tightly letting the tension irradiate throughout his musculature—he did not wear a weightlifting belt. He sipped the air as he lifted the 140kg off the rack pins and began his descent. He always went full depth, before pushing through his heels for the ascent.

The weight bore on him like a giant's thumb as the veins throughout his shoulders, upper chest and neck stood out in bold relief. At the top of his reps, the thighs displayed a remarkable muscularity.

He fought through the burning pain of the final two reps. It took almost the last of him to step forward and re-rack the bar. He leant against it pretending not to notice the surreptitious looks from the other gym patrons, including a couple of the women on static bikes in the reflections of the mirrors. He leant down to his small training holdall to take out his pre-prepared protein shake when he noticed a message waiting on his work phone.

'We need to talk. Use a phone box,' it read.

Connor continued his training throughout the following months. He was tested every day, physically, mentally and spiritually. That he was the only recruit on the course felt alien to him. On every training course in the Marines, he had always been surrounded by other lads. Here, aside from the instructors, Connor was alone. None of the directing staff ever extended him any familiarity. He was not being screamed at or insulted, and every criticism was constructive and measured.

Still, he was not being encouraged either.

The line between instructor and student was not ever crossed, by any of them, nor had it been by him. He did not want them to be his friends, not while he was 'on course'.

Every morning began with either weapons training or unarmed combat. This would be followed by memory training, learning about key personalities and the structures of different terrorist or organised crime threats. Surveillance training, driving at speed, basic Arabic and lock-picking were hammered in. There were lectures and practical lessons on agent recruitment and handling. The complex geography of major cities in the UK and Europe had been impressed into him day after day.

Sometimes his brain felt akin to a left-over lasagne.

The fight training often left him feeling vulnerable and in pain, but he loved it. Everything stretched him, making him better for his new profession.

Connor felt a definite purpose he had not felt in years. He knew that this was the real reason the Scotsman had included him on the mission before he completed his training—to let him know that the skills he was learning would be used.

It bothered him that in the Marines some of the more arduous training might never be used. He knew of Sergeant Majors with twenty years of service, who had been to Belize and Norway several times in their career on exercise, having never had the opportunity to complete an operational tour in jungle or arctic conditions. Though he had heard it argued most of the skills in those conditions were transferrable to any environment, it had still bothered him.

Also, McQuillan had probably wanted to see if he could kill someone up close, which was different to engaging the enemy with a rifle at range.

However, he also knew McQuillan wanted to let him know he would be making a difference. Connor was aware that this was what he wanted to do with his life and thanked providence.

This morning, when he had walked into the dojo, he saw another man in addition to George. The man was about an inch taller than himself, stocky, with a shaven head and prominent features.

With the man prowling around in the corner of the cage wearing black and red Lycra fight shorts, Connor could sense why he was here.

The man thankfully did not make eye contact. Connor thought it was ridiculous to try and win a staring contest with a man he was going to punch the fuck out of anyway.

The man looked South American, possibly Brazilian, with every muscle clearly defined.

"You will be fighting this man under *Vale Tudo* rules," said George.

Connor stripped his training vest off revealing his tattooed torso. He made a conscious effort to remain non-emotional. He turned to face the man.

"No eye gouging, fish-hooking, biting or tearing ears off. Other than that, it's no holds barred," George announced.

Connor's adrenaline spilt out like cold liquid around his internal organs. He controlled his breathing and reminded himself to keep his defence tight and not to over-reach. They circled one another, and Connor threw a couple of sharp jabs to test his opponent's reactions. He kept switching the angles and kept off the *centre line*.

Feinting the jab, Connor sank a thudding right to the body which fired out the Brazilian's breath. Connor ducked the whipping left hook, sliding to his right before clattering his fist off the bald head. The man stumbled, righted himself and threw a swift kick to the thigh. Connor blocked its path with his shin—the adrenaline switched off the pain that would throb later through the bone.

His opponent shot out his hands to grip Connor only to find the hollow of his eye smashed by a headbutt.

By his reaction, the Brazilian had forgotten the lack of rules.

Connor seized his opportunity with a hard knee to the stomach, raining punches and knees both to the head and body. Captured by both legs under his arse, Connor was elevated into the air. He could not wrap an arm around the opponent's neck quick enough, so had to break his fall by smashing the mat with both hands.

The wind vacuumed from him.

He wrapped his legs around the Brazilian's waist and crossed his ankles together. Fighting to survive the moment, he blocked the incoming blows with hands and forearms.

He shot up and threaded his arms underneath his opponent's armpits, pulling him tight to his chest. Releasing his hooked feet, he jammed them between the Brazilian's thighs. Like a pair of pliers, he opened his opponent's legs and tipped him onto his back. His elbow smashed onto the skinhead's jaw and he whipped his legs either side of his chest. Connor reared up to give himself room to hammer the Brazilian's face with punches.

The skinhead made a grab for one of Connor's wrists. Connor snapped his grip onto the wrist of his opponent's outstretched arm and swung tightly around to trap it tight between his legs. The skinhead had managed to grasp both his own wrists. Judging by the corded muscles of the forearms, it would be difficult to release the grip by wrenching it apart.

Connor smiled.

The bottom of his fist hammered onto the skinhead's nose. His opponent released his grip and Connor cranked on the arm bar. The skinhead frantically tapped Connor's leg and the mat in submission. The thought flashed through Connor's mind to break it because of his surliness at the start but instead he let it go and lay there sucking for breath. He was elated, though—he had survived.

George shouted, "Next!"

10

Carl exited the hotel and approached Pierre's car.

He had changed into a light grey business suit, not dissimilar to the style that Pierre wore and had noticed some of the women's looks as he made his way through the hotel.

When he got into the car, Pierre informed him that any question he wanted an answer to, he could ask. It was then when he knew that there was no going back. They would not let him walk away from the job and live once he knew the answers to the questions he was about to ask.

The car began to move.

"Who runs the show within the organisation in London?" Carl asked.

Pierre tilted his head back before answering,

"Monsieur Ravil Yelchin, born in Minsk at 1960. He made his reputation during the eighties where he greatly specialised in the export of contraband oil and precious metals from Russia. It is unclear when he joined the Bratva."

"How did he become so powerful?"

"Years before the collapse of the Berlin Wall, he was selling western goods in Eastern Europe. How he managed to continue the enterprise, year upon year, without falling permanently foul of the KGB, is a testament to his individual discretion and guile. Any Russian crime organisation he may have been a member of back then wouldn't have been powerful enough to protect him."

Not many organisations would have been—thought Carl as Pierre continued. "He slowly built his wealth and contacts, keeping the right people satisfied financially and investing in legitimate businesses. Then around the mid-nineties he began to, how you say, diversify into money laundering, prostitution, extortion of government officials with seemingly stunning success, and has continued ever since."

"How powerful has he become?"

"He was next in line to become the Pakhan for the Moscow faction which would have made him—officially—the most influential member of the Russian Bratva. However, in a shrewd—I like this word—shrewd move, I think he negotiated a deal in which he took over the London…faction."

"Why a shrewd move?"

"Being the Pakhan for Moscow is massively lucrative with the other Pakhans kicking up a percentage. But it also puts one in an isolated position. Corruption is large in Russia which helps protect the Pakhan from law enforcement," said Pierre, leaning forward slightly, "the political manoeuvring is much with constant threats of a takeover having to be put down. London affords greater freedom and less stress. I believe he voluntarily took himself out of the running for the appointment, in exchange for fewer constraints being imposed on his London brigade."

"What makes you say that?"

"His brigade is a lot larger than other cities—excuse moi—than in other cities."

As the Parisian streets blurred by, Carl looked out of the window in thought—*How did Pierre know all this?*

"How have you been given a golden pass with regards to the inner workings to the Russian Bratva? I was led to believe it was either a highly secretive organisation or wasn't nearly as structured as what you're saying. That there are thousands of factions across the globe that are just known as the Russian Mafia?" Carl asked.

"To answer your first question, I have not been given a golden pass, as you say. I have contacts everywhere, Mr Wright, and I cross-reference this information continually for accuracy," answered Pierre haughtily. "No one in the Russian Bratva has ever told me more than I needed to know. That some doubt its structure is a testament to its efficiency. It may be a surprise to you but Interpol privately considers it the most far reaching, powerful and profitable organised crime syndicate in *le monde*—the world. And Ravil Yelchin is its most powerful member no matter who ever resides on the Moscow throne. He wants to take over the world, Mr Wright, and I guess that he is now ready to do so."

Connor skirted around the mat dragging oxygen into his system. He tried not to show his opponent how depleted he was. He used feints while waiting for a second wind that could not come quick enough.

Connor had cursed to himself when he realised he would have to face another opponent—*I am meant to be training to be an agent for this not learning how to be in the fucking UFC.*

He banished such thoughts from his mind. They did not help. He would fight until it was physically impossible to resist any longer—*I am a Bootneck.*

This opponent was an inch or so shorter but stockier, well-built with disproportionately large, muscular thighs. A handsome man with wavy blond hair and an anvil-like jaw. Connor guessed him to be American by the way he carried himself and his glowing white, straight teeth. The man had not yet spoken.

Also, Connor deduced that he was a wrestler with the way he moved low in a crouch. Unlike in Britain, wrestling was a staple sport imparted in American schools and colleges. Connor pushed him away with a teep to buy time.

Mr Blond was doing a commendable job of checking Connor's low kicks. It was a painful thing to do but checking kicks did not usually disable the recipient like solid kicks to the thighs could. Connor let him come closer and fired a chopping right to the temple forcing him to one knee. With the power of a rushing bull, the wrestler shot in on his leg, took grip and wrenched it off the floor driving forward. Connor hopped backwards while pushing down on the blond's head, trying to break the hold. The grip was now too tight.

He toppled.

Reed associated 'punching it out' as the true way to fight. He hated wrestlers who used their wrestling to simply 'control' an opponent on the floor. The fist of Mr Blond bludgeoned into his cheek before he had even mounted him—Connor then knew that just controlling him was not his intent. Connor quickly used his hips to twist and scrambled up. The Marine's mood darkened. He was determined he would not let himself be taken down again.

Up quicker than Mr Blond, he smashed a knee into his face. Mr Blond stumbled back onto his behind, a weird vertical cut split his left cheek. Connor ran up and tried stamping on his face as Mr Blond rocked onto his back. Thrashing arms thwarted the stamps.

Connor stood over him, feigning attempts to get past his feet but was slyly taking the opportunity of a breather. After a minute, he backed off, and Mr Blond wearily got back to his feet. The Yorkshireman began to jab and step around him, giving him different angles. He started to feint and found himself beginning to hit Mr Blond. Nothing devastating, but he was landing and Mr Blond was not.

Connor sprawled away from a couple of takedown attempts by shooting his legs back as Mr Blond shot in for them. Looking for an opening, Connor found it with a whipping long right uppercut to the face. It landed like a mallet on a slab of meat as Mr Blond stumbled forward with his hands outstretched. Connor took a hard grip of his hair before raining obliterating knees and punches into Mr Blond's face. Follet dove in to save the unconscious and bloodied Mr Blond.

Bruce drove his M3 towards George's house, cutting through a quiet residential area. George sat beside him dressed in jeans and his training sweater.

"Anything else?" Bruce asked George after discovering Connor had overcome his two opponents. His performance surprised them both. They had been two young professionals who had regularly paid George for private sessions.

The exercise had been designed to push him to ascertain whether or not he would surrender in the face of a task he could not succeed in. Instead, he had neutralised both opponents; almost breaking one's arm and bludgeoning the consciousness from the other. They resembled car crash victims when Bruce saw them, and he had had to financially recompense them.

"He's got ruthlessness about him. I would say viciousness. He would have kept pummelling that American if I hadn't dived in," said George to Bruce.

"How do you rate him?"

George continued, "It helps he's had a solid background in boxing and judo, and he responds well to tutelage. I'd back him against most."

"Thank you," said Bruce, "a guy who can handle himself tends to be more confident going about this business, and it could save his life one day."

As Bruce said this, he thought back to when one of his undercover operatives died. It had been in a brawl with a Turkish gangster in the backroom of a club. It had not been because he had made the gangster suspicious of his identity—it had been because he had beaten him at the card game they were playing.

Makar Gorokhov sat in a charcoal Skoda Fabia. He was parked on the street overlooking the majestically lit Mandarin Oriental London Hotel.

It was a 'work' vehicle; a car he used to keep a low profile. The scene from a film in which Al Pacino's character impressed the benefits of being underestimated, came to his mind—*I am a surprise. They do not see me coming.*' Makar knew the importance of this, realising that it was one of the reasons for his success in this career.

But it had become harder to be underestimated as the years went by and his reputation grew. He knew he was feared.

This fear was most evident to him when meeting people in this business for the first time. Some hid it better than others, but he had been able to read people ever since he could remember. The change in body language, behaviour and dialogue of individuals, however subtle, gave away their nervousness.

The surveillance task he was currently engaged in was one others in his position would delegate, but Gorokhov chose not to. It kept him sharp.

He was the *Avtorityet* (Brigadier). The role of an Avtorityet had similarities to a *Capo*—Captain—in the Italian-American Mafia. An Avtorityet would oversee a crew of around ten men. There were four Avtorityets to a major city's Bratva, ruled by one Pakhan.

Ravil Yelchin had made allowances for Makar. London still had the requisite four Brigades, but the other three had five Boyeviks (warriors) apiece and five to six Shestyorka (associates). Makar had ten of each.

The other Avtorityets stayed in line; happy to be a part of the most lucrative Bratva in the entire Solntsevskaya Bratva. They were also aware that one of the driving factors in the London Bratva's prosperity was Makar Gorokhov's ruthless professionalism. An undercurrent of fear helped too.

Makar stood six-feet one-inch, appearing a well-built man in clothes. Underneath lay a fearsome physique. The muscles were thick, hard and dense with none of the water-retained size which some steroid abusers carried. This density of muscle was why he did not look conspicuous in his standard suited attire.

He had a strong face made up of a square jaw with the alert eyes an unusually intense shade of blue. He would have changed his eye colour if he could—they were too memorable. He had a full head of brown, wavy hair cut into a fashionable but not eye-catching style.

Makar's gentlemanly manner had prevented anyone who did not know him from finding him threatening upon initial meeting. It had been advantageous, causing him to be underestimated by literally hundreds of adversaries throughout his thirty-nine years. Makar rarely exuded any intimidating behaviour, himself preferring to let his actions do the talking. It was the actions that made others talk of him.

The membership of the Russian Bratva revered Makar. Most were acutely aware that he would have been a Pakhan, had he held that ambition, including Ravil Yelchin himself. Makar's long and distinguished past career as a KGB agent had given him a skill set far beyond most of his contemporaries, both in and out of the Brotherhood.

Today he was observing Hassan Saki, the head of the most profitable Turkish organised crime syndicate in the United Kingdom. Saki was a principal in the transportation and distribution of heroin onto the Isles and had been for years.

Makar had followed the hulking Turk as he wandered the local market stalls earlier in the day. As he watched him converse with market stall patrons and locals, Makar had admired his apparent common touch despite being worth millions.

Hassan Saki was one of five major crime figures in London that Makar's Bratva had been surveilling— *'Getting your ducks in a row'*, being the English term that the Russian liked.

The time for change was on the horizon.

11

Grace opened the door and shone a smile at Connor. It had been over a week since his last visit.

"Back so soon?" she said. She gave Connor a closed mouth kiss. He liked the warmth of her face and breath just before they kissed.

"I'm just finishing up with a client, will take a few minutes," she said, leading him inside.

"Client? You on the game finally?"

"If I were, I'd be living in a mansion in Monaco by now," she replied. He couldn't hide his smile.

Grace had a small room where she tattooed clients, separated from the living room by hanging wooden beads that covered the doorway. She was sought after as an artist, but her commitment to the hospital prevented her from becoming even more renowned.

From the sofa, he watched her as he pretended to peruse a magazine from the pile she kept for clients. He doubted that Grace herself would read 'Now', 'Woman's Own' or 'Woman's Weekly'. Her niche of only tattooing women proved popular. He guessed there were some women who found the thought of tattoo parlours intimidating.

She was tattooing the small of a thirty-something-year-old woman's back, who was sat on a swivel stool. Her upper body leaning on a leather-covered rest fitted to it.

Connor watched Grace, her face a picture of studied concentration. Her red hair was up in a clip, baring her elegant neck. She was wearing jeans and a willowy white shirt, as her latex gloved hand moved the tattoo gun in small circles.

Connor had read a few books on human brain function. Although people tended to be either left-sided (more logical and analytical) or right-sided (more creative or intuitive), a person could develop both sides of their brain to an equally high degree. One book he read stated that the most famous example of that was Leonardo da Vinci. On the one hand he sculpted and had painted masterpieces such as the Mona Lisa. On the other, he had conceptualised helicopters and tanks, as well as outlining a basic theory on plate tectonics, amongst other things.

The best example of a person developing both sides of the brain that Connor had been in contact with was Grace.

She was the most intriguing, mentally stimulating, alluring and sexy girl he knew. She had the ability to make any person feel special, like the woman she was tattooing now. Despite her beauty, the warmth of her manner could completely disarm stand-offish women.

She finished, dabbing away at the tattoo with kitchen roll damp with soapy water and let the client know she had finished.

The lady let out squeals of delight viewing it in the mirror. Grace gave her a broad smile and snapped a few photos with her client's phone. She showed them to the woman, who gushed with appreciation.

Connor began to silently curse the woman as she began to make small talk with Grace—*sense the atmosphere and fuck off!*

He had been getting hard in the car on the way over. His head became deliciously light as Grace tactfully shortened the conversation and began leading the woman to the door. Connor got up and followed a few steps behind.

Grace had tried hard to forget Connor was waiting and concentrated on the tattoo.

She had always drawn, ever since she could remember, sketching in lessons as a school girl. Now she would sometimes draw alone in parks or libraries.

For her tattoo work, she would listen to what the client asked for in the initial consultation, perhaps subtly steering them onto an alternative if she was not too keen on it. After this, she would draw a template which she transferred to the body to work off it.

She knew artists, excellent ones too, who would simply draw on the client's body with a biro and it always made her cringe. After fighting the urge to rush she finished the tattoo twenty minutes after Connor arrived. She cleaned and took some photos of it on the clients' phone.

"Oh, it's gorgeous Grace! I'll post them up. Can I tag you on my wall for advertisement?", the client asked as she pinched her knees together and bounced.

"It's OK Shirley. I'm not on social media. Word of mouth is more than enough."

"Oh…I am thinking of coming off it myself, to be honest. It's all what people ate for their tea…that and pictures of injured animals. I mean, I just don't want to see it on my wall, Grace. I just use it to keep in—"

"Shirley, this client has booked in at the last minute, and I have to get cracking, Luv" smiling again to diffuse her interruption.

"Oh yes…. OK Grace…thank you very much."

Grace's heart beat harder as she saw Shirley to the door as she noticed Connor stand and follow her.

As soon as Grace closed the door, she felt a firm grip on her arm spinning her around and slamming her against it. She exhaled, either with shock or relief. The fingers on one of his hands gripped her face, and she was physically forced, though mentally willing, into a deep, probing, and open-mouthed kiss. She felt his rough stubble. As her hands came up to clasp his hair, she was spun around again, her wrists grasped by his hands, her palms put against the door.

She felt herself getting wet as the blood rushed to her brain. Her head forced to one side, his mouth was on hers again—hard and insistent. Her belt was prised open, and the buttons of her jeans pulled apart. His hand plunged down her knickers, and his fingers found her wet pussy. It amazed her at how wet she had become. The realisation fell that she had begun to 'feel it' from the moment he got up to follow her to the door.

As her jeans and knickers were torn down, his mouth left hers, and her arse cheeks were pulled apart, exposing her to the cool air. She gasped, letting out a guttural moan, as his probing mouth mashed against her. He began to lavishly eat her pussy before tracing his tongue to her arsehole.

She pushed back against him like she could not get his face deep enough. His fingers entered her pussy and began driving in and out. Just as she felt the stirrings she craved, she was whirled around with his body crushed against hers. She could smell herself on his face. His hand found her throat. He took a grip of her hair and began to force her to her knees.

She did not care about anything else now but him. She received a slap, the noise reverberated and the pain being just right. It was she who liked this—he was a little reluctant in the beginning. It was more the sound of it that turned her on—what it symbolised.

"Look at me," he said.

She did so, near adoringly. He was the best she had ever had, being able just to know what she needed. In these moments she fought the urge to go too far with her verbal endearments.

The other men she had made her feel weird with some of her requests. Many of them indulged her out of sheer gratitude. With him, slapping aside, she had never had to ask him to do anything. That was what turned her on about him: a masculine confidence and complete inhibition not born from just how he looked.

She was on her knees, and he prised open her jaw forcing himself into her mouth. She began to suck, letting the saliva spill over him. Her mouth was making lewd sucking noises as he fucked her face. He gripped her jaw, sliding his cock out before spitting in her mouth.

Pushing her away, they stumbled through to the living room, kissing as they went. He pressed her onto the Persian rug, tearing her jeans down, and fumbling them over her heels. Taking off her knickers, forcing her legs wide, he plunged inside her as she cried out.

He kissed her hard and deep.

He gripped her hair as she clawed at his back. She came hard around him, and he gave her a moment or two to enjoy it.

He put her shapely leg over his shoulder and drove himself into her again. He did not stop, pounding into her until he came with a muted roar. She wrapped her legs tightly around his waist, staring at him.

The man walked along London Bridge admiring Big Ben, a magnificent landmark of London.

He had a kind face, despite rarely smiling. His short black hair gently receded on the crown. His suit was expensive and well-fitting, drawing the attention of the keener-eyed Londoners; the rest were in too much of a rush to notice.

The only clouds in the sky, white and non-threatening, seemed to frame the giant clock tower.

No doubt a student of Freud would make a correlation between his thirst for power and the phallic-like nature of the piece, he thought. Nevertheless, Ravil Yelchin admired all kinds of architecture around the world. The clock tower at the north end of the Palace of Westminster was known to the masses as Big Ben. He knew Big Ben referred to the bell within it and not the entire structure itself.

Yelchin had the sort of enquiring mind that wanted to know everything about anything relevant to his world. At times, information that seemed useless to others had helped him when he least expected it.

He had spent lots of time reading about London's attractions, even the lesser known ones. It fascinated him to learn of the clock's mechanism, the design and architecture of the clock tower itself. It was renamed the 'Elizabeth Tower' in 2012 to celebrate the Diamond Jubilee of the current Queen of England. It amused him to discover that in 1949, the clock slowed by four minutes as a flock of birds perched on the minute hand.

He wanted to know every nuance of the city. London would be Ravil's world, and he would be the master of it.

Now fifty-one years old and although incredibly influential, he felt it was time to stop shifting from place to place. He had to set roots and build a fortress.

The acquisition of this type of power could not be rushed, and it had been a slow, laborious process.

The Russian rarely reminisced as he did not want to waste time living in the past. However, as he was about to rise into a position of true power, he could not help but lament on the journey that led him here.

He had no illusion of what he was—a criminal, and had been since he was young. The ironic part of Ravil's childhood criminality was that his parents were upper class, with his father being a distinguished banker. At around twelve years old, Ravil began to go out on weekends causing mischief. Eventually settling in a little gang—*a banda*—made of youths from twelve to fifteen. They stole from warehouses then sold the goods on the street, stole cars and fought vicious running battles with other gangs. He loved all of it.

He often wondered why he was not caught or that his parents did not question him. Perhaps the former was down to luck, and the latter to denial.

Still, he did well at school and outwardly had seemed the typical teenager. When he reached the age of sixteen, Yelchin came to the attention of a gawky local waiter named Sergei Mikhailov. The charismatic Sergei was not just a waiter. He was a local criminal. To Ravil's surprise, Sergei encouraged him to stay in school and afterwards move on to University, saying, *'Young Ravil, the authorities see what they want to see, they are prejudiced like everyone. Men with real, high powered professions are almost invisible to them.'*

Ravil followed his advice and obtained a PhD in Linguistics at the Modern State Linguistic University, specialising in German, Spanish and English. In Ravil's absence, his old friend Sergei had gone to prison, following a conviction for fraud. He came out and founded the Solntsevskaya Bratva—The Brotherhood.

Ravil arrived back into the criminal underworld in time to prove himself in a bloody war with the Chechen Mafia, who were challenging the Bratva's dominance. Ravil, who had never killed anyone before, killed three of six Chechens in a shoot-out at the Kazakhstan cinema. The battle also saw four of his Bratva brothers die. Ravil escaped, carrying one of his compatriots on his back while shooting at the remaining Chechens—and his legend had been secured.

Sergei, reasoning Ravil had a fluent grasp of German, English and Spanish, sent him to Western Europe. He would take advantage of any opportunities that would present themselves in the wake of the collapse of the Berlin Wall. Ravil agreed, although he also thought it was a play by his mentor to get him out of Moscow, where he might have challenged Sergei's leadership.

Yelchin's contemporaries liked to think of themselves as businessmen for whom crime was a necessary endeavour; that it was no different to what corporate types did anyway. Ravil did not lie to himself though—he was an out and out criminal and liked it.

Though, he did not accuse himself of having a complete lack of morality. There was always going to be crime—it was human nature—but a 'good' crime lord could do more to uphold order than a 'bad' Police Chief Superintendent. The chaos in Russia during the nineties had convinced him of this. He had seen more than his share of 'bad' policemen, bankers, and politicians to know criminality came in all forms.

At least he did not deny what he was. Ravil knew he was not destined for sainthood. He liked amassing power and wealth for himself and the people he cared about. Drugs, prostitution, robbery and extortion were in existence before he came and would still be long afterwards. There were things one needed to be capable of, certain levels of brutality that had to be reached to keep order. It was part of the business.

Yelchin saw Britain in the words of Al Pacino's Scarface, *'as a great big pussy just waiting to get fucked.'* Britain was full of corruption at the highest levels, and the media influenced the opinion of the masses. He marvelled at how the powers that be within the country could distract its population. His theory was that long-term perspective was always the mark of a great man. The dregs of any society only ever made decisions that affected them in the short term—*'What will I eat tonight?' 'Where will I go this weekend?' 'Where shall I spend this year's holiday?'*—That was about as far as they went. The great men set seeds in the present that would not bear fruit for years, decades and sometimes not even in their own lifetimes.

Ravil had dreamt of this sort of power for just over two decades. It had taken him that long to climb the rungs of the ladder. Unlike his contemporaries, whose impatience had cost them their lives, wealth and liberty; he had set the foundations for his own success long ago.

The UK was not like Russia, where the underclass had to be suppressed through poverty and an oppressive regime. The people who controlled Britain were much subtler. They did it by pacifying the public into a comfort zone of consumerism and reality TV from which the populous did not want to escape. This kept them from rising to their dangerous potentials. Like a woman in denial regarding her cheating spouse, the British were in denial about the golden cages they were in. Potential widespread social anger from issues like tax evasion, homelessness, bankers' bonuses, and judicial corruption were suppressed with sensationalism, entertainment gossip and free internet porn.

A black man gets shot by police, the underbelly riot, shoplift and vandalise. The media whips it up for weeks and all the while the people are blind to the real picture, but Ravil knew. He knew that if the Government wanted every man and woman to be a master of his own destiny, they would teach financial astuteness lessons in school. Their news would have highlighted the success stories of working class men and women who had risen to prominence within their local communities, but they hardly ever did.

No ruling system wants its underlings getting above their station—a country needs its 'worker bees' and consumers for the multinational corporations to survive. He saw a nation transfixed with tabloid news that had no direct effect on them, keeping them amused enough to work jobs that were unfulfilling to buy things they did not need.

Ravil continued his walk through the busy and impersonal city that was London, deep in thought. He had been enthralled as a boy reading about the swashbuckling, vast British Empire that had ruled half the planet. He always enjoyed coming to Trafalgar Square with the history behind it. He had avidly read about the Napoleonic Wars. While some felt Nelson reckless to the point of arrogance to be dressed in his full Admiralty regalia on the ship's deck at the time of his death, Ravil knew why he had. To inspire one's men in crucial battles was vital. Nelson had died during the battle of Trafalgar having already implemented his unorthodox campaign tactics. It was left up to his second in command Vice Admiral Collingwood to ensure the battle was won. Now every true Englishman knew who Horatio Nelson was, even centuries on.

He stood before Nelson's column considering his own tactics. He would make no apologies for taking advantage of what the once great nation had become.

Connor and Grace lay naked on her Persian rug in front of the fireplace. She smirked as she felt his cum sliding down her thighs, realising that she should probably now get her rug cleaned.

He had never been straight-laced with her, not even in the beginning. He seemed to instinctively know she was not either. That surprised her; usually, men were very vanilla in the beginning, as not to be seen as depraved or weird. It was different with him. He seemed to sense she would like it—or maybe he didn't care. There were a few minutes of silence.

"What did she have done?" Connor asked.

"Who?"

"The woman you were tattooing?"

Grace sighed. "A butterfly on her lower back, I couldn't talk this one out of it. She says it's a memorial to her deceased sister who loved butterflies. I didn't think bringing up the term 'tramp stamp' was appropriate."

"I wonder how many butterflies have a picture of a fat, unemployed woman above their arse," he said.

"Oi. She's the head anaesthetist at work, and she's not fat."

"OK…we'll say she's extra medium. I'll wind my neck in."

Grace shook her head at him keeping her face straight. Shirley was a bit overweight, despite being on a new fad diet every week.

"When are you going to let me tattoo you?" she asked, stroking her fingertips over the Superman tattoo on his chest. She liked the scratchy feeling of the hair on it.

"When a design jumps out at me. Besides, I'd be frightened of you etching your name into me as a deterrent to the rest of the harem."

She gave a derisive snort. "You'd need a harem to compare to me."

He smiled. "Any chance of a cup of tea since that was the main reason I am here?"

"Since you performed adequately, I'll stretch to it."

Connor watched Grace walk to the kitchen donning her shirt on the way. Connor did have tattoos: a Superman logo on his right pectoral and a half-sleeve that covered his left shoulder and upper arm.

In the Royal Marines, a lot of the lads got particular tattoos referred to as *'Pusser's stamps'*. Connor never fancied having either of them as he thought them to be the height of unoriginality until one of his *oppos* pointed out that only Royal Marines could have this type done.

Still, considering the line of work he was embarking on, he was glad he never had.

12

Carl Wright rode the Eurostar from Paris to London as the hum and his thoughts washed through him.

The general concept of what he was being asked to do was not much different to what he did for a living anyway, he mused. Nevertheless, he did not want to have anything to do with the kidnap and the probable murder of one of the most dangerous men on the British Isles. He felt frustrated being put in this position, then frustrated at being frustrated—*I can't make a living from killing people and expect a life of sunshine and roses.*

He looked at the young Asian woman sat adjacent to him. She was wearing a veil that covered her head and neck—a hijab—which framed her pretty face. She caught him looking and gave him a shy smile which he returned. She looked out of the window. Carl thought back to what made him join the military in the first instance.

His father Finn had regularly taken him to see the Detroit Lions Football team ever since he could remember. Finn's affection for the Lions and the famous Barry Sanders had rubbed off, and he enjoyed going to the games with him even deep into his teenage years. Carl remembered the last game that he saw in 1999 for two reasons. One, the Lions' losing effort to the Washington Redskins would be the last time the Lions made the playoffs.

The second was his father's murder in a mugging two days later outside a local bar. The suspects were caught and were found to be a part of the Lebanese gang culture that had begun to grow in Dearborn. This lit the touch paper that led him to enlist in the 75th Ranger Regiment.

He could not have envisioned, as a young recruit, the position in which he now found himself in.

Back then he had been exhausted, hungry and deprived of sleep. But he had been fulfilled then. Every day passed was one step closer to becoming someone more than he was.

Now he felt very different.

"Makar, come, how are you brother?" said Ravil standing to greet Makar with a handshake.

"Very well, sir," answered Makar, returning it. This was their custom: Ravil would forgo any address to his hierarchal superiority, whereas Makar would make a point of it. Makar would use the word 'Pakhan' when assured of their privacy. Here they spoke English with the dialects removed. Makar's English was flawless and Ravil, although his English was superb, had been finding contractions like *he'd, I'd, I've* difficult. It was what had prevented him sounding like a native.

They sat down together at a small table in the outdoor section of one of Kensington's most private clubs. Tall trees danced in between the canopy lighting, bathing the area in a simmering orange. The leather seating wrapped the occupant in comfort, overlooking the centrepiece of the small pool and Jacuzzi.

Striking, statuesque women, dressed so demurely upon entrance in cocktail dresses, now frolicked in the pool with just their underwear on. Suited gentlemen— with jackets removed and ties relaxed—looked on.

Ravil wore a light blue shirt enclosed by a grey patterned waist coat with the dark blue tie relaxed. Makar wore a darker blue shirt with white patterned flecks throughout. His dark grey trousers held up by brown braces. The ensemble should not have worked, thought Ravil, but it did. He had noticed a few of the women glancing at his masculine countryman.

"Cheers," said Ravil, holding up one of the whiskey snakebites he had ordered for them both. They had been made with an imported Canadian Club 100% Rye. Makar clinked glasses with him.

"So, what do you think?" asked Ravil, referring to Makar's meeting with Pierre Gaultier.

Ravil and Makar always kept conversations of this nature vague and in code when in the open like this. Parabolic listening devices had become ever more sophisticated.

Makar took a sip of the snakebite. "He's smart and ambitious. He knows he's not able to dictate terms to us, but he knows his worth."

"What is his worth?" asked Ravil, wanting to confirm what he already knew.

"He's perhaps the best businessman of that speciality in Western Europe. With our help, he could become a very formidable ally."

This concurred with Ravil's own assessment.

"Your agreement to his proposition was unexpected my friend," said Ravil, referring to Makar's calculating nature which often erred on the side of patience.

"This gentleman the Frenchman wants to be removed, if the stories are true, will have had to be dealt with one way or another, considering our goal."

"To retaliate first so to speak," said Ravil, remembering he read that somewhere. "I have asked our friend by the river for his thoughts and he has agreed. He has asked you to contact him to work out a plan of action."

'Our friend by the river' was a highly-placed contact for the Russian Bratva known only by Ravil and Makar.

There were a few moments of silence before Makar spoke, "So it's true?"

"Yes."

A smile threatened to break out on the ex-KGB agent's mouth. "I'd heard rumours on the demise of certain highly placed individuals and organisations being down to a mercurial ghost. I could never discover a name."

The laughter from the pool reached a higher crescendo and Ravil noticed two beautiful dark-haired women in an embrace. He thought them to be attempting to catch his Avtorityet's eye, who seemed to pay them no heed. A few of the men around the pool were not as oblivious to the scene.

"Well our friend knows his name among other details," said Ravil.

"Is this where I ask the name and you let the tension build with a theatrical air?" Makar said with a smile.

Ravil smiled back, they never said names aloud unnecessarily. He would not have appreciated the jibe from anyone else, but Makar had been instrumental in his success.

Ravil had already been adept and prosperous in criminal enterprise prior to the mid-nineties when he had first met the KGB agent. Back then, Ravil realised his favoured crime from a business standpoint was the extortion of officials. It was preferable not to extort them of their own money but to persuade them to tap Government funds—typically for projects with the appearance of legitimacy. Ravil preferred to gain this co-operation through uncovering a transgression: an affair, drug addiction, or crime. This way the individual could look upon the blackmail as a form of penance. There was nothing sexy in that sort of criminal enterprise and Ravil did have a certain nostalgia for his 'rooting tooting gun toting' days, as the Americans liked to say. However, he surmised the more shoot-outs you had the more likely you would be shot eventually. He already had plenty of those and embezzlement rarely led to gun fights.

Makar had come to see him in the summer of '95 regarding fifty-two million roubles that Ravil had extorted from various Moscow officials. After dispatching two of Ravil's armed henchmen with his bare hands—mercifully leaving them alive—he made Ravil an offer: to pay back part of the money and take Makar on as a consul of sorts. The alternative was to 'suffer a fever'. Ravil agreed in principle.

After a few negotiations on specifics, they began a partnership that precipitated a rise within organised crime; the speed of which had rarely been seen.

"I have been provided with a lengthy file," said Ravil, handing a small memory stick out to Makar. "It's all in there."

Makar took it. "Give me the bullet points so to speak."

"After a troubled youth, he got involved in Judo and made the national team as a teenager." Ravil looked at Makar. He knew Sambo to be a derivative of it, and once remembered the former KGB agent describing Judo as 'the best kept secret in martial arts'.

"Go on sir."

"Joined Britain's Parachute Regiment at eighteen after training. His mother died when he was twenty."

"How?"

"Suicide." Makar did not say anything and Ravil continued, "Passed what they call 'selection' at 23 years of

127

age and joined the SAS. Our man told me that there is a…how do they say… 'crème de la crème' unit within the United Kingdom's Special Forces, and this man entered it. It was from there he was recruited into his current position."

Makar said, "There's a unit some term 'the increment', made up of experienced special forces soldiers drawn off both the SAS and SBS to carry out highly sensitive operations."

"You have encountered these men? In your earlier days?" asked Ravil, more of a statement than a question.

Makar gave a non-committal shrug before asking, "Why isn't he more well-known?"

"Our man says this man has almost complete independence now," said Ravil, observing out of the corner of his eye the men on the far side of the pool remonstrating with the girls in it. Despite Makar's angle, he knew his Avtorityet must have noticed it too. "He thinks that we are going to assassinate him. In fact, he is demanding of it."

"He demands it," corrected Makar.

"Yes, thank you. He demands it."

"That's understandable he should want that," said Makar. "How's your Brazilian Jujitsu training, sir?"

"Very well my friend. The first six months was not pleasant though," answered Ravil, thinking of how inept he felt during those months. It had been oddly refreshing too; it had been a long time since Ravil had felt anything approaching inferiority.

"It's a constant learning curve. One I reckoned would appeal to your enquiring mind," said Makar. It was he who suggested that Ravil would enjoy it.

"Oh it is. There is a phrase drilled into us: 'Position before submission', quite relevant to our current plans," said Ravil raising his glass.

As Makar raised his glass a loud, English private school voice cut through the air.

"To what are you gentlemen toasting?"

There stood a large gentleman, sipping a cocktail while swaying slightly.

"A conclusion of a business arrangement," answered Ravil.

"Aha, I am a businessman myself, maybe you would like to share with me the nature of it?"

"Maybe we wouldn't," answered Makar curtly.

"I do believe I was asking this chap," said the stranger, with a slight shrill to his voice. Two of his companions appeared on his left close to Makar.

"Gentlemen, without wishing to be rude, my friend and I have a lot to discuss so—" said Ravil before he was interrupted.

—"You said you had concluded your business deal? And now we can't help you celebrate?" said the man.

Makar stood up abruptly causing the three men to flinch but they remained rooted in place.

"Perhaps the background music is affecting your ability to hear what my friend is saying. Perhaps if we all step outside the premises I can explain it to you more clearly?"

Surprise lit the man's features before quickly returning to their mask of arrogance. "Are you quite sure, my man? There's three of us?"

Ravil noticed people on the veranda and around the pool honing their attention on the scene. He remained seated. He had watched a few derivatives of this scene before and knew Makar was in no danger. He felt a mild excitement warm his belly. Makar placed his thumb and forefinger on his chin and furrowed his eye brows.

"You're quite right chap," mimicking the man's accent, "the numbers do appear to be unfair...perhaps you would like to call upon the rest of your friends?" indicating to the other three men looking on from the far side of the pool.

Bemusement, then anger befell the men's faces. Makar hit the one closest with a crunching right elbow to the jaw. A pulverising left hook fired into the point of the next opponent's chin. Both men fell away into untidy heaps. He stepped toward the original protagonist. The man's feet made a step as if to run away before stopping themselves. He lashed out clumsily with his right hand, the liquid from the glass arching into the air. Makar slipped inside the blow, grasping the wrist with his left hand. The crook of Makar's right arm smashed up underneath the man's left arm pit. His hips whipped underneath with violent torque as the Englishman was spun like a rag doll into the air. The eyes bulged with the thudding landing. Ravil noticed Makar's hand underneath the man's head—the only reason he did not lose consciousness. Makar's knee pressed into the side of the man's face. The on-lookers stood in silence including the slack-jawed women. He quickly found the man's wallet and removed a driver's licence.

"OK, Mr Malone of Number Two Virginia Water in Surrey. Has your hearing improved now?"

"Yeh...ye...yessssirrr," he croaked.

Connor drove 'up the line' in a six-year-old Audi on the motorway towards Leeds. He was not far away now. He smiled as the M62 parted in two and washed around Stott

Hall Farm. The myth was that during the motorway's construction in the 1960s, the stubborn owner refused to sell his land to make way for the development. Therefore, the engineers built around it. However, Connor knew it was due to a geological fault beneath the Farmhouse. He also grinned at the memory of himself and Liam as eighteen-year-olds hurtling past the Farm in a Porsche Boxster. This one, they had not stolen.

Liam had visited Connor in a pub he bartended at in the small nearby village of Hipperholme. The man who owned the bright yellow Porsche was a regular in his forties, and Connor had overheard he was going *'through a midlife crisis'* and liked to *'flash his money'*. At the end of his afternoon shift, Connor called out to the man jokingly, "Phil, fancy swapping cars for a bit?" Connor had driven a two-year-old Golf at the time.

Phil laughed. "Well…are thee insured?"

"Yes," came the unflinching reply. Connor had not been sure if his insurance covered another person's vehicle.

"Well, I guess ye can take it for a spin for half an hour," said Phil in an avuncular tone, and nonchalantly threw Connor the keys. "Just half an hour mind."

He and Liam could barely contain their excitement when they climbed in, and the engine growled. The monster violently coughed, bucking the pair forward as Connor stalled it.

"Fucksake mate, couldn't you have done that further down the road? He looks like he's about to have an aneurysm," Liam had said. He indicated with a jut of his chin to Phil's anxious mask peering behind one of the pub's curtains.

"Trust me, all he cares about is for us two to come back gushing about how awesome his car is to everyone, so he doesn't have to," Connor had said. "Fuck me, it feels like a Go-Kart with how low it is."

"Well make sure we do come back...alive! Because it's not a Go-Kart and my IQ must be low getting in with ya, you've only just passed your test you mad bastard."

"Stop being melodramatic. Yer like an old woman."

After weaving through the residential areas, passing the disconcerting looks of pedestrians and fellow motorists alike, they had hit the motorway. When Connor pressed his foot down, it reminded him of the 'Star Trek' scenes when Captain Picard ordered *Warp speed*. Within seconds the digital dial read '163 mph' with Liam's exertions of, "Fucking slow down!" getting louder as Stotts Farm blurred by.

He and Liam had swapped seats after the Saddleworth turn off, and the car was driven back with more care. They both laughed about the incident afterwards. More so because they had been deliberately nonchalant about the vehicle's performance in the pub later, which had visibly pissed off Phil.

Connor now felt a ripple of melancholy spread through his chest as he thought about his deceased friend. The main reason Liam got into that car was to make sure Connor did not kill himself. He was heading to Leeds to visit Rayella, and he hoped to lift her spirits.

13

Bruce felt a warm glow in the presence of his two nieces, Millie and Sarah, within The Honours restaurant. He took them to the famous Edinburgh restaurant whenever the chance arose. The Honours had soft yellow lighting warming the polished timber walls. A zebra crossing of light and dark wood made up the floor mirroring the white shirt with black waistcoat attire of the pleasant waiting staff. The food was always full of flavour and well presented.

Millie, the younger of the sisters at eighteen, had taken this opportunity to introduce her new, older boyfriend, Richard. The foursome sat at a corner table at the end of the room. Bruce faced the door, a habit which he shared with everyone he knew in his profession. The girls were his younger sister's children or 'weans' (pronounced 'waynes') as they said in the west of Scotland, and Bruce spoilt them whenever he got the chance. He knew this was in part because he did not have any children himself to spoil. Still, he was also proud, and a little relieved, of how they had both turned out. Sandra, his only sibling, suffered from a bipolar disorder that he thought she handled heroically. Their mother Kathleen had had a bipolar disorder which had not ended well.

McQuillan ran background checks on any new boyfriend the girls brought home. He did with this current one earlier that day before arriving to meet the girls. McQuillan did not even have to access *ACRO* for criminal record information before being perturbed.

Typing 'Richard Eric Dowling' + 'Kilmarnock' into Google and reading the 'Daily Record' article made him pinch the bridge of his nose.

One of Kilmarnock's primary drug dealers was jailed by the High Court in Edinburgh this week. Richard Dowling, 26, of Sidlaw Place, Kilmarnock, was sentenced to four years and two months after a Police raid on his house resulted in over £37,000 in cash and a large quantity of heroin found.

Mr Dowling, who has previous convictions for assault, aggravated burglary and theft, pled guilty to possession with the intent to supply class A drugs.

The sentence was welcomed by prosecutor Marie Taylor.

She said: "This is positive news for the local community. Drugs and the resultant crime it brings are a misery to the area. The sentence is a warning that drug dealing will not be tolerated."

Bruce still held hope that maybe D owling had been rehabilitated. He knew many a criminal who had. Nevertheless, he was aware of many more who would never be. Bruce made a call to Derek Hammonds, the Director of Investigations at the National Crime Agency. It was a professional relationship only, and calls were abbreviated to the necessities.

"Hello."

"Hi, it's me."

"Giving or wanting?"

"Wanting—information on a Richard Eric Dowling of Kilmarnock. Out of Barlinnie a couple of years ago after a stint concerning the supply of class A drugs. I want to know of any charges that he hasn't been convicted of, and if he's gone straight since coming out of prison."

"Give me half an hour." And the line went dead.

Thirteen minutes later Bruce's phone vibrated.

"Hello," Bruce answered.

"He had a charge of sexual assault as a twenty-year-old dropped due to lack of evidence. The alleged victim withdrew her statement. Currently subject of a surveillance investigation into the supplying of class A drugs throughout Ayrshire. He has links to our favourite Gorbals crime family, but he's relatively small time. He's still a player to answer your question. Get all that?"

"Aye."

"It's a long-running investigation, and the boys downstairs want him kept in play for a while, if you don't mind."

The line went dead.

And now Bruce sat across from the thickset, expensively shirted thirty-three-year-old Richard Dowling and restrained any outward sign of distaste for him.

"How's Uni life?" Bruce asked Sarah. She was in her final year of her social work degree.

"Naw too bad, the end is in sight, so it makes it easier."

"That it does," he answered before asking Millie. "And you?" She had just started her HND Graphic Design course at Glasgow Clyde College.

"Aye, good thanks. Excited. I ken that'll wear off after a year or two in," she replied, with a toothy smile.

"Was o'time if ye ask meh. Thir's nae dosh in'it," piped up Richard.

Bruce pressed his toes into the ground while keeping a neutral expression on his face. Sarah glanced nervously at her uncle, and he knew she was expecting him to lambaste Richard. He did not—he needed to gain the man's confidence. Hiding his aversion for the man became a small challenge as the evening wore on. Bruce did not like the way Dowling shied away from eye contact, laughed too hard at his jokes and how sugary his compliments were. On top of this, he had a strong regional accent. Bruce was proud of his Glaswegian heritage and was happy to allow his accent to return when in his native Scotland. However, he felt a lot of Scots from areas around Glasgow blindly wore their thickly-accented slang as a badge of patriotism.

Bruce felt a little disappointed that he had not influenced Millie enough to see through Richard's façade. He knew women almost always, especially when they were young, allowed their emotions to cloud their good sense. The male libido had the same effect on men.

The atmosphere had an undercurrent to it, and he noticed that the elder Sarah treated Richard with indifference—*at least one of you has your head screwed on.*

"Millie tells me you'd like tae go beating," Bruce said to Richard, referring to the sport of using dogs and people as beaters to flush out birds for shooting.

"Aye, ah wid like tae wan day."

"Well, am going the morra if you'd like to come?"

"Aye, that wid be guid, cheers," Richard nodded enthusiastically.

"I'll pick you up from Balmoral Road around eight, OK?"

"Aye, cheers," said Richard looking bemused as Millie smiled next to him.

Bruce smiled too. He knew Richard was trying to work out how Bruce knew where he lived but did not want to ask.

The Jaguar XKR glided up to the third floor of the multi-storey car park under Makar's deft driving. It slid up and halted before an athletic man with soft brown hair. The man wore a lightweight, black leather jacket over a white t-shirt with dark jeans and brown boots. Only reasonably sturdy looking under his attire, Makar knew the man to be hugely muscular underneath. The muscularity befitted his years as a gymnast of international standing from a teenager into his early twenties. Makar had seen him in competition years ago at Crystal Palace on the rings. As Roderick held the Maltese cross, his shoulders reminded Makar of a bunch of bananas.

Roderick Smith—or Rod Smith—now in his early thirties, still moved with a feline grace—like a leopard embodied in human form. The English-schooled Russian climbed into the purring piece of engineering, and it pulled away.

"I was able to source a significant amount of information on the subject but it had to pass through more than one pair of sensitive hands, hence the fee sir," said Roderick in English that sounded like he was a native. He had lived in England since he was seven years of age.

Makar gave a slight nod. He knew this information would not come cheap and good intelligence was always worth its weight. Roderick was an ex-undercover *SVR* agent who maintained close links with the organisation. Makar had known him for the better part of a decade.

"Give me the highlights first," said Makar in the same tongue while he merged the vehicle into the midday London traffic.

"Carl Wright. Born October 1983 in the Dearborn area of Detroit. His father was murdered in a street robbery by a gang of Lebanese descent in 1999 when Carl was sixteen years of age. Enlisted in the 75th Ranger Regiment at nineteen years old. Passed 1st of his class and specialised as a sniper."

"Were the gang caught? And if so what happened to them?"

"Three found not guilty and two convicted of aggravated manslaughter, paroled after six years." answered Roderick, "Wright joined Operation Enduring Freedom in Afghanistan and made several confirmed kills as a sniper, including a shot of 900 yards or metres, whichever you prefer."

"A yard is 0.914 of a metre. A significant difference when there's 900 of them."

Roderick nodded and continued. "He came to the attention of our friends at SAD's SOG mainly as a sniper and other surveillance tasks. Over the next eighteen months he saw action not only in Afghanistan but Pakistan too. I could not obtain the specific details of the missions without attracting suspicion but after eighteen months he was accepted for formal training at The Farm. Despite not having a Bachelor degree."

Makar absorbed the information as they waited at the traffic lights. Roderick remained quiet.

The SAD was an acronym for the CIA's Special Activities Division, responsible for the Agency's more delicate covert operations. It was made up of SAD/PAG (Political Action Group) and SAD/SOG (Special Operations Group).

Two things had struck Makar while listening. Firstly, it was the first time he had heard of an individual not of the SEALS or Delta Force being recruited. SOG was a highly elite paramilitary group and thus recruited almost exclusively from these two 'Tier One' units. The Army

Rangers, while highly respected, were considered a level below them.

Secondly, it surprised him that the American had been selected for training to become a Paramilitary Operations Officer without a Bachelor degree, which was usually a requisite.

"Did he succeed?"

"Top six of an initial annual intake of 79. Only a third completed the course."

"The full eighteen-month course?"

"Yes."

Makar said nothing.

"In the next fifteen months he completes missions in Nigeria, Iraq and back to Afghanistan before resigning from the CIA," stated Roderick. "Again, I could not obtain details on any of the missions."

"Any indication of the reasons why he resigned?"

"No sir, other than it was his decision."

"Then what?"

"It appears that he spent two years travelling the world before turning to his current employ. He's been off the radar for the last three years until his dealings with the Frenchman."

"I have some specific questions," said Makar, freeing the Jaguar from the shoal of city centre traffic onto the carriageway. For the next twenty minutes, Roderick answered them all.

Connor had turned up unexpected but was warmly received as always by the Scott family.

"She seems to have perked up a bit since you last visited, but she's still not herself like," Mrs Scott told him in the living room as he nursed a cup of tea. "It's not healthy her spending so much time in her room. Thought it was that school at first but she says she likes it."

Rayella had passed her Eleven Plus exams and now attended the local Grammar school. Connor was terribly proud of her for persevering with her academia given what she had been, and was, going through.

"She's just becoming a woman that's all Ann. Stop mithering all the time," said Mr Scott gruffly.

"It's no wonder she doesn't comes down to talk with us with an attitude like that."

Connor could not make out what Mr Scott mumbled under his breath. He thought him a wise man not to antagonize an upset Ann Scott.

"I'll go and speak to her," said Connor as he polished off his cup of tea and made his way to her room.

Connor gently rapped on Rayella's door.

"Yes?" Rayella called out.

"It's Connor." The door opened, immediately revealing a smile that although sincere, didn't quite reach the eyes. He stepped in and closed the door.

"Take a seat. I have something to show you." She stared numbly at him and sat on her bed. He sat next to her, taking out his android phone.

"Try not to get too upset until I've finished OK?"

"OK…I won't," she replied meekly.

He felt his heart lurch. He knew enough to know that what had happened to her was going to affect her, in one way or another, for the rest of her life.

He flicked on to his Google Chrome and pulled up an article on Hardcastle's suicide. He saw her flinch when the MP's picture came into view at the top of the screen and he put his arm around her. She stiffened but after a moment, cuddled into him.

"Do you want to read it or shall I read it for you?"

Her answer surprised him. "I'll read it."

He handed her the phone. Seconds later, she quietly sobbed, "Was this you?"

"All that matters is that he got what was coming to him. He died in agonizing pain. He got justice."

After a while, in a quiet voice she said, "I love you, Connor."

He could feel the moisture creep under his eyelids and he blinked rapidly.

"Well you're not a *figure eleven*," he said and then, ignoring her quizzical look said, "Look at me Rayella," and when she did he continued. "Listen, tomorrow I want you to tell your Mum what's happened. You need to be brave. You can't keep carrying this around by yourself. She will get you the help you need, OK?"

She looked at him with watery eyes. "Could you tell her with me Connor?"

He smiled pretending to rub sleep from his eyes. "Of course I can. You ready to do it now?"

She took a deep breath and smiled. He thought he could see a bit of her old self smile through.

"Come on. Remember, what is important here is that we all love you."

He held his hand out to her and she took it. He mused whether breaking news like this to such loving parents was going to be the hardest thing he had ever done. They had been through more than their fair share.

"Can I get anything else for you?" asked the young waitress as she set down the coffee. She took her time setting down the cup and saucer as Carl kept eye contact. The top two buttons were undone revealing a hint of her youthful breasts encased in a black bra.

"No thanks," he replied, accentuating his American accent and giving her a tight smile. She matched it with a wider one revealing a set of straight, white teeth. He took the opportunity to peruse her tight posterior as she sashayed away.

He sat outside a café in central London with the day's temperature being sixteen degrees. The light breeze sieved through his white cotton shirt and light blue suit trousers. He sipped at the dark liquid and watched the hum of the impersonal bustle of London pedestrians and traffic.

London was one of his favourite cities. He appreciated the mix of historical and modern architecture throughout the city, loved the busyness, the undercurrents and the mix of people here. Carl often enjoyed a leisurely lunch or coffee when first arriving in a city to take in the ambience, especially in Europe. All the while he was conducting his counter-surveillance duties. These countermeasures involved memorising people, ensuring they did not pass twice, and scrutinising all the static individuals in the vicinity. He remembered how mentally draining it had been during the surveillance package of his training at 'The Farm'. Now it was just second nature. He took his time sipping his coffee and did not return the young waitress's glances towards him. He was here on business.

He sensed the hand before he felt it on his shoulder. He looked up to see a pretty brunette, early thirties, wearing jeans and a brown summer jacket over a white top.

"Excuse me, can you point me in the direction of Chicksand Lane please?" she asked.

"I'm sorry lady, but I'm not from your great capital," he replied.

"Not to worry," she smiled brightly and walked off.

This was the pre-arranged signal that Carl should finish his coffee before following a man with a white baseball cap and green jacket. He put on his suit jacket and left the cash plus a large tip under the saucer.

The man appeared along the pavement within a minute of the lady disappearing. Carl followed him at a distance of fifteen feet for a few hundred metres to an underground car park. He found the man studying his phone by a Silver Mercedes E class, then he walked away. Carl opened the door and sat beside a stocky, suited gentleman he guessed to be around his early forties.

"Mr Wright, a pleasure to meet you," he said, with a trace of a Russian accent. The man extended his hand giving Carl's a gentlemanly squeeze.

"My apologies, but you are required to wear this for the journey," and he produced a blindfold.

As the darkness covered Carl's eyes, he tried to figure out if this was a good thing or not.

Bruce sat in his car outside the large terrace house and beeped the horn. The curtains of the house next door and opposite house twitched. Brand new BMWs were not common in this area. Or perhaps they were, given Richard's associates.

Richard's face popped out from behind the curtain, a scowl painted on before it disappeared as Bruce made eye contact. Richard gave a small wave and gestured he was coming out. After a couple of minutes, dressed in a sports jacket and jeans, he walked hurriedly to the BMW.

Bruce saw dark shadows underneath the eyes.

"You alright? You look a wee bit upset?" asked Bruce.

"Aye, ma Staffie bull terrier bolted aff lest nicht…He'll caw up am sure."

They began the hour and a half drive to the Campsie Fells.

After a time, they made small talk about football until Bruce invited Richard to rest his eyes. The Campsie Fells were a range of hills in central Scotland with the highest point being the Earl's Seat, measuring 578m. They gave way to some beautiful, scenic views of parts of Glasgow.

Bruce glanced over at Richard; he was a couple of inches shorter than Bruce, albeit muscular in a bloated sort of way. Bruce guessed Richard was using Dianabol in an amateurish 'bulking phase'.

Bruce had taken courses in physiology and sports science to gain a better understanding of the human body. He understood that most body building training increased the muscle size primarily by increasing the 'polyfilla'-like sarcoplasm between the muscle fibres. This differed from the training employed by Olympic and Powerlifters whose regimes mainly strengthened the tension-inducing myofibrils of the muscle. That and the central nervous system and tendons. It was the reason why gymnasts possessed massive physical strength in relation to their bodyweight whereas the opposite was true of most bodybuilders he knew. There were always exceptions, but Bruce doubted this Maori-tattooed drug dealer was one of them. And he reckoned on odds of fifty-to-one that he took any regular cardiovascular exercise either.

He thought of how his life would have been if not for the intervention of his first Judo Sensei Martin Dunn. He had hoped that he would have had the strength of character not to turn out like the low-life in his passenger seat.

The BMW snaked through the Glasgow traffic and pulled off at the junction for the small town of Kirkintilloch.

He had always liked Glasgow. It was a visceral city that produced down-to-earth, hard, dry-humoured but warm-hearted people. Still, there were always bad apples in any community. Bruce smiled to himself. Of all the girls Richard could have had, he chose one with a member of the family such as Bruce. There must only be a handful of men of his ilk in the entire Isles; who possessed the combination of being so high up in a law enforcement— or law-breaking—organisation to know what Richard was involved in with the capacity for premeditated, cold-blooded violence.

Finally, the car threaded through the village of Lennoxtown and ascended a road to the Fells. Bruce pulled into the small car park overlooking the local village.

"Wakey, wakey, eggs and bakey," called Bruce and Richard woke up, scrunching his eyes in a manner that reminded Bruce of a toddler.

"There's a wee bit of a trek up that hill, a bit of a walk and we're there."

"Might as well be Mount Everest tae me," Richard chuckled.

"Ye'll be fine, come and help me with this," Bruce replied as he opened the boot of the car. There inside was a long-back *DPM bergen*.

"Ah will tak' that, am over ten years younger," said Richard shouldering the bergen. Bruce took the comment as a compliment—the age difference was nearer twenty.

"Whit have ye got in this?" Richard asked, jumping up and down.

"It's a surprise," Bruce said, shutting the boot and setting off briskly. The sun peered around the clouds, and the wind whistled around the Fells.

Bruce hid his contempt as barely ten minutes into the estimated twenty-minute hike to the top, Richard started to wheeze. The image appeared in Bruce's mind of rust flaking off the lungs. He regularly stopped to allow Richard to catch up before immediately setting off when he did. After half an hour, he reached the top with the rasping Richard a few minutes behind.

He took a few moments to catch his breath before asking, "Where's this gun range fae here then?"

"Oh, there is'nae one," said Bruce, letting it sink in. "I lied to you. Like you having been lying to Millie about what you do for a living."

There were a few moments silence.

"Whit th' fuck ur ye talking aboot?" asked Richard aggressively.

Bruce smiled. "Well, we'll get on to that in a moment. First things first, there's something yer'll be needing to get on with. I suggest you tip oot tha' backpack and get cracking wee laddie."

Richard stood with his eyebrows reaching down for one another, staring at Bruce. His face cycled through the masks of anger, bewilderment and concern.

The wind filled the silence between them. Richard slipped off the bergen, set it down and undid the two buckles at the top.

"Go on, tip it out."

Richard tipped the bergen upside-down. Out slid a Staffordshire bull terrier's severed head. Its body, and a child's plastic spade covered in blood followed. Richard stood back, his mouth hanging like a swing.

"You see, I know yer ill treatment of tha' dug has led to it becoming dangerous. You have set it on a few people, including one of the fifteen-year-old lassies who used to mule drugs for you. Now, she may never walk properly again. Couldn't be having that now. The poor dug was beyond rehabilitation, so I severed its head with a Samurai sword. Nice, neat and nae pain." Bruce stared into Richard's perplexed eyes and continued. "So dry yer fuckin' eyes, ye scumbag."

He purposely did not tell him he had anaesthetized the canine before the beheading. Richard's breathing became shallow and erratic, his eyes darting from Bruce to the divided animal remains. Bruce fathomed that he was psyching himself to attack, but fear was rooting him from moving forward.

Back in the familiarity of Kilmarnock, the thug was a 'face'. Now, the drug dealer was fighting to draw breath on top of a blustery hill, alone with a man who had severed his dog's head from the body, both of which now lay at his feet. Bruce had expected a reluctance to act might occur and had a contingency plan to push the gangster to attack. Bruce's moral compass dictated he could not attack him first, but he could defend himself as ruthlessly as he chose.

"We're no leaving 'til you have buried the poor wee lad. It's only right you do. Get on your knees and get to it, I didn't want to be here all day ye boggin scrote," Bruce said with his smile stretching into his cheeks.

Richard ran at Bruce with flailing arms. The whites of his eyes showed above and below his pupils. Bruce ducked under a wild right hand and fired a short right uppercut into his stomach. Pivoting as Richard bent double slightly, he delivered a scudding left hook to

147

Richard's kidney. A boot shove on his arse sent him sprawling.

"They don't make scumbags like they used to, ye couldnae lead a young team, ye bawjawed fanny," Bruce guffawed.

Richard got up raising his amateurish guard. The anxiety shone from his face like a beacon. Bruce pumped two piston-like jabs catching him in the eye. Richard dabbed his eye as he reached out with his right hand to 'catch' another pair of jabs. Good boxing coaches taught fighters to 'parry' jabs close to the face as not to open themselves to powerful hooks. Richard's attempts resembled a cat pawing at a suspended ball.

Bruce picked his moment, feinted a jab before slinging a long left hook that staggered the floundering Richard. Bruce's right fist ricocheted off the point of the jaw with the speed and force of a baseball bat. It felt like punching through warm butter with the shadowed chin offering no resistance.

Richard fell.

He lay barely conscious like a fallen elderly lady in a supermarket. The confusion ironed onto his face. His size and thick neck saved him from blacking out. He spent a few moments pawing at the ground like he was searching for dropped glasses. He feebly kicked out like a wounded animal at Bruce's legs. The older man watched him with no expression.

As he turned onto his front to get to his feet, Bruce seized the leg, trapping it between his knees just above the ankle. Richard began to struggle. Bruce wrenched his leg to one side and the ankle snapped. The scream turned into wails. The wails turned to sobs. His hands hovered over his ankle as if terrified to touch it.

"Fucking shut up you," said Bruce. The drug dealer had turned ashen but still whimpered.

"I said shut your fucking geggie before I stamp on your ankle, you little fuck."

Richard's sniffling receded.

"Your maw, Mavis, lives at 104 Burnbank Street in Darvel. Your wee sister Ashley lives at 88 Forres Court in Durham," said Bruce.

The younger man looked at Bruce like a schoolboy at a Headmaster about to cane him. Bruce knelt and took out a black Heckler and Koch USP Compact from an ankle holster. He levelled it at Richard.

"I want you to take a good look at your dog and ask yourself if you want your maw and your sister to end up like it. You're going to finish it with my niece. Say you're married, and if you have any contact with her whatsoever after that, I'll murder your entire fuckin' family. Do you understand?"

Richard nodded numbly.

"Dinnae worry. I'll take the dog away and bury it for you because I am a nice man aren't I?"

Richard just stared.

"Hopefully, a dog walker will find you, unless you want to hop it down to the road. You'll tell them that you twisted your ankle up here, and this will be the last time we meet. Unless, of course, you decide to ignore me and contact Millie again. Then we will meet again, and I'll get to keep your skull on the mantelpiece as an ornament."

He stooped to pick up the dog's body and put it back in the bergen. He grabbed the head and fit his hand inside it like a glove puppet. Moving the dog's head in time to the words, he growled, "Next time, it'll be your head."

Fear plastered Richard's face.

14

Carl blinked with the removal of the blindfold.

He took stock of his surroundings. The car had stopped in a driveway enclosed by a back lawn opposite a Victorian mansion. It had two floors, with two short towers rising another ten metres from the roof. The high polished wood balcony skirted the upper floors. Surprised by the number of windows—he presumed these people used it often and wanted as much discretion as possible.

Then he noticed that you could not see into them. "Apologies for the discomfort Mr Wright," said the man beside him.

"No apology necessary, security isn't a dirty word," he replied.

"'Security is not a dirty word'. I will remember that one for myself," the man smiled. "Mr Wright, the gentleman we are about to encounter is our 'Security Officer'. He will have the details of your role in the action upon we are about to embark. I would suggested— suggest—you ask any questions you have now as he will be happy to answer them all. He will only meet you face to face once. Then, any questions you have must be relayed through Mr Pierre, and there may be a time lag to your answers. Do you understand?"

"Yes."

The door to Carl's side was pulled open for him to his surprise. *How did the guy who opened the door know the interaction was finished?* The door-opener briskly frisked him.

The small mansion overlooked fields as far as he could see, with woodland to his left, deep and stretching a few hundred yards along the side of the meadow. The fields had a few cows in them and a hill a quarter of a mile away. There was a small lake around a hundred yards to the right and a pen of geese thirty yards from the mansion. Carl knew geese made a better early-warning system for intruders than dogs.

"Come Mr Wright."

Carl followed the man up a small flight of stairs and entered the house as the man held the door open for him. The Bratva member led the way into a large, decadent room with smooth yellow-tinged lighting illuminating the cream decor and brown sofas. There stood a well-built man of a height of six-feet one-inch, in a perfectly fitted, three-piece light blue suit with the tie removed. He stood with an authoritative ease as his open palm pointed at Carl.

"I apologise for the clichéd look, but I have just returned from a function," he said as Carl felt his firm handshake. It felt like the handshake of a man not gripping too hard so as not to hurt the recipient.

"I would enquire about the comfort of your trip, but that would be trite, considering you had a blindfold tightly squeezed around your face. A necessary precaution, I am sure you'll understand."

There was no accent to his voice, which Carl could only describe as neutral.

"Of course, I'd be more alarmed if you hadn't," replied Carl.

"Quite. Please, take a seat Mr Wright."

The two men sat on the opposing sofas, with the Russian from the car sitting to the left of them. Carl noticed a painting of a grand old ship from British colonial times on the wall behind the man and wondered who had it put up.

"Mr Pierre informs me that you have heard of this man we wish to acquire?"

"Only the inexperienced in my profession have not heard of him. Or the myth, so to speak," said Carl, refraining from asking the Blue Suit what his name was.

"Yes, a very dangerous man. Your reluctance of being in any way involved in any unfortunate incident that was to happen to him is understandable." Carl leant back by way of response and the man continued. "I understand this is small comfort, but you have been told you are not killing him, or indeed killing anyone."

"So, why am I here?"

"We have an asset close to the subject who will provide us a target location. Your mission is shoot him with a tranquilizer dart, subduing him for his rendition."

Carl was perturbed.

Law enforcement agencies around the world used Tasers for subduing humans. Tranquilizers were too risky to the victim's health. An anaesthesiologist studied for years to a doctorate level, in order to be able to determine the amount needed to render a person unconscious without killing them.

As if reading his mind, the gentleman in front of him spoke again.

"A Taser will not be used as he will be taken in a daylight setting. This would arouse too much suspicion. A gentleman falling over from a heart attack and taken to the hospital wouldn't cause a civilian to alert the police. As regards to the tranquilizer, it has been specifically synthesised and tested. You have my guarantee of its effectiveness. If he were to die from it, you would be absolved of blame. This is as much as I am willing to divulge on this particular subject."

Carl gave a small nod.

The man continued, "The gentleman to your left will provide you with the finer details. Is there anything you want to ask me before I leave?"

"No thanks."

"Mr Wright, after the job has been completed, you will be free of us in any involuntarily capacity. I am aware you have no reason to trust me, but it is in my experience that men allowed to live freely don't come back to haunt an organisation like the dead. Whatever happens it is unlikely we'll meet again."

At that, he shook Carl Wright's hand as he rose to meet him, and left the room.

Bruce sat among the whirr of the Glasgow pub with Nick Flint across from him. It was a Saturday with the football on the three big screens overlooking the punters. Celtic were playing Dundee United.

"Like their football up here don't they," said Nick eyeing the horde of men glued to the screens.

"Aye, a lot calmer though since Rangers went to the fourth division. They are nearly back up now, and it won't be long until the Old Firm games are lighting up the city again."

"Why do they call games between Rangers and Celtic 'Old Firm' games?" asked Nick.

"They say, the commentators at one of the early matches described the two teams as 'old, firm friends' but no one really knows for sure."

Nick Flint had been working for him for eight years. Bruce found him to be highly professional and dependable if a little nonchalant at times. This he could understand. Nick was a family man and in this line of work because he was good at it as well as affording him a good living. Bruce got the impression the youthful enthusiasm that he came to him with had begun to ebb a little.

Still, he was Bruce's first pick for the most sensitive and important operations, being dependable when making decisions. He had again proved his reliability with his extraction of Hardcastle from Connor.

The background of Scottish whirred throughout the pub helped to mask their low voices.

"We're due to touch base with Jaime in the next few days. He'll tell me the location on the day of the races, so I want you down in London on Wednesday," said Bruce, referring to his tech genius Jaime. The name pronounced 'Hi-me' befitting its Latin owner, a magician with everything and anything to do with computers.

"He's paranoid that man," said Nick.

"He's careful, hence why he is still alive and off the radar."

"We walking to the meet as usual?"

At that Bruce studied him, without knowing why, "You know we'll work that out when we find out the location."

"Yeah, of course"

Bruce felt something clench in his stomach.

Makar sat on his bed in The Actor's Penthouse at The Corinthian Hotel, enjoying the bed's softness while staring into the flickering gas fire. He admired The Actor's Penthouse: the colours, the layout, decor, the red and white flowers and the ornaments of animals and ships—well-presented without being pretentious.

He especially liked the balcony, although he had to fight the feeling of exposure and vulnerability when he ventured out on it. However, he felt not going onto balconies to avoid would-be snipers overstepped the threshold of being security conscious into paranoia.

Makar's thoughts regarding vices were that if they were controlled, they were not vices but pleasures—*what is the point of living if you cannot feel alive?* A pleasure indulged in too often was less a pleasure, and more a controlling addiction. Not only did addictions rob a man of his power, but they were also things that a potential adversary could use against him. He had seen it all over the years. Handsome, youthful, smart and ambitious men turned careless and indulgent by their early thirties then ravaged and/or obese by middle age. Drugs, women, gratuitous spending, alcohol and gambling were just some of the few compulsions Makar had seen claim professional potential and in his business—lives.

Still, he thought it weak to abstain completely from the things that gave pleasure, as long as you ruled it not the other way around. Makar's pleasures were gorgeous women, great food, expensive hotels and luxury or fast cars—clichés he knew. All these things he indulged in but only after a period of abstinence. He compromised on some of these pleasures as not to draw unwanted attention. Makar strived to strike a balance, so instead of buying fast cars, he would hire them out for a week or two before returning to public transport for a time. Makar had driven an Audi R8 Spyder, Aston Martin DB9, Bentley Continental GT Continental Sports, and a Maserati Gran Cabrio amongst a plethora of other cars. The constant change of vehicles also made surveilling him more difficult.

The Russian compromised his desire to be involved with a woman on a permanent basis by dating regularly. Never the same woman more than three times in a row.

Another option would be to hire high-class escorts, often just for a night but never more than a fortnight.

Now and then, he would indulge in a luxury hotel room. He resisted some of the more expensive suites and grand hotels to remain the *'grey man'*. As these next few weeks required his full attention, he decided to get his release now.

There was a knock at the door, and Makar rose with anticipation. He opened the door to two gorgeous women. He greeted them with a handshake and made way for them both to step inside. They were escorts from one of London's premier agencies who Makar had used on occasion. He would have used them all more, but his protocol was to avoid patterns.

One of the escorts went by the name of 'Victoria' and the other 'Elizabeth'. The perfume they wore smelled intoxicating as they brushed past him. Victoria looked to be in her mid-twenties and curvier of the pair: English, voluptuous and around a height of five-feet eight-inches, she had platinum blonde shoulder length hair, blue eyes and a heart-shaped face. Her manner was one of confidence. She wore a figure hugging all-in-one, white dress with the skirt coming down to her mid-thigh.

Elizabeth, a Czech according to her profile, seemed to be the younger by a few years. She was slender and petite with straight jet-black hair. Makar thought her stunning, with her large brown eyes and athletic legs. He liked her sense of fashion; she wore a denim sleeveless dress with a large white collar. The dress ended higher on the thighs than Victoria's, and she wore brown fur-lined heel boots.

"Ladies, would you like a drink as you take a seat? I'm not bad with the cocktails," asked Makar in a faultless upper-class English accent.

"Ooh let's see what your Cosmopolitans are like, please," answered Victoria with a wry smile.

"And you?" he asked Elizabeth.

"May I haves a vodka mixed with cranberry juice please," she replied shyly. The Russian found her accented English pleasing.

"Of course."

The two ladies took a seat together on the dark cream sofa. Makar went to the bar and began to prepare the drinks as the girls quietly talked among themselves. It was true he was quite adept at mixing various drinks—the KGB had sponsored him to be taught as part of an undercover operation.

He returned with the triangle of three glasses in his large hands, his being malt scotch.

"Hmm," hummed Victoria, as they both looked at him with approval sipping their drinks.

"We'll savour these before we savour you." She winked with the straw in her mouth.

Makar felt a jolt in his groin at her crass forwardness. He smiled back. "You'll savour one another before that."

"That could be a plan," replied Victoria.

Elizabeth looked at him with shy but interested eyes. She may just be a supremely talented actress, he thought. The best ones always were. They soon finished their drinks.

"Where would you like us?" Victoria asked, seemingly the boss of the duo.

"On the bed, I want to watch first if you don't mind," he said.

Both girls smiled.

"Of course, we don't mind," answered Elizabeth assertively to his surprise. She led Victoria by the hand over to the bed and took the English girl's face in her hands. She kissed her, lightly then steadily getting deeper and harder.

Makar raised his eyebrows as he watched her scrabbling Victoria's skirt up. She grabbed her ass hard, spreading the cheeks and exposing Victoria for his gaze.

Makar took a seat as he watched the role reversal intently.

Elizabeth spun the blonde around and bent her over with surprising force. Victoria's hand reached out to steady herself on the bed. The Czech gripped her hair yanking her head back. The blonde's face gushed with pleasure as fingers entered her. After a few moments, she pulled Victoria upright and took a grip of her jaw with one hand. She turned the girl's face and began to kiss her, open-mouthed and hard. She looked at Makar as she did this before she forced Victoria to her knees.

"Come here," Elizabeth commanded him, and he did.

15

Connor stood in the car showroom in Essex admiring the new silver Mercedes CLA 180 sport, placed apart from the rest of the cars. He was not particularly mechanically minded. He remembered this highlighted when attempting to help his maternal grandfather fix a car at age twelve. His grandad was leant over under the bonnet as Connor's lack of knowledge of the names of tools became apparent.

'What do they teach you at that school of yours?!' he had asked him.

'Maths, English and Science…err, food technology and resistant materials,' Connor had answered

'Food technology!?...you mean cooking.'

'Yeh. That's what they call it.'

His grandad had just shaken his head.

Connor now shook his head too. He knew his grandfather had taught himself car mechanics by stripping down and building back up car and tractor engines on the farm he grew up on—not at school.

Connor appreciated that cars like the CLA were a feat of evolutionary engineering and an attractive piece of sculpture. He had never been particularly materialistic and therefore did not have a keen interest in sports cars.

In the last few years, Connor had developed an appreciation of a better driving experience, with hours spent driving up and down the country for various military courses. Attending courses, he guessed, was going to continue under his new profession.

What was the title of his new profession, again? An 'Agent'? Like Bond? Except Bond killed terrorists in exotic countries with a silenced pistol—*I have killed a Paki accountant in Cheshire with a hammer*. Still, everyone had to start somewhere. Maybe one day he would have a 'wow' car.

"She's a beauty eh?" said the faint Scottish lilt behind him.

"She is," replied Connor, "Maybe it lacks foresight meeting your agents here. It might tempt them to strive for cash they don't earn?"

"A materialistic type of character doesn't need any tempting."

"We'd better go," said Connor, drawing Bruce's attention to the moustached salesman that was approaching them.

"Nah, might have something for me," said the older man as he smiled. Connor half smiled back at the attempt of a 'Dad' joke.

"Mr Murphy, here are the keys you requested. Your car has been parked around the corner in space D11 as requested," said the salesmen, handing the keys to Bruce.

"Thank you very much. It's been a pleasure, as always," said Bruce.

"Come on," he said to Connor and made his way outside. He clicked the keys and the beep emitted from a shimmering black Audi A7.

"Nice," murmured Connor.

"Yeah, got to enjoy the finer things in life or else yer'll become disgruntled. Then, disgruntlement turns to anger and envy. It's that that leads to striving for cash that you don't earn."

"I see…where's my Ferrari?"

Bruce ignored the quip. "The trick is never to allow these things to become your master. Be the type of person who could lose it all and not care, you understand?"

"So, you would be happy to go back to driving a clapped-out Fiesta?"

"Aye, well, maybe not happy," Bruce answered, "but I wouldn't be devastated. I have been penniless and worse. What about you?"

"Well, I drive a clapped-out Audi with which I am happy. So, the answer is yes."

"You don't drive a clapped-out Audi. This car is only a year old."

"What do you mean?"

"It's yours," he replied holding out the keys, "so you don't attempt to strive for cash you don't earn."

Connor stood motionless for a moment or two. "Thank you."

They climbed into the Audi and Connor made the adjustments to his seat and mirrors. The former marine drove onto the road and began the drive down south as Bruce had instructed. The Yorkshireman tried to hide the thrill at the knowledge that the car was his.

He had refrained from the whole, *'I can't possibly accept this,'* speech he always went into when his Nan used to slip him money.

He would have a cousin of his check the car for bugs when back in Leeds.

"I have your final training scenario before you're considered an official unofficial operative," said Bruce.

"OK," answered Connor nonchalantly. He felt a butterfly bounce around his stomach.

"You'll begin surveillance on a Nicholas Flint over the next few days at 22.00 hours tomorrow night. He's the man responsible for apprehending you. He was also present when our friend combusted. You'll report back what you can on his movements. If he spots you, you'll be held back for remedial training. Understood?"

161

"Yep," he replied. His mind anticipating the difficulty of carrying out surveillance alone on someone he had already met.

"Here," said Bruce, as he handed Connor an envelope, "A dossier on him, including a couple of photographs."

"Does he know of this exercise?"

"Naw, he doesn't, that would be unfair."

"How will you call EndEx?" Connor asked, meaning the end of the exercise.

"I'll call."

"Roger."

Carl Wright sat the 'The Duck and Dog' off a side street in Soho. He lamented there were not many establishments like this in the US, with its tapestry flooring, dark red leather seating, mirrors and soft lighting.

Being midday, the pub was not busy so counter surveillance was straight forward. He was admiring a picture of a British Redcoat with two hounds. Given his current predicament, he empathised with the dogs—hunting another animal for a more powerful figure.

One thing he liked about the British was their long history and the traditions left over from it. America's history was still in its relative infancy—*well, white American history is*. He remembered overhearing a conversation between a British Royal Marine and a US Marine back at the huge Kandahar military base in Afghanistan.

'So, how long have the British had Marines for man?' the US Marine had asked.

The British Marine had laughed. *'Mate, our Corps is older than your country!'*

Carl smiled at the recollection. A lot of his countrymen did not even have a passport. With the country's vastness, many never considered owning one. They did not comprehend events outside the States as neither had he before joining the military.

The blonde barmaid with blue eyes and high cheek bones smiled at him. He returned it as he ordered a lager. Pretty and friendly bar staff were always good for business in a bar—good looking women attracted the men and the men attracted the women. The blonde gave him another shy smile as she returned his change. He sensed it was more personal than professional. Although not the 'pussy hound' as most of his old Army Ranger comrades had been, he had his share of women over the years. That share had grown with his affluence especially in London where his accent seemed to break the ice. He had envisioned settling in the UK after this line of work was over. He ground his teeth—*that would no longer be happening now.*

He sipped the crisp beer and allowed himself to daydream about the vacation he was going to take. He had not made his mind up where yet but the Caribbean was tempting. He planned the rest of his evening while waiting for an email notification on his phone.

He did not like the feeling he was getting, and he had not liked it from the beginning. He was committed now, though. What was about to happen was going to create a shit-storm, and he wanted to be far away from it. They were paying him £750,000—*over 1million for firing a shot, maybe you should get over yourself.* That compounded with what he already had in various accounts, meant he could live comfortably for a while.

This life and profession had an expiration date—now more than ever. He could re-train to be whatever he

163

wanted and begin a second career. One that would dramatically increase his chance of a longer life.

He decided this would be his last assignment. He had had a good run, and it was time for change. He prayed this would go off without a hitch and he would make a clean break away. He realised that this positive self-talk was taking an effort and he took another sip.

Connor stood on his left leg in his red and white boxer briefs. His core tight with his right leg and arms, coiled with muscle, at a ninety degree angle to his torso. He descended smoothly on his rooted leg until his butt rested a few inches from the floor. He ascended efficiently, his exhale sounding like a pressing machine. He repeated the action nine times, each being a mirror of the last.

As a teenager Connor had been inspired to master them when he read a book by an American fight conditioning guru named Ross Enamait. Watching his exploits on YouTube made him a believer.

In the beginning, he would open a door, loop a bathrobe belt around both handles and hold on to the ends to steady himself. Eventually, he managed to perform one unaided, his left leg taking a while to catch up to his right. Now he could grind out sets of ten, hugging a twenty-kilogram plate to his chest. He used them when he could not get to a squat rack, or wanted to give his spine a break from being compressed by a bar.

Reed pitied people who felt they needed to buy this gadget or must use that machine for exercise. He managed to make a lot of household items useful for strength training: chairs for dipping or press ups, books to increase the depth for handstand presses, towels hung over doors for pull ups to name a few. People just lacked the long-term discipline especially in this time of instant gratification. People bought into the twelve-week programmes punted by various fitness and bodybuilding magazines with steroid-laden models on the front cover. He believed in books over magazines; that the information in a book was more trustworthy than a magazine article written under a monthly time constraint.

He began his repetitions with his right leg and began to smile. It felt like it was sinking in—he had killed three men, one after torturing him. Instead of being locked up, they offered him employment. The alternative may not have been attractive, but he would have jumped at the chance regardless.

His smile faded—*I am not employed yet.*

Bruce got through the door of his London apartment after returning from a run. For the sake of his joints, he knew he should be using the elliptical trainer stood in the living room corner. It had resembled a towel rack since its purchase. Exercising on static cardio machines bored him, feeling like a hamster on a wheel. He had commenced bodybuilding recently when a doctor told him a sign of healthy ageing was the retention of muscle mass.

He still loved running outside. He had got over feeling faintly ridiculous wearing a bum bag—called a 'fanny pack' in America—when running. It concealed his Smith & Wesson M&P45C which held eight rounds. It may not have been the best handgun in the world, but it was small and accurate. Importantly, it had been stolen from a Turkish gangster and untraceable to himself.

He walked into his hotel-like bathroom, stripped off, threw his clothes into the laundry bin, and stepped into the glass cubicle. Cold showers had been his routine for years. It had taken him two years to abscond from warm showers altogether. He had seen it written in several articles and books; cold-water exposure helped produce more white blood cells. Indeed, he could not remember the last time he had been ill.

He finished, dried off, dressed and walked into the small dining room. Sitting at the small table, he unlocked his laptop. After a few procedures, he located an encrypted email from Jaime.

Jaime Rangel was a twenty-five-year-old Peruvian computer genius living in the UK. He had been studying at the Imperial College London when Bruce first came across him. The Chameleon Project chief would never know the number of institutes, organisations, and people whose computer systems Jaime had hacked before their first meeting. However, it was Russia's SVR intelligence agency that eventually managed to locate the student. The SVR, though not the force their precursor the KGB had been, was nevertheless very formidable and dangerous.

Most in the Intelligence community believed them to be behind the assassination of Alexander Litvinenko. The former KGB Agent had fled to the UK for political asylum in exchange for information. In November of 2006, Litvinenko fell ill and was hospitalized with radiation poisoning dying three weeks later. The message had been clear—death will not be quick nor painless for traitors. Bruce respected that.

It had been Jaime who contacted Bruce. He deciphered an encrypted email and was aware the SVR were about to move in on him. He needed an ally and wanted it to be Bruce. Bruce remembered how perturbed he felt that Jaime knew of him. After putting in the necessary precautions, he met him at the British Library on Euston Road. He still remembered how scared the thin

Latino had looked back then, sunk into his ill-fitting cardigan. Offering him protection in exchange for the use of his cyber skills seemed a natural discourse. So began a professional relationship that was extremely valuable to Bruce, and financially lucrative to Jaime.

Jaime was security conscious to the extreme. Nick had used the word 'paranoid', but Bruce did not agree. The precautions were not only smart but also provided security for everyone involved. Bruce knew he could afford to replace any individual in his team, but he would be hard pressed to substitute the loyalty and skill-set of Jaime. Bruce had picked up skills from the 'techies' that had enhanced his working knowledge of computer hacking. Enough to realise Jaime was a master—maybe 'the' master. Cross-referencing his work with some of the official hackers on MI5's pay roll confirmed it. In a few instances when they had reviewed some of his feats, they had been convinced some of the work was impossible.

Jaime would only deal with him, never any other agencies. He also insisted he always pick the meeting place and choose the route for them. He could tap into the CCTV cameras and track Bruce—and anyone who might be following.

Jaime performed a multitude of tasks in his role: tracking funds, intercepting emails, monitoring electronic chatter. He would report in every three weeks unless he had something pressing, where he would immediately bring it to Bruce's attention. Despite being so technologically advanced, he insisted on giving his findings to Bruce in person if he deemed it an emergency or ultra-sensitive. Now the email was asking him for a meet in Chatham. He would give him the precise location nearer the time.

Bruce usually brought Nick along with him as backup to meetings with contacts. They had a prearranged messaging system that covered them in the event of one being apprehended or worse.

There had been something about Nick's demeanour that had unsettled Bruce, but he could not explain it. It was not dissimilar to knowing the answer to a test question but being unable to recall it under exam conditions. It gnawed because he could not articulate it to himself and therefore could not act upon it.

He remembered when he first felt a pang of unease. It was when Nick had asked him if they were walking to the meet. Ordinarily, Nick would only ask where he would have to be, at what time and with what kit. Nick had always been dependable. There was not anyone else he had trusted more, so he decided to suppress his reservations.

Ravil strolled across Walton Heath Golf course with his two bodyguards doubling as challengers. He guessed the cold crispness of the day was the reason the course was sparse of players. The bodyguards played against him regularly with the offer of £5,000 for any game they could beat him in. In eighteen games, one had managed it but only once. When he had been younger, Ravil could not understand some people's obsession with golf, but the older version understood; the walk in the open air, relaxed conversation and a game that was a supreme technical challenge. Ravil now had a handicap of eleven—a sticking point he was determined to overcome.

He had been told most Brazilian Jiu-jitsu practitioners quit soon after obtaining their blue belt Most hit their first real plateau at this grade. He knew how learning curves worked. First, you improved rapidly, then the improvements slowed into increments which took time and effort. There was an American term that he believed originated in wrestling circles: 'Embrace the Grind'—an apt expression.

Golf rid him of the stress of this career without being too relaxing. He needed a stress release in his life. He was mindful to unwind even under the most trying of circumstances. He had seen many of his contemporaries become the victim of the 'sinkhole syndrome' by not observing the necessary balance between work and play. He had seen a clip on a news channel regarding a sinkhole and how they were caused by a collapse underneath the surface layer. He realised this happened to high performing people if they did not take a break—they imploded or simply burnt out.

Ravil observed how one of the bodyguards set up to putt for the fifth hole. His feet were shoulder width, slight bend in the stomach, thumbs on the flat section of the grip and the shape matched the angle of the forearm. Ravil knew he was going to putt it.

As the ball sank in, Ravil clapped twice in congratulations. He was behind now. He dismissed the notion that it could be an omen. The last time he had been amidst such a precarious time was over a decade ago. That was when Ravil single-handedly plunged the entire Russian Bratva into civil war.

Traditionally, only a repeatedly jailed convict could become a 'made man'—a *Vor*—within the Russian Bratva. To be crowned involved approval by several Vors and the newly made man would be marked by a tattoo during the ceremony.

Ravil had been the first to object to the ideas of jail time and tattoos which had caused an uproar. He had a vision, and a brigade full of ex-prisoners with identifying tattoos ran against it.

After fourteen months of paying a few of the right people, and killing a lot of stubborn dissenters, Ravil achieved his aim of policy change within the Brotherhood. However, it had taken its toll with Ravil falling prey to tiredness, colds, migraines and insomnia. He realised the importance of taking time out to pursue enjoyment during times like this.

What was about to occur was going to send shock waves through the British establishment and beyond. The first step was nigh: the kidnap and interrogation of the man he and Makar referred to as *Opekun*—'The Guardian'. Ravil was perturbed that Opekun had gone under his radar until recently. One day one of Ravil's contacts ensnared a recording of Opekun. Ravil questioned whether Opekun knew he was being recorded.

"I am responsible for the protection of the British people. I do not care what these people do in other countries. It's not my responsibility. The people who empathise or appease them only make the matter worse in the long run. Greed is a basic human trait, and if you allow these people an inch, they will take a mile. Germany could still control most of Europe to this day if Hitler didn't get so greedy. I will fight any one man or organisation who think they can set roots here. Until they kill me trying."

Ravil felt a surge of admiration when he had listened to it. His admiration grew when he learned that the contact who had recorded the conversation had drowned in a fishing accident two weeks later.

Connor had tracked Nick for a full day now.

Nick had not left the hotel he was staying in thus it had not been a challenge. The headache would come when he had to track him on the move. Connor had taken a calculated risk. He knew he could not stay awake at all hours waiting for the target to leave. He needed a plan. He had walked into the hotel and drew the attention of the young manager behind the reception, noting the name on the tag.

Connor took out his Naval Identification Card. It used to irk him that it was labelled 'Royal Navy' and not 'Royal Marines'. To give it some semblance of authority, he had put it in a plastic holder meant for his railcard. Showing the manager the card he announced, "Military Police sir, is there somewhere we can talk in private?"

"Errr...yes...erm...follow me."

He was led into a small office and took a seat in front of the nervous-looking Jason Reynolds.

"Mr Reynolds, I'll be brief because time is of the essence. There is a guest within this hotel who we have reason to believe is involved in a drug trafficking ring."

Reynolds's lower lip detached itself from the upper and Connor continued. "Because at this juncture it is only suspicions, we are unable to maintain a twenty-four-hour surveillance on the hotel. There simply aren't enough human resources. I would need your assistance, sir."

The Manager leant forward. "What...what can I do to help?"

"All I need you to do, is to call me whenever this gentleman leaves the hotel...not just checks out, I mean whenever he steps foot out of that door sir," said Connor before he unfurled a picture of Nick.

"Is that OK? I will see to it your assistance is appreciated".

"Yes...happy to help."

"Thank you, Mr Reynolds. Circulate that photo among the staff on reception. Ensure the next member of staff on shift is briefed by the previous. The man isn't renowned for being physically dangerous, so there's no need to be nervous. Could you pass me the pad and pen behind you, and I'll give you my number. My team and I are staying at the 'Lock and Key' across the road."

Connor had written down his number, made the reception manager call him on his mobile to confirm it.

"Thank you for your assistance," he had said. He had shaken the manager's hand firmly and left.

Now he was sat back in his room across the street, bag fully packed. He watched 'The Jeremy Kyle Show' in a kind of morbid amusement. Connor had come across people like these guests when he had visited his dad and went 'debt-collecting' with his uncle.

Connor thought about his father's side of the family, where hardness and ruthlessness were a necessity.

16

Bruce drove on the M25 towards Basildon, exhaling again at having to stop with the rest of the traffic. He would rather continuously crawl along at fifteen mph, even if he got there later. Still, the BMW provided a comfortable drive.

He had just finished a hands-free call to his niece Millie, which had helped to pass the time. She had been upset. Her ex -boyfriend Richard had ended it after admitting to being married. She lamented on what a scumbag he was and what a lucky escape she had. Bruce had regurgitated the usual cliché quotes.

As the traffic coughed along, Bruce was getting drawn into listening to a topical debate on Radio 2. It centred on the social comparisons of attitude towards the elderly between the UK and countries like India and China. Bruce had seen a bit of that himself: the old people of an Asian family were taken in by relatives which was almost unheard of amongst white Britain. The common discourse was professional home care followed by a nursing home. He was just about to listen to one woman's counter argument over the air when his phone rang.

"Yes," he answered.

"It's me. Ken Follet. Be at The Lemon Tree tomorrow at 13.00. It's near the railway station. Got it?"

Bruce knew instantly who the electronically distorted voice belonged to; 'Ken Follet' was one of the various author-based code names agreed upon by him and Jaime.

"Got it," answered Bruce, and the phone cut off.

The cream pattern ceiling contrasted with the burgundy veneer of the walls and soft carpet. The bowls of lights on the walls drew the eye to the various esteemed paintings dotted around: contemporary artwork of soft eroticism juxtaposed with the centuries-old canvases of battleships and historical figures.

Stanton and his companion lounged on the brown leather sofa chairs, as they nursed scotches. They had met in this exclusive London private members club to ensure discretion: a public meeting between the Director-General of the Security Service and the Commissioner of Police of the Metropolis would attract attention.

Commissioner Sir Antony Adamson was a nondescript man of average build. His white and grey hair buzzed short, with a moustache retaining much of its original soft brown. His grey eyes remained bright and inquiring. His Portsmouth—'Pompey'—accent lightly garnished his voice in relaxed company.

He looked at Stanton. "Dark clouds are looming Roger. Three of the most powerful crime figures in London have disappeared within the space of a week. Tommy Lloyd's body was found last night in a rubbish skip in Islington after a tip-off to one of our officers. The media are going to dine out on this. I was hoping you may have some ideas?"

Tommy Lloyd had been the head of one of the most powerful white organised crime syndicates in London. Marvin Amos, the leader of the Tottenham Mandem Gang and Wei Cung, a prominent figure within the Sun Yee On Triad organisation, had also disappeared.

Stanton cleared his throat. "Isn't this type of gang warfare typical every ten years or so. Re-structuring so to speak?"

"Indeed, but it's usually the rooks and knights who bear the brunt of the bloodletting. These three are all major players."

"What does our friend at the NCA say?"

Stanton was referring to the Director-General of the National Crime Agency Meredith Jones. He was aware relations between Adamson and Jones were frosty.

"She said she couldn't speculate. We'll see if she's willing to impart more at the meeting tomorrow. I wanted to see if you had anything I could filter down to my guys beforehand."

Adamson was referring to a multi-agency meeting scheduled for the next day's afternoon. Representatives from the Ministry of Justice, NCA, Scotland Yard, the MET and MI5 were to attend.

"Tony, this has been a surprise to me also. We've had our hands full with other things frankly. I'll look into it and get back to you."

Adamson took another sip of his Scotch. "There was one thing Meredith and I did agree on. Whoever are behind this, they are very smart, very professional, ruthless and worse—ambitious."

Connor's father had been the criminal kingpin around Leeds in Connor's youth. The foundations of him becoming such a lethal figure were inadvertently laid by Connor's Grandfather. Connor's paternal grandfather Frank was a former Army Commando who served during the Suez Crisis, at a mere seventeen-years of age in 1956, and boxed extensively for the army.

From what Connor could ascertain, his grandfather had moved back to the Burmantofts area in Leeds after his time in the army. The story was Frank had beaten up members of a local crime family single-handedly who had tried to take over a pub that he frequented. The family tried several times to avenge this dishonour to no avail. They stopped when his grandfather crippled two of them. Connor never could correlate the image of this fearsome fighter to the grandfather who would sit on the floor and play draughts with him as a child.

Soon, his reputation spread and landlords sought him out. Frank put the word out that these pubs were under his wing and made the occasional appearance. This alone would be sufficient to deter any aggravation. He soon had six pubs from which he collected reasonable wages. He refused to take on any more—'*greed could be a man's downfall*' he would say.

The confident twenty-four-year-old Frank met a blonde twenty-year-old Paulette at a local dance. Both were smitten from the beginning and they married five months later in the St Agnes' Church. Despite it being five years until their first child, Paulette went on to give birth to five boys; the middle child being Connor's father Gregory Colin Ryder.

Greg had apparently been naughty as a boy and the strongest character of all the brothers. Paulette had once told Connor that, '*Your Father was always the most wayward...a rascal! He was the leader of the brothers even then. He used to drive your poor old Grandfather around the bend!*' before she lowered her voice conspiratorially, '*Was his favourite, mind*'.

Frank took Greg to the local boxing gym for an outlet for his natural energy and aggression. Greg had his first boxing match at eleven years old and went on to accumulate an 89-7-2 amateur boxing record resulting in the light-middleweight senior ABA title at nineteen. He was a charismatic, black-haired, self-assured man with bright grey eyes. Touted for big things in the professional ranks, the ABA final was Greg Ryder's last competitive amateur boxing match.

A local gang of youths had entered a pub where Frank was drinking. Frank well over fifty now was more affable and compromising than in his youth. The gregarious quartet had begun touching up the young girls, intimidating the boyfriends, refusing to pay for drinks and being outwardly threatening to everyone.

Frank confronted the unruly foursome asking them politely to calm down. Immediately set upon, after a short but furious fight, he found himself on the floor as boots and bottles rained.

He was taken to hospital with lacerations and bruising on his face, fractured ribs and skull. He was put into an induced coma as a precaution for the brain swelling he had received.

Before this incident, the brothers were as law-abiding as the next man. This would change—and would lead to the incarceration of Connor's father.

Damian Adamik kept a three-car distance between himself and the white transit van as it weaved through the traffic.

The Pole had been working for Makar a little over five years now. Being tall, heavyset and square-jawed with his brown hair in a crew cut, a lot of people mistook him for one of Makar's henchmen. However, Adamik had been a six-year veteran of Poland's *GROM*, the country's premier Special Forces unit before leaving the military for pastures new. He had left GROM six years previously at the age of twenty-six, having run out of steam. He left the unit, planning a year to himself—to relax before deciding what to do with the rest of his life.

After a few months of not being disciplined by the military system, of being made responsible by the professionalism of the unit, Adamik's drinking binges had got out of control.

One drunken night in Warsaw, Damian decided he had not had his money's worth from two whores he had brought to his suite. He took his money back and turfed the pair out into the corridor.

"You make big mistack...you be fucked up!" screamed the voluptuous Filipino in broken English.

"Yes, you have a big problem now," said the calmer Ukrainian in better English.

He shut the door on the pair and face-planted onto his bed and drifted into an alcohol-induced stupor.

His eyes cracked open with the gentle knocking at the door. He had been unsure how long he had been asleep for. When the knock got louder and more insistent, he flung the duvet off and moved bleary-eyed to the door. Upon looking through the spy hole, he saw an unremarkable man in the hotel's uniform.

"Hello Mr Adamik, I would like to speak to you please," said the gentleman in Polish.

Instinct clicked in through the haze—the accent did not sound quite right. Damian used his right hand to push the door handle down with his left forearm braced as he unlatched the door. He pushed the handle down, and the door smashed through and knocked him back a step. He was still on his feet as his left arm had taken the brunt of the impact. Ramming a seventeen-stone shoulder into the door, rewarded him with a dull thud.

There was a grunt of pain as he pulled back the door to see one heavy-set man reeling back. Two more burly

178

men rushed to take his place to get at Damian. The pair slowed one another down in their lack of cohesion, and that was all Damian needed. He threw a ferocious left hook at the first assailant. The blow fractured the man's cheekbone and smashed his head off the door frame. He was unconscious as he fell. The Pole crouched avoiding the punches from his left side, throwing himself at the assailant with his meaty left forearm up to protect his face.

Damian despatched him with a thudding elbow from underneath and a short chopping right to the temple. As the second assailant fell to his knees, Damian's knee dished his face in. A right arm slid around his vast chest snaking for his neck. Damian clamped his hands on the man's sleeve and plummeted onto his knees landing on the first assailant's shins. The man looking for the strangle fell untidily in front of Damian. A huge wrecking ball punch crushed the man's nose flat across his face. The head was pinned like a vice between the Pole's knees as three punches landed like lamp posts being dropped from the sky. The man was comatose by the second blow.

Adamik stood catching his breath. He surveyed the scene of the three bloody and unconscious men. The adrenaline still flowed through his veins like bolting greyhounds. He began to take stock of the situation. He thought it unlikely the hotel would call the police. The man in the spy hole had been a member of staff confirming his suspicions the hotel had an arrangement with this vice network. Still, he did not think it prudent to stay much longer. He sped to the bathroom and grabbed his wash kit, stuffing it into his black rucksack. Although he used the hotel towel to wipe his finger prints off everything he might have touched, he knew this to be a redundant effort—they would find evidence of DNA somewhere in the suite.

He ran over the stirring bodies down the stairs and was away. He did not realise this incident would change the course of his life

.

17

"Hello, Detective Reed?" said the voice on the phone.

"Yes," answered Connor.

"Hello, the gentlemen you…ahem… required is about to leave now."

"Thank you for your assistance sir. It's much appreciated."

"Happy to help."

It was now 10.36 A.M and Connor had been waiting in his car, a hundred yards away from the hotel, since around seven o'clock. He saw Nick leave by the front entrance, taking notice of Nick's quick, subtle glances of his surroundings approaching the car. This was one of the most tension-filled moments of Connor's life of which there had been many. What happened next would determine the rest of his career, and his life. Connor cracked a smile as relief coursed through him. Nick had not checked the underside of the vehicle for trackers.

"He's parked in an open entrance industrial building right on the corner of Southside Street by the north entrance. He's closed the shutters. I can't go in because it will arouse suspicion but there's only one door on the side other than the shutters," said Damian in excellent English.

"South Side Street, north entrance comrade?" relayed the digitally distorted voice. Even though it was distorted, Damian knew it was Makar. He had used the word 'comrade' to identify himself.

"Yes," he replied, and the phone went dead.

Connor shadowed the tracking device for twelve multi-cultural miles into Croydon. He kept out of sight of Nick but not too far away as to lose him. His cousin had sold him the tracking device and neither had asked the other undue questions.

The time when he would be most susceptible to losing Nick would be when he parked his vehicle before moving on foot. Connor would have to quickly locate a parking space and potentially run to catch up, which could look suspicious. Added to that was Nick knew what he looked like. Connor had thought about dying his hair black but, not trusting the results, opted for a baseball cap instead.

The tracking spot on the monitor began to flit on and off. He felt a spike of panic that was assuaged when he saw Nick pulling into a multi-storey car park. Another stroke of luck when Nick simply parked his car without implementing the basic security measure of driving to the very top before doubling back. Connor began to feel a pinch of paranoia.

He had been taught during the agent-handling phase of his training how to park strategically. In this case, Connor would have taken the last available space so that the occupant of any vehicle following could be ear-marked and later spotted when travelling on foot. Not a fool-proof scheme but one that made life difficult for 'shadows'.

Nick had not done a quick loop around at the beginning of the journey as he would have done. For a vehicle to follow you back to your original starting point would be highly suspicious. That the operative had not done any form of 'cleaning run' perturbed Connor.

Cleaning runs consisted of techniques to identify or prevent being followed: Cutting down a one-way street. Stalling at the lights and putting on the hazard lights and letting the traffic pass. Pulling into a cul-de-sac and seeing if another vehicle followed you. That an experienced agent did not employ any of these techniques seemed strange to Connor.

The best counter surveillance was always covert. It involved not letting the tracker know you were aware you had been spotted or *pinged* as the Marines would say. It was a case of the better the devil you know instead of alerting the tail and it being replaced by another. Surely Nick would be doing his counter surveillance? Or maybe he was so good that he wanted to keep Connor in his sights until he ditched him?

Connor quickly put those thoughts from his mind—they were not going to help him. He picked Nick out on the bustling street and began to follow him.

Bruce sat outside a café sipping black coffee. He spotted Nick walking down the street towards him. Both dressed casually; Bruce in a dark blue nylon jacket and jeans, and Nick in a brown leather jacket and a scarf.

Bruce carried out the usual drill of looking around for anything suspicious, specifically if Nick was being followed. He took note of Nick's body language. They had prearranged the signal of subtly rubbing one's hands together if under duress or surveillance. He could not see anything yet, which meant Nick had shaken Connor off as expected. That or the former marine had managed to transform into a ghost and keep Nick under surveillance.

The exercise was to enforce into Connor that following a lone target needed a lot of human resources, along with specialist equipment and adaptations to vehicles.

He was never meant to succeed.

McQuillan had decided after Connor's Vale Tudo fight performance, he was going to employ him as an operative. And that he had performed well during the assassination of the money launderer. He had performed almost too well, as Bruce recalled the moment he had crashed into Abeeb Zahid's room. Seeing the myriad of Abeeb's disintegrated skull along with Connor's blood splattered face. He clearly recollected the Yorkshire man's laugh amid the carnage—not a hysterical giggle of adrenaline but a release of genuine pleasure.

Nick sidled up and took the seat. There was a feeling that stopped Bruce asking Nick the question of whether or not he had spotted Connor. He was supposed to ask Nick the question before texting Connor to tell him to pull off task and await his decision. If Nick had seen him surely he would have told Bruce anyway. Nick reached out for the cup of tea already in front of him.

"Any dramas?" asked Bruce.

"Nah," Nick said, "You know the address yet?"

This question caused another spike of unease in him. Nick had never asked him before.

"Not the building but it's on South Side street, why?"

"Just making idle conversation I guess."

After a few moments, Nick excused himself to use the café's toilet. Not long after he returned, Bruce's phone bleeped. He looked at the screen.

"That's him. Let's go."

"Pull the schematics for South Side Street on my screen now and forward them to Damian," said Makar to his bespectacled technician. They sat in a safe house office, twenty miles away. It took a few moments.

"Highlight the building 205, according to the council listings the room is without tenants. The sniper should have a clear view of the street."

The technician sent Damian the highlights along with the information.

Makar remembered how he had met the foreboding Pole. He had been conducting business in Warsaw. The report got to him that this Polish character had put three of his lower level enforcers out of action. Makar had the bank card Damian used to pay for the hotel traced and ran him through a background check. He was impressed with what he had found, in addition to Adamik's performance in dispatching the three single-handedly. He also knew that before he could employ Damian, a certain level of respect had to be gained.

It had taken two days to find the ex-GROM member and after another three of tracking him, Makar accosted Damian outside a bar. He had made sure it was on the way in and not out so there could be no ambiguity regarding the Pole's state.

It had been necessary for what he had planned.

"Damian," he had said in Polish as the bear of a man had been about to enter the bar. The Pole had stopped and studied him for a moment or two.

"Yes?"

"I have a proposition for you," Makar had said raising his wrist revealing a Hublot Big Bang Shiny watch. It had cost him £14,000. "If you can take this from me, you can have it…there will be no police charges, regardless of how you go about it."

Damian seemed surprised, before he had smiled. "You can't guarantee that…there may be witnesses when you die."

Makar had returned the smile. "No doubt you believe that Damian Adamik. I am sure you received sound tutelage in unarmed combat in the Group Operational Manoeuvring Response Unit."

Makar had watched Damian digest the fact that at least part of his background was known to Makar.

"Why do you want to fight me?" he had asked simply.

"You'll find that out after you wake up."

Connor had struggled to keep up with Nick through the busy commercial street. The throng of the crowd was pushing him back like waves. He resisted the urge to run and catch up. The surveillance experts said a 'shadow' should never run; that it would just mark the shadow out to any '*dickers*' in the area.

Nick turned a corner into a side street, and Connor knew he had lost him—by the time he would have caught up Nick would most likely have changed direction again.

He persevered anyway.

As he rounded the corner, he saw Nick picking up oranges that had scattered across the street. They had fallen off a food van delivering to the back entrance of a local shop. The deliveryman lavished Nick with a series of 'thank yous' as Nick assisted him before smiling and continuing on his way.

Connor shook his head—*what were the chances* he thought as he carried on shadowing the target. Was there such a thing as fate or luck? He had a flashback to when he was thirteen years old. He would wait at the bottom of the street he lived on to get picked up to go to boxing eight miles away. The father of another boxer drove them both there, and Connor never missed going. Except for once.

Connor had been involved in a fight with a local heathen after school. The youth from another estate had come onto the school grounds looking to make a name for himself. He *'side-winded'* Connor unrepentantly. Connor had immediately gone on the attack, punching the antagonist to the floor before gripping his ears and smashing his head on the concrete. It took his ex-prop forward headmaster to wrench him off the unconscious youth.

The lad came around eventually unbeknownst to Connor who spent the entire afternoon in the police station. He had been genuinely concerned, but more for his liberty than the heathen's health. His father came, picked him up and to his surprise, defended him in the face of his mother's scorn.

The next day, Connor discovered the father and son who customarily gave him a lift had died in a road traffic accident—half a mile from the Boxing Club.

Damian sat in a Volvo—a work car—his phone screen displayed to the American assassin beside him. The screen showed the schematics of the building the American was to occupy, along with a more general overhead view of the area that he was to be 'working' in.

"Do you need these forwarding to your phone?" Damian asked, with only a hint of an accent.

"No, thanks."

187

As he watched the American get out of the vehicle, he made a quick text to Makar to confirm his entering the building.

Damian, though trusted, was still kept out of the details regarding the target and the implications. That was the way it was in the Russian Bratva; a need-to-know basis governed everything. However, he could sense it was important as Makar was handling the operation personally, which he almost never did. They had also brought in an outsider—this American. Still, Makar knew what he was doing—he always did.

Damian remembered the proposition Makar had made to him outside the bar when they had first met. It had been that he could have his watch 'without any legal repercussions' if he could take it off him. He had laughed to himself at the thought of tearing this businessman's head off. This ceased when the Russian let it be known—in Polish—that he knew his name and was aware of his former unit. The man's demeanour was off-putting too. The stranger, a little shorter and around ten kilograms lighter, exuded an eerie calm.

Damian had taken a short mental checklist and noted the bulbous knuckles and slight cauliflower ear. The sharp jaw signified a low body fat percentage despite the stockiness of his physique. Still, it was a fight and Damian had won countless of those and not lost since his school days. The watch must have been worth five figures alone. He knew about these things.

Damian had nodded his consent. His smirk now forced as the man led the way around the corner. They had walked around the corner down a small alcove where the deliveries were brought in. Makar took off his suit jacket, folding it neatly before laying it on the top of a bin.

He had placed his watch upon it. Instinct had told Damian not to rush his opponent and they circled one another.

Damian threw out a double jab. He had been startled at the Russian's speed, as he had slipped to the right and fired a left-handed blow into Damian's mercifully tightened solar plexus. Damian had managed to pivot before the follow up. He feinted with a right and threw a jab. Makar ducked it but Damian had caught hold of the back of the head with his bear-like palm. He was astonished to find his thrusting knee was blocked by a stabbing elbow. His gripping hand was thrown off with the web of the man's right hand.

The Russian's head thudded off his cheek bone with a resounding crack. His cheek was hot with the pain that would later come. Damian briefly wondered why his adversary had not gone for the finish as the ram-like butt had dazed him.

He stuffed down the sliver of panic and began to feint his quicker opponent for openings. He was not doing himself any favours by going first with the attacks all the time—better to 'draw the lead' and counter.

The suit took the hint and led off with combinations of punches, thrown in a deliberate sequence rather than mere haphazard flurries. These crunched Damian from all angles before he found a perfectly placed thudding left uppercut. It landed on the point of the shorter man's jaw, sending him skittering back a few paces. Damian went for the finish with a cannonball right hand. He found himself flying as the man employed a shoulder throw—an 'Ippon Seognagi'.

He almost lost consciousness upon his head hitting the ground.

He had felt a pain in his right ankle as the man trapped it under his armpit. He had felt his leg lifted by his opponent's hooked arms.

"Surrender Damian, and you'll still retain the ability to walk," had said the man.

"Fuck you. Break it," spat Damian.

The man raised his eye brows with what looked like approval.

In a swift motion, his trousers were gripped and Damian had been spun onto his front. His head was lifted by his hair and his ankle released. The forearm had punched its way around his throat and Damian knew it was over.

As his fingers had clawed for the man's fingers, he had found himself unable to wrench them from the man's clasped bicep or the back of his own head. All he had left was defiance. Despite his desperate efforts the world around him had faded to black.

He had awoken to a text message, *"When you have decided to be part of a brotherhood again, call me."*

The Hublot watch had been wrapped around his wrist.

Bruce and Nick walked along the street, carefully observing their arcs without moving their heads. They kept a light conversation going between themselves. Talking about something benign was a psychological trick which would reflect in their body language.

Jaime had sent a text message to Bruce directing him to the general area of the meeting. He always did this upon Bruce's arrival. Then he would give the directions to the specific location.

Bruce glanced at Nick. He still could not shake his feeling of unease. His instincts had been developed over three decades of being in this business. This did not include an adolescence spent in one of the rougher areas of Glasgow.

In British military doctrine, soldiers were taught to observe the 'atmospherics' of the surroundings. A typical example of this would be entering an area that seems unusually sparse of locals, indicating their knowledge of an incoming attack.

For Bruce, the feeling of danger felt like a breeze of vulnerability down his neck and behind his ears. He had it now, and it centred on Nick somehow. But what was he going to do? He could not stop now and confront him. He had to get this done. *Besides, confront him with what? Asking too many questions?*

Bruce scanned backwards and saw a figure trailing about a hundred metres behind in a green bomber jacket.

He guessed who it was and felt a little more secure.

Carl set the snooker case down. He stood at the entrance of the block of flats he was about to enter. There was a light rain coming down in London. This was to his advantage, making the few pedestrians around the area rush and not pay any attention to him. Thus shadows— or pavement artists as they were known—were easier to spot in the rain.

The snooker case, with a couple of snooker ball pictures emblazoned on the surface, contained a DAX-13 tranquilizer rifle that the Bratva had given him. Carl had test fired and zeroed it in a secluded wooded area east of Greater London. He had been amazed to find himself

191

hitting a man-sized *Figure 11* target at 200 metres away with a less than two-inch grouping in ten shots.

He had never heard of a DAX-13 rifle and concluded that it was either exceedingly rare or worse—custom made, meaning the weapon could potentially be traced. Still, the priority was the accuracy of the rifle, and that could not be faulted.

Masking his use of a lock-pick gun with a bunch of keys, he made entry within seconds. Carl grabbed the case and made his way up the stairs to the appropriate apartment room. There was nobody on the landing. He masked the lock pick with the keys anyway and unlocked the door.

"Hello?" he sounded out in an English accent opening the door.

Satisfied there was no answer, Carl entered the small flat and closed the door quietly. He made a quick but thorough check that the rooms were empty.

If anyone were inside, Carl would have explained that their door was ajar, and he feared a burglary. He would have cracked a joke regarding using his trusty snooker cue as a weapon. His brief stated that the apartment was absent of people, though fully furnished. He relocked the main door.

He had applied a silicone-caulk to his fingertips to disrupt any prints but was still careful not to touch anything. He used his knuckles to push open the doors.

The flat contents were cheap, but it was clean and tidy. The comfortable-looking green couch formed the centrepiece of the room facing the small flat-screened TV. Ornaments of cats and scenic pictures adorned the room, although thankfully no religious paintings—he did not want Jesus's eyes on him for this.

Peering out the window, he saw he had a clear view of the target street. Providence was on his side as he went into the bathroom. The window had the option of opening a small gap feature that slid from bottom to top. It was not as noticeable as a full opening of the window.

After confirming that straddling the toilet made a workable firing position, he broke out the rifle from its case, he quickly assembled it before he dialled the number in the call log, and as the phone was picked up, he clicked off. A missed call denoted that he was in position. A blank text would have indicated that it was unsuitable, and he was coming back down.

He sat and waited.

Despite the difficulty, Connor had managed to follow Nick to the café. It had surprised him to see Bruce sat at one of the outside tables. He made a quick pass down a side street; a risk as he gave up a visual on them, but Nick had sat with a cup in front of him.

He turned out his reversible jacket, stuffed the baseball cap into one of the pockets and put on sunglasses. Then he decided against the glasses. They would draw attention to him—no one would wear sunglasses with a green bomber jacket unless they were 'Jack Bauer'. He walked back, entering a charity shop overlooking the cafe from a hundred metres away. Bruce and Nick were still drinking coffee and conversing.

He perused the books.

Connor was the only person in there, and the elderly lady behind the counter gave him a glance before getting her nose back into her Danielle book. On one of the shelves was a book he wanted to buy written by Sven

Hassel. Seeing Bruce and Nick standing up to leave, he cursed not being able to buy it.

As they made their way down the road, Connor slipped out of the door and followed from the opposite side.

'Mr Negative' began to chatter again. It was going to be doubly difficult to escape the attentions of the two men now.

Bruce felt his phone vibrate with a text.

"150 yards to your right on South Side Street. Industrial warehouse. Take the entrance facing north. I am in a white BT Van inside. Come alone. Leave your man outside."

Bruce tucked the phone away.

"He wants you to wait outside," he said to Nick.

"Why?"

"He didn't say."

"Did he tell you where it is?"

"It's here."

Bruce entered the warehouse. There was a van with the side door open, and he stepped in.

"Ah Bruce, take a seat," said the light caramel-skinned South American.

Jaime wore jeans, a white shirt and a grey cardigan with his black hair fashionably dishevelled.

Bruce recalled that when he first met Jaime he had a patchy beard, ill-fitting clothes and some strange ideas with regards to colour scheme.

The Scot took the swivel seat amid the computer and surveillance screens. He felt anticipation. It was the first time Jaime had asked him to sit without any pleasantries exchanged first. Jaime sat by a small desk holding an expensive coffee maker. He had converted the former BT van so he could get to and back from the driver's seat.

Jaime exhaled. "You have a major problem, a'ma afraid," in his machine-gun like prose.

"Enlighten me."

"There are members of the security services in collusion with the Russian Bratva."

A few icy moments of silence.

"OK, give me their names and the evidence."

It was bad, but Bruce had dealt with traitors before.

"You don't understand Bruce," Jaime stated, pausing in hesitation. "They are very high up in the food chain. And I think they might have penetrated The Project"

Bruce felt a chill in the air.

"Do you have names?"

"Not yet."

"Then how do you know?"

"Through intercepting these Russian criminals' communication traffic. They speak in code *naturalamente*. I have highlighted some of the transcripts and cross-referenced them—'a friend in the seat of power'—is Russian Bratva code for a friend in the Government. 'The Scotsman', I presume that is your monkey?"

"Moniker," corrected Bruce.

"This one here," said Jaime stabbing his finger on one of the pages, "*'Birds high above the Scotsman have given us a gift within his inner circle'. This is not good, not good at all.*"

"Calm yourself, Jaime," said Bruce. "Could any of this be disinformation?"

"Why would they feed disinformation when we were not onto them in the first instance?"

Good point thought Bruce. "These high above birds…are they MI6 or MI5?"

"I do not know at this point," replied Jaime.

195

"What's the end state?"

"For the Russian Bratva with the aid of friends here to eradicate the other elements of organised crime."

"If they get entrenched, they will be near-impossible to get out."

"Well that is another thing, my friend, they may already be entrenched. This a recording I 'fished' from an e-mail sent to Ravil Yelchin. I could not trace the sender, but it must be one of his informers. The voices are distorted," said Jaime.

As he clicked the mouse on his desk, a robotic voice came out of the speakers.

"He's the majority share owner in Juntech through a dummy company. No one knew for approximately three years after all the products were implemented."

"What are the implications of that, in detail?"

"Firstly, imagine the fallout politically if certain people within our Government discovered that the very systems we use are owned by arguably the most powerful, and certainly the smartest, Russian Mafia boss in the Russian Bratva's history? Secretly replacing them would cost the sort of money that would be missed. We don't know how much he knows, how far the system has been penetrated, nothing. The tech guys say it's highly unlikely that it could be but it's got certain people rattled to the point of negotiation. And to be honest, what this Ravil character is offering doesn't seem to be the end of the world unless you're an idealist."

"What is he wanting and offering in return?"

"Immunity, or at least for any investigation into his activities not to be as vigorously pursued as much as they would be."

"That doesn't sound outlandish."

"There's more. Ravil wants to take over organised crime in London and Greater London with the view of expanding an empire. His selling point is that there's always going to be organised crime, why not let him control it and bring order? Better the Devil you know

so to speak. He says that within six months he could clean out the Turks, Yardies, Chinese, Triads, and bring any domestic gangs under his control."

"What's the decision?"

"It's looking like a yes, but certain people will never accept it. They will need to be dealt with."

"Bruce McQuillan?"

"Unfortunately yes, because it's suspected that he has independent sources, funds and people. He's too dangerous even to be made aware of this."

The tape stopped, and Jaime looked at him for a few moments.

Bruce breathed deeply.

Currently, the greatest threat to UK sovereignty was dissident republicans in Northern Ireland, despite the media coverage of extremist Muslims. Still, Bruce knew the day would come where the Russian Bratva would make their move on London. He did not think that day had been so close. He had heard of Ravil Yelchin but had kept him low on his list of priorities.

It dawned on him this was due to the shrewd Russian keeping a low profile while he arranged his pieces on the board. That the highest people within the UK government and the security service were colluding with this upper echelon, high-tech, ruthless criminal constituted the gravest threat he had ever faced.

He thought of something he had read recently.

A man had had his arm trapped by a rock in a canyon where he had fallen from his bike. After five days, he had freed himself by applying enough torque to his arm to break it. Using a knife from his multi-tool, he had sliced through the flesh, tendons, and splintered bone. He had applied a tourniquet to cut off the blood flow with the tubing of his 'camel back' re-hydration system. He had hiked for miles, starving and dying of thirst until he reached safety. The story reminded Bruce of one thing: It did not matter how bad things got, you could always improve your position if you remained alive.

18

The shadows of a derelict shop doorway encompassed Connor.

He was stood 150 metres from Nick who had not appeared to spot him. This apparent incompetence gnawed at his instincts. Nick's body language seemed alert, but his focus was on the door Bruce McQuillan had gone into, mixed with quick glances of the road in front of him—*Why would Bruce use this shit bloke to watch his back?*

If indeed that's what he was doing?

Bruce opened the door leading out onto the street and approached Nick. An invisible man punched him hard in the crevice between his shoulder and clavicle. He looked down and saw a tube with a red tail sticking out—a tranquilizer dart. He pulled it out, and it clattered to the floor as he ducked between two parked cars on the street.

"Nick! Contact!" he shouted.

That was when he knew Nick was part of it—there was no urgency in his meander towards him. He needed to send a signal to whoever was looking on that this bastard was the enemy.

Whatever now raced around his veins had already begun to take effect. He fell to the floor on all fours.

"Nick! I have been shot with a tranquilizer…move to cover!" he rasped.

Bruce braced his hand against the rear bumper and coiled his weight onto the balls of his feet. He could not risk anything requiring fine motor skills now. Nick appeared at the side of him, and Bruce launched himself forwards, forehead hurtling towards Nick's face.

Nick reeled as his face felt like a concrete-filled pan had hit it. When he regained his equilibrium, he could see Bruce on one knee, one hand on the pavement trying to fight the effects of the drug—*the hardy fucker should have been unconscious by now.*

A black Volvo pulled up, and the powerfully-built driver shot out of the car as soon as it came to a stop. Wrapping his massive arms under the armpits of the unresponsive McQuillan, the driver dragged and lifted him into the back of the car. The Volvo burred away, and Nick watched it disappear. He let out the breath that he did not know he had been holding. They had him now, and it was no longer his responsibility.

His heart plummeted.

He did what he had had to do. Bruce was one of the genuine good guys of the world, but he was too stubborn. And too much of an idealist.

Nick felt the blood trickle from his nose and knew he had to get away from the area. As he began to look around for any potential witnesses, he saw a flash of movement in his peripheral vision. He began to react when his feet whipped from under him.

Connor had intended to sweep Nick, but as his target turned, he switched to a sliding tackle. His jeans tore along the pavement. He got up, winded from the sprint and rammed his boot down towards Nick's head. The tread dug into a pair of barricading forearms. Connor's knee landed like a dropped bowling ball onto Nick's sternum.

They both felt the crack of the ribs.

Fists smashed into Nick's pain-covered face.

The third blow took his consciousness.

Connor looked around while sucking air into his depleted lungs. It had been easier than he thought. The element of surprise was essential in these situations. He thanked whatever guardian angel watched over him when he spotted the bonnet of a mid-nineties Toyota Corolla parked in the alley.

He roughly patted Nick down and found his Glock 17.

Connor scanned the area, particularly the windows. There had been a few people walking along the street in the distance at the small T-junction. There did not seem to be anyone paying attention to what had happened, such was the nature of London's busy and impersonal people.

Surreally, even given the adrenaline coursing through him, he still had a pang of disappointment that he did not have time to buy the Sven Hassel book. He took a grip of the comatose Nick, and as he hauled him into a fireman's carry—he prayed he would not awaken while on his back. As he ran for the car, he had a flashback to his Marine training when carrying another soldier a hundred metres, both wearing a rifle and webbing, was a test requirement.

He dumped him on the pavement and took out a 'bump-key'. The key was designed to open cars and start the ignitions. He knew they were only effective with cars over twenty years old or so. He had been taught about them during his agent training and was told he would only receive a bump-key once he had finished the programme. He had already possessed his own for years. They had been discounted to him by the same cousin who sold him the tracker. Inserting it into the keyhole of the boot, he felt the rewarding click, and it opened. He looked at Nick and realised he did not have anything to tie him up with.

He had the element of surprise this time, but the next time he would not. He considered resting Nick's leg onto the bumper and snapping it. He stopped himself—a captive that could not walk and needed to be helped everywhere would be more of a hindrance and danger. Besides, Connor had a Glock and Nick did not. And he was sure he had cracked at least one of his ribs.

Connor lifted him into the boot and took a look at Nick's unconscious face. An illicit giggle bubbled in his stomach, and he punched Nick square in the face. Connor slowly craned his head back and laughed as he saw the tongue protrude out. He shook his head—*for fuck sake. There was a time and a place.*

He closed the boot and opened the driver's door as easily with the bump-key. Now was make or break time. He did not have a screwdriver or a wire stripper that made hot-wiring easier. He put the bump-key in the ignition and twisted.

His heart soared as the motor coughed into life.

The sunshine illuminated the golf course, and Ravil felt at ease. He had heard it said the art of meditation lay in focusing on a single thing to the exclusion of anything else. In that the mind finds peace.

The Pakhan of London believed he got the same effect from golf, which he had become addicted to despite himself. When alone, sometimes he would practice his swing without his golf club in his hand. An instinctive feel for the game was developing, and he relished games that pushed him. His opponent was Henry Costner, a power broker within the British Government.

Ravil found the Brit likeable enough though he did not trust him—he did not trust anyone unless it was necessary. He had to trust Makar as his operations would collapse if he did not. That was as far as it went and even that had taken a significant amount of time.

He felt his phone vibrate in his pocket and cursed it interrupting his swing.

He answered it. "It's done," said the voice before clicking off.

Ravil had also taken years to develop these contacts within the British security services, judicial system and Government. His most powerful contact had insisted he kill Opekun and Ravil had pledged to do so.

Opekun's real name was Bruce McQuillan.

Ravil was not going to kill him immediately, though. He was going to bleed Bruce McQuillan for information first. Having the Scot within his possession felt akin to catching a mythical beast. A beast whose very existence had been doubted.

The rumour was Mr McQuillan held a treasure trove of evidence that related to the corruption and shame of high echelon figures within the British establishment. He had used this evidence to armour himself and for leverage. Any information was useful information, but dirty information regarding powerful and supposed allies would be priceless. Behind all the façades they were snakes.

"Good news?" His playing partner enquired.

"Yes, my friend, achieved without error and no witnesses."

"And so?"

"And so my friend, you will, as they say, 'batten down the hatches'. Control the media output, feed my organisation intelligence," commanded Ravil, "and we will clean up your streets and monitor criminal activity from now on."

"And release us from any blackmail?"

Ravil looked the politician in the eyes. "You know that we will not do that."

"No relationship survives without trust."

"Maybe not my friend,' said Ravil, hitting the ball sweetly, "but plenty of business partnerships do."

Bruce woke in darkness. The blindfold wrapped tightly around his face. Quickly, he became aware his hands were tied. He tried not to move. He had hoped to get his bearings or any information before whoever tied him realised he was conscious.

There was no such luck.

The influx of light made him squint with the removal of the blindfold and his retinas fought hard to absorb it. Before him was a gentleman dressed in dark corduroys, with a cream shirt covered by a tweed suit jacket. He was an inch over six feet, thickset with a sharp jaw line. The eyes stared at him but not with any attempt at intimidation. Instead, they were flickering between determination and what looked to Bruce like a hint of sadness.

The man carried a certain aura even though there were just two of them in the room—an internal confidence that showed even when not consciously expressed. The stranger spoke.

"Mr McQuillan, I am an associate of Ravil Yelchin. My name is Makar Gorokhov. We have come to an arrangement with individual members of your government and security services to control organised crime in London and beyond,"—Makar shook his head— "It's those members who saw it fit to betray you to us."

The two men stared at one another for a few moments. Makar continued, "We don't trust traitors that betray their own people. You, of course, can appreciate the worth of real intelligence. We need all the information you have about these people and your organisation. I risk sounding redundant but if you give up the information willingly, I will give you a quick death. This merger is going to take place, it's inevitable. It's senseless to put yourself through what will follow if you refuse to co-operate. To protect the same people who have orchestrated your demise. The very people who would have ordinarily provided you hope of escape have proven their true colours Mr McQuillan. I have no desire to torture and maim an individual who I respect."

Bruce just looked ahead with a neutral expression. After a few moments, Makar spoke again. "Very well Mr McQuillan, the interrogation will begin shortly."

Connor had pulled up to a deserted country track and finished tying Nick with some black rope purchased from a hardware store. He had flagged down a young teenager to go in and get it for him, explaining the central locking had failed and he could not leave the car. The teenager had agreed to the ten pounds then and there, and ten pounds upon giving Connor the rope and insulating tape—*the necky bastard*.

Now Connor wrapped the insulating tape around his mouth several times.

The Glock had gained Nick's compliance.

His eyes stared as Connor was about to close the boot.

Connor stared back and slammed down a fist which broke his captive's nose. He banged the boot lid down not caring Nick would now struggle to breathe—a mild retribution. Connor thought about where this pleasure of hurting bad people came from. His recollections took him back to when he had been fifteen years old running through the local park. He saw a youth a year or two older than himself gripping a young girl by the hair. The thug had brought his face menacingly close to the girl's as his cronies surrounded her. When he saw the youth spit into the girl's face, the red mist had descended. Connor's anger eradicated his fear, and he tore into the 'screamer' like a jungle cat. He had pulverised him to the floor. The others stepped back in a collective adrenaline-induced shock. Still, Connor could not leave it there, and after ensuring the girl was fit to return home, he had removed the would-be gangster's jeans, trainers and underwear.

He had got pleasure afterwards from two thoughts. One had been that this 'wannabe gangster' had met a real one and not one of his so-called friends lifted a finger to help him. Mostly the thought that the embarrassment of being half stripped while unconscious would burn into the bully's psyche, probably for life.

Connor also knew it was his father's wish for him to be a force for good as his grandfather was. His grandfather died when Connor had just come out of Borstal. The funeral was to be a private affair, as was his wish. However, hundreds turned up with the vast majority having to wait outside. There were some 'gangster types' there, but mostly it was people from the local community and beyond paying their last respects to Frank Ryder. Greg Ryder was not a religious man, but Connor remembered him once saying, "Do unto others as you would have done to yourself. How much further to religion do you need to go?"

His grandfather Frank was the epitome of that.

Connor had once asked his dad if it was '...*ok to hurt bad people*'. His father had replied, '*Hurting bad people, or hurting people for bad things, is a bit like striking a child for being naughty. It's a last resort and essentially means that you have failed—failed to teach them correctly.*'

'*So there's no time you can do it?*'

'*I didn't say there's never a place for it,*' he said, '*being a pillar of your community, trying to help heal dysfunctional people, teaching your kids rather than continually punishing them, helping a person knowing that they may never be able to repay you – these are the marks of a true man. Unfortunately, some people are too far out of reach to be saved no matter what idealists say. They're a cancer to other decent people, and need to be dealt with. Sometimes, they need to be dealt with in a manner that sends a signal to other baddies.*'

Connor used to smile at his father's use of the word '*baddies*'.

Now he was driving a car he had stolen, and in the boot was a '*baddie*' of a Government agent that he had assaulted and kidnapped. He felt his nerves bite but he could handle that. He had learnt to live with them long ago and he knew what he had to do. He needed somewhere private to take Nick and he knew who to call as he began to look for a payphone.

He no longer trusted the phone he owned.

Makar knew it was not going to be quick. This was going to be especially difficult as all the techniques they tried were known to Bruce McQuillan, who had probably performed most of them himself and at least witnessed the rest.

When the captive did begin talking, the initial dialogue would be lies and half-truths. Still, getting the

207

detainee to say anything gave you a foothold. That they had even opened their mouth let you know they wanted a way out.

A Hollywood myth was that there were men who were unbreakable. This simply was not true. All it took, as with anything in life, was time, skill and effort.

Bruce McQuillan would know that.

Nevertheless, he would also know the longer he held out, the more chance a miracle might occur. A skilled interrogator could stretch it out over a lengthy period without a detainee becoming incoherent. But it was more difficult than generally imagined.

In war, where time was of the essence, the longer it took to break a captured soldier the more time it gave the enemy to change anything mission sensitive. Some militaries now taught their soldiers to bleed out information slowly to their captors for this reason.

Time was not a major issue here as no one would be coming to the rescue of Bruce McQuillan. As far as the British conspirators were aware, Bruce McQuillan was dead. Ravil had them by the balls anyway. It had surprised Makar that Ravil had pulled this off. He had thought the computer system ruse was too farfetched to work—but it had been a master stroke. Though Ravil helped finance the manufacturing, he did not have access to MI5 files or activities through them. However, the British establishment did not know for sure. Makar originally thought Ravil had a mole inside the security services. That Ravil had insinuated to the establishment that he knew of certain sensitive information through an imaginary 'bug' he had planted in the computer systems.

Makar had at first believed the British conspirators had panicked into an unprecedented agreement based on a bluff. When Ravil revealed to Makar the truth behind the betrayal, he was depressingly disappointed. He also, despite himself, felt a worm of injustice.

He had had McQuillan placed in a sensory deprivation tank. Makar, who himself had been placed in one during his KGB training, knew that hours felt like days. A man of honour like McQuillan should not be in there, but life was not fair. Makar had made peace with that fact a long time ago and felt happier for doing so.

"What's 'appenin' my gee!" said Louis in an exaggerated Caribbean accent.

He walked up to the car which Connor was leaning against, parked off a side street in Peckham. Connor smiled. He did not know his friend's exact ethnicity except that Louis had told him he was 'African black'—not from the Caribbean.

Louis was tall and very well built, a lot more so than when Connor had last seen him. Some would think he had been 'on something', but Connor knew that Louis Allen was one of those annoying men who was not only a natural sportsman but could also look at a barbell and put on muscle.

Louis wore a white plunge top under an expensive black leather jacket, grey jeans, brown leather loafers and a black cap. Connor thought him irritatingly good looking.

He had two *stacked* and intimidating looking men with him who he made stand back with a gesture with his fingers.

Louis Allen and Connor had been in Royal Marine basic training, then the Corps and Navy Boxing teams together.

Louis was born and bred in Peckham and his real accent matched. He had left the Marines after the minimum four-year engagement and two tours of Afghanistan to become a personal trainer. He was not just a commercial gym trainer but had been hired by a few B-list celebrities. Connor knew by his social media he had been doing well for himself.

Louis was also a criminal for the fun of it—armed robberies were a favourite. Connor knew because they committed several together.

"Call me boy again and I'll one-bomb ya. You won't be able to look your homeboys in the eyes after being dropped by a cracker," dead-panned Connor.

"If you coulda, you woulda," replied Louis who would normally edge their sparring sessions being twenty-five pounds heavier, "What do you need anyway brother?"

"What I need is a room or a space where I won't be disturbed, and loud screams won't be heard, and I am being serious."

"Can you tell me what this is about? And before you say anything, you couldn't make any chick scream loudly fam'."

"I can in my Louis Allen mask," Connor smiled. "It's a bit of a long story"

"Well, you have time. The place I'm taking you is far away."

Carl Wright approached the table where Pierre sat. His eyes burnt into the Frenchman. The man had promised him he would be released from any blackmail once the assignment had been completed. Now he found himself being summoned again. To make matters worse they met here in Istanbul and Carl hated it: the congestion, the constant blare of car horns, the smoke and the stress of the people in this particular part of the city.

210

He took a seat and stared at Pierre. The bodyguard sat at a forty-five-degree angle to him but Carl's anger clouded any fear he had. Pierre was leant back looking at Carl with his chin raised. He dressed in a blue shirt with the sleeves turned up to reveal his tanned, sinewy forearms and a Balme and Mercer watch.

"Well Mr Wright, it seems you failed. Well, at least partially failed."

"Impossible, I saw him bundled into the car you dick."

Pierre raised his eyebrows, "That you may have, but your brief was to provide over-watch and now the insider has gone missing. The reports suggest he was captured at the scene."

"No, I didn't fail you fucking liar. If your insider can't look after himself that's your problem, you Monday-morning-quarterback."

"Watch your tongue Mr Wright, or—"

"—fuck off! What you going to do? Gun me down in the street for stating a fact?" Carl knew that ultimately Pierre had a hold of him but that did not mean he had to eat shit, "It's your problem now."

Carl could see his disrespect getting to Pierre. He realised that no-one had probably spoken to Pierre like that for a long time.

"Actually Monsieur Wright, it is your problem. You don't want to be looking over your shoulder for the rest of your life, because if there is one organisation that still holds honour at heart, it is ze Russian Bratva."

Carl replied, "True, but you don't want the connotations that would happen if I refused. Therefore, I want 700,000 euros for this, half now, and half later."

"Why would I agree to this, Mr Wright?"

"Because I may not have the finances to escape the clutches of the Russians forever but I do have the finances to dedicate myself to tearing your operations apart. That's if I do not simply decide to kill you."

"Mr Wright, these threats are so American, so Hollywood. Please cease with them before you get yourself into trouble or worse...to be boring to me."

They stared at one another intently before they resumed.

"What's the captured man's name?" asked Carl. Pierre smiled broadly before answering. "Nicolas Robin Flint. I will email you all the relevant information. Now we have to depart."

Pierre and Carl stood up.

As Pierre and his bodyguard turned to leave, Carl asked, "Weren't you wearing a Berguet watch last time we met? Has it seemingly gone missing from your hotel bedside during the night as you slept by it?"

Pierre stopped still, turned and stiffened to see Carl casually throwing his $150,000 Berguet from hand to hand. He threw it to Pierre, forcing him to scramble inelegantly to catch it.

"You may want to re-evaluate how well protected you are. Then decide to pay me the first half of what is a now 800,000-euro bill before I set foot in London."

He turned and walked away from a stock-still Pierre and his bodyguard.

19

"Now I know you ain't gassin', that's a *dit* even you couldn't make up," laughed Louis, as he rubbed his back against the seat. "My gee, this is some stone-cold conspiracy shit, but couldn't you have got a better car? Anyone sees me in a clapped-out shit-wagon, I won't be able to live it down."

They had decided that Louis would drive.

"You're an oppo though, why do you think I called you?" asked Connor.

"Eh, because you don't got no friends other than me down here, ya northern monkey!"

They both started laughing before Connor replied, "Not touching that one."

He looked out of the window as the Toyota bumped along the country track. The sun had gone, leaving a darkened blue sky illuminating the rolling hills that Connor did not even think existed down south.

He could see in the distance that they were coming to a large farm house with several stables and other huge farm buildings.

"What is this place," asked Connor.

Louis replied with a smile, "It's for growing plants."

Connor shook his head, but he did not find cannabis distasteful, although he had seen people adversely affected by it. One of his friends, sharp and in the top classes in secondary school, had seemed like a stuttering idiot a short few years later when all he seemed to do was smoke pot. Then again, Connor knew high-flying corporate types who smoked it without seemingly any adverse effects.

Maybe it was all down to the quality and the frequency used.

Connor surmised lethargy and lack of ambition came first and the abuse of weed came afterwards.

Sativas was a strain smoked by a friend of his who claimed it made him more creative and energetic. This was opposed to Indica, which was the cheaper and the more common strain distributed. Indica leaves were short and broad which made it more suitable for growing indoors.

"How long has this set-up been running?" Connor asked.

"A few years bruv, we can see for miles here. Anyway, the police might already know of this place but I reckon they aren't too vexed as long as it's not in their yard."

"You know mate….not to judge but it's not as if you need to do this, you have that personal training business. You know they'll get you eventually. Maybe you can grow your PT business and leave this behind?"

Louis looked at him sideways, "This the same Connor Reed I'm talking to? Robbing, even if it is from drug dealers, isn't legal either," referring to some of the work they had done together, "I am providing a service…anyway, it's weed gee. It's legal in civilised cultures."

"I know…I've just been thinking lately."

"'bout what?"

"About the fact that every time I get the buzz from a score and get away with it, it encourages me to do it again. The probability of getting caught goes up each time. I don't want a buzz for a few years then prison for decades…a pretty face like mine wouldn't do well in there. Besides, I've got a new career now…or I thought I did."

214

"Will be hard to walk away from bruv…believe me." Louis paused as if thinking. "Besides, don't you give your money away to charities?"

"Yeh, but only some of it. I used to think of myself like a Robin Hood. The truth is, it stops me feeling guilty."

Louis said nothing.

The car reached the gates. A hooded black guy ushered them through when he spotted Louis.

"I don't know how long it's going to take with this lad Louis," said Connor

"Take as long as you need in'it." The car stopped outside the warehouse. "Stay in here."

Connor watched Louis approach the tall, skinny yardie-looking youth who came out of the entrance to greet him. He noticed the outline of the pistol under his shirt tucked into his belt. A few words were exchanged with the adolescent looking over furtively. Connor could tell by the body language Louis was the leader of this operation.

He returned and got back in the car.

"We'll go around the back. There's a small door into a tool room and they're clearing it out just now. My boys have been briefed to leave you alone and ignore any noise."

Louis gunned the car and drove it around the back. The pair got out and Louis took out a Windicator revolver and pointed it at the boot. Connor opened it and took a step back. He saw Nick bound and squinting, struggling to breathe through his broken nose. They took a grip of Nick under his bound arms and lifted him from the car. Nick neither helped nor hindered their efforts before being dumped unceremoniously on the wet gravel.

"Let's take his shoes off," gestured Connor, then to Nick, "Walk to the door twenty-five yards from your eleven o'clock. I hope you give my friend an excuse to knee cap you."

Nick began to walk.

As he stepped over the threshold, Connor's boot thudded into the small of his back. It sent him face first on the floor with a sound of dropped meat.

The tape was torn off Nick's mouth, which Connor had bound all the way around his head. Nick grimaced but did not cry out. They threw him onto the single chair. A trickle of blood leaked from his eyebrow.

Connor turned to Louis, "Can you grab us both a chair, I don't like not being able to see his hands. An' a hammer."

Louis left the room.

Nick spoke, "You don't know what the fuck you're doing son or what you've got yourself into."

"Don't call me son, we're about the same age you fucking dick," said Connor, "but you're right, I don't. That's why you're going to tell me."

Louis came back in with the chairs, sitting one down at an angle in front of Nick for Connor.

"You having t'is or shall I?" Louis asked, raising the hammer.

"You, mate. You seen the film 'Payback'?"

Louis smiled. He raised his chair over Nick's head to plant it behind him. He let one of the legs hit him in the face. Connor kept his smirk at bay as Louis set down the seat behind the detainee.

"I am going to ask questions and if you refuse to tell me, or if I think you're lying, my friend here is going to hammer your toes one by one. Apologies for the lack of sophistication, but part of me gets a kick out of mutilating you for what you've done."

Nick scrunched his eyes, "And yet you don't know what I have done."

"You helped someone kidnap your boss, no doubt for money or because they coerced you."

"You ignorant fuck, you don't know anything."

Louis's chair scraped on the ground like nails on a blackboard. Connor sat him back down with a gesture.

"Why don't you enlighten me?"

"Where're your phones?"

"Why?"

"Because I want to see them switched off before I tell you this." Connor and Louis looked at one another— *was this a ploy?*

Connor removed the pay-as-you go phone he had bought the previous day, powering it off and Louis did the same. They showed Nick.

"Start speaking," said Connor.

Nick took a breath. "Bruce McQuillan's death was ordered by certain people high up within Government."

"Lies, you've done this for fucking money, no other reason."

"It's true."

"Why?" asked Connor, and when Nick did not answer. "If you hold back again, a little piggy will go to the market you prick."

Nick looked back at him. "The Russian Bratva is taking over all organised crime in London. Probably the UK as a whole after that, with the help of people within the Government."

Connor looked at Nick and immediately saw that he was telling the truth—*it is too out there to be a lie*. He felt his stomach lurch.

"Why?"

"I don't know. Perhaps it's better the devil you know? Too many resources spent trying to track too many different groups."

"Or maybe it isn't the organisation as a whole, maybe it's a select few they have managed to coerce, you fucking weasel," Connor spat.

"We can talk all day long, but my orders were given to me by my superiors."

"You sound like an SS Officer."

"You heard yersen. Had you completed training, Bruce McQuillan would have asked you to do some questionable things to say the least."

Connor looked at Louis. "Louis, would you hold him steady and cover his eyes my good man?"

Nick blanched as the hammer was passed to Connor. One of Louis's python-like arms whipped around and clamped the struggling Nick's chest like a vice. Louis covered Nick's eyes with a tight palm. Nick kept shifting his feet until Connor pressed a gun-mimicking pair of knuckles into his kneecap.

"Toe or kneecap, five seconds to make your choice."

"Why are you doing this?" shouted Nick.

Connor replied, "I'll explain in a minute but in the meantime, I suggest you stop moving your feet."

Nick stilled his feet. His little toe on his right foot splattered with a clanging thud, leaving Nick roaring. Louis let him go as they watched him take huge swallows of air.

"Stop crying you fanny. They do worse to themselves on 'Jackass'," sneered Connor, "and in answer to your question, Bruce McQuillan did take me on a mission requiring me to kill someone. He made me question why and gave me the reason, so don't pull that shit with me again. Now answer me this, why did he need to be kidnapped?"

Nick, still smarting from the hammer, looked at Connor. "He wasn't, at least they told me that he was just going to be killed in the street."

"We'll get to why he wasn't later but first, what reason was given for killing him?"

Connor guessed Nick's tongue might have been loosened by the toe splattering.

"They told me that this partnership with the Russians was the future... that Ravil Yelchin was someone they could deal with, that he was a businessman not a psychopath and this 'relationship' could cut organised crime in half. You're talking about millions of pounds that could be funnelled back into the NHS, Education, and public services. Bruce McQuillan would never accept that and to even float it to him would be dangerous given his independent resources. He needed to be taken out."

"Who are these superiors? I thought we...you only reported to Bruce?"

"They have eyes on my family man...I'll never tell you who."

"Which toe now?" said Louis.

Connor shook his head.

"Why wouldn't he accept it?" Connor asked,

"Because he just wouldn't. He sees things in black and white and he wouldn't—"

"—wouldn't accept elements of the British Government and its security services being in collusion with Russian gangsters? Yes, he sounds like the nutty one doesn't he," said Connor.

Nick's head just hung slightly, and Connor continued, "Let me tell you something Nicholas. Let's say this does go forward and there's a 'relationship'—so to speak—with these Russians after a great war with the Turks, Yardies, Chinese and British gangs. Let's say they overcome them all and bring order to the UK, because this Ravil character is an all-powerful yet reasonable guy. Tell me what happens when he goes. If he dies, if he falls ill, what happens?"

"What do you mean?"

"What I mean is that we would have to be pretty fucking fortunate that his replacement would be just as *'reasonable'* as you say. If he wasn't, you will have given him an infrastructure that's nearly impossible to dislodge."

"How do you know that? You're half Royal Marine, half fucking criminal? You don't know how it's going to play out."

Connor smiled, "It's because I come from a family of criminals that I know how it's going to play out. This Ravil character might be the Frodo Baggins of the criminal world but I doubt it. It sounds to me a lot like the Munich appeasement of Hitler. Hypothetically though, let's say that he is. Once he's gone, his replacement will have the infrastructure to bring the country to its knees. It's the classic 'all your eggs in one basket' don't you see? And that's why we have to stop it."

"What the fuck are you talking about? There is no stopping it, it's already taking place. It's the most influential people in this country and the most powerful Russian mafia boss forming an alliance. Who's going to stop them? You and Wesley Snipes here playing 'White Men Can't Jump' with guns? You'll have more chance spit-roasting the Queen, ya prick."

Connor and Louis smiled, in admiration at the outburst. Connor thought for a moment.

"Let me tell you a story. Thailand is the favourite place for Royal Marines to go to relax and I use that term loosely. Anyway, there's an element in the Marines named ASG—the Armoured Support Group—and they cut around in this amphibious, all-terrain vehicle called the Viking. It's a great bit of kit. You heard of it?"—Nick said nothing, and Connor continued— "Anyway, they'd be away six months of the year in Afghanistan, and an oppo of mine, a friend rather, would just go to Thailand any chance he got. I mean, it could be a four-day weekend, and he'd go, and eventually he ended up in over £40,000 of debt. I used to ask him how he was going to get out of it and he'd replied, *I'll think of something*'—not bothered like. Just before he went to Afghanistan, he took out a shed load of life insurance with injury cover with various insurance groups. He came back, we went into the woods with a hammer and chisel, he placed his hand against a tree and using the hammer and chisel I chopped his little finger off—at his request of course. It took two whacks. He didn't take any painkillers as he didn't want it to look suspicious. He ended up getting around £80,000. Used the excess to start a profitable private security business. So you see, there's no jam impossible to get out of."

Nick looked at him with bemusement etched on his face. "You're fucking crazy."

"That doesn't mean that I'm wrong."

Bruce McQuillan sat back in the room after his stint in the sensory deprivation box. It felt like he had been in there for hours, unable to see, hear or to move. It was impossible to tell how long. He understood a man could go mad in there. He also knew that was not what they wanted. He would have to be lucid or at least semi-so. It was a mental battle that ultimately he could not win, unless

221

he escaped or a cavalry came. His goal was to draw it out as long as possible.

The Russian's words had briefly penetrated his psyche.

If it were true people high in the security services had orchestrated this, a cavalry would not exist. Still, he knew he would resist until he had no strength left. Not because of pride but because it was the only way to give him any semblance of a chance of turning this situation around.

He was lying to himself about the pride part. No way would he go to his grave without tolerating what he could withstand past his absolute limit. This was the life he chose, and he knew the risks. To crack to spare himself pain would be like the Mafia members who swear an oath, only to turn 'rat' in the face of long prison sentences. He had seen more than a few of those types. They had been extremely useful to him, had indeed helped to save lives, but he still found them distasteful. He remembered one staunch member of the IRA who would not be swayed by money, the loss of family, reputation, immunity or anything. In the end, Bruce had had to kill him. As he squeezed the trigger, Bruce looked into the Republican's eyes, feeling a weight of admiration and sadness wash over him. He almost owed it to that enemy to go out the same way. As long as he had control of his mind, he was winning.

The door opened.

"I want any information that will help me get him back," said Connor.

"I told you, he's dead. Those were the orders."

"Nah, if they wanted him dead, there's any number of ways they could have done it—hit and run, poison in his tea, mugging gone wrong, anything. Instead, they put this elaborate plan in place and kidnapped him alive."

"Why?"

"I am guessing that the Russians don't much trust their new partners and are looking for any leverage they can use against them."

"They have all the leverage they need."

"How so?"

Nick did not say anything and Connor's voice boomed, piercing the air. "You fucking stop again and it'll be your big toe on the same foot. You'll be walking like your mother after a session with Louis and his mates."

Louis shook his head straight faced.

"Ravil owns the computer systems that have been installed in MI6's headquarters, or at least he has part-ownership. Now he's coercing some very influential people with this. He has already gleaned information about the inner workings of the Government and UK Security Services."

"This doesn't make sense. Why does the Russian need to interrogate Bruce McQuillan then?"

Nick said nothing.

"Be that as it may, you're going to tell me what you know Nick."

"I know they used an arms dealer by the name of Pierre Gaultier. He's the middle man to hire the assassin who was meant to take out Bruce."

"But he wasn't taken out."

"Well, it looked to me like he was shot with a tranquilizer dart."

"Why didn't you fucking say that? Surely that's enough to convince you it was a kidnap?" Connor stared at his captive incredulously.

Nick returned the gaze contritely.

"And this Pierre character can help us how?"

"He could lead you to them maybe. But you need help—technical support," replied Nick.

"From who? You?"

"No, someone who specialises in these things. He's more than a specialist. He's a wizard when it comes to anything to do with computer systems."

"Why should I trust you or this 'Q slash Gandalf'?"

"I can't make you believe me, but I'll say it anyway. This guy would do anything to make sure Bruce is brought back safe. He is your only chance now."

Connor processed a few thoughts before asking, "Not that I know him well, but from what I have seen, surely it's more than a possibility that Bruce will end your life for betraying him?"

"Yes, but I guess I am dead anyway. I thought I was doing the right thing," Nick exhaled, "but as you say yourself, why did they kidnap him? Why not kill him as briefed?"

"Because they don't want an alliance. They want total control."

"Right. So I'll help yer."

20

Jaime Rangel drove banging his hand on the steering wheel. Yesterday, he had observed Bruce McQuillan's kidnap through a temporary surveillance camera he had set up in the warehouse overlooking the street. The Peruvian felt an invading army of fear and despair march through him. That traitorous bastard had a hand in it, and that was bad news. Bruce had told Jaime he divulged more information to Nick than anyone else.

Jaime had made his escape driving through an exit that had not yet been up-dated on any schematics held with the local council. He would never know if this had saved his life or not.

He had to drive somewhere safe and begin to monitor the electronic 'chatter' to ascertain Bruce's location. What was he going to do if he discovered it? Either MI5 or MI6 had been compromised, perhaps both. Who could he trust now? The police, if they were to use their Armed Response Unit, would have to alert MI5.

Jaime had only ever trusted Bruce McQuillan. Now he had been taken, and Jaime felt like a stalked gazelle. He had to do something, and at that moment in time, the only thing he could do was try to acquire Bruce's location. Of that, he was confident in his abilities.

A strange twist of fate led him to have the most unlikely of aces up his sleeve. The Russian Bratva did not know he had been following them for weeks. He had intercepted a coded email from a French arms dealer to a contract killer.

He was not sure he believed in a higher power, but this had the feeling of fate around it.

Ever since he had got involved in this murky world of espionage and crime, Bruce McQuillan seemed the only man to be impervious to having his principles shaken. Jaime had to find him and pray for a miracle, whatever form it came in.

"I'll need to contact him via payphone," Nick continued. He had been watched over throughout the night.

"You think I am going to trust you to do that?"

"What else are you going to do?"

"Why the change of heart? Because he was kidnapped rather than killed?"

Nick took a breath. "It's like you say—why did they take him away instead of inducing a heart attack or running him over? Maybe it's a ruse. Maybe they don't have the leverage they say they have. I am a patriot. Don't you think it's haunted me, having to give up Bruce McQuillan to the wolves? The man should have the title Lord High Protector like Cromwell. But he was getting in the way of change, change for the better, or at least, so I was told."

"Who the fuck is Cromwell?" asked Louis.

"He was a bloke who raised an army and defeated the King's forces back in something like the 1600s," answered Connor.

"Lord High Protector? Did he get a *chuck up* for defeating the king?" Louis laughed. "Thought that was the one dem jocks all cream over…the Braveheart one."

"William Wallace, he was the other one," Connor smiled. "I'll spin you the full dit before bed tonight. Can you get me a car?"

"Safe, brother. Am in this now, and am in this all the way."

"You've done more than enough. I can't be getting you further involved in this, Royal."

"I am not asking you, am telling you. If you think you're duking it out with Russian mobsters all to save the UK without me, then you're crazy, ya get me?"

"Yeah, on second thought, maybe I could use you to pose as a Russian to get in with them?"

They both laughed. Nick looked on with an alarmed look on his face.

Bruce last slept thirty-six hours ago, and his mind felt sluggish. He had gone nights without sleep many times. He knew willpower could only overcome the need for sleep to a point. Once past that, slumber overcame a person, especially when you were in an inactive physical state as he was now. Unless you were being kept awake with white noise like he was being. He tried to focus. Why had Nick betrayed him? *For money, probably. Or was he ordered to? If so, who by?* He discounted Stanton. The man had always gone to bat for him, and Bruce could not see the motive. It must have been Miles Parker; the MI6 Chief must have waited all this time to get even.

In walked the smartly dressed Makar. He took the seat in front of the haggard-looking Bruce and gave him an almost avuncular sigh.

"Mr McQuillan, I see you're holding up to this initial 'softening' phase."

Bruce said nothing.

"Without wishing to be a James Bond cliché, what you are doing—this resisting—isn't only futile, it is damaging to your cause."

227

The Russian paused to sip the water from the plastic cup he had brought in; Bruce had not had water for over twenty-four hours.

He continued. "Our British allies, or I should say ally as one man was the catalyst…well, he has been spinning a tale that your security computer systems have been penetrated. A tale of how Ravil Yelchin was a secret partner in the manufacture of the overhaul of computer systems, that he already has enough information because of this to bring the establishment to its knees. He whispered in the right ears, and now backs will be braced, eyes averted, and cheeks turned while we systematically take out all the organised crime gangs who resist change and control those who embrace it," Makar sipped at his water again, "however, the sad truth is all of this is based on lies. Depressing isn't it? All it took was £75 million for this individual. In return, he courted several influential men in your government for a few years. They told them the sensitive information had come from the computer systems hacked by Russian Bratva and surveillance." Makar swirled the water in the cup, "This is the institution you want to protect? Brought to its knees by money?"

He watched Bruce, looking for any sign of weakness at these words. All he saw was a stony impassivity. Makar fleetingly wished that Bruce had been born a Russian.

"We are the solution Mr McQuillan. If we could have trusted you, we would have used you, but I know men like you will never compromise. You will always seek to attack what you see as crime and injustice. However, there's no escape because there's no-one who knows you're still alive, no-one willing to help anyway. It's just substituting British, Jamaican, Turkish and Chinese gangsters for Russian ones. Why continue to resist?"

Bruce's rasping voice cracked the silence, and Makar felt a sliver of triumph.

"There's no crime organisation that isn't a cancer. You may think that your Russian mafia is different, or at least your Bratva is. Maybe at this moment, it is built on a sense of honour. But it never lasts. Frustrations flare, egos clash, grey areas appear, plotting begins, and weak links become evident. Every organisation ends up like that. You already know that. Maybe you and your boss can contain that or maybe you can't, but what happens when you're gone?" said Bruce, as he looked Makar in the eye. "You see, I don't mind many moving parts. I don't mind many gangs competing over the same pie. It makes them easier to take out or control. They prevent one another from getting too large. You will have left something that's impossible to take down—a monopoly. This time in Britain's history will go down forever as the time where Russian gangsters staked their claim to these islands and never let it go. So you see my friend, I will hold out to the bitter end."

The two men stared at one another.

"I admire you Mr McQuillan. Enough to make you one concession. Would you like to know who the inside man was?"

"Of course—it'll make it easier to kill him."

Makar smiled and told him.

Carl Wright travelled back to London via the Eurostar. His destination was Ashford International in Kent. Usually, he enjoyed the 180-mph trip but not today.

What he hated was someone having control over him, particularly against his will. He had got used to it during his military career and at times even welcomed it.

He enjoyed the structure and discipline, just turn up on time, dress appropriately, and do the job that you were assigned to do. However, that was a voluntary choice, unlike now. Now he was being threatened and manipulated. At first, he almost respected Pierre Gaultier for how he entrapped him. Carl carried out the mission calculating that doing it was less aggravation than not. And that included taking into account Bruce McQuillan's reputation. Now, he could see that Pierre viewed him as a commodity to wield until his usefulness had drained. He had to get that monkey off his back. If it were not for the threat of the Russian Bratva, the American would have just targeted Pierre himself and have done with it. He had to figure a way out of this now, or he was dead. Until then, he would have to just go along with the programme.

Jaime's heart began to race as he checked the sub-compartment on his computer. He kept encrypted voicemails in there. He was in an apartment he owned near Chelmsford, a quiet place where no one bothered him. He had a few places dotted in and around Greater London— *'never set patterns'* was what Bruce told him. Only one person had this email address, and that had been Bruce McQuillan, as far as he was aware. The two scenarios were the Scot had either escaped or the Russians had extracted the information from him. Neither seemed likely.

Bruce would have surely told him if he had told anyone else. Jaime thought it would have taken longer for the Russians to prise it from him. He opened the email with biting nerves and played the recording. The voice was loud and clear.

"Hello, I am sure you are aware of what's happened to a mutual friend of ours. I was trying to make contact to probe your interest in helping me extract him. I will be on the corner of Firth Street near the bank, next to the payphone at eighteen hundred if you wish to help me. I understand you have no reason to trust me."

Jaime listened to the message three times before exhaling, sitting back and rubbing his temples. Although he did not recognise the voice, he could tell that it belonged to someone from the north of England. It was not the traitor's voice though. His mistrust had kept him alive and meeting a stranger like this was something he would never have done in ordinary circumstances.

Jaime was not a field agent. He was into computers and affording a pleasant lifestyle. The challenging work, learning technical nuances, keeping up with the latest trends, picking out the relevant information from the cyber world, was his Ying. The lifestyle, the excellent restaurants, holidays in hot countries, nice cars, good clothes, was his Yang. There would not be computers or first-class waiter service in a Russian mafia interrogation room. The practical side of his mind began to work and was leaning towards him meeting with this unknown voice.

What would Bruce do? If he could not get Bruce back, he would have to deal with all sorts: wealthy Arabs, Russian oligarchs, billionaire drugs cartels, unscrupulous corporate enterprises to name a few. What was now an extreme vigilance in his counter surveillance would manifest into an intense paranoia. There was another reason he knew he wanted to help Bruce—he liked and respected him. And he saved him from prison. The more he found out about him, the more he was aware Bruce McQuillan's primary purpose was to protect the innocent or indifferent from the bad or evil. Sometimes the line got

231

blurred, or mistakes happened, but the man's intentions were pure. One of the ways Jaime knew that was because millions of pounds had passed from Bruce's hands into operational accounts. In the years that followed, the accounts were solely debited to fund operations against the enemies of the UK citizens. They had been emptied on more than one occasion to do so. These were off-the-books accounts that only Bruce had access to and known only to them both. Jaime, for a selfish reason, knew that he could not turn his back on him. He would never make peace with himself, and that is why he was going to make the meet.

Connor had insisted to Louis on going alone.

"You're not going there on your own bruv," Louis had said.

"Nah, I have to. I don't want to spook him…no pun intended."

"Listen, jokes aside…you can't go alone. There might be a team waiting, Gee."

"If there's a team then they will be enough to take both of us out anyway. It needs to be just me. Besides, we both go, that's all our eggs smashed in one basket."

Now, he stood next to a telephone box as the sky turned to dark blue and the raindrops clattered around him. He felt a nervous energy growing in him as the seconds ticked towards 18:00. The feeling was not dissimilar to a teenage boy waiting for a girl to show for their first date.

Now 18.06, he told himself he would hold on for no more than ten past.

Throughout the drive over, he reflected as to why he was even here. Surely the threat of prosecution for

Hardcastle's murder would vanish with Bruce. He could just fall off the reservation. Maybe he would just be left alone. Deep down he knew why he was here. He had seen more destruction to society by wicked men than any other person he knew. He had seen men and women with potential in one area or another get fucked long-term by drugs or alcohol abuse. They passed it on to their children who passed it to theirs. He had seen the feral animals disguised as humans who would rob, rape and beat the young, old, infirm and weak.

He had also seen greed on a monumental scale—greed of the wealthy and powerful, greedy for more, no matter who they hurt, what damage they caused or who they had to remove.

He knew he was risking his life for two equally compelling reasons. One was Bruce McQuillan himself, whereas that misguided knobber Nick had spoken about the Scot as a blind idealist, Connor was convinced he was a highly intelligent man with a steadfast moral resolve—not unlike his own father.

The other reason was Connor had seen first-hand how power corrupted anyone who did not have the strongest of moral codes. He had been around enough criminals and was enough of a criminal himself, to know. He was worldly-wise enough to know if the Russian mafia controlled London, they would never stop.

Connor's heart jumped a little as the phone vibrated. This was it now, no turning back. He did not need religion to know what he was doing was right. He did not need anyone's opinion to help his decision to fight evil until his last breath. Criminal greed was evil—it did not stop for anything or anyone.

He answered the call.

"He's making a mistake you know," said Nick.

"Ya know, I didn't see this conversation 'appenin'," replied Louis. They were sat facing one another with Louis in the seat Connor had used.

"This agreement has already gone through. If I am reading this right, your mate thinks he's going to rescue Bruce from the Russian Bratva's deadliest brigade?"

Louis laughed. "Connor is crazy, that's why I love him. Well, that's one of the reasons."

"You'll love him 'til the point he gets you killed and probably after being tortured."

"You think I'm helping this white boy because I'm sure he's going to succeed? Let me tell you something. I have been through a lot with him. Eight months of basic training. We did a six-month tour of Afghanistan while we were still sprogs. He's the least *jack* man I know. He would cut off his arm if you needed one. You wouldn't understand." Louis leaned back, pulled out a can of cola, cracked it open and took a swig when the hiss died.

"I'll tell ya a 'ickle story. When we came back from Afghan, we had six weeks' leave, and Connor and I decided to rob these drug dealers from Wolverhampton. It was proper 'Behind Enemy Lines', 'White Men Can't Jump' shit with burners an' balaclavas, as ya say. It was just 'im and me too. £120k between us. Mine went on a brand-new BMW, clothes, jewellery and a holiday to New York. All sorts, man. You know where his cut went?"

Nick shrugged.

"£25k got split between his local boxing club, the Salvation Army, a youth project, and an elderly person volunteer group, all anonymously. The only reason I know is that we shared the same money launderer for that job. He knew me better than Connor," there was a pause as

Louis edged closer to Nick and lowered his voice, "so if you ever question my loyalty to my Gee again, I'll take one of ya fuckin' eyes out, ya get meh?"

Nick blinked repeatedly, defeated.

"Listen to me very carefully. You will let go any sense of self-preservation and answer my questions fast and truthfully because believe me, this goes against every professional instinct I have," said the voice on the other end of the phone.

Connor took a breath as he realised he was going to have to give up the very thing his recent training had taught him to preserve: his anonymity.

"OK."

"What is your full name and the last four digits of your bank account number?"

"What the fuck is this…a Nigerian cold calling scam?"

"Just answer it."

"Connor Andrew Reed, 8998."

"What's the name of our mutual friend?"

"Bruce McQuillan."

"And why do you want to help him out of his current predicament?"

"Let's just say I am a Clint Eastwood fan. I still believe in bad guys, good guys and the rest in-between."

A short pause.

"Head north and take the third turning onto Albion Road."

Connor almost shouted, "Wait."

"What?" said the voice sounding startled.

"It's cloudy. Which way is north?"

Another pause.

"To your left."

Stanton clicked his phone off.

He began to pace his office, something he had never done before. Now he could not reach either Bruce McQuillan or Nick Flint. He calmed himself—*you have not got to this point by panicking.*

He grimaced and made another call.

Connor walked, scanning the area as he did so. The rain pattered around him, and the car tyres cut through the sheen of wet. London even smelled differently from his native Leeds. Connor fought the urge to make the mental connection between danger and this city. Perhaps he shouldn't fight it.

He rounded the corner into Albion Road, and after thirty metres a white van with 'Shore and Son' emblazoned on it pulled up beside him. The passenger door opened to reveal an almost pretty Latin man.

"Get in."

Connor got in only to feel a prod in his side. He knew without looking down it was a gun as a hand clamped onto his shoulder.

"Open up your jacket slowly," said the man, with a South American accent.

He opened it, and the man patted him down.

"Now lean forward," commanded the Latino and patted Connor's lower back.

"Show me your ankles."

Connor did so, and the man put away the gun. He pulled the van out into the road. He noticed a slight jitteriness to the Latino's movements, and in his voice a barely noticeable tremor. He wore a light blue denim shirt with dark denim jeans along with suede loafers. The ensemble worked against the man's caramel skin.

"My name is Jaime. I provided Bruce with his intelligence and surveillance support."

"I was told you might be able to help me."

"You mean, you were told we have a common interest and may be able to help one another."

"Apologies for the wording, but yes."

"Tell me, who told you this?"

"An associate of Bruce's by the name Nick Flint.

Jaime jerked the steering wheel a little.

Connor asked "What?"

"And you trust him?"

"Not especially, which is why he's being watched over in a warehouse in the middle of nowhere, nursing a broken nose, cracked ribs and a hammered toe."

A set of red traffic lights held them, and Connor watched two locals smoking outside a pub despite the rain.

Jaime said, "Good, how did that happen, step by step?"

"Bruce put me on to Nick to carry out surveillance on him. He said it was the final exercise before I went operational. I stuck on Nick for a couple of days, followed him to a cafe in Croydon where he met with Bruce. They walked off together, and Bruce disappeared for about ten minutes around a corner. I couldn't see from where I was without being compromised. Nick appeared to be standing guard."

This was the first time Connor had recalled it all. The lights turned green.

He continued, "I see Bruce walking up to Nick, but then his shoulder looked as if it was punched by an invisible fist, he was stumbling about, seemingly

237

disorientated. As Nick approached him, Bruce head-butted Nick, but Bruce fell to the floor. A car pulled in. I was already running towards them at this stage, but I was a distance away. I saw Nick help an unknown man who got out of the car and bundle Bruce into the boot...wait...no the backseat. The car drove off, leaving Nick on the street."

"Then what?"

"I apprehended him."

"Apprehended?' said Jaime almost to himself. "Before we get into details, how did you not know Bruce was—how to say—disorientated, head butted him, and two strangers had not just offered to take him to the 'ospital?"

"Then why didn't Nick go with them?"

"Yes," Jaime nodded, "tell me step by step how you apprehended him."

Connor took a breath. He controlled the desire to smack the driver's head off the window. He hated the way he was interrogating him and the tone of his voice. However, he understood why he was doing it—he was scared.

"I reached him as the car disappeared around the corner, he was facing the same direction. I took his feet from under him. I dropped my knee into his sternum and punched his face until he was unconscious. I carried him to an early-nineties Toyota parked thirty metres away, using a bumper-key to open the boot. He went inside while I used the same bumper-key to start the vehicle. Off we went."

"Can I see this bumper-key?" Connor took it out and showed him.

"A car that old and easily accessible just happened to be parked there?"

"Yes, it was Lady Luck. Besides, it was Croydon, not Surrey."

"You took him where?"

"To a friend's."

"What—who—is your friend?"

"I am not telling you. Risking myself with you is one thing, risking my friend is another."

"You do not hold any power in this Mr Reed. I am the one with knowledge and means to locate Mr McQuillan, not you. I suggest you remember that."

"But you'll need me to do the extracting because you can't trust anyone else, else you wouldn't have met me."

"I do not trust you."

"Then why are we having this conversation?" asked Connor.

"Because you is—are— the lesser of the evils."

"Exactly, so let's not make threats, eh? My friend is going to remain anonymous until further notice."

Jaime frowned, and they were quiet for a half mile.

Connor broke the silence. "Do you know much about this Russian Mafia outfit that has taken him?"

"They are members of a particularly professional unit of the Russian Bratva. Although they have remained low on the list of Interpol's priorities, I can assure you that they are the most dangerous criminals in Europe. The leader, a Ravil Yelchin, is a very shrewd man."

"Do you know of any known safe houses?"

"I think know where Bruce McQuillan is being held."

Connor straightened his back. "OK, tell me and I will—"

"—will do what? Rescue him from a highly professional group of ex-Spetsnaz, and ex-KGB criminals?"

"What do you suggest?" said Connor. "And stop flying off the handle all the time like an old woman."

Jaime sighed.

"Bruce is guarded by highly professional, well-armed and very ruthless men. Even if you had the manpower, the right plan, the professionalism to by some miracle overcome them, they would just kill him before they let him be taken back alive. And that is a 'no-no'. He is the only one who might just be able to reverse this disaster."

They hit a long dual carriageway, and the yellow of the street lights beaconed their faces as they sped past.

"What do you propose?"

"The Russian Bratva is the same as any organisation. It fits to its, how do you say, area of operations. It is a large group, but has to cover large areas. It is not infinite in its manpower, finances and resources. No organisation is, despite what some would have you believe. Now, this particular brigade's resources have been directed towards the guarding of Bruce. They do not know what friends he may or may not have so they are taking no chances. And while their resources are put to guarding him—"

"—they are not being used to guard Ravil Yelchin."

Jaime looked at him, "You learn good Mr Reed. Now, Ravil Yelchin has never been heavily guarded, preferring not to draw attention to himself. However, his Security Officer Makar Gorokhov is overseeing the interrogation of Bruce. The feeling is Ravil is quite safe now the agreement between the security services and the Bratva is set. However, he will still be watched over by very ruthless and professional men. He is the bargaining chip for Bruce."

"Surely he avoids setting patterns with his movements?"

"Sure he does, and I have an idea about that, but there's something else that needs your attention."

"Enlighten me."

"Well, there's been a strange twist of fate. Bruce's kidnap was first muted by a Pierre Gaultier, a French Arms dealer who has gathered a considerable reputation in recent years."

"Why?"

"We will get to that," said Jaime. "Either the Russian Bratva contacted him regarding sharing the workload, or maybe it was the other way around. Pierre Gaultier blackmailed an American hitman to shoot a tranquilizer at Bruce. It seems that your kidnap of Nick Flint has thrown a spanner in the workings. Against his will, Mr Gaultier has contracted him to find Nick Flint."

"And so?"

"And so, I think he can be turned to our side for the correct offer."

"And what would that be?"

"That Pierre Gaultier is killed and the Russians' hold on him is undermined. For good."

21

Carl Wright dodged his way through the throng of commuters. He had alighted from the train at the London Paddington Station three minutes earlier. Now he made his way to the Praed Street entrance. Walking up to a pay phone, his eyes flickered into the semi-reflective advertising boards to check faces behind him. He put in the money and dialled. He heard the answer of a digitally distorted voice.

"Mr Wright, a gentleman will introduce himself to you. He is wearing a green sweater with brown shoulder patches and jeans. You will greet him like a friend. He will make you an offer that comes from me."

Carl turned around. The described stranger stood before him. His intelligent eyes met Carl's.

He had sandy hair and strong, regular features on a face that Carl would guess women found attractive. The man spoke in an accent that Carl recognised to be of the north of England.

"Don't look so glum. I am not happy about having to meet face to face either," said the man.

Carl gave a smirk of acknowledgement. "What do you want, Mr...?"

"My name's Connor," said the man. "Let's walk and talk."

"Walk where?"

"You choose. I am just here to make a proposal to you."

Carl set off out of the Praed Street entrance.

"What is it?"

"Firstly, if it's agreeable to you, I will lay out your predicament. You can stop me at any time to interject. When I am sure of my facts, I can make this proposal."

There were a few moments of silence—confirming or refuting any information went against his professional grain.

"Go ahead."

"Take this," Connor ordered, handing Carl a recorder. "It will prove a point later."

"There's an alley over there, let's go walk to it," Carl said, and when they reached it he said, "Put your hands against the wall so I can frisk you."

Connor did so, and Carl thoroughly searched him. He looked at Connor sharply when the Englishman emitted a sex noise as Carl used the back of his hand between the legs.

"That was a joke. I apologise."

"Good one. Now you can start talking," Carl said, as he led them off down the street.

"You were contracted by international arms dealer Pierre Gaultier who had uncovered your identity. Using the threat of exposing your anonymity coerced you into carrying out the tranquilization of Bruce McQuillan for kidnap. You carried this out on the understanding your part of the agreement was complete. However, Mr Gaultier informed you a Nick Flint was captured at the scene and now, again against your wishes, you are to find him. Naturally you had some grievances, but the combined threat of Mr Gaultier and the Russian Bratva has forced your hand. You are cursing the fact that you are in someone else's pocket, which is where you don't want to be, is it mucker?"

"Mucker?—Motherfucker?"

"No, it's slang for…never mind, it's not an insult. So, am I right?"

Carl said nothing for a few moments and then, quietly, "He may keep his side of the bargain this time."

"Press play on the recorder," said Connor, and Carl did so. There was a faint whirr and, despite the quiet background noise, Pierre Gaultier's accented English as plain as day, emitted:

'This American belongs to me now, and if he is well paid, he will do as he is told. Come the day his usefulness expires, then so will he.'

'And when will that day be?' (A voice with thick Middle-Eastern accent).

'I have already put it into motion so do not be troubled.'

The recorder clicked off.

Carl looked at Connor. He held his nerve.

"So?"

"So I need your help, and if you give me a hand, I'll assist you."

"Go on."

"What if I said that with your help we could remove our friend Mr Gaultier from the equation, and make that Russian connection disappear?"

"I'd think you were overconfident in your abilities."

"Maybe so, but what other choice do you have left?"

Bruce sat in the cell-like room, more taut and tired than he could remember. He had not slept for three days, being forced awake by the head-splitting white noise resounding throughout the room. He had been stripped naked and beaten with a rubber hose at periodic intervals—the hose being preferred as it did not break bones or pierce the skin, so the risk of infection was minimalised. The beatings left welts though, making staying in any position for long difficult.

Makar had told him electric shock treatment was to follow. That was something he fought hard not to dwell on. Being told this initially filled him with both relief and dread. Relief, as he knew they would eventually have to let him sleep. Not to do so would just reduce him to a jabbering wreck, and that was not good for them. Also, they probably would not start taking limbs because if he held up there was nowhere else to go. The victim can enter a kind of mind-set where he or she cannot bear to think that they have lost fingers, feet, arms or ears for nothing. Thus they become tough to break. Bruce had had the experience of witnessing this early in his career, and Makar would know that.

He began calculating whether they would use the drug scopolamine, commonly known as 'Truth Serum' which he had seen to be remarkably effective. However, he had also seen it kill a victim which was why these Russians, if they had it, were probably reluctant to use it yet.

Electric shock treatment was a battle winner in these situations. It was relatively easy to control, potentially everlasting, and agonising.

Although the Russian had not actually asked yet, he knew what they wanted. They wanted the files that he kept on high-ranking officials within the Government and access to his operational funds accounts. As soon as he gave them up, he was dead.

The white noise cut off suddenly, and he mentally braced himself. After a few minutes, he let sleep take him.

Connor, Carl and Jaime sat in the back of a caravan that the computer tech had procured. It felt bizarre to Connor as he scanned the ornaments dotted around the edges: little birds on branches, flowers, and a snow dome to name a few. These were the kinds of ornaments of which his nan had been fond of. Nostalgia swept over him remembering the almost permanent smell of her baking in his grandparents' home.

Instead, these ornaments decorated a caravan where he sat with a Latino Machiavellian cyber-hacker and an American hitman, planning how to extract the chief of a British black ops team from the clutches of the Russian Mafia—*I couldn't have made this up*. His brain was too focused on the task at hand to process the surrealism of it all. It reminded him of the Chinese saying, *'May you live in interesting times'*.

"So," said Carl. "Ideas?"

He was aiming the question at Jaime.

"Do you still have the rifle you used to tranquilize Mr McQuillan?" Jaime asked, looking intently at the American.

"It's reachable," he answered.

"Well, I suggest you will reach for it, as Mr Yelchin may have to suffer a heart trouble soon."

Connor smiled, he had had the thought himself.

"OK, tell me more," demanded Carl.

"Mr Yelchin is security conscious but seems to believe he is invulnerable while playing golf in a club—a golf club. His security only accompanies him to the gates and no more. What makes him do that I am not certain. Maybe it is his way of, how do you say, not assoc— disassociating himself with that part of his life? That is the time to take him."

"How?"

"Mr Yelchin will be struck with a dart inducing a mild seizure. The club's first resident medic attending to him will call an *ambulancia,* a call routed to me. The ambulance that will arrive will contain Mr Reed here."

"I am more than happy with the scenario, right up until they spot the dart in his neck."

Jaime laughed. "He is of little faith. Not if you fire these." He fished something out of the case beside him and opened his palm to reveal what appeared to be four wasps.

"What the fuck?" Connor whispered, a slight furrow appearing on his forehead.

"CIA budgets were so large in the wake of 9/11 they even developed these. The retractable wasp dart. It plunges the fluid in on impact then falls away. Apparently, even the recipient feels that he has just been stung by a wasp."

"And you can verify this?"

"Not personally, no, but they been tested in the field."

"Before we get to that, where's this mysterious ambulance going to emerge from?" Connor asked.

"You two are going to steal one." Connor and Carl looked at one another.

"Surely it would be easier, not to mention more morally justifiable, to steal a van, siren, and have Doctor or Ambulance emblazoned upon it?" Connor questioned.

"See? Thinking outside the box as you Brits would say. I like it," replied Jaime, his accent coming through more, "but authenticity is the key. There's no room for taking unnecessary chances."

"I am not stealing an ambulance for some old lady to die because we have it, end of story," said Connor.

247

Jaime looked at Connor for a moment and replied "Fine. I will just have to buy one."

"Buy an ambulance?" Connor asked.

Jaime said nothing.

"My escape?" Carl asked.

"Mr Reed will pick you up. You'll be far enough away that there shouldn't be any witnesses watching you get into the ambulance."

"What about the Russian's security?" asked Connor. "When they see an ambulance scream up to the club, won't their natural instinct be to check on the boss?"

"I can't anticipate their actions, Mr Reed. You will have to deal with that situation as you see appropriate. You are the…how do you say…field agent. The priority is to have Mr Yelchin in our possession."

"OK, I want to know for sure when this Ravil character gets shot, he thinks it's a wasp and doesn't start screaming 'I've been shot'," said Carl.

Connor pitched in. "I have an idea about that. We'll talk after this." He switched to Jaime. "When is this going to take place?"

"On Sunday."

"That's four days away. We can't wait that long."

"Well you'll have to. You will not be able to get near him until then, trust me, Mr Reed. And besides, I read Royal Marines believe in concurrent activity?"

"Very good. What's the concurrent activity?"

"A trip to Brussels."

The ringing awakened Nick and his eyes focused in on Louis.

"Yep… Yeah… Eh… OK," he heard Louis say into the mobile phone. With that, he stood and walked to Nick.

"Seems like the main man wants you to have some fresh air," and Nick felt the cold metal of the revolver against the back of his neck. "I shouldn't have to tell you, blood, if you go for it, your Adam's apple will bounce in front of you."

"Thank you for making me aware mate," replied Nick, as he felt the plasticuffs loosen off and the barrel leave his neck.

"Stand and move to the door."

Nick did so but winced as the blood rushed into his crushed toe.

"Now, kneel. Open the door and shuffle out on your knees."

"Why?" asked Nick, bemused.

"Because it'll be harder for you to slam the door in my face and scram. Be a good boy and do as yer told because the next question you ask, Mr Revolver will answer it in'it."

Nick knelt, opened the door and began to shuffle out while his toe throbbed. He got two yards then let out a painful cry, slapping his hand to his neck.

"Fuck, I've been stung by som'mat."

Makar stood with Damian in a room of the abandoned farmhouse. They were watching Bruce in another room through a monitor. They spoke in English, as the Pole was learning to get rid of his accent.

"He is the toughest westerner I have seen but I still think we can push this motherfucker harder," Damian growled.

Makar knew Damian deep down resented him. No matter how well Makar saw to his financial needs or how much he treated Damian more as an associate and less of an underling, the Pole would resent him. He would resent him because Makar was a Russian.

Acrimony between Russia and Poland dated back to the sixteenth century when Poland sided with Lithuania in conflict with Russia. Relations between the two countries had been a roller coaster ever since the fall of communism and Poland's entrance into NATO. Indeed, as a KGB agent, Makar had spent a significant amount of time in the country. Enough to know most Poles held a dim view of the Motherland. Still, Makar knew better than to let national relations prejudice his view of another, yet was aware Damian did not share his open mind. He was also aware that Damian not yet being made a Vor created resentment. Making him the first pole to become the first *Vor v Zakone* could only have one of two effects; either make him more belligerent or calm him. Makar was not sure which. Damian had not yet done anything substantial to test his patience. It had been only subtle undermining comments or questions—*but that is how it starts*. He had already defeated Damian physically and tried to make the Pole feel a valued member despite his short service within the Bratva.

Abraham Lincoln had made political allies of defeated opponents. How he turned his once enemies into a cohesive team influenced Makar to take the same approach with vanquished foes. This method had proven spectacularly effective in the past but as the British liked to say—*There is always one*.

Makar replied, "Pushing him too hard too early would have a counterproductive effect. He'll resist harder or become incoherent. The trick isn't to break them but to more make them run out of steam. It's a process that cannot be rushed." he turned to look at Damian. "It will be worth it in the end.

"Can I ask how?"

"He has information that can tilt the balance of an uncertain allegiance in our favour."

"Is this before or after we tear the heads off these soft Britishers?"

"Whenever we need it. We have already taken out three significant leaders in our game. In a few days, our offensive begins but the 'soft Britishers', as you call them, can wait until we deal with some of the more ruthless gangs residing here. Then our Pakhan's golf trips will have to be curtailed."

"He will not like that."

"I would have loved to fuck the local women when I visit Africa, but I don't—some risks outweigh the reward."

Damian just smiled at the comment. Makar knew that the Pole would probably take the risk anyway.

Three sets of feet surrounded Nick Flint.

"Mr L, this is … Mr X. Mr X this is Mr L," said Connor.

"Mr X? Is that the best you can do?" asked Carl.

"I am not having a code name of Mr L!" said Louis.

"What would you two suggest?"

"Just called me Ken," said Carl.

"Alright Ken, just call me Louis. I may tell you my real name once I get to know yer." Connor inwardly smiled at his friend's risky but oddly clever decision. "And who are you?" Louis continued.

"I am a friend."

Connor gave a nod to Nick and said, "What did this one say just then?"

Louis shrugged. "He said he'd been stung,"

"Must have been some fucking wasp, though," said Nick.

Connor and Carl looked at one another.

"Yep, it was," said Connor, picking up the dart.

"Happy?" he asked the American.

"Suppose so."

"What the fuck is that?" asked Nick, as he concentrated on the wasp rotating between Connor's fingers.

"It's a wasp dart from the CIA."

The Londoner began to laugh. "And you decided to test it on your man here?"

Connor shrugged, "Listen, brother, can you hold him for a couple of days, I need to make a trip?"

"What trip?"

"We need to take care of something."

"Alright, Royal."

Ravil sat in a clinical, white high-rise office around a long oak table surrounded by a consortium of investors. This meeting was to discuss making a bid for a major electrical goods chain throughout the UK. Ravil had learnt to cope with the tedium of these deals long ago as they were a necessity. They made money, they provided alternative streams of income, and they gave him a corporate persona which helped protect him. The financial gurus called this 'diversifying your asset allocation'.

Ravil also knew he was a criminal and enjoyed it. He himself had come from an affluent beginning but his mentor Sergei had risen from utter poverty to become the original Pakhan of it all. Ravil had little empathy for some of the drug addicts whose lives were destroyed by the drugs he brought in. No one in this western society was without choices. If they wanted to damage their health, or kill themselves with drugs, then he was happy to make a profit. He scoffed at the notion that he should feel guilt towards a British population. The majority were near zombies—hypnotised by football, X Factor, social media and tabloid newspapers. With a significant percentage feeding off the state, the rest spent their time complaining about them, seemingly oblivious to the corporate white collars—such as the ones he was currently sat with—that raped the economy regularly. Part of him knew on some level that not all the population was of that mentality, but he vanquished the thought. Now was not the time for procrastinations. He was going to take this once great island and use it. It would start tomorrow with the murder of certain Turkish kingpins as well as the kidnap and torture of some of their families. The Turks would be removed first as they were the most feared, powerful and ruthless of all the gangs currently operating in the UK. He liked to checkmate the King in as few moves as possible.

Ravil could not create a dynasty without committing necessary evils, and he had little empathy for other criminal gangs. Neither did he have sympathy for the career politicians that were going to form a 'partnership' with him. Once he had Britain in his grasp, he would bleed it and filter the fruits down to The Brotherhood. The Bratva was the one thing he believed in—the true loyalty from its members.

Connor stood in a Waterstones bookstore perusing the sports section. He had liked doing this since he was in his early teens. He would catch the bus into Leeds town centre or The White Rose Centre, get a coffee and just browse books. That was when he had not been stealing from there. Connor was enjoying himself, but he was getting the urge for sex. He knew why: his sex drive always got stronger when he was about to embark on something dangerous. He would have loved to have seen Grace but she was all the way up in Leeds.

Luckily, he had a *pre-recorded* not far away in Basildon. He had met Lauren while attending the annual Army v Navy rugby match in Twickenham. Or the 'Fiji v Navy' game as the lads in the Marines and Navy liked to say. Lauren was a cute, very curvaceous brunette and an army engineer. After some Northerner v Southerner banter, he ended up back at her hotel. Connor had been inebriated but could hazily recall that she had enormous tits. They had exchanged texts back and forth for a while. It had dwindled to a couple of messages a month recently—but he never burnt his bridges.

He found her number and heard it ringing, hoping that she had not got shacked up or was away with work.

She answered, "What the fuck do you want Reed? More nudes?!"

"Erm… I was wondering if I could get your Mum's number because the toilet door it was written on has been replaced."

"Oh, I'm not sure about that, she told me that she sees you when she's desperate but she always ends up hating herself afterwards."

"Hates herself that she's not woman enough to pin me down to a monogamous relationship? You, however, are grateful for what you can get, which brings me to the reason why I am calling. I am about twenty minutes away from your neck of the woods, and was wondering about a brew as you Army folk call it?"

Lauren laughed. "I don't know if twenty minutes will be enough time to prepare for the God-like Connor Reed?"

"Just how long does it take you to make a cup of tea?"

"Cup of tea? Yeah, right!" she exclaimed. "I'll text you the address, Royal."

"Roger."

22

Hassan Saki lay back in the barber's chair. He enjoyed the skilled strokes of the razor as it glided against his skin removing the rough black beard behind it. Hassan was a Kurd who arrived in London as a seventeen-year-old in the mid-nineties. London Turkish gangs were predominantly made up of Turkish Cypriots and Turkish mainlanders that had arrived in London ten to twenty years earlier than the Kurds. Hassan had seen London as a haven; a cultural melting pot full of promise and riches. He knew from the start he was going to carve out his corner of it.

He started off as a drugs mule, transporting cannabis for a drug dealer out of North London. He had learnt the ropes. After a year, he stabbed the Cypriot supplier in a frenzied attack and took over his customer base. He could have made the kill a lot cleaner but the more wounds, the more powerful the message he had surmised.

After warding off a couple of unhappy associates of the supplier, Hassan again kept his head down, growing his business and associates. Then he moved into cocaine and heroin, on a much larger scale.

Although now one of the top three UK drug importers and a multi-millionaire, Hassan always kept close to the street. People thought it risky for him to expose himself, but he knew better. On these streets, to be out of sight was to be out of mind.

Hassan had formed links with the Bulgarian Mafia and the Kurdistan Worker's Party, or its Kurdish acronym the 'PKK', along with corrupt local politicians and law enforcement officers which kept him busy. He had had to become increasingly savvy, articulate and professional to deal with such a myriad of different groups and personalities. Yet he retained the characteristic that got him to this point: a terrifying ruthlessness.

He still made visits to grocers, local businesses and in this case his local barber shop. He had been coming here for years, and it was one of the few places he felt safe.

Hassan was a heavily built man with a shaped beard covering his square jaw and his thick, hairy, muscled forearms protruded from the barbering gown. His midriff was a little bigger than he would have liked, a concession for a love of good food.

He normally had his shave done by the owner but the proprietor insisted on breaking in a new guy and the crime boss had allowed it. He had not spoken to the trainee but was impressed with the deftness of the man's hands. With a few strokes to go the man broke the silence, speaking in Kurdish.

"You know, I hear that a man's beard still grows weeks after death."

Hassan smiled and replied, "It appears to, but it is that the skin becomes sunken, and the growth already underneath becomes more visible."

The Kurd felt a sharp pain slice across his throat followed by a warm wetness. His hand went to his throat, and he stared at it in bemused horror as he saw it covered in blood. His vision began to blur as he vaguely made out the voice.

"I will be at your funeral Mr Saki, on behalf of the Albanian Mafia, to see just how thick your beard grows back."

He saw the barber stood over him firing a pistol into the ceiling.

He died before he slid to the floor.

Lauren opened the door in her Wasps Rugby top and jeans. Her brunette hair bounced over her shoulders. She reached up, wrapped her arm around Connor's neck and gave him a peck on his cheek.

"Get inside before the neighbours see ya, I wouldn't be able to live it down," smiled Lauren, ushering him into the warm living room. He took a seat on one of the chocolate sofas. The walls were a mix of cream and beige with a 32" flat screen mounted on the wall.

"What? A white man being in your house for once?"

Lauren laughed. "It's London baby, and we're no longer stuck in the fifties with our views OK, *Kes*?"

"I think that's more out of necessity from what I've seen," teased Connor.

Lauren sighed. "As much as I like discussing politics with the apparent new leader of the English Defence League, what are you doing here?"

She was funnier than he remembered.

"Well put the kettle on, and I'll tell you, won't I."

Lauren smirked and went into the open plan kitchen.

"So, what have you been doing with yourself? How's the Marines?" she asked, putting the cup of tea down in front of him.

"It's fine thanks. How's the Army?"

"Good at the moment. We're getting deployed on exercise to America soon."

"Thanks for confirming that it is, in fact, just an exercise," he replied in playful sarcasm. "There was me thinking we were about to invade."

"You're such a dick," she exclaimed in her London accent. "Anyway, you got a Missus yet?"

He briefly thought of Grace.

"I have too much respect for women to make one of them my girlfriend. Besides, I wouldn't be here if I did."

Lauren laughed. "Pretty sure of yourself Mr Reed. What on earth do you think is going to happen here?"

"Well, I haven't come around for your southern take on a cup of tea, it's as gash as your banter," he said with a wink.

"If it's that bad, why don't you chuck it down the sink and join me on the sofa?" she said, as she got up and sauntered over to the plush couch in the corner of the room.

Connor did not throw the tea away, just set it down to cool and followed her—*it will be ready to drink by the time I have smashed her.*

He sat, slipping his hand under her arm, for which she subtly made space, and put it on the back of her neck. He could smell her perfume. They kissed slowly. He felt her tongue slide into his mouth, and her nails ran along the back of his T-shirt. He felt her tits press into his chest, and he slipped his hand under the back of her top, unclasping her bra.

"One hand, I'm impressed," she murmured, before straddling him.

"This isn't my first rodeo," he replied.

He took a grip on her hips as she grasped the bottom of her shirt, arched her back and slowly pulled her top up, exposing her tits barely held back by her black bra. She slid her bra off, and her magnificent breasts bounced free.

Connor smiled as she ground herself on his hard cock, slipping her hand around his head and bringing his mouth to her nipples. He felt a flash of guilt as Grace entered his mind, but he quickly shunned it. He could be dead in a matter of hours, and he was not dying wishing

259

he had had one more fuck. And he was going to fuck Lauren—hard.

"It's begun," said the voice over the phone. "Hassan Saki had his throat cut in his regular barbershop this morning."

"Yeah, I heard. The Turks seem to be blaming it on the Albanians though," answered the government official.

"That's another thing. Albanian mob boss Florim Againi was shot dead today in what they believe to be a revenge attack."

"These Russians have the cunning of a hundred foxes. You ought to be careful."

"I'll be retiring soon enough."

"You are a loose end, and you're vulnerable if you retire. They won't need you."

"£75 million can protect you from almost anything if you know how."

Carl and Connor sat together on the Eurostar heading to Brussels. The American felt more uncomfortable than he could ever remember in his time as a freelance assassin. He was about to light the fuse on a piece of dynamite that was going to explode. How much he was to catch was dependent on a lot of factors beyond his control.

He hated that.

He looked around the carriage playing the game of guess the Brits from the Frogs before he had heard them speak. He was normally good at this game. Brits had a different demeanour and their dress sense was not as European as a rule. He was not as good guessing Jerries from Frogs on the trains between Berlin and Paris. Still not bad, though.

Two men sat at his eleven o'clock. One had a shaved head, with olive skin and a blue Italia tracksuit top. The other had an oriental look about him. His dark hair brushed into a Mohawk with the tips highlighted. Carl knew they were French, not just in the way they dressed but in the physical contact they had with one another. They were open in their sexualities in a way that gay men in England would find awkward, even in cosmopolitan London.

Carl's thoughts drifted to the task in hand. Here he was now helped and directed by people he did not know and therefore could not fully trust. Then again, he had not trusted anyone since leaving the military. He looked at Connor perusing a magazine. The good-looking Englishman with a confident demeanour. He had relatively short, blond-to-brown hair and was just over average height. Nothing too physically out of the ordinary. There was just something about him; a certainty that whatever life happened to throw at him he would deal with it. It was to Carl's annoyance that Connor seemed remarkably calm—alert but still at peace.

As much as Carl hated the lack of control, he was looking forward to this. The more he found out about the target, the less he liked. He knew to feel this way about the arms dealer was ironic; he himself was a man who ended lives for money. He had already decided to leave this life if he succeeded, but that was a big if.

He leaned forward.

"You know, it's either he dies, or we do."

Connor looked up from the magazine at him.

"What made you think I thought there was another way?"

Two carriages down, Damian Adamik was attempting not to draw attention to himself. Remaining inconspicuous took an effort as his height and build frequently resulted in a second look. He deliberately slouched and avoided people's gaze as not to intimidate them. A face that caused a strong emotion in someone was more readily remembered.

He was to visit the French arms dealer to emphasize the importance of finding out what had happened to the British mole. He was ordered to ensure that progress was to be made. Damian would have much rather been in the thick of it in London. At this stage of his life, he should be running his own team, not taking orders. He had been a member of Poland's most elite military force. He should not be taking orders from a Russian either. Their inbuilt superiority baffled and irked him. That nation had become a superpower due to the country's vastness, and little more.

Makar paid him well, but Damian was worth the money. There would be a time though when he would rise.

As he picked a discarded magazine and began to scan it, he shook his head. Ravil, who he had met once, had been right. The United Kingdom was a nation brainwashed into being absorbed in fake breasts, stupid diets, fake romances, and stupidity.

It was a country ripe for the taking and deserved it. There were some people of character in it, thought Damian. The one Makar had in the farmhouse cellar being one. The man had remained resolute despite the hopelessness of his situation. He was an exception.

The majority were hardly the calibre of people who had helped to win World War Two. He doubted they as a nation would be able to stand together like that again. He was sure his native Poland could.

Connor and Carl disembarked at the Brussels-South railway station after an hour and forty-five minutes of travelling.

The American—a frequent visitor of Brussels—engaged a nearby taxi driver in French and they were on their way to the centre of the city. Less than five minutes into the journey, Connor could piece together that the cab driver was spouting off about the Moroccan and Turkish populations in Brussels and how they were taking jobs.

Connor smiled.

He bet he could find a similar version of this story all around the world, even in an economy as robust as Brussels. He did not doubt the man believed what he was saying, yet he also understood the man, who was in his early thirties, would reach sixty and still be complaining about life.

Connor had read it referred to as 'The Snow White Syndrome', these kinds of people always expected someone else to save them. He thought of the quote put on his old boxing club's wall: *If you are good at making excuses, it's hard to be good at anything else'.*

Knowing the driver could not speak English very well, Connor roared, "If you spent more time improving yourself and less time complaining like an old woman you'd get on more in life, you fat fuck."

He kept a smile painted on his face.

"Yes my friend, yes," the driver simply replied. Carl remained impassive in the front passenger seat.

As they hit the greater ring road of Brussels, the sun pierced through the old and new architecture. They stopped off in the centre of Brussels, and Connor just stared at the old, grand buildings lit gold against the dark blue sky. Carl paid the taxi driver and indicated for Connor to follow him.

As they walked along the sparsely populated street, Carl said, "Maybe it's not a good idea to insult the local people who may be potential witnesses in the future," in his American drawl.

"I am a Brit aboard, though. It would be suspicious if I didn't," said Connor.

After ten minutes of walking, they checked into The Crowne Hotel. Connor expected something less lavish, especially since he was not paying. Jaime had given them both a bank card and the hotel details.

Carl looked at him, said, "I am not complaining, I could be dead tomorrow."

Connor looked at him in pleasant surprise and said, "My sentiments exactly, still, can't get drunk can we?"

"Hell no."

"I'm still going out though."

"No you're not!"

"Yes, actually I am. What's your problem anyway?"

"Because you'll risk exposing yourself. We're picking up the vehicle at one in the morning."

"Who am I exposing myself to? They have never seen me. It's more suspicious us leaving past midnight like we're off to a gay swingers' party to get covered in goose fat. You should come out too."

"What the fuck, goose fat? And why does leaving at midnight make us gay?"

"Never mind. I am going out, you coming?"

"They have seen me before."

"I know, but Jaime is adamant that this character doesn't get to Brussels until well after noon tomorrow. If we don't trust him then we're sat here like pricks waiting to be ambushed. We can't physically rehearse anything now. Besides, there are over a million people in Brussels, the chances of anyone seeing you in the few hours we're out is minimal."

"That's the thing you see. Why risk it?"

"Because there's a difference between living and existing and I know which I am going to choose. I haven't been to Brussels before. I want to get a few drinks, get turned down by some birds, and come back." He turned to Carl. "Now are you coming or not?"

You feel like you are spinning in the darkness. Each shock is agonising. You are trying to disassociate your body from your mind. It is just a body—a vessel. Let them shock it, cut it, tear it to pieces for all you care, just do not let them have your mind. Any voice that even hints at capitulation, fuck it off again. They just need a foothold on a ledge of weakness, then you are on your way to spilling and your death. Just hold out, for as long as you can. You will laugh about this when it is all over. It is character building. That is if you do not die first. Stop. You are not going to die. You are going to live. And you are going to kill everyone who has had a hand in this. You scream as another shock hits you.

23

Ravil sat behind a massive oak desk in a study overlooking the Thames. This study was one of the three rooms where he sat to conduct business meetings. The outside walls were panes of reinforced glass, and a few old paintings of English and Russian ships hung around the inner edge. Sat across from him was a suited gentleman looking cantankerous but trying to hide it. Unfortunately for him, Ravil had developed a keen eye for human body language a long time ago—*How had this man gained such great responsibility?*

"I take it you have had a hand in these clashes between the Turks and Albanians in London?" asked the man in the suit.

Ravil smiled inside. This gentleman had come to him to talk after Ravil had rejected the request for neutral ground. He had already displayed his weaker hand.

"Presumption is a dangerous thing. Besides, our arrangement was that we would handle it from here on in."

"The arrangement was to keep one another involved so we could mutually support each other."

"You know to do that would be to unnecessarily expose our operation. There are powerful people not yet under our control who could try to usurp us."

"Exactly, that's why you need to tell me, so I can run interference."

"Your interests lie with yourself, your retirement and your money. Mine concern the expansion of my organisation. You let me deal with interference, and if I need your assistance, I will tell you."

"I see. You want me to retire in disgrace. You want that to be my escape."

"On the contrary. It would not benefit our cause you retiring anytime soon."

The suit looked aghast. "Excuse me? I'll be retiring shortly. That was always the plan."

Ravil's voice took on an edge. "You will retire when I say you can retire. No negotiation."

The man glared at him. "I think you're getting above yourself. You're known to us now, and I can shut your organisation down whenever I want to."

"An empty threat," Ravil replied. "Then you must explain how seventy-five million pounds made it into your accounts. And the secretly recorded discussions between you, myself and certain other men. Take the one you had last Wednesday, beginning at 08:12, detailing how you would spend your millions. Try explaining Maisie, your illegitimate fourteen-year-old daughter in Australia of which your wife does not know. She, of course, would have to hear about it. The media may ambush her at Derrydale High School, yes? You don't want that sir, almost as much as I do not want you to retire in this moment. Understand?"

The gentleman sat there, and murmured, "One is not punished because of his sins but by them."

Ravil said nothing.

He considered the emotionless eyes of the Russian, and mumbled, "I understand."

Connor and Carl sat in a bar they had found hidden away at the end of a narrow passageway in the city centre.

The room was laid out with three rows of tables all pushed together. The patterned wood walls came halfway up, while the various artworks which hung above the panels glimmered in the soft lighting. The former Royal Marine had convinced the former Ranger that *'one would not hurt. It will be spacers after that'*. They were sampling refreshing white beer in a stone jug and munching Ardennes ham sandwiches. The bar began to fill with the hum of soft, French chatter.

Connor had noticed Europeans tended to eat as they drank, thus slowing the inebriation process. It seemed a bit more refined than the behaviour of Brits, except for the 'Hoorah Henry' areas of the UK and sections of the larger cities. That was one of the reasons why he would not emigrate from Britain—he would miss it too much. There was all the action, all the excitement.

He knew people thought the British were reserved. He noticed how Americans, and to a lesser extent Europeans, could curse and get in one another's face. They could take a verbal slanging match much further than the British would. Connor knew two Brits would start punching one another as it reached those sorts of verbal crescendos.

Still, there were things he liked about Europe. People seemed more chilled out. The food was excellent, and the women had an exotic quality to them—like the two he was looking at now. The women were both fairly tall. One had free flowing brown hair with a hint of red in it. She was pretty, wearing a cashmere top with trousers that Connor thought looked a bit like horse-riding jodhpurs. He could hardly take his eyes off her companion. He thought she was gorgeous, with her black hair cut into a bob bringing out her alluring cat-like brown eyes. She wore a white casual suit jacket with black embroidery, black jeans, and zebra print high heels that took her only a couple of inches off Connor's height.

"How many times have you been to Brussels?" Connor asked Carl. He sensed the hitman was still pissed off at him.

"A few times, just passing through. Never stayed for any length of time."

"What do you tell people?"

"What do you mean?"

"What do you tell people you do for a living?"

"I say I am a salesman. I specialise in metals."

"Couldn't be more imaginative than that?"

"If it was good enough for Robert DeNiro, it's good enough for me. Why? What do you say you do?" Carl asked.

It was then Connor realised Carl did not know just how inexperienced he was at this type of work.

"Dolphin shaver, biscuit designer, penguin picker-upper is a good one. You need to be more creative."

"You're telling me you convince people you shave dolphins for a living?"

"Well, most people. I am alright at convincing people."

"Oh yeah?"

"Yeah, convinced you to come out didn't I."

"Any other tricks then?"

"I reckon I can convince those two chicks over there I am wildly charismatic."

"I would like to see that," sniggered Carl.

"Fine."

Connor drained off the last of his pint, stood and made his way to the two women. Carl stared after him.

The two women looked at him as he stood in front and between them. He gave the redhead a nod and smile and turned to the black-haired beauty.

"Excuse me, I don't mean to be rude, but my friend over there bet me a hundred euros that I couldn't get one of the two prettiest women in the bar to accept a drink off me. How about we just spend his money?" Connor said with a wry smile.

She broke into a huge smile and said, in a light French accent, "One of the two? Very smooth."

"Well, do you think you could convince your friend here? Because the other woman is the other side of the room and it's less convenient for me to get over there," he said.

She looked at him for a few moments taken aback, before hiding a smirk and extending her hand in a ladylike manner.

"My name is Helene."

"Nice to meet you, Helene," said Connor shaking her hand and turning to her friend. "Yours?"

She took his hand. "Zoë, and I will have a vodka and orange blossom if you—" she said before Connor interrupted her.

"—whoa, I just made up the line about the bet and drinks to get talking to you. I can't spend money on women I barely know. It would cheapen it for if I did buy you one," he said with a wink.

"Aha, who's to say you'll get a chance?" mused Helene.

"Well, if you dismiss me simply for not immediately buying you a drink, then I know you're not the woman for me," he said, as he made full eye contact with Helene. She laughed.

270

Connor continued. "Forgive me for being rude, but can I introduce my friend? He's over there on his own."

"Of course, but you better hope you don't go into battle with him. Shame on him for letting you talk to two maybe crazy French women on your own. You are very brave," Helene said.

"I know."

Connor beckoned Carl over, who stood with a slight shake of his head. Connor knew this was not what the assassin was expecting to happen. He would be uncomfortable, possibly even nervous. It was not talking to women per se that was the problem. It was because this was so far removed from what he would usually be doing the night before a job. *Fair play to him, he's not letting it show.*

"Ladies, how do you do?" Carl said.

"Ah, an American," enthused Zoë, as she touched her hair. "I've always wanted to live there."

"We'll switch passports," he said. "My name is Robert, by the way."

He shook hands with the two girls.

"So, I suppose we'll get, let's say, the formalities out of the way. What do you do for a living?" asked Helene, directing the question at Connor.

"I work predominantly in Arctic conservation."

"Arctic conservation? How do you mean?" Her eyes were enquiring.

"Well, for example, I was in the Arctic for six weeks there picking up Penguins that have fallen to one side. During the coldest months, they go into a cryogenic sleep and remain stuck until they thaw out. That's fine if they stay standing. However, if they fall on their side due to Arctic winds, during the couple of months they are in this sleep, their internal organs can become compressed, and

271

they die. So we go around standing them up, packing their feet and keeping them alive," said Connor.

Zoë looked a bit bemused but impressed. Carl gritted his teeth and rubbed his mouth. Helene had a smile dancing on her lips. She tilted her head back to look at Connor with her eyebrows raised slightly.

"It's a fantastic story, and you tell it with such verve and conviction, but surely, as a conservationist and lover of penguins, you would know that they come from Antarctica, not the Arctic."

Connor did not know what to say for a moment but already decided that he liked her more than just physically.

"You got me, I'm a salesman. I specialise in metals," he answered, as Carl shot him a look before relenting into a grin.

"I would just prefer it if you broke off any unnecessary engagements, Ravil," said Makar.

They were both sat in the back of a customised luxury sedan overlooking the Aquadrome lake. Ravil leaned back involuntarily at the intensity of Makar's gaze.

"I understand your concerns Makar, but this 'cleansing' process will take many months. I am not going to hide for that amount of time. Besides, it will look suspicious if I do."

"And I understand, but you have had that golf game booked for two weeks in advance. I am just advocating more short term and random bookings for appointments of that nature."

"I am not pulling out of this game Makar, it's with one of my most important contacts. Besides, as you say, the Albanians and Turks still don't suspect our hand in it.

When they do I will run my engagements past you prior to making them."

Makar was unhappy but knew this was a compromise Ravil would not move from. You did not become the most powerful Pakhan of the Bratva by being indecisive.

"How is our friend at the Farmhouse?" asked Ravil.

"He's still holding out, but he can't forever."

"I am sure you appreciate we do not want this to take forever. The resources we have are not limitless, not to mention that you are needed elsewhere. That need will only increase as our hand in this war is revealed."

"It's not a process that can be rushed. Besides, when he breaks, it'll increase our leverage threefold."

Ravil sighed. "Every day that man is alive is a concern. He should have been one of us—born in Moscow and not Glasgow."

Makar allowed himself a brief smile. "I was thinking the same thing, and that's why I have to be there. His sense of purpose and bravery make him every bit as dangerous as his knowledge is useful."

Connor and Helene walked through the city centre, her arm threaded through his. Connor briefly smiled as he thought back to how Carl's outgoing character had come out as Zoë lavished him with attention. Connor and Helene had left the pair back at the bar. It was Helene that decided she was tired and wanted to go home. He offered to walk her back, and she accepted. Connor briefly thought of how brazen the two women were being, allowing themselves to be separated by two strangers. He recalled how they went to the bathroom together and had likely worked out a safety procedure between them. It was probably a text sent within a certain time.

"Look Helene, my friend will be expecting me to text him at an appointed time so if you lead me anywhere and try and force sex on me at knife point you'll be in trouble."

Helene burst into laughter. "You really are the strangest man I have ever met."

Connor smiled—she had an infectious laugh.

"The English phrase is 'darkly mysterious'."

"Maybe that's the phrase for Monsieur Bond. A Strange Man is the right phrase *pour toi*," she said with a twinkle in her eye.

They walked for a little while. Connor found himself intoxicated by her perfume and tried not to let his good fortune show on his face. Her arm tightened around his, and a gentle wind blew her hair across his face, tickling it.

"This is *moi*," said Helene with a smile.

They stood outside a terraced row of gothic looking townhouses that were four floors high. Connor guessed the floors split into flats. He turned back to face the stunning vision before him, desire overriding any fear of spoiling the moment.

"Goodnight, Helene," he said grasping her waist, bringing her closer as they kissed. He felt a thrill course through him as she slipped an arm around his waist, her tongue flickering gently into his mouth.

They broke, and Helene said, "Would you like to come in for a coffee or, as you English seem to like, tea?"

Connor gave her a tight smile. "You see Helene, I have to be somewhere soon, and sharing a...coffee...with you isn't something I would like to rush. Is there a chance we could rearrange?"

Helene's large brown eyes looked into his.

"Of course we can. However, Connor, something that's rushed is sometimes better than nothing at all. So tell me, just how quick can you be?" she asked, with a devilish smirk.

Connor felt a surge through his cock. "In and out," he winked, "like a Commando."

"Eh, maybe not zat quick, Englishman," and she turned, lightly gripping his hand.

She unlocked the door and he admired her tight arse, following her inside. She turned around and they melted into a kiss. He removed her jacket, pulled out the bottom of her blouse and ran his hands up her waist, unclipping her bra and kissing her harder. She responded, unbuckling his belt and sliding her hand onto his ass, pulling him in tighter.

She pressed her pussy firmly against the bulge of his cock.

He took his top off and she lightly bit his chest, sliding her tongue over his nipple.

Connor, realising the time, manoeuvred her to the wall and began to strip her naked as she looked at him open-mouthed. He removed his shirt, leaving only his jeans on. She was just as stunning without clothes: hints of definition, olive skin and a flower chain tattoo curving around her upper thigh. Her supple tits rested high on her chest above a flat stomach. Her pussy was neatly trimmed atop a pair of toned, shapely legs. Connor took her hand and backed her into the living room.

She squealed in delight as he picked her up into a standing sixty-nine position. Connor gripped her tightly then put his face into her wet snatch. She let out a moan and her mouth engulfed his cock.

They stayed like this for a minute until Connor began to think of a way to elegantly put her down. Not finding one, he dumped her untidily on the sofa as she giggled. He quickly scrambled above her, kissing her hard and thrusting into her as she cried out. He began to fuck her hard as she moaned excitedly in French. He gripped her hair, hooking her leg on his shoulder, running his other hand all over her body. He put his two fingers in her mouth as he fucked her harder. Her nails scratched the back of his shoulders as she came, only a moment or two before he did.

Carl had arrived back at the hotel almost an hour ago, impatient and fighting the urge to be angry. Connor had texted him telling him he was on his way.

He had shared a respectful kiss with Zoë outside the bar before getting her number. He saw her off in a taxi, regretful to watch her leave. He was surprised with how much she responded to him and was secretly grateful that Connor had introduced him.

He had to admit, he liked the Englishman from the little he had been around him. However, professionally he made him anxious. His unpredictability set Carl on edge.

He had packed his things into his small suitcase. There was a premeditated knock at his hotel door that he and Connor had worked out between themselves. Still, Carl stood back and to one side of the door.

"Yeah?" he called.

"It's me," said Connor.

After a quick check of the spy glass, Carl let him in.

"Where have you been?"

He was trying hard not to sound like a scolding mother.

"I walked her back. Why? We still have plenty of time."

"Your things packed?" he asked.

"Yes, I did it before I went out."

"OK, cover your fingertips in this," said Carl handing him a small tub of silicone caulk. "It'll dry quickly. Meet me outside the hotel entrance when you're done. We best leave now."

With that Carl left the room.

Pierre looked at the huge Eastern European standing in his office. Two of Pierre's men flanked the man with one at his rear covering the door.

He had met many large, intimidating men in his time, indeed his three bodyguards in the room were big men and plenty experienced. Still, this member of the Bratva exuded an aura of danger that was palpable.

The man took a seat in front of him without waiting to be asked. Pierre stiffened at the underlying insult.

The man said in English, "Mr Pierre, an intelligent man such as yourself should know that if we wanted you dead, you would die. If we wanted you hurt, you would be hurt. You would not see our faces. So please, remove your three apes from the room or I will remove them for you."

There was a deathly silence.

Pierre donned a blank mask but was furious, confused and little unnerved. He was not a man who got edgy easily. Pierre gestured to the three guards, and they left while looking daggers at the man.

"What can I do for you Mr...?"

"Mr Adamik. You can give me a detailed report on the progress of your search for Nicholas Flint."

"The handling of that was mine, and mine alone."

"That is true. But it affects our interests, and now you are to be accountable to us."

"I do not react well to threats, Mr Adamik."

"You will not react well to one of your legs being sawn off while you are to watch, Mr Gaultier." The threat was delivered with such booming fearlessness that Pierre could not respond. Adamik continued. "Now I will give you this one chance to tell me," he said, holding up his finger for effect.

Pierre had dealt with violent men all his life and could read them easily now. The man was in Pierre's domain surrounded by his armed men and, still, he exuded an air of utter confidence that bordered on nonchalance. It was unsettling to the Frenchman.

After a turn, he answered. "We have despatched the man who tranquilized the previous target to clean up his own mess. He is in contact with a cyber tech who is searching for leads."

"Good, when and what was the content of his last check in?"

"Check in? He checks in when the job is done."

There were a few moments of silence as Damian frowned.

"You contracted a man who had already failed to eliminate a loose end to an extremely delicate operation, and you do not know where he is?"

Pierre bristled indignantly and cursed himself for letting this henchman gain the psychological upper hand.

"Mr Adamik, you are admittedly a member of a very powerful organisation, but you are a subordinate. I doubt you have ever had to head an organisation like mine. You are in no position to question my expertise."

"Mr Gaultier, you are in no position to question my expertise either, as you do not know of it. I am not here to justify myself to you. I am here to collect information and report on your progress. So far, you are to tell me you have no idea of the progress being made. He could be

278

dead, and you do not know. It is, as they say, ridiculous," rebuked Damian, with the same icy tone.

Pierre was now visibly trying to control his anger. It had been years since anyone had spoken to him in such a manner. After a brief moment he answered. "He is due to check in tomorrow, by email at two o'clock."

"Good, I will be with you until then, and you will explain the situation more to me."

"Both are not necessary."

"I am afraid it is for both of our respective health." Pierre forced a smile.

Connor joined Carl outside. They walked briskly through the quiet night of Brussels down an assortment of side streets. They would stop every so often so that the American could check the GPS on his phone, while also acting as a counter-measure for any possible follow up.

After twenty minutes of walking, they came to a dimly-lit, make-shift car parking space, outlined by unshaped granite stones behind an industrial building. There was a single vehicle inside: a metallic blue Ford Transit, with a company logo of 'Store de la Senne' written on the side.

Carl walked over to one of the stones and, whilst under the pretence of tying his laces, lifted it to retrieve a pair of keys that were hidden beneath. Connor initially thought it risky leaving the van unattended, considering what was meant to be inside. Then it occurred to him 'they', whoever 'they' were, would have eyes on the vehicle at least until Carl and Connor were in possession of it. He made a note of the buildings with windows facing the car park. He was increasingly impressed with this Jaime character.

Following a cursory check of the undercarriage after 'dropping' the keys, Carl unlocked the doors.

"Shall we drive it somewhere new and check the contents at a different location?" Carl asked.

"Yes."

Connor was mildly surprised the hitman had asked his opinion. He considered the American to be his superior. Not only older but Connor knew Carl had many years of experience under his belt. That was as much as Jaime had divulged to him. It occurred to Connor that Jaime probably did not divulge anything to Carl regarding Connor's professional career. Carl's confidence in him may shake if he knew of his relative inexperience. Although, Connor realised, Jaime did not know just how prolific a criminal he was—*or had been.*

Carl got into the driver's seat with Connor sliding in beside him, opening the envelope that had been left for them in the glove compartment. Connor took in the new-car smell as he began to rifle through the documents and photographs. He began to prioritise the information before relaying it. Carl pulled out onto the R20 road and by the time they joined the N8 road twenty minutes later, they had begun to discuss the mission.

Connor smiled as he read what weapon systems were in the back.

After a time Connor asked, "Did you get that bird's number?"

"Bird?"

"The girl who I left you with. Zoe."

"Oh...yeh I did. Why do they call girls birds in England?"

"Because they're always chirping."

"Oh, OK. Did you get your 'bird's' number?"

"Yeh. She was a nice girl."

280

Carl raised his eyebrows. "I bet she was,"

"Don't be crude. It doesn't suit you."

"I am not saying anything."

It took thirty minutes to reach the town of Ninove in a rural part of Belgium. After a further twenty minutes they found a place to stop. They cut down into a dense piece of woodland for a hundred yards, wound the windows down and cut the engine. They remained quiet for two minutes, listening out for anything untoward and exited the vehicle.

They opened the back and climbed in, shutting the doors behind them as they did so.

Immediately, the most noticeable thing was the gun mount bolted onto the reinforced floor of the van. It was a twin mount and so could fit two weapon systems, complete with a cast iron protective plate which shielded the firer's centre of mass. They began to open the assortments of cases one at a time and check the weapon systems in each one.

Connor smiled as he opened the first one and saw that it was a General-Purpose Machine Gun, before opening another box and discovering an identical one. The GPMG was the heaviest weapon of a British infantry section, and it was often referred to as a 'Battle Winner'. Connor had remembered the reassuring sound the gun made when it was fired during contacts with the Taliban. He had been made to take responsibility for it part way through his first tour, when the original gunner had snapped his ankle. He used it during several fire-fights and loved it. It fired the 7.62mm round which was designed to kill men rather than 5.56mm, which was designed to put men out of action.

In the eighties, the British Military had begun the switch from the Self-Loading Rifle (SLR), which fired the

281

7.62mm, to the SA80 firing the 5.56mm. Connor had heard that this was because a man hit by a 5.56mm would not necessarily die, at least not immediately, thus diverting his comrades' attention and resources to him during a fire-fight. The smaller round also created less recoil thus was more accurate, more ammunition could be carried and generally, the smaller the round, the lighter the weapon system. The GPMG, however, did fire the 7.62mm round and at a rate of 1200 rounds per minute at an effective range of 800m in this light role.

Connor smiled as he remembered an incident when he was a recruit. At the beginning of the first lesson they had had for the GPMG, the instructing Corporal threw it into the air to demonstrate its robustness. Yet, one of the bi-pod legs had snapped, much to the amusement of the class and the instructor, who swore them to secrecy.

Connor looked at the six boxes of 200 rounds and felt excited.

Makar looked at Bruce with admiration, although he did not show it. They had to push him dangerously close to the point of no return because of the Scotsman's unflinching mental robustness. Makar knew the signs he was displaying were approaching the realms of losing him completely. He was slurring the words that he was speaking to himself, the eyes switching from darting to staring, almost like he was in a waking nightmare.

Makar felt the frustration inside him but dismissed it. Feelings were just feelings—it was only the actions you took that mattered. First, though, he had to let the subject rest and recuperate.

24

The sedan snaked through the steady and polite traffic of Brussels, in a convoy of three—a van protecting the rear and an official-looking Mercedes to the front.

The sedan and the Mercedes each had darkened windows. The van at the rear was to protect the sedan from fire from behind and held three hardened men of Pierre's security team including the driver. Their eyes darted around assessing any potential threats. These actions mirrored the behaviour of the rest of the security detail in the Mercedes and sedan.

Damian was sat in the front passenger seat of the sedan next to the driver, while Pierre was sat alone in the back studying his phone. Damian felt a flutter within him and did not know why. They were on a two-lane road, not including the hard shoulder, separated from the mirroring road for opposing traffic by a man-made grass central reservation.

Damian had taken the opportunity to wear the new type 3 bullet proof vest. The London arm of the Bratva had purchased it at great expense. They were a Chinese development and capable of stopping 7.62 mm rounds. It was heavy but not nearly as heavy as it should have been due to a material weld technology and lack of side protection. He would not have got away with it in the summer months, but this part of Belgium was having a particularly cold November. He felt it was inconspicuous underneath his sweater and jacket. Some of the security detail might guess, as might Pierre himself—he had not always been a suit. Yet, no one gave Damian any indication that they knew. For that, he was pleased; it would afford him an edge should Pierre's indignation at his manner overcome his sense. Damian had been deliberately belligerent to unbalance him, and he could sense the Frenchman was seething.

Damian scanned the road as a van sped along side and past them.

Time slowed.

The van had what looked like a large, reinforced bumper which piqued his attention. It cut in front of the Mercedes before slowing.

"Cut into the left lane!" barked Damian.

The van's lights glowed red as it stuttered towards stopping. The Mercedes smashed into the reinforced bumper. The sedan and the rear van piled in after it. Damian had braced himself just before the smash by tensing his entire physique and gripping the seatbelt away from his clavicle. That took a lot of the whiplash and shock out of the collision for him.

He clicked the internal locking mechanism off. The rear shutter of the van snapped upwards.

The reverberation of heavy machine gun fire, smashing glass, and the tearing of the vehicle's bodywork erupted.

A crescendo of sound pounded in his ears.

Damian flung himself out of the sedan. An articulated lorry blocked his escape to the other side of the road. He turned to his left and began to run down the side of it. His heart pounding and his back riddled in vulnerability.

With two yards to go from cutting in behind the lorry to safety, three sledgehammer blows thudded into his back and shoulder. They flung him forward five feet onto his front as his forearms took the impact. A burst of fire shredded one of Pierre's security as he exited the rear van. Damian, with a massive effort, rolled himself into the gap made by the now somehow static lorry and the car behind it. His back felt dished in as he dragged himself into a crouch. He took out his Smith and Wesson customised 686 revolver.

The gunfire stopped, and Damian took his opportunity. He extended the gun and began to guide himself around the corner of the lorry. The ex-Special Forces soldier saw to his muted alarm why there had been a pause—a grenade sailed through the air and landed in the sedan. He ran for the cover of the lorry. The grenade exploded, shaking his bones and sending a ringing in his ears.

He made out the battle scream of "MOVE!" as it pierced the air.

His instinct screamed at him to fight back.

He fired in the general direction before he even looked around the corner of the lorry. He picked up his aim on the now-moving van. He fell to a crouch and zeroed in on the baseball-capped head along with skull face mask above the machine gun barrel. He knew it was a lost cause as he fired off three more rounds in quick succession. The head had already disappeared behind the armoured plate as the first round struck, about a fist's width away from the opening.

The van roared away.

Damian surveyed the carnage.

Horns blared, and people ran screaming. He waited until the van disappeared left at the cross roads 200 metres away and ran over to the sedan, already knowing what he was going to see.

He peered inside to see the grotesque, mutilated and charred bodies of Pierre and the driver. The smell of cooked pork assaulted his nostrils.

There was something he was not expecting: Pierre's Android phone, undamaged on the floor, opened on his emails. Damian picked it up and read the latest one, sent at twelve fifty-six from an unknown address: *'Pick up the R21 road, further instructions will be forwarded.'* Damian immediately understood. He pocketed the phone and looked for an escape route.

The distant sirens wailed.

The speed of Carl's driving pressed Connor into the seat. Symptoms of what he recognised to be adrenal-comedown coursed through him. There was a mixture of relief and endorphins. He knew the next stage would be drowsiness. He fought against it.

He smiled recalling *vittling-up* Gaultier's security team. The Frenchman was a man who made his living from war.

Carl pulled into the beginning of a back road that began to climb. After several hundred metres, they pulled into a small alcove where a small Nissan lay parked. Carl got out and opened the boot of the car, taking out a metallic jerry can of petrol and four separate solar showers. In turn, they stripped and bagged the clothes. They used a nail brush to scrub themselves clean under the solar showers before drying themselves. They dressed in new clothes and threw the old ones and towels into the back of the van. Both completed the entire process in under five minutes apiece. Connor had confidence that a human would not smell any propellant on him—*a fucking dog would though.*

Connor went into the back of the van, finding the lead-encased box storing the phosphorous grenades. They had re-applied the silicone caulk to their fingertips before the assault. Carl poured part of the can over the front compartment and the rest all over the back. He got into the driver seat of the Nissan, gunned the engine and turned the vehicle around.

Connor activated a phosphorous grenade, launched it into the back of the van and dove into the Nissan. Carl shifted through the gears back down the hill. They could hear the firework show as all the remaining munitions began to catch alight and explode.

Damian hid in an alleyway about half a mile from the chaos. He had called his Brussels Bratva contact and had sent through his GPS location.

"Stay in place for twenty-five minutes," was the response ending the call.

Too risky to move now anyway he thought, especially not with three prominent tears in the back of his tweed jacket. Damian tapped in the memorised number and heard it ring. If anything happened to him now at least Makar would know who to look for.

Makar's digitalized English came on the line after two rings, "Report."

"The convoy was ambushed. One man was operating a machine gun from the back of a driven van. The Frenchman is dead. I got his phone and found a message. I think the American turned on him."

"Where are you now?"

"Awaiting pick up from our friends. I am around 800 metres away from the site of the ambush."

"Check in with me as soon as our friends have you at a safe house," said Makar.

Jaime sat in his study in the countryside of Surrey. It was a small room built underground and offset to the large country house that he owned. There were two projection screens built into the wall along with three computer systems, one on either side of him and one in front. That was all he needed.

Jaime had been fascinated with computers since his childhood in the early nineties. His father, a wealthy government official and property developer had taken him on a visit to the Kennedy Space Center in Florida. Jaime was mesmerized by the technology, the missions, and the vastness of the place. One of the technicians told him, *In the future, any piece of information will be able to be obtained by anyone—in seconds—through a computer that almost every western household will have.*

His father had encouraged him to watch English speaking videos to improve his grasp of the language. Watching films like 'Hackers', 'Sneakers' and 'War Games' compounded the young Jaime's interest in information technology. Soon, the internet exploded, and Jaime never looked back. That was nearly twenty years ago.

Jaime, now in his late twenties, was rich verging on wealthy and one of the best in the world at what he did. At this moment, he was sat in his fiefdom scanning police radios and checking CCTV confirming what he already knew—that the two men he had sent had completed their mission. He estimated within fifteen minutes the initial reports would be all over the news.

Jaime felt a creep of admiration for the pair. It was their plan, and even though they had needed his technical assistance, they had carried out their part.

He began to search for the online chatter that Pierre Gaultier's death would generate.

Connor and Carl kept scanning the crowd searching for any signs of undue interest in them. They were at the Calais terminal of the Eurostar, with the train due in a quarter of an hour. Nervous and excited chatter hummed among the people as the news of the shooting spread through their smart phones. Brussels was a mere two-hour drive away.

This was the time when they were most susceptible to capture or being arrested; being closed in by civilians, any plain-clothed police or agent approaches would be harder to spot. They sat at opposite ends of the station. Remaining separate until they boarded the train was a tactical measure to look out for one another. It might also afford one the chance of escape if the other was detained.

The train pulled in, and Connor made his way from the furthest side, walking past Carl to the train. A young woman sat on the far side, set down her magazine, and pulling out her phone, keyed in a memorised number.

"Louis man, why we babysitting this joker? Coppers gonna be looking for him fam."

Jay was Louis's right-hand man. Despite standing over half a foot shorter with a slim build, he had a fearsome reputation. He sported a curly top, low fade hairstyle with a straight-lined tapered beard. He wore a black leather jacket over the top of a black plunging T-shirt, dark grey jeans ripped at the knees and grey trainers. They were stood outside the warehouse, smoking.

"It's favour for a friend," replied Louis laconically, his face illuminating orange as he took a drag of his cigarette.

"The white boy from Winterfell?"

"He's from up North yeh. Can't wait until you finish Game of Thrones man."

"He a good friend in'it? Din't you say there was two of em? Two bad boys of the North."

"Ye man, one died in Afghan, name was Liam. Ma man's not been the same since. They were tight."

"Need me to do anything for you, bruv?"

"Nah, jus' keep things smooth."

Connor and Carl sat at the opposite end of the carriage in view of one another. Connor felt relieved that there had not been sniffer dogs at the Calais station. He knew it was unlikely that they would be employed at the arrival station. Still, he felt a keen awareness about his person—an instinct that had developed over the years, both with the Marines and in his criminal life.

His first foray into crime had started with shoplifting in The White Rose Centre in Leeds at eleven years of age. He and his cousin would lift mainly clothes and sometimes books. One trick was to remove a security tag and plant it on an unsuspecting shopper. As the customer would walk out, they had set the alarm off and attract the attention of the security guards. With the guards' attention elsewhere, they would walk past them with an array of stolen goods in their bags.

Connor had made the leap onto stealing cars and joyriding, or 'twocking' (taking without consent) as the local youths called it, soon after. By fourteen, he had joined one of his older cousins in a gang specialising in robbing warehouses. He made what would have been serious money for an average twenty-one-year-old.

He had first kept it hidden in a small safe in his room, later putting it into a bank account he had opened at the minimum age of sixteen. His mother thought his opening of an account admirable. She did not check his mail wishing to treat him as an adult and was not privy to the amounts being deposited in there. However, he was aware that that amount of money was suspicious and thus invested in a security box from the bank. In it went expensive jewellery and specifically Swiss watches because he knew they did not lose much value over time.

As his money increased, so did his methods of laundering it. He would always disguise his inquiries as mere curiosity before discreetly acting on any information he received. Connor could not understand why his father had not confronted him as surely, being the 'Don' of Leeds and beyond, he would know about his excursions into crime. Maybe it was because Connor had never dealt drugs. He did not like the idea anyway thinking it to be boring, scummy and unromantic. Being a robber had a different air than being a drug dealer he thought, and Connor liked stealing when he was younger. He loved being part of a gang as well as the risk, and the money.

When he was fourteen, Connor made a serious mistake. He burgled a house with his cousin in an affluent area of Leeds. He got away clean with a lot of expensive jewellery, or so he thought. Two days later, he set foot inside his father's house to visit. He turned around from locking the door, he saw a flash of a fist and heard a crunching thud. He felt his brain sneezing blood after being rattled off the inside his skull. It took a few moments through the haze to realise his father had decked him. Next, the tread of his dad's shoe pressed into his face.

"Think it's acceptable to steal from hard working people do you eh?"

Connor's heart seemed to freeze in his chest.

"Stand up." Connor did so, unsteadily. He had never seen his father so angry.

"Want to go for it?" asked his father.

Connor was not surprised at his own disinclination to fight. But he was surprised as to the reason why. It was not just fear that stopped him from accepting his father's challenge—it was the shame.

Connor could not believe what happened next. His father drove him around to the said property to be welcomed by a middle-aged professional couple. His dad had visited the couple after being made aware of the burglary. Connor never found out how he knew.

He was made to sit there while the couple told him of their humble beginnings.

The woman had come from a council estate in Huddersfield, being one of five children. She became a social worker and then a behavioural therapist in her later years. The man told him of his being orphaned at the age of seven and put into a children's home. It took eighteen months to get his behaviour under control before being adopted by a foster family from the Headingly area of Leeds. He described how he worked hard through college and university to become a geologist. The point was that they had earned what they owned. They had scrimped, saved, studied, and worked for the nice things they had. They were benefactors to various local charities, and when Connor heard one of these was his beloved boxing club, his stomach churned. He had invaded their home in the middle of the night and stole from them. Connor did not have to don the mask of contriteness.

This time, he had genuinely felt shame.

When his father demanded that Connor work the weekends for them, they had refused. Instead, they made Connor promise never to burgle people's houses or steal their possessions again. Connor had made that promise and kept it.

Nick sat alone in the room.

His mind was in turmoil—*surely there were some mistakes you could not make amends for.* In fact, his mind had been in turmoil ever since he had agreed to help remove Bruce. He had to try and right this wrong, but how? Connor, that closet psychopath, was not going to trust him. Not unless he had reason to.

He heard a car outside before the engine cut out. Moments later a black youth with a snapback cap came in with a fish and chip supper. Nick made out the pistol on his hip.

"Dis is for you," the youth said.

"Thank you."

The youth unfastened Nick's cuffs and backed away. Nick ate the supper ravenously. All he had eaten until then was a Pot Noodle over twenty-four hours ago.

"Can I use the toilet? I haven't had a shit in two days," he asked when he had finished.

"Err...yeh."

Nick stood and started for the door.

"Wait!"

Nick turned around, painting an expression of confusion and concern on his face.

"What's up?" he asked stepping towards him.

293

The youth had drawn his pistol. "I have to keep you covered with this when—"

Nick snatched the pistol barrel with one hand while palm striking the wrist. The gun was torn from the youth's grasp. A pistol-weighted backfist struck his face staggering him to one side. Nick levelled the handgun at him.

"Throw me the keys."

After taking a moment to get over the shock, the youth fumbled into his pocket, and the keys sailed through the air. Nick caught them with his left hand.

"Stand up, let's go."

He had the barrel pressed into the youth's spine and the collar was bunched into his fist. He marched him to the black BMW parked outside.

"Get on your knees slowly."

Pressing the unlock button on the keys, the lights of the BMW flashed with a beep.

"Your boss still inside?" He asked, prodding the youth with his foot. He nodded in affirmation.

"Call him. Tell him to come outside immediately and then click the phone off. If you do anything other than that, you'll die, understand?"

"Yeh."

"Go ahead."

He rang the number and Nick could hear a voice answer. "Yeh fam, can you come outside right now yeh?" said the youth before clicking off.

"Alright, lay face down."

When the youth was prostrate, Nick placed the pistol on the roof and held his hands palms out at shoulder height. Louis burst out of the door with his pistol levelled at him.

"What's the crack?" he asked, taking in the scene.

294

"Well, I could have lamped this amateur across the temple and driven away in his car, but I didn't."

Louis nodded. "OK…why didn't you?"

"Because I want to help."

Louis stared at him for a few moments and slowly lowered his handgun.

Connor's Android phone vibrated in his pocket, and ephedrine bolted around his insides as he read the message.

'American C been spotted. British C does not appear to have been detected yet.'

A picture of a Damian Adamik along with his bio uploaded to his phone. It was not good reading. Connor perused the Pole's Special Forces career, perceived fighting skills and physical characteristics. He looked a brute of a man. Connor looked at the pictures again and in a few seconds realised this was the man who had fired at him from behind the large lorry.

The only advantages they had now were that they were aware of Adamik and that Connor had not been spotted—or it might seem like he had not been. Connor had worn a bandana across his mouth and a peak baseball cap whilst he was *brassing up* the vehicles. He looked up and made eye contact with Carl, feeling a stab of guilt. If Carl had completed his initial task of returning Nick Flint, then he may have been free of this. Now, he was being targeted by the Russian Bratva, and the pair were returning to London. He was beginning to like Carl too.

His phone vibrated again.

'Their organisation unable produce numbers to take Am-C. DA set to take Am-C himself in London.'

Connor looked and made eye contact with Carl. He knew what he was going to do.

Connor had picked out Damian. The Pole was following Carl through the horde of the station crowd. Connor noted the surveillance cameras at intervals throughout the station and began to speed up—he was going to have to make his move outside the station. Connor passed the Pole and Carl, exiting through the station's double doors.

Halting by the cigarette bin, he swilled saliva around his gums and mouth. Swilling saliva, as well as deep, slow breathing, tricked the system into helping control adrenaline; he could not afford to have his fine motor functions going haywire.

The American broke through the exit door with the Pole not far behind him. Connor began a course to intersect the giant from an angle so the big man would only see him at the last moment—hopefully he would not see him at all. The Pole looked every bit as immovable as his bio had suggested. As Connor closed the distance, he felt the fear lurch in his stomach mixed with a shot of excitement.

"Damian?" he called out like a long-lost friend.

In the split-second window of engaging the Pole's brain, his steel *kubotan*-filled fist, whipped through an arc smashing into the point of Damian's jaw. It was a perfect 'side-winder'. As the towering hulk collapsed, his head hit the pavement with a sickly crack. Connor dumped his kubotan back into his pocket.

"Help! Help! This man has collapsed!" shouted Connor.

An elderly couple looked at him perplexed.

Soon they were joined by a small gathering crowding in on the scene. Nobody challenged Connor—*thank God for London haste*. A portly woman broke through the rapidly expanding crowd and began to attend to the Pole. There was blood seeping from the head.

"I have a first aid kit in my car around the corner. I'll go get it." said Connor.

He jogged off without waiting for a reply. Around the corner, he spotted Carl standing at the driver's side of a Black Vauxhall Astra. Connor raced to the passenger side, and they both got in.

"Short and sweet," said Carl.

"Yeah, a bit like how I fuck."

25

Makar stood looking out of the farmhouse window in thought. He had learned a long time ago that panic never solved things. Nevertheless, this deserved his undivided attention. He had received a call from Damian. The Pole's tone had continually shifted from contrite to angry as he explained what had happened. Pierre Gaultier had been audaciously mown down in Brussels, along with his entire security detail. Then, Makar's go-to man had been unceremoniously prevented from his apprehension of the culprit by another unknown entity. Damian could not explain what had happened, other than he had awoken on the street surrounded by people and his throbbing jaw had been cut open. Damian had been treated by one of the surgeons on the payroll—six stitches but miraculously the bone was intact.

Makar did not know who he was dealing with. Maybe Ravil's supposed partners had thought better of their deal and were trying to usurp it using the American as a cover? Perhaps the American really did turn by himself but had friends? There could be no way to know unless Makar took a chance. He could instruct Ravil to use the supposed friendly elements of the UK Security Services to help locate the American. But if they had orchestrated this then all they would do is undermine his efforts.

Makar needed manpower and technical support to find Carl Wright. He had thought of leaking it to the Turks that this man had been involved in the Hassan Saki assassination, but he decided against it. It was unlikely a hundred amped Turks could find an alert professional assassin who did not want to be found.

Makar was still unclear of the intention of this team. Perhaps their target was solely Pierre Gaultier. Makar's instincts told him it was not—*Why would the American return to London? Surely he would try and slip away quietly, at least until the fallout died down?* Suddenly, realisation surged. They, whoever 'they' were, had come to London to derail the agreement the Bratva had entered in with a section of the UK elite.

Although Makar's priority was Ravil, if these British co-conspirators were taken and they were not already part of a plot against the Russian Bratva, they soon would be. This was unless they were assassinated, which would mean the agreement collapsing. The London Bratva would have to fight an underworld war without the protection or support of these establishment figures.

Makar needed all the men at his disposal now. This left him with the challenge of what to do with Bruce McQuillan. He could kill him. However, if their British 'friends' had betrayed them, the information the Scotsman held could be even more vital. He was too dangerous to be left with one of Makar's soldiers. In that moment the solution came to Makar.

He left his seat, entered the hallway and made his way down to the basement. He gestured for the *Byki* stood beside the door to unlock the bolts. Makar drew his pistol as a precaution and stepped back from the door as it opened towards him. McQuillan was still fixed to the chair in the centre of the small room and Makar stepped in towards him.

"Mr McQuillan, where do you keep your information on individual members of 'The Establishment'?"

Opekun did not speak but just looked through him. Makar put the barrel of his pistol on Bruce's right knee and pulled the trigger.

Ravil was being driven to The Royal Blackheath Golf Club in a silver Maybach Cruisero Coupe. He was impressed with the V12 Engine, which powered the nearly six-metre luxury business Coupe with 605 horse power. The only customisation was the bullet proof windows. The Royal Blackheath was Britain's oldest golf club, and generally Ravil would look forward to visiting.

He was playing with Henry Costner and this was a dangerous time. He could usually decipher a person's motives without even having to meet them; their lifestyles and past gave evidence to what drove them. However, sometimes reading a person's body language when they were under pressure allowed greater accuracy. He had to ascertain whether Costner and the others had reneged on their agreement. A business arrangement built on this amount of mistrust was not ideal. Added into the equation there was a team seeking to derail the entire thing along with an underworld war, and it amounted to a situation.

Ravil did not reach the level he was at by panicking in the face of such events. He knew he had what psychologists call an *'internal locus of control'*—a sense of responsibility regarding his reaction to things that happened to him. The weak who put the onus on anything or anybody other than themselves had an *'external locus of control'*.

The Maybach pulled up outside the club's grounds and his driver got out. After a cursory scan of the area, he opened Ravil's door. Makar had at first insisted they take a full security detail with him wherever he went, but Ravil had overruled him. Whether Costner had betrayed him or not, a full complement of ex-Spetsnaz bodyguards would send out the wrong message, particularly in this club. He did make a concession and increased the number from his usual single man to two. In addition to the capable Roderick who doubled as his bodyguard and driver, he had included one of Makar's main *boyeviks*, a Pole named Damian Adamik. He had debated with Makar whether to use him or not as Ravil questioned Adamik's mind-set. He was too emotionally involved since he had been embarrassingly blindsided outside St Pancras Station, Makar himself had argued it was for this reason he should be assigned to Ravil's protection detail—he would be on hyper alert to catch the culprits. This did indeed seem to be the case.

They turned in from the main road into the long country lane leading to the golf club. The Pole asked to be let out of the car to Ravil's mild puzzlement, his tone indicating a demand rather than a request. Roderick pulled over and Damian disappeared into the surrounding woodland.

The large club house overlooked the golf course. It was made of red brick, with four great pillars guarding the main door, along with four parallel chimneys on the roof.

The club was busy today, which had both its advantages and disadvantages from a security point of view. People acted as obstructions to not only potential attackers but also the security detail.

Ravil found the debonair Henry sat alone at one of the tables in the bar. He was dressed in a navy-blue knitted body warmer over a white shirt, with chequered blue and white golf pants. His hair was immaculately coiffured. Ravil took his seat opposite him on the same table. The politician shifted in his seat and Ravil remained still.

301

"How are we Mr Yelchin?" asked the Prime Minister's advisor.

"I am fine Mr Costner. Are the halls of Westminster proving stimulating enough for you this week?"

"More than stimulating, thank you. Would you like a drink?"

"If it's agreeable to you, I would like to proceed to the green"

"Of course."

The temperature was warm but the air remained crisp, with only a hint of a breeze.

Ravil teed off.

Roderick doubled as his caddie, and the Politician's minder—an equally unassuming-looking man—did the same for Henry Costner.

"So, how's progress in our mutual area of business?" Henry asked.

"Ah, there's been progress, but there's also been a complication."

Henry hit a sub-par tee-off which the Bratva boss took to be a good sign. If he had struck a perfect stroke, it may have indicated he already knew of the issue.

"OK, can you give me a rundown please?" asked the politician, as they took a stroll down the fairway.

"The assassination of the Turk was leaked to be the work of the Albanian Mafia. They are locked into eliminating one another for the time being. However, a cleaner, contracted by Pierre Gaultier has since turned on him. He was involved in the assassination of Bruce McQuillan. He was responsible for the shootings in Brussels. They arrived back in London last night, where they managed to escape our apprehension. Now, we have to think their aims are wider than merely the elimination of Pierre Gaultier."

"Jesus Christ man, the carnage in Brussels was because of this?"

Costner's shock seemed authentic to Ravil. However, the Englishman was a career politician—well versed in lying.

"I am afraid so."

Ravil strolled up, measured his swing, and struck the ball well. It floated and rolled to a stop within three yards of the hole.

"Well, if this American has now assassinated Pierre then he has tied a loose thread for us?" pondered Henry aloud.

"My reasoning was initially the same. However, the American has returned to London. It would be in our interests to discover his motives."

As Costner walked to his ball, Ravil felt an invisible finger give him a hard-flicking sting just under his collar bone. He felt a jolt—the small impact indicated to him that he had been hit by something. He looked down to see a wasp was falling away from him. The grass underneath him came rushing up to smack his face hard. His hearing became muffled, and he was spinning in that dream-like state just before slumber. Sleep washed over him.

Connor sat in the ambulance a mile away, awash with anticipation. He would not let nerves show. He could not change or improve the situation he was in now. Carl had to fire 'The Wasp', and because a paramedic team of one looked suspicious, Connor enlisted the help of Nick Flint, who could still drive despite his injuries. The blackened eyes from the broken nose Connor had given him were not ideal. Louis had explained what had happened—that Nick could have easily escaped but did not.

Connor consulted with Jaime regarding using Nick on this, and the South-American reluctantly agreed. Connor could have brought in Louis to help, but he could not allow his friend to become any more embroiled in this than he had to be. He made up a story to Louis that Nick needed to be there to identify Ravil, although Jaime had already provided him with pictures. Nick did not know what Ravil looked like either.

While Connor believed Nick to be sincere in his desire to help, he had Jaime discover where the Salford man's close family members lived as insurance. Back came the addresses of Nick's elder sister and his niece who lived in Brighton. Connor contacted Louis with the information, who then sent a particularly menacing looking member of his crew on the long drive to the house. The guy took a photo on his Android phone of himself outside it. When showing him the image, Nick exhibited surprise and what looked to Connor to be a mild disappointment. But not the alarm or fear that would have sounded warning bells.

Now they waited for Jaime to ring. He was due to do so after he intercepted the call from The Blackheath to the emergency services. The tech wizard would mimic an operator and despatch Connor and Nick to pick up Ravil.

Connor felt a wave of clarity come over him. Like a window had opened to allow him to feel what he should. He knew himself well enough to know how he reacted in a crisis. He always made the right choice in a way that he could not explain because other areas of his life needed consistent discipline and effort. In most areas, he was still way off the mark. Though he was making headway in some ways, controlling his temper, even with minor things, was a constant struggle. He thought of the area that he made little progress in—womanising. It was the real reason why he did not have a girlfriend. He had developed 'standards' in the last few years, but that was about it—*how could a man be satisfied with the same pussy for decades on end?* That was something he was still wrestling with. He mused that maybe he simply had not fallen in love, the love Celine Dion sang about—*although she was twelve when she met her future husband.*

However, in the thick of action signifying great danger, Connor could never remember flapping. He also noticed that things like his marksmanship significantly improved. He remembered a contact in Helmand Province. He somehow managed to land a bomb from his Underslung Grenade Launcher, onto the head of a Taliban insurgent from 300 metres away. It was also an 'off-the-cuff' decision to throw the grenade at Pierre Gaultier's motorcade. There was also his reaction to witnessing Bruce McQuillan's kidnap. All driven by an instinct that had not let him down.

The internal phone rang.

"The call has gone through. Wait four minutes and retrieve the package."

Damian stalked through the woods on his clearance patrol. His feet made outward sweeps to clear debris that could snap. He decided if he were to take out Ravil, he would do it with a sniper rifle from this area.

His ears locked onto a muffled 'phut' and instantly knew what it was. He fought the instinct to rush to the sound. The shot had already been fired, so what was done was done. Damian could yet apprehend the assassin, but he was not going to accomplish that if he was dead from rushing into the path of a bullet.

He moved cautiously. He estimated the firer to be around forty metres away through the overgrown trees. The former GROM operative stalked forward with his pistol pointed at the ground at a forty-five-degree angle. If the pistol was held out to a ninety-degree angle, he could give his position away.

He came to the edge of the thick bramble and launched out from behind it.

Everything seemed to slow as he saw the American assassin, levelling a pistol at him. He leapt to his right while simultaneously firing his own pistol in the general direction of the target. Damian was obscured by a thick oak tree listening to the American's voice giving instructions.

"Been compromised. If I am not back at the appointed time, leave without me."

There was a radio beep and a "Roger" in reply.

Damian knew he had to act now. He exposed his shoulder for a split second before spinning around to his right, dropping to his knee and using the tree as partial cover.

He spotted the American behind a tree, just before the American spotted him. Damian fired a hammer pair—two shots in rapid succession—striking the American's upper left pectoral and shoulder. The returning bullet clipped his ear just as Damian ducked back behind the tree. Ignoring it, he edged himself back around the other side of the tree in case the American was lucid enough to use his pistol. He saw legs awkwardly stumble away into dense bushes. He knew it was a matter of not getting careless now. The American would be his, one way or another.

He wanted to take him alive to question him, but that was extremely dangerous. His target was now a wounded animal—an armed professional assassin.

Damian followed the blood trail and flattened foliage. He spotted the horizontal legs and a part of his torso. His prey had stopped trying to drag himself away. The Pole could see by the rise and fall of the chest he was still breathing. He kept his pistol levelled at the American's stomach, his head and torso still partially obscured by the tree.

As he got to within a few steps, the warm blood flowed down his cheek and neck from his torn ear. The torso came into view, and Damian could see his shot had incapacitated his left side. The American was trying to roll to pick up the pistol that had fallen from his grip. As the turn completed, Damian put his boot on his right shoulder blade to prevent him from rolling back.

"So, Mr Wright, second time lucky. This time your friend is not here to save you."

Damian Adamik's lower jaw disintegrated, and his corpse toppled over like a felled tree.

Connor watched the hulking figure collapse like an accordion and felt relief. The Bratva's henchman had been pointing his pistol at Carl as Connor took the shot. The former Royal Marine, who's breath was erratic due to his dash to reach the scene, took aim at the point where the spine met the skull—at the medulla oblongata located in the lower half of the brainstem. The medulla contained, amongst a host of things, the messaging centre of the body's nervous system. Shooting it prevented the death twitch of the big man's trigger finger. He did not truly expect to hit it, hence the relief pushing through his veins.

He and Nick had been inside the ambulance in a small parking area which served as the rendezvous point. Then Carl's transmission had come over the net informing them that he had been compromised. Connor knew the smart course of action was to leave as he already had Ravil in his possession. That and he did not necessarily trust Nick despite the threat he held over him to his family. Leaving Ravil with Nick would be a tactical mistake born out of emotion.

During his agent training, he was told of a study where they had simulated a war game to test the performances of two groups at commanding their respective virtual armies. Top tier US Generals made up one group with high performing stockbrokers making up the other. The results were shocking; the stockbrokers outperformed the generals in every scenario. This was due to their ability to see numbers, not people. Ironically, they sustained fewer casualties en masse. Connor knew all of this and still could not bring himself to order Nick to drive off and leave his now oppo.

He handcuffed Nick to the steering wheel amidst his protests. He knew that if the Chameleon Project operative was truly determined to do so, he could escape. Now, he was looking at Carl, who was struggling and bleeding from the shoulder.

"Bet you wish that we stole a real ambulance now, eh?" said Connor as he rifled through the Pole's pockets. He did not find anything.

He located and collapsed the sniper rifle into the tactical case. He manoeuvred the former Ranger to lift him.

"Luckily, I was wearing a vest. But he caught me in the shoulder—"

"—hey," said Connor abruptly. "I have my own problems," then smiled.

"What took you so long?" said Carl, who smiled back.

"That's rich coming from an American."

The hitman grimaced as Connor hoisted him up, holding the tactical case in one hand. After a few minutes the rendezvous point appeared, and a euphoric feeling came over Connor—the ambulance was still in place. He opened one half of the double doors to reveal a comatose Ravil and his bodyguard with part of his head missing, blood splattered all over the wall.

"What happened here?" asked Carl, as Connor set him down.

"Insisted on coming, didn't he? Nothing I could do," replied Connor nonchalantly. Connor ripped open one of the first aid boxes producing two pistols.

"Keep both of these on you. This pistol's mag is empty. I have to drive, and Nick has to try and treat you. Have this one in his sight and this one hidden. If he goes for this gun, you'll know where his loyalty really lies. That's what the loaded pistol is for."

The two men looked at one another, and Carl gave him a slight nod. "OK."

Connor left the back of the ambulance, closed the door and made his way to the driver's side. He smiled inwardly as he saw Nick still in the driver's seat, but his handcuffs were removed.

26

Makar fought to control his anxiousness. He had made two phone calls: one to Roderick and the other to Damian. Both had rang out. He then made a call to Ravil himself. There were five rings and an English voice answered in a tone of a call centre operator.

"Hello, Ravil Yelchin's phone."

"Who is this?"

The tone of the answering voice changed, "I am the person who will slaughter your boss and send pieces of him to your Mafioso brothers in Moscow. Unless you do exactly as I say."

"Why should I care?"

"Because if you are who I think you are, it would highlight your failure in protecting him. And you don't want that now, do you Drago?"

Makar took a breath, and answered, "I'm listening."

"I want to know the details of who is involved in this collaboration of yours, and I want Bruce McQuillan back."

"He's dead, I am afraid," said Makar, hoping he could break McQuillan for an advantage.

"Well, you better bring him back to life before Mr Yelchin here follows the same fate. Do not lie to me again."

Makar frowned—*how does he know I am lying? Has Ravil told them?*

"When?"

"I'll be in touch."

Connor clicked off the call. He was outside Louis's warehouse in the van his friend had procured for him. The rain began to drizzle. His phone rang, and he answered it with a quick, "Hello."

"That will have been Makar. Ravil's right-hand man." It was Jaime, speaking of Connor's last call.

"How do you think he'll play it?"

"He is a very clever man. He knows he has to retrieve Ravil and a swap for Bruce McQuillan is reasonable. It is the request for information that he will not give up. It goes against the Russian Bratva's *Omerta*," said Jaime's distorted voice.

"Even information regarding people who are not members of the Bratva?"

"Yes, even then."

"Any ideas of how to play it?"

"We wait."

"What do you mean, we wait?"

"He cannot go to his friends in Moscow, at least not until he has exhausted all other avenues. He will go to whoever they are dealing with here. Then I will find out just how far and deep it goes."

"How exactly do you plan on doing that?"

"I have a few suspects, and when he reaches out, I will be listening."

"Then what?"

"It is your country. You tell me."

Connor thought for a moment. "Trials of powerful men get so convoluted, and those trials cost the taxpayer money."

After a moment or two, "I agree," came over the line.

Makar clicked off the call and steadied his breathing. He began to contemplate his options. The real enemy was faceless. Carl Wright could not have been a part of this in the beginning. He had to have been recruited by an unknown entity. Whoever they were, they had technical support good enough to intercept CCTV and unsecured emails—*how else would they know of Pierre Gaultier's and Ravil's movements?*

They were ruthless too. Damian and Roderick were two of the most capable men in the London Bratva, and both now were presumably dead. He fought the urge to curse Ravil for his lack of care and stubbornness; he knew anger would not help him. The voice on the phone gave him pause for thought too. It seemed to belong to a relatively young man—one completely devoid of fear.

However, they had made a tactical mistake. In asking for the details of who was involved, it revealed that they did not know or at least were not sure themselves. That meant that Bratva's UK business associates had not let their morals get in the way of their greed. And that meant he could still use them. He dialled a memorised number.

"So you're saying that Henry Costner isn't a traitor?" Connor asked, incredulously. He and Carl were back with Jaime in his caravan.

"We made contact yesterday. I told him to call me on a secure line. I had counter traces on there and recorded the call. Listen to this." Jaime replied, pressing play on the recording.

'Tell me how you were propositioned and why you didn't report it immediately.'

'I was propositioned at a private club by someone who's name I won't mention over the phone. This was over the course of two

*meetings— one to feel me out and one to proposition me. He told me
that, with the influx of domestic Jihad terrorism, the security services
were getting stretched to breaking point and organised crime was
about to spiral out of control. He told me that it was 'better the devil
you know' and indicated that the Russian Mafia could take control
of organised crime in the UK. He also inferred that they might help
manage our domestic terrorist threat. All this would be in exchange
for protection by the security services and a few highly placed people
within the Government. All of this sounded misguided, but almost
noble until he mentioned money. £75 million for the both of us.
That's when I knew.'*

The recording clicked off.

"How did he manage to contact you? You strike me
as someone who keeps well under the radar," asked Carl.

"He did not. After Bruce had been taken, I began
working to locate and de-encrypt his various email
accounts looking for anything that may help us. MP
Costner had emailed him on the day he was kidnapped
attempting to warn him. Bruce had not opened it before
his kidnap."

"What do you think? Can we trust him?" asked Carl.

"Mr Costner transferred twenty-five million pounds
into an account of my choosing yesterday."

"How the fuck did you get him to do that?" asked
Connor.

"I asked him to."

"How did he know you are who you said you are?"

"Before I came to work with Bruce, I was being
hunted by the SVR. Desperately reaching out for friends,
an unknown source directed me to McQuillan. That
source turned out to be Henry Costner."

"And he's proved this?" asked Carl.

"Yes."

Connor and Carl looked at one another but did not pursue it further.

"What about Makar?" asked Carl.

"He is very smart, ruthless and this word—meticulous. He's much of the reason why this Bratva is the most profitable in the world."

Carl rubbed his palm with his thumb while Connor remained impassive.

Jaime continued. "We need to put in extra precautions. Also, he may or may not have recruited the help of his British contacts."

"Wait, why wouldn't he have recruited them?" Connor looked bemused.

"Because he may not trust them. He may not be sure if they got cold feet or if they were ever truly on his side. This is a fanciful hope, and we have to presume he has contacted them for help."

"What's that mean for us?"

"That we have to put in countermeasures. But remember, any support given to him cannot be too overt. Makar is a shadowy figure, but no one gets to his level without being noticed. Interpol, the SVR *naturalmente*, Mossad, and MI5 all have files on him, even if they are light on detail and sometimes inaccurate. But, he's known, and if the link is made between him and them, that's not good for them."

"Whoever they are, they are done for anyway," replied Connor, his eyes opaque.

"I know who the original traitor is now," said Jaime.

They both stared at him expectantly.

He told them.

Makar was back in another hotel room when the vibration of the call he had been waiting for came through.

He answered it swiftly.

"Merrywood Industrial Park, 22:00, tomorrow night, south entrance. You and whatever security detail you want, but you'll inform me of the numbers beforehand. In answer to your inevitable stalling to obtain the information I require, let's just say I have taken certain pictures of Mr Yelchin," said the voice. "Let's also say that what goes on between Mr Yelchin, an unknown man, a dildo and a pair of rubber gloves is his own business, but that will only remain so as long as he co-operates once out of my custody. I can't imagine the dent to your organisation's image if those pictures got posted on the internet. He suits the pink dress by the way."

The phone clicked off, and Makar stared at the screen.

Whoever was behind the voice knew exactly the best way of hurting the Bratva—attack its reputation. He briefly wondered why he was being allowed a security detail. It came to him; they wanted the men where they could see them. He knew the course of action to take.

Roger Stanton wore an expensive charcoal suit. He sat in the rear of the Jaguar XJ in a secluded location overlooking the lights of London. He smiled—*my London*.

One thing Roger Stanton enjoyed more than anything else was the combination of money and power. He had both, although he could only overtly enjoy the latter. If he flaunted the wealth he had amassed over the years, there would be suspicions.

The Russians naively thought they were the ones pulling the strings but, Roger knew what he was doing. He had given them the perception of control over the most influential city in the world. They would do anything to hold on to it, including turning on one another such is the criminal mentality. He had had to accept the seventy-five million pounds for the show of it, but he planned to take so much more. He had made Ravil believe he wanted to retire.

After the Bratva took over control of the underworld, he would begin to tax them. This would be in exchange for keeping them out of the grip of law enforcement agencies, anti-terror organisations and intelligence agencies both in the UK and internationally.

Having the head of MI5 watching your back would be too much of an ace. No matter how much they tried to coerce him through blackmail, he would force them to pay, as not to do so would be strategic suicide—they needed him to retain his position. Now, there was a complication. Makar had requested a face to face meeting, and his tone had been one of insistence.

At first, Stanton suspected an assassination attempt, but Makar had allowed him to select the location and agreed to arrive alone—a small reassurance as it was.

When Stanton asked him about Ravil's whereabouts, Makar had explained that the meeting would revolve around the same question. This answer sent a bolt of concern through Stanton: *What had happened to Ravil? Was he dead or simply missing? Did another authority have him in their possession?* The first phase of their plan was underway, and the Bratva leader was needed now more than ever.

Stanton decided to wait until Makar arrived before jumping to any conclusions. One thing he had learnt in almost three decades within Britain's Intelligence Service was not to lose energy over speculation.

An aqua-blue Chrysler Crossfire pulled up beside the Jaguar, and the formidable-looking, smartly-dressed Russian got out and made his way to his vehicle. He opened the door of the Jaguar and took a seat next to him. Stanton took a breath to speak, but Makar had already begun.

"Ravil was kidnapped by an unknown team at the Blackheath golf course yesterday morning. They killed two of my men, and they have called twice today. Once was to confirm that they have Ravil in their possession and the other to agree that they would exchange Ravil for Bruce McQuillan."

Stanton could not keep the shock off his face. "How... how do we even play this with McQuillan dead?"

Makar smiled. "Bruce McQuillan isn't dead. We have him."

"Why on earth would you do something like that and keep it from me?" spat Stanton in an exasperated fury.

The Russian replied calmly, "The same reason you made me come alone to a location of your choosing— because there's a lack of mutual trust. Besides, you needn't worry. He hasn't given us anything, despite our best efforts."

Despite the Russian's calm aura Stanton could not contain his enraged panic. His voice came out strangled, louder and a few octaves higher.

"It's not just the things he knows. It's the things he's willing and capable of doing. He has friends—friends I do not even know about. If he's in any fit state, he will come after us, however long it takes. Christ, why do you think I told you to take him out before we proceeded?"

"Do not be troubled. I do not want Mr McQuillan alive any more than you do."

Stanton took a few moments to compose himself. "What do you want?"

"What do you think I want? I want support so that this goes smoothly."

"Smoothly hand over Bruce McQuillan? So you can obtain your boss?"

"Mr Stanton, please rest assured that I would rather Ravil die than Mr McQuillan be handed over alive."

Roger Stanton just stared at the Russian, and it clicked into place.

Connor looked across at the Russian's impassive face staring back at him. The man looked like a bank manager at first glance; except a bank manager would not be looking at a guy like himself with such a lack of emotion after being kidnapped. They were in the back of a Mitsubishi Delica with the seats facing one another. They did not speak.

Connor had a while before getting 'into character'. In these moments of reflection, he realised that since this began, despite the danger and the odds stacked against him, it was the happiest time of his life. Perhaps it was because of the risk and the odds against him. He knew that was only part of it, though. He was aware that systems and laws governed the world. Some were a necessity, to prevent anarchy, but others were manipulated to suit the desires of a select few. They targeted the downtrodden masses. Influential people in positions of great responsibility, who turned out to be corrupt, were the worst in his eyes.

Honour was something his father had cherished and had passed on to him. The trouble was, he knew there were very few honourable men in crime. It was all fun, games and excitement until one had to face a lengthy custodial sentence, and then true characters were proven depressingly thin on the ground. The fact the people you were protecting with your silence were unlikely to return the favour lessened one's resolve.

Still, that was not the case in the Royal Marines. It was ingrained in a Royal Marine recruit to look after his comrade or his oppo. The 'buddy-buddy' system, in which you constantly looked out for your 'buddy'. It spilt over into the day-to-day life when Marines were together. Harsh training and operational environments strengthened this philosophy. Therefore, he had accepted Louis's offer of assistance who was now driving the Mitsubishi.

Connor remembered his circle of civilian friends becoming smaller and smaller when he did not recognise that quality in them. He would keep the ones who at least entertained him. It was the reason why many former-marines could not mentally let go of the Corps. They would feel a lack of loyalty most civilians have for one another.

He thought about Roger Stanton. For a man to be the head of the nation's security service, only to collude with the very people he was meant to be protecting the country against made him break out into a cold fury. Still, now he could fight back.

They had had more success than was rational. This thrown-together team had managed to take out one of the most powerful arms dealers and kidnap the most powerful crime lord in Europe. All this while being unsure if elements of MI5 were tracking them. Still, it did not matter how many battles you won unless you won the war. That was a long way off yet.

Though Roger Stanton was the one he wanted to make suffer, he knew the Russian in front of him had caused a lot of suffering himself. He stared into Ravil's eyes and decided—*I am going to kill this cunt too.*

Roger Stanton stood in The London Library perusing some of the rarest and oldest European history books. Usually, he liked to come here for the quiet. He began flicking through a book he was not interested in borrowing—not that he was interested in borrowing any book today. He had come to see a man who had selected the library for the meeting.

"It's a classic, 'The Campaigns of Napoleon by David Chandler'. All leaders should read it," sounded a voice behind him,

"So that they don't make the same mistakes of overreaching?" answered Stanton.

"Maybe, although he will be remembered for centuries."

The MI5 chief straightened up. "Let's take a walk."

The man who fell into step alongside him was a bespectacled man of average height, early forties, wearing a tweed sweater. His physique frail and his hairline a touch receding. His demeanour was every bit the University Professor that he was. James Fisher taught Computer Sciences at the London Metropolitan University and had done since the early nineties. However, that was not all he did. Professor Fisher also provided tech support to Stanton personally for off-the-book operations.

"I have a problem that I need your help with," said Stanton cautiously.

"OK," replied Fisher.

"Ravil Yelchin has been taken by an unknown team. An exchange has been bartered for. It's due any time."

"Yes?" said Fisher.

Stanton found the professor's way of processing this kind of information without emotion startling.

"The individual in question is Bruce McQuillan."

Fisher remained silent for a moment or two and Stanton observed him—this was not processed without emotion. He knew the academic was piecing it together. Stanton was taking a gamble now. He recognised Fisher understood that he had broken the rules and lined his own pockets, but this was different. He was going to have to tell him the story, maybe not the full story, but at least some of it. He knew, as did a lot of men, the best lies had a high degree of truth to them. He would leave out the vast sum of money Ravil Yelchin had paid him. Stanton would add, when the Russian Bratva had wanted to rid the UK streets of the most dangerous criminals, he had fully intended to clear them out too. Fisher did not necessarily have to believe it entirely— he just needed to believe it enough to allow his mercenary side to overtake his conscience. Stanton always paid him well.

"Well," replied Fisher, "you best tell me the story."

"Why doesn't he just tell the PM and have done with it?" Connor asked. He was on the encrypted phone to Jaime. He rode in the front passenger seat of the Mitsubishi now with Nick driving. Louis had switched into the back with Ravil.

"He cannot just accuse the eight-year head of MI5 of treachery. You need evidence. Besides, he does not know how deep this thing goes. None of us do."

"He's about as far as it can go, isn't he? Unless you're suggesting the PM is in on it."

"No, anything is possible, but I doubt the Prime Minister is in on this. No western political leader wants to risk their term of office ending in that sort of…of *escándalo*."

"I guarantee you, if you cut the head off the snake, the body will die. It doesn't matter how long the snake is."

"We cannot just murder him in a shoot-out. This is the head of MI5. No matter how corrupt he is, he is not just some European arms dealer."

Connor thought of the adage, *'It's easier to ask for forgiveness than permission.'*

"So, how can Henry Costner help us in a practical sense?"

The unknown number lit up Makar's phone—*This was it. Whatever happened, in less than twenty-four hours this would be over.*

"Yes?" he answered.

"One A:M…That means one o'clock in the morning. There's a warehouse on the Thames. You'll be sent the exact location and grid via text, once this conversation ends. I'll allow you a security detail of six men to help with your nerves, but no more," said the confident voice. The phone call cut off. He expected the call's brevity, but the allowance of a security detail surprised him. After a moment, Makar got it. Six men present were six men accounted for—they were not able to remain in the shadows. If Makar did not provide the allowed number, then the voice on the phone would know he was planning something. He felt his phone vibrate and looked at the message that read the location and the grid reference. He turned to the seven men in his presence. The men were all compact and sharp looking. They wore civilian attire. Uniformity would have attracted attention. There was a relaxed alertness in their eyes. They were all Vors.

"That was them. I have the location. They'll change the venue at the last moment but check it out anyway."

The men dispersed.

27

Nine men alternatively stood or sat in the empty warehouse preparing for battle. Connor Reed went through the familiar routine of oiling his assault rifle. In basic training, they taught the recruits to buy cheap, plastic spray bottles for the Ox24 gun oil. He sprayed the oil over the gas parts of the weapon system. He pulled the cocking-handle back, exposing the breech and the extractor, spraying them from inside the magazine housing. Keeping the trigger depressed, he used the cocking handle to move the bolt back and forth, spreading the oil through the inside of the rifle. The action was familiar and relaxing to him. He looked around at the rest of the men and felt a sense of unease.

In addition to Carl, Louis and himself, Jaime had provided a half-dozen Dutch mercenaries. One of Louis's men had taken Nick to the hospital to have his injuries treated—but he was not told the location or the details of the plan. The mercenaries had originally been members of a Dutch Special Forces unit nicknamed 'the Black Pyjamas', who specialised in house clearing and urban combat. Connor knew why the mercenaries were not British. Dead foreign mercenaries were easier to cover up than domestic ones. When Jaime told him he was to command these men, he felt an initial fleeting sense of inadequacy. He had not been in the SBS or SAS, and these men were the Dutch equivalent. He quashed this sense.

He had had operational experience in the Royal Marines, an elite albeit conventional force. He had undergone months of training under MI5 instructors. He had helped assassinate one of the world's most prosperous arms dealers and managed to capture one the Russian Mafia's biggest crime lords. He was more than equipped for this.

In a few hours' time, this would all be over one way or another.

Makar drove in the bouncing rain that became visible in the rushing street light as it came out of the dark. He had insisted he would drive the new Mercedes S-class. He trusted his operatives, but not as much as he trusted himself. Besides, Makar had the feeling something finite was about to happen. He was very impressed. The handling was smooth with the car almost driving itself. Yet he knew he would have gotten bored after a long while. Material possessions were not his poison.

It was now 00:48. Maybe the oncoming warehouse was the place. As this faint feeling of hope settled, his phone rang.

"New location. Pausedon Docks. I'll text the details. You have twenty-five minutes exactly, or in a few months bits of him will be delivered to different Russian Embassies," said the caller's clipped voice, before hanging up. Makar pushed an intercom button.

"They have changed the location. Pausedon Docks. We have twenty-five minutes. Yuragi, start looking for any possible sniper position they might use from across the water. Andrei, begin a clearance patrol that encircles a 150-metre space around the area of the meeting."

Sometimes you could only play a poor hand as well as you could.

Connor looked out onto the black water as the street lamps cast their electric, yellow shadows across it. He doubted Makar would be on time. It would be a game to probe how far he could push him. He had already decided to give Makar a three-minute window before he began to peel parts of Ravil off, starting with his ears. A part of him knew it was inhumane and wrong. Another part of him began to wish that Makar was overly late, so he would have the excuse. If he were to die tonight, then he would have at least done something to the Bratva crime lord.

Connor was self-aware enough to see the irony in his distaste for Ravil's criminality. He was a criminal himself. Even in the Marines he had taken part in armed robberies, drug-dealer taxation, and assaulted those he considered 'bad' people. He always used to have to rationalise each one until recently—*until I set that paedophile politician on fire in the boot of the car.* That was real justice, and he doubted he would ever feel guilt over it. It had set off a chain of thoughts, which made him question just how 'Robin Hood' his crimes were. *'Every action has a reaction'* Bruce had said. Connor just had not looked that deeply into it before. He did give a lot of the stolen money away but not all of it. Also, the armed robberies he had committed or helped to commit would have an adverse effect on the economy. Not a major effect, after all, the most Connor ever got from a heist was £60,000, but he was still contributing to any downturn. The drug dealers he ripped off, he knew some of them would be embarrassed enough to keep silent. Others would not. Others would burn with humiliation— *and what does a thug do to get over a seared ego?* Violence begets violence, and there would be innocents, directly or indirectly, caught in the crossfire. There were the two men he crippled for making threats against his cousin. He remembered seeing one in a wheelchair in the centre of Leeds, being pushed by his poor, caring mother. What had she ever done to him? Apart from raising a stupid, misguided, violent kid. Maybe like his own mother had.

Connor was not too hard on himself, though. He was not a drug dealer, a pimp, a rapist, a murderer of innocents or anything else of that ilk. He had a code of honour. He had had it ever since his father had taken him to face that lovely, upstanding couple whose house he had burgled. That is why he could feel angry about all of this. It was not the bound and now hooded figure in the back of the car he was angry about. The Russian was a criminal doing what criminals do.

It was Roger Stanton. The man swore to protect these isles from threats to its security. The man who put in place a plan to help the most ruthless organised crime syndicate entrench themselves here. *All for fucking money. The treacherous, self-serving, repugnant cunt.* Connor was surprised by his own sense of emotion towards this man who he had not even met. He might—if forced—have to let Ravil go this time in exchange for Bruce McQuillan. However, he would never rest until he had put Roger Stanton in the ground. He did not care how long it took, and he would take the first opportunity to do so.

The thought faded as the black SUV came into view, on time.

Roger Stanton locked himself away in his large house in Surrey. He could not sleep and so sat in the large dining room, nursing a neat scotch with his wife dismissed to bed.

The radio on low provided a distraction. He looked out into the huge black shadows of the trees dancing on the back lawn. Time now was going to feel like an insect crawling between his brain and skull as he awaited a phone call.

Makar slowed the car to buy time—anything to give Yuragi and Andrei even an extra minute. He began to pick out the men—four of them, all wearing skull masks over their mouths and nose alongside plain black baseball caps. They were spread out with hands by their sides, but no weapons in them yet.

Makar slowed the car and stopped with a thirty-metre distance from the other car, as instructed by the message he had received from the voice. Bruce McQuillan was slumped in the back unconscious, with his hands cuffed onto the roof handle. A silenced pistol pressed into his side. The windows of the other vehicle were blacked out, as were his.

Makar got out of the vehicle. He had his first look into the eyes of the man who he instantly recognised as the leader. The man's youth surprised him. He looked in his mid-twenties. The man's eyes were not on his at first, presumably because he had not expected Makar to be driving. Makar wondered how recent any of the pictures they had of him were. The man's eyes snapped on to him and held them for a moment or two. His voice cut through the air.

"I'd want to drive it too."

"Have to take your pleasures when you can."

"My thoughts exactly. He in there?" said the man indicating to Makar's car.

"Wouldn't be much of an exchange if he wasn't. My man in there?"

"He may or may not be. You'll have to release Mr McQuillan to find out."

There was a palpable tension that rippled among the surrounding men on both sides.

"A little unfair I think. An exchange is an exchange."

"True, but you know that I want Mr McQuillan alive. I can't be sure that's your intention for Mr Yelchin here."

The intelligence of a fox, thought Makar.

"You have a suspicious mind. However, I fail to see how that affects our agreement."

"You're not having him until I have McQuillan alive, so I know that he's safe."

"The obvious question is, why should I trust you to hand Ravil over?"

"My vehicle is boxed in here. It would be difficult for my team to remain unscathed. Now, we both know my hand is stronger. McQuillan to me is a 'nice to have', Ravil Yelchin to you is a 'must have'. So, stop fucking around and get him out."

Makar knew his stalling was up. He jutted his chin to one of his men who turned towards the vehicle.

"He's unconscious, and his knee is shattered," said Makar.

"Why did you feel the need to do that?"

"Don't be naïve."

The man nodded.

Makar raised his left hand seemingly to indicate that Bruce was to be taken out of the car. The man's eyes were averted to Bruce McQuillan as he was lifted out. One of Makar's men lifted Bruce McQuillan in a fireman's carry. When he was within a few feet of the man, he made a run at the enemy leader. Just as planned, his man obscured the

329

protagonists' vision and Makar made a dive into the driver's seat of his car. The bullet smashed into his right hand, at the base of his little finger.

Carl cursed. His finger still depressed on the trigger of the sniper rifle as he watched Makar escape into the car. It seemed his entire upper left torso throbbed painfully. He should have been in a hospital bed resting. There was a huge bruise covering the left side of his chest. The Ultra High Molecular Weight Polythene had spread the impact of one of the rounds fired by the Pole, mercifully preventing it from penetrating his breast plate or even fracturing it.

Connor had managed to stitch the shoulder surprisingly well. Carl was reminded of how in an action movie, if one of the good guys were shot, it was always a flesh wound to the shoulder. He had often lamented it was unrealistic. Luckily, the wound and bruising were on the side of the hand that supported his rifle, not the side that squeezed the trigger.

There are a few techniques a rifleman, let alone a sniper, needs to employ in carrying out a good shot. His position and hold should face naturally onto the target. If there is time, the shooter will take his shot in the natural pause following an exhale. He will squeeze the trigger without anticipating the shot as opposed to snatching it. He will make sure the shot is fully followed through with his trigger finger, not relaxing it too early.

The Russian's swift movement put paid to all of this. Carl Wright had had to take a snap shot. He fired a few more, knowing it was useless. The windows did not smash. The vehicle started towards Connor and the unconscious Bruce McQuillan.

"Lock the doors," Connor screamed, as he pulled out his Glock 17.

As the Russian tried to throw Bruce onto him, he shot the gangster through the stomach. He outstretched his arm to break Bruce's fall. He pumped another few rounds into the Russian. The car came towards him. Connor hurled himself and Bruce to one side as gunfire disintegrated the quiet of the night around him. The car smashed into the vehicle that contained Ravil. Its engine whirred in reverse.

He was up, dragging Bruce a distance with him to get behind a large steel rubbish skip. Half the Dutch mercenaries leapt to the boot of the car to grab the assault rifles. The other half covered them with their now drawn pistols. The compact area erupted in noise and light. He knew what had to happen now—he had to brave exposing himself to suppress the enemy. That was the only way to win a firefight. As he looked to his right, he saw the Dutch mercenaries and Louis doing that. Louis had his own M4 assault rifle which he was firing in a three-round burst mode.

Connor's task was helped by the fact the Russians could not move due to the American's sniper fire. However, Makar had reversed the vehicle so as to give his comrades cover.

The former marine was wearing an earpiece linked with the former Ranger. The American's voice sounded in his ear, "Half left, forty-five yards."

Connor, like a meerkat, poked his head out and the pistol jolted his hand. He shot the Russian taking aim at one of the Dutch mercenaries. He snapped back behind the cover. The side of the steel skip reverberated with a hail of return fire.

"You're obsolete now. The Russians have pulled back, so your pistol is ineffective, but their assault rifles are not. Hang tight," said the sniper's calm voice in his ear.

Connor knew that all he could do was to stay and wait. His morale took a dive as Carl's voice came back on the line.

"Two more vans are about to pull up."

"Two more vans are about to pull up" warned Carl, as they screamed around the corner on the Russian's side. They pulled up, throwing out several smoke grenades. Smoke needs time to build for it to become an effective screen.

In their haste to enter the affray, the armed men poured out before the smoke could mask them. Their heads detonated into a red and pink mist as he picked them off.

The rest positioned themselves behind the vehicles, making it difficult to get clean shots. The smell of propellant filled his nose.

He caught a Russian shoulder blade as he was taking aim at the Dutch security team. He fell, exposing his head. It exploded across the floor like a red paintball as he put a round into it. All he could do from this vantage point was to suppress them and hope they exposed themselves again. It was difficult to tell which side was in ascendency as the firefight raged. He thought he heard a sound behind him and began to turn to look. Before he could, everything went a thudding black.

As smoke built, Connor could see Makar's car creep forward. The rest of the Russian criminals fired and manoeuvred in pairs behind the various boxes, metal containers and tips dotted around the area. The Russian's car smashed into the sedan, trapping a screaming Dutch mercenary underneath it and dispersing the rest.

Connor resisted the temptation to fire on the vehicle; he knew it was pointless. The Mercedes repeatedly crushed the sedan. He thought Ravil was probably dead at this point. It was confirmed when he heard the loud bang of the grenade that had been launched through the sedan's shattered window. He had known all along that Makar's priority was that Ravil could not remain captured, not that he lived.

The police sirens wailed in the near distance and Connor knew they would be forced to make an aggressive push for their second priority; Bruce. It occurred to him that if he were Makar, he would simply turn the car in his direction and run the pair of them over.

He gripped the Glaswegian under his armpits, heaving his inert body. He pushed it into the gap made by the upper edge of the huge steel rubbish skip pushed to the wall. The Mercedes turned in his direction. Connor felt a pump of adrenaline even in his already epinephrine-soaked body. He over-rode every fibre of his being to stay rooted to the spot. He pretended not to notice the vehicle now accelerating in his direction. If he moved now, the vehicle would just hunt him down. The armoured luxury car careered towards him. He waited.

At the last possible moment, he dove to his left. The Russian's vehicle crashed through heavy oak doors with wrought iron bars criss-crossing the frame. Connor scrambled for the driver's seat door, pistol in hand as the

333

car halted. The door shunted open knocking him backwards onto one knee. He brought his pistol down on aim. The Russian was already out of the car and kicked it clean out of his hand. The metal clattered away as it slid underneath another steel skip. Connor kicked the leg that the Russian was standing on. He made a scramble on top of the felled Russian. He was blocked by a raised knee.

Connor stood up a fraction of a second quicker than the larger, heavier man who was on his knees. Connor's kick to the head was deflected by steel forearms. The palms rushed up and slammed the younger man back a few paces with astonishing speed and strength. Makar made a running escape through the damaged doors of the large warehouse.

Connor quickly looked around—there was no-one. Everyone had left as the wail of the sirens drew closer to the carnage. Only Bruce McQuillan's body remained and he was not sure if the Scot was alive or not.

He did not have time to reach his pistol. If Makar was armed, then surely he would have shot him when he pushed him back before making a run for it?

He made his choice.

He pulled Bruce's body from under the skip into the open—the police would call an ambulance for him. He felt a touch of relief that Bruce seemed to stir but Connor had run out of time. He could not escape from the police carrying the Scotsman anyway.

He ran after Makar a split-second before the first police vehicle arrived on the scene. Connor chased Makar through several industrial buildings, all with a similar layout of containers, work benches and small offices.

The Russian exited through a side door across a quasi-road into a single building with the Englishman in pursuit. Connor slowed at the door suspecting a trap. He kicked the door open with his head snapping right then left as he stepped inside. Makar stood seemingly implacable facing him in a clearing in the middle of a warehouse. The building was two hundred metres away from the scene of the shootout. The warehouse was around half the size of a football pitch. Large, metallic isolation containers, around three metres tall and eight metres long, with gaps of different sizes separating them, filled the floor space. The place smelled faintly of tobacco.

"The distance we have put between us and the scene will give me enough time to kill you," said the Russian, emotionlessly.

Connor's adrenaline hit his blood stream like a high-powered motorcycle ripping through a tunnel.

"I can't think of anything 'Clint Eastwood' enough to say," he replied.

This part was always the worst part he knew. The part where it is just about to begin, and you do not know what exactly you are up against. Makar extended his arms with his hands open at chest level. His chin was down but he was upright in posture.

Connor tucked his chin so he could see the outline of his eyebrows, raised his guard and hunched his shoulders closer to his jaw.

He knew an average street fight was usually over in the first blow or two—that or else it disintegrated into an ugly brawl. It was usually too fast and shocking for a skilled martial artist to have the time and space to employ feints, footwork, head kicks and two-phase attacks.

Big, simple attacks that did not test the adrenaline-disturbed fine motor skills tended to work best—a well-delivered right hand or left hook, a smashing head butt or crushing knees. However, this was going to be a match fight—an 'anything goes' battle. He believed the Russian when he calmly stated his intention to kill him.

He swilled the saliva around his gums and breathed deeply through his nose—*be patient and do not overreach*.

He took a step forward.

His opponent was larger, heavier and maybe that would be a good thing. Perhaps he would over-commit himself to impose those advantages. No emotion showed on the Russian's features at all. Connor began to close the distance between them.

He began by feinting with a jab while stepping around the right of the Russian. He fired a jab and a short right. Makar evaded and blocked the blows. Connor decided not to risk anything but punches at this moment. He jerked his shoulder, springing forward with a three-punch combination. The last screw shot impacting on the Russian's philtrum.

Makar smiled. He nodded, seemingly to himself. Connor threw an inside leg kick at the front left leg. It missed as Makar switched into a southpaw stance. Connor felt the dull thud of a right fist on his cheek, knocking him back a step.

The Russian's next punch smashed into his right elbow which was protecting his ribs. Connor retaliated with a swift, hard right uppercut to the jaw then cannoned a vicious head butt cleanly into the face. Makar took half a step back under-hooking Connor's left armpit with his right arm and hurled him airborne. He landed with a thud and continued with the roll to create distance.

A chorus of nerves sang in him; this was the first time he had felt fear during a fight. He had experienced it, to varying degrees, before most fights but not during. Sensing the Russian's strength, quickness and technical savvy, fear bolted through him.

He overrode the negative thoughts and countered them—*He is older than you. He would not be as fit as you. Target his body. You can outlast him.*

He sprang to his feet just before Makar descended on him, punching a right fist into the solar plexus and a left hook to the ribs. He spun away, catching a slicing elbow on the top of his head. Connor felt the hot blood trickle down his head, tickling his face.

He blocked a vicious low kick with his left shin. Glanced a thumping right fist off his shoulder while swaying away. He hooked another hard left to the larger man's flank. It was evident now that the Russian wanted to overwhelm him.

They exchanged punches, kicks and knees several times. The exertions, the exhales, and the wet sounds of fists against faces echoed off the walls. Connor came off worse every time. He would land more shots but not enough to negate the weight disparity.

Makar's face showed the signs of Connor's swift and crunching punches. There was a slice under the eye, puffy cheeks and a bleeding lip. Connor knew his own injuries looked worse. There was still no sign of tension on his opponent's face.

Makar stepped forward.

They exchanged vicious kicks, punches, elbows and knees that left Connor's legs unsteady. He had never seen a man this big move this fluidly while hitting so hard.

'A good big man, will always beat a good small man', was the old boxing quote, yet he loved smashing up men much larger than himself. This man was something different. He was not just a 'run of the mill heavy'. He knew how to fight.

Connor tried a hook off the jab, both of which were blocked. He sliced a leg kick in the thigh but found himself on the receiving end of several hard blows. He held his arms tense, ducking and diving while the blows smashed his own fists and elbows into his head and body. He caught the hurtful oncoming knee, holding onto it for dear life. He drove forward with all his might like a rugby prop forward and hooked his foot around Makar's standing leg. He toppled his bear of an adversary. The piston-like legs pushed Connor away like levers, stopping him from gaining a top position. Connor levelled kicks to his thighs knowing now that if he let this machine up, he would lose.

He did not fancy grappling with him on the floor either. The way the Russian defended his attempt to mount his hips, had proven that he had at least a semblance of technical ability on the ground.

The thought flashed through his mind to run and to live to fight another day. He dismissed it—*this ends now, one way or the other.*

He went for another soccer kick, but Makar rapidly shifted his body on a tilt. The Russian's right leg hooked around Connor's left thigh with his left foot pushing on the inside of his right thigh—Connor toppled down on top of him.

Connor punched his right arm under the Russian's left leg to grip the trousers of the right. Trapping the thrashing lower limbs in place, he began to climb the body. Elbows and fists stabbed into the top of his head. Passing the hips, he jammed his knee into his opponent's solid stomach. He rose to pound away with his fists. The Sambo master simply formed a human bridge, flicking his hips and Connor was scrambling to stand again.

He heaved desperately for oxygen. The fight had lasted a while, and his adrenaline ebbed, allowing him to feel the damage. His face was hot and swollen. His thighs, especially his left, were weak and in pain. Every part of him seemed to ache. As he saw the Russian already standing, he knew he was going to lose—*therefore, I am going to die.*

He stood as straight as he could and smiled to himself. He felt serenity now—he hoped Valhalla was everything he thought it would be.

Still, he would continue to fight. He would not just accept his death willingly. He would rather die fighting for his life. 'Rage against the dying of the light' he heard from a poem somewhere.

Besides, he could not physically run now even if he wanted to.

The Russian looked into his eyes. "If your leaders had as much resolve as you, your country wouldn't be so weak. I will make this as quick as I can," he said.

"I bet you say that to every woman you fuck," replied Connor, as he took a fighting stance.

The Russian's face afforded him a small smile. "Not quite Clint Eastwood was it?"

He moved towards his prey.

His throat exploded in a geyser of blood. The echoing boom of a gunshot pierced the air. The falling Makar revealed Bruce McQuillan, leant against the back wall. Connor's pistol was in his clasped hands.

"Let's go lad" he ordered, in his familiar Scottish drawl.

28

Four Months Later

The moon glittered off the tops of the crashing waves. Roger Stanton lounged aboard his luxury yacht, nursing his brandy tumbler. The boat floated off the Northern Coast of Venezuela and was thirty-two metres in length. Powered by two CAT diesel engines, it could reach speeds of sixteen knots. It had five cabins, with the other four occupied by four members of his security team. No sense in taking an unnecessary risk. He would have preferred something larger but did not want to attract attention to himself.

Relocating to Venezuela was always the contingency plan of escape if his scheme failed. He had contacts here, a secure bank account and he spoke the language fluently. It was near the sea and the women were divine. Venezuela had a disproportionate amount of Miss World winners in comparison to its relatively small size.

He had left his wife in the UK, saying he was on secondment to Australia. It had been a marriage of convenience for a long time but he had left her enough money to get by. She did not know anything worthwhile and the house had been sanitized.

He also had insurance policies in place should he be assassinated by the UK Government; the dark, dirty secrets of very powerful men and women. These secrets were regarding people from the Cabinet, international security services and the ultra-wealthy. They were hidden in places and with people to be released in the event of an 'accident' befalling him. Bruce McQuillan had taught him that.

It was not the same as his dream of domination and power, but with millions secure in various banks he could afford to lounge around and consider his options. He would let the dust settle and eventually lever his way back in.

Right now, he could enjoy himself after decades of service. He finished off the rest of his brandy and eased himself off his lounger. He made his way to the stairs leading below deck to the bar cabinet. As he turned the corner he froze.

There lay the head of his security team, his throat cut with the pain and surprise still etched into his face. There was a rapidly expanding dark red pool emanating from beneath him. An open-mouthed Stanton turned around just in time to catch a flash of the oncoming fist.

The shivers pulsing through his body awoke Stanton.

Pain throbbed through his jaw. His head hung as he stared at his naked thighs and cock. The tourniquets excruciatingly bit into his upper right arm and above the knee of his left leg. He lifted his head and terror leapt from his stomach, internally gripping his throat as he saw the torsos of his entire security team minus their arms and legs. He felt tears water the edges of his bottom eyelids.

He heard the voice. It was a voice he recognised; well-clipped with a subtle Glaswegian drawl running through it.

"Good evening, Roger."

The terror started whirring throughout Roger's exposed body as Bruce McQuillan stepped into view. He limped a little. Stanton had never discovered what happened to Bruce after that fateful night.

"You can't... you can't kill me. There will be an avalanche of information that goes to various media outlets throughout the world and—AARRRRRGH!" Roger screamed as he felt his ear being roughly torn from behind by what felt like rusted garden shears. He watched in horror as his detached, bloody ear fell to the floor. The pain pounded the side of his head, and his jaw slackened.

"Be quiet Roger. Mr Ellis in New York, Mr Williams in Cheshire, Mr Suberov in Minsk and Mrs Taylor in Melbourne have all submitted the 'evidence' to us. There won't be an outpouring of evidence to any media outlet unless we direct it. But thank you for collecting this information for me, I do appreciate it. It will come in useful to get things moving in the right direction."

"There are others," Stanton lied desperately.

"No there aren't."

Stanton began to open his mouth again but was silenced by a bone-crunching punch. The metallic taste of iron filled the back of his throat.

Just as Roger's rapidly blinking eyelids cleared away the tears, another hand reached around and grasped his broken nose hard. He began to choke for the air that this hand was denying him. Pain pounded his face before the hand released his nose. He inhaled giant gulps of air like a landed fish.

After a few long minutes, Stanton managed to compose himself. If they wanted him dead, he would be dead by now.

"What do you want?" he asked.

"We want to know your answer to this question: Do you want to die, or do you want to live, minus one of your legs from the knee down, and one of your arms from the elbow?"

Stanton looked at Bruce in horror and bemusement.

The subtle Yorkshire brogue came from behind him. "Just to remind you, there are plenty of British Servicemen who have lost limbs in Afghanistan in service to their country, not from betraying it."

"Please… " Stanton begged.

"We'll give you a minute to decide," said Bruce. He stepped behind Stanton as he began to shake and convulse. In what seemed like an instant, Bruce stepped back in front of him.

"Time's up. Which is it?"

"Just kill me. Please, just kill me."

"Well, that's up to you. You can remove the tourniquets with the hand we'll allow you to have if that's your wish."

As Stanton looked at him with confusion the sound of a chainsaw pierced the night and echoed over the simmering water.

EPILOGUE

"Before I go I'll tell you a joke...listen...I was on the beach the other day when I saw a man frantically splashing in the water shouting 'Help, help, shark, help!'...but I just laughed...I knew the shark wasn't going to help him!" said the voice on the phone.

Rayella laughed, "Good one! Dingbat!"

"You sure you don't need it explaining to you?" the voice teased.

"I am sure."

"Good. Got to go kiddo. Congratulations again on smashing those first year exams. I am only a call away."

The call ended from Connor's end, and she put down the receiver to the house phone. Bounding the stairs to her room, she realised she was smiling—her first real smile in a long time.

The first few weeks after that day at school had been the hardest. She did not know how to tell anyone. The feeling of utter isolation even when surrounded by her school friends and family had been suffocating.

She had escaped through daydreaming about the past; to a time before it had happened and a time when her brother was alive. He would take her to the swimming pool before she could swim properly. She would kick out and laugh uproariously as his watery image slid along the pool's bottom before grabbing at her legs, pretending to be a shark.

Even escaping to that memory could not get rid of the heavy weight on her chest or the feeling of cold bleakness that now splashed her entire world.

Then Connor had visited, and she remembered the feeling of relief when telling him of what had happened—the feeling that she was a little less alone. He came down with her to tell her parents and stayed with her through their disbelief, questions, and sobs. Stayed with her when the police came to interview her. Before he left, he had told her to remember it was not her fault and some men were just sick.

He told her not to lose her faith in people.

He had written letters to her several times over the months, and these had helped lift her mood. A few weeks back she realised she had not been reading them as often—she had not needed to.

Bruce sat in the driver's seat of his BMW outside a motorway services. He nursed a flask of black coffee. He waited for Connor to finish a phone call and join him in the car.

He had picked Connor up a few hours ago from the Military Correctional Training Centre—MCTC—in Colchester, where he had spent ninety days for going *AWOL* from his unit. Bruce saw to it that he be discharged from the Royal Marines too.

Connor had vigorously protested when Bruce told him of his future detention in Colchester—*'What the fuck?! I saved your life, and now you're sending me to get marched around army style like a spaz for three months?!'* Bruce explained it was the least suspicious way he could leave the military and work for him.

The Yorkshireman had seemed in better humour upon his release, likening his time there to that of 'The A-Team', and referring to Bruce as 'Hannibal'.

Bruce flexed his reconstructed knee.

The months of pain, swelling and rehabilitation had passed. The doctors ensured that he could partake in any activity that he had before. He did not delude himself—nearly fifty years old with a resurfaced knee—his field days were over. He was almost relieved.

He saw his young apprentice put his phone in his pocket and wander back to the car. He got in and produced two empty Styrofoam cups, and said "Here, pop the coffee in them. Don't worry, I chucked a quid into the charity box."

"You've only been out a few hours, and you're already dipping into crime."

Connor sighed. "Meanwhile, back in the real world. What's going on with everything?"

"Define everything," said Bruce, starting the car and pulling away.

"Carl?"

"Handed over to our American cousins in Langley. I believe they insinuated to his family that he was still on their payroll and died in a black operation."

"What's happened with the Russians, what's going on with Nick, what's happening with your 'Ninja' group?"

Bruce joined the speeding traffic.

"With Ravil and Makar out of the equation, the London Bratva are on the back foot —they've had to agree to terms with the Turks and Albanians as it came to light they were behind the murder of Hassan Saki."

"I wonder how they found that out," said Connor rhetorically.

"Quite. Nicholas has left my team though I said he could stay. He's working close protection for a Saudi Prince now."

"That was magnanimous of you after what he did."

"He had his reasons," Bruce sipped his coffee, "and I, with Mr Costner's and Mr Parker's influence, have the now official position of 'Chief Liaison Officer' between MI5 and MI6. Meaning, someone else must take the lead on being the man on the ground."

"Congratulations. Who's my new boss?"

Bruce looked at him. "You're going to be that man on the ground."

Lines appeared from Connor's eyebrows. "I can't do that—I am twenty-six."

"Aye well, you didn't think you could do a lot of things until you did them. Don't panic, I'll be here to hold your hand for a bit."

"What about the rest of your lads?"

"They know what you did and respect that. Yer'll still need to prove your worth, though."

Connor was quiet for a few moments. "What if I wanted to bring Louis in?"

"It's your team. We might be able to work something out."

They drove listening to the radio for a while. They were on the M25 making their way to Oxford. Bruce had procured Connor a flat there.

"Was you on the phone to a lassie before?" asked Bruce.

"Yeh but not like that. It was Rayella."

"How is she?"

"Her Mum says she seems better now. She sounded chirpier over the phone. How she passed her eleven plus exams back then while coping with what she has been through I will never know."

"She's made of stern stuff," said Bruce. "It's good you looking after her. Brings balance to your life."

"What do you mean balance?"

Bruce looked at him, "Lessens your karmic debt a wee bit."

"You still believe in that?" said Connor shaking his head, "As far as I have been led to believe, you have spent your life trying to protect people from criminals and terrorists. Yet you were tortured for days and shot through the knee cap. What did you do to deserve that?"

"It may be years before you are ready to hear this but violence, doesn't matter how well intentioned it is, is still violence —it always comes back on you."

Connor narrowed his eyes. "Then what the fuck are we doing?"

Bruce thought for a moment. "We are buying humanity time to get its act together."

AUTHOR'S REQUEST

Please leave a review of The Bootneck

As a self-published author, Amazon reviews are vital for me getting my work out as many readers as possible.

By reviewing it means I can continue to write these books for you.

Thank you so much

Quentin Black

The Bootneck Review

GLOSSARY

Actions on— Predetermined procedures that are to be carried out if certain events were to occur during the missions.

ACRO— ACPO (Association of Chief of Police Officers) Criminal Records Office.

AWOL— Absent without Leave.

Bergen— Large rucksack used in the military.

Brass up— UK military slang for shoot a target or person(s).

Career laugh— A fake laugh designed to further your standings on the career ladder. Used primarily to laugh at superior's jokes and vaguely funny comments so you keep in their favour.

Centre line— Imaginary line projecting directly forward of the opponent; to be off the centre is to place one's self at an advantageous angle of attack.

Checking kicks— The most common defence against a low kick is known as 'checking', where the leg is bent and brought up to protect the thigh. This causes the kicker to slam their shin into the defending fighter's shin or knee.

Chuck Up— Royal Marine slang for compliment or honour for work.

Dickers— Originally a slang term given to IRA lookouts by the British military. Some use it to describe hostile lookouts of any operational area.

Dit— British military slang for 'a story' i.e. 'Spin us the dit'—tell me the story.

DPM— Disruptive Pattern Material

Eejit— Scottish slang for idiot.

Enforcer— A man-portable cylindrical battering ram used for forced entry into buildings and rooms.

Figure eleven— Standard man-sized target used by the British Infantry and Royal Marines on the shooting ranges. Made of wood thus the phrase, *'You're not a Figure eleven'* equates to 'You're not made of wood'.

Fish-hooking— Inserting the fingers inside the opponent's mouth and pulling. Done with the intention of tearing the surrounding tissue.

Flap— To panic i.e. flap like a headless chicken.

Flashbang— A non-lethal grenade which is used to disturb the senses of enemies by its loud noise and its bright light.

(The) Grey Man— To play 'the Grey man', is to act and dress in an inconspicuous manner to blend into the background.

GROM— Poland's elite counter-terrorism unit.

Jack— Royal Marine slang for putting yourself before others. Singularly the worst name to be tarnished with within the Corps.

Kes— 1969 film drama about a fifteen-year-old boy from Barnsley.

Kubotan— is a genericized trademark for a self-defence weapon developed by Sōke Takayuki Kubota in the late 1960s. It is typically no more than 5.5 inches (14 centimetres) long and about half an inch (1.25 centimetres) in diameter, slightly thicker or the same size as a marker pen. The material is usually of a hard high-impact plastic.

Mong— One lacking in intelligence, with **Turbo-Mong** meaning one really lacking in intelligence.

Omerta— A code of silence about criminal activity and a refusal to give evidence to the police.

Oppo— An affectionate term for a friend within the Corps—an opposite number.

Pinged— Derived from the sound the World War Two submarine detector made when a submarine was identified. In Royal Marine and Navy parlance, it means to be found out, or 'volunteered'.

Point— Pointman, as in the first man.

Pre-recorded— A mortars term. A mortar is a barrel used for firing bombs at high trajectory and usually at long distances. Long enough that grids had to be used rather than just aiming them at the target. When the mortar fire was 'brought on' to the target sometimes the grid was marked and recorded. If the enemy engaged from that position again, the mortar fire can be fired immediately without the necessary adjustments having to be remade. This was called a 'Pre-recorded target'. Royal Marines also used the term for women they had already had sex with and knew they would be willing to do so again.

Pussers stamps— In the Royal Marines, the word 'Pusser' was often put in front of words to indicate a belonging to the Ministry of Defence. Pussers stamps were a pseudonym for tattoos denoting military service.

Rolling— Originally from the Brazilian Jiu-Jitsu slang 'rolar', to engage in BJJ practice.

Shit-bloke— A man who is professionally inept.

Side-winded—To attack an unsuspecting victim from the side.

Stop-short— A military tactic used for stopping and remaining still for a period of time to detect any follow up from the enemy.

Spacers— A non-alcoholic drink consumed between alcoholic drinks, intended to limit intoxication. A 'spacer' will often be disguised as an alcoholic drink.

Stacked— Well-built and muscular.

SVR— tr. Sluzhba Vneshney Razvedki—Foreign Intelligence Service of the Russian Federation.

Teep— A front push-kick used in Muay Thai predominately as a defensive technique.

Vale Tudo— A Portuguese term that translates to 'anything goes'; derived from the full contact unarmed combat events that were first made popular in Brazilian circuses in the 1920's.

Vittle up (or brass up)— UK military slang for shoot a target or person (s).

Vor (Vor v Zakone)— Thief (Thief in Law)—an elite position with the Russian Bratva, like being 'made' within the Sicilian and Italian-American Mafia.

NEXT BOOK

Available on Amazon

The following is the first chapter of Quentin Black's follow up novel—*Lessons in Blood*

1

She spent a few minutes in that state between unconsciousness and being awake. Finally, her eye lids fought against the light before relaxing open. She recognised first the smell of the hyper cleanliness of a hospital. The sterile white interior and the thin, plastic cannula tube emerging from the back of her hand confirmed it.

She searched her memory for how she came to being here but found nothing. Her memory had often not co-operated in the past haze of alcohol and drugs. In those instances the recollection used to taunt her from the recesses of her mind. This was different—there was nothing at all, and uneasiness coursed through her.

Pain throbbed in her lower abdomen. Her shaking hands gingerly lift away the white sheeting. The twelve-inch blood-concealed scar circled her navel like black insulated wire. The searching of her memory became a frantic racking—*Jesus, what did I do to myself this time?*

Her breath began to come in exasperated spurts. After a few moments, the curtains to her left were drawn back to reveal a white surgeon's uniform wrapped around a smiling middle-aged gentleman. His hair, seemingly confused as to be either grey or white, highlighted his artificially orange-tinted skin. The tan emphasized perma white teeth.

"Easy Miss. How are you feeling?"

"Where am I?"

"You are in Braeson Private Hospital. You were found by social workers unconscious in a derelict house in Hackney three days ago. They brought you here, fortunately," the smile seemed painted on.

This information calmed her a little; it sounded depressingly likely, and that she was fortuitous for where she now lay.

"Have I been stabbed?" she asked. That too seemed a dark possibility.

"No," replied the white coat as he picked out a file from an acrylic holder at the end of her bed, "after initial tests were performed, an emergency nephrectomy was performed due to your kidney being irreparably damaged."

"A nephrectomy?" her eyebrows squashed vertical lines between themselves, "that's impossible. I had a full physical by the London Bridge Hospital less than two weeks ago. All the tests came back clear?"

The coat's expression now matched her own,

"London Bridge Hospital?" he said, repeating the name of London's largest and award-winning private hospital.

"Yes, my father insisted after I came out of rehab"

The man eyed her warily, "Who is your father?"

"Ahem, Darren O'Reilly."

"Darren O'Reilly? Where have I heard that name before?"

"He owns Verbatum Cyber Securities."

"I see," the man replied, "excuse me."

During his absence, the question began to turn over in her head constantly—*Could I have really irreparably damaged a kidney in twelve days?*

Could she have been struck in one of her heroin-induced comas? Her boyfriend was many things but he had never been violent towards her; probably because he was high more often than not. She, with money siphoned off her credit cards and cash allowances from her father, had kept the pair of them in their preferred drug-induced state throughout their dalliance.

The gentleman in the white coat returned. She felt threatened without understanding why. His smile had gone. He reached up behind her and she saw him turn on a valve.

"Excuse me, what is this? What you doing."

In response, she felt his palm press down on her chest. No sooner had she begun to thrash, it seemed like she was laying in an invisible vat of honey. Her eyes felt like they were sinking into their sockets before her vision blurred into black.

2

The tall, broad-shouldered Bruce McQuillan sat relaxed but straight-backed in the mahogany tufted chair. His striped shirt ran flat down his still trim physique with the dark trousers finishing with subtly patterned brown lace-up shoes.

The soft yellow of the various lighting dotted around the room illuminated the dark reds and browns of the interior.

This was one of London's most exclusive private men's clubs and thus Bruce was unsurprised at the other patrons' surreptitious glances; he was an outsider, and glad to be so. However, his companion's presence assuaged any hostility towards him; MP Henry Costner was fully enmeshed within the establishment.

The Glasgow-born Bruce and the Eton-educated Henry had forged an unlikely alliance in harsh times over a year ago.

Henry dressed in contrast to his role in the upper echelons of Parliament, and more out of the pages of GQ. His shirt, intricately chequered white and blue, contrasted with his light blue suit. The forty-year old's blond hair verged on foppish atop his youthful face.

"How are you Bruce? How are you dealing with the bureaucracy of your new official role?" asked Henry.

"A necessary evil. An evil nonetheless."

"You miss being under the radar?"

Bruce's past involvement in UK security would never officially be acknowledged. The activities of the clandestine unit known to a select few as 'The Chameleon

Project' was far too sensitive. However, in order to provide his unit more top cover, Bruce and Henry had agreed that a more official role within the British Security services was appropriate. Through various petitioning and leveraging, Bruce received the role and title of 'Chief Liaison Officer between MI5 and MI6'.

"It had its advantages," said Bruce taking a sip of his black coffee, "what do you need Henry?"

Henry inclined his head as he regarded Bruce, "I do not know why I am a little offended at your correct assumption that this isn't merely a social meeting."

"If that was the case you'd invite me to an establishment that permits the presence of women."

Henry nodded slightly, "Ah, I see"

"And so?"

"Do you know of a Darren O'Reilly?"

"Owner of Verbatum Cyber Securities Darren O'Reilly?"

"What do you know about him?"

"Created cyber security systems seemingly years ahead of their time. They have been taken up by Government contractors and commercial businesses alike. Personal wealth well past the half a billion pound mark. Gives generously to charity."

Bruce saw Henry resist the urge to look around furtively; the Scot had told him off for doing so in past meetings.

The politician began, "Darren O'Reilly, also a generous donor to various power players in Government. It was his financial contributions to the last election campaign that kept the Prime Minister in power. The man has many important friends."

"Go on."

"His Daughter Jessie was found dead in a drugs den in South-East London. Overdosed on a drug named Fentanyl."

Bruce had been aware of the girl's death and of how O'Reilly had used his influence to keep the circumstances out of the press.

He also knew of the increase of Fentanyl on the streets in recent months. The synthetic opioid analgesic gave off an effect similar to morphine, except it had fifty to a hundred times the potency.

"Then Mr O'Reilly has my condolences"

"Mr O'Reilly had a private autopsy done Bruce," replied Henry sipping his Scotch, "she was a day removed from kidney removal that she apparently didn't need."

"So we're not talking about some kind of macabre tearing out of the kidney. You're talking about a nephrectomy?"

"Yes."

Bruce nodded, "What did the police say?"

"They determined that Ubaid Almasi, an Egyptian national, with a proclivity for raping, killing and then mutilating young girls to be responsible. An addict, he was found dead in his flat in Luton. Heroin overdose—laying in the bath for a week. He had detailed the murders, including Jessie O'Reilly's, in a diary."

Bruce rubbed his chin, "This apparent savage kept a diary?"

"Yes."

"Where was it found?"

"Under his mattress."

Bruce paused for a second, "Police ruled out any foul play?"

"Yes."

360

"How did the police come to track down Almasi to the murders? DNA, witnesses, CCTV what?"

"I am not sure."

"OK, and Mr O'Reilly doesn't accept that Almasi was her killer."

"How do you know that?"

"Because you've brought me here to ask me to look into it for your friend, the 'Old Boys' Club in action."

Henry sighed, "She was a young girl Bruce, and he's a grieving father."

Bruce liked Henry on the whole but still—*he was forever the politician.*

"A grieving father who is also one of the richest men on the Isles, is he not?"

Henry looked at Bruce for a few moments before shrugging. "Well, yes. O'Reilly came to me with his concerns. He did not wish to continue down the more traditional route of justice."

"I see," Bruce stared, "meaning he wanted the real culprits to pay with their lives and not a lengthy custodial sentence…and you told him you knew just who to come to?"

Henry gave him a rueful look. "Bruce, I haven't mentioned you by name."

The Scotsman finished his coffee, "Where does he want to meet me?"

"How do you know he wants to meet you?"

"A businessman like Mr O'Reilly would never pour his money into an investment without knowing exactly how it is to be used, however upset he may be."

Henry blinked a couple of times, "He says he's happy to meeting you at his home. You know it doesn't have to be you who meets him, given your new 'legitimate' status so to speak."

361

Bruce thought of the men and women within the Project who could handle this. And then he thought of his quasi-protégé before dismissing him; despite all his promise, Connor Reed still had some rough edges—a ferociously smashing hammer not yet fashioned into a razor sharp, efficiently wielded blade. No, he had to look into this personally, besides, his favoured agent had enough on his plate for now, especially tonight.

"I'll meet him. Midday tomorrow."

Waseem Khan sat in the back of the Jaguar XJ, his ring-adorned fingers tapping on his knee. The stillness of the night amplified a growing impatience. His shifted his bulk amid the leather interior, the fabric of his grey shalwar kemeez crinkling. Waseem, now forty-three, had possessed a physique of a fine cricketer almost a decade ago.

However, the influx of money and notoriety had stripped away the desire of hard physical exertion and a temperance of diet. Women, respect and fear were bought now.

He watched his two hulking bodyguards approvingly—they were an advertisement of his status. They stood on a white carpet of snow, cutting menacing silhouettes in the dim glow of the deserted industrial estate. Rashid Kumar and Varun Singh, were feared within the Asian community in Birmingham and the City's underworld.

Both stood over six feet two inches tall with their black leather jackets straining to accommodate their steroid-ramped physiques. Rashid was particularly feared — the eighteen stone, black-bearded and dark-eyed gangster had a fondness for machetes. His victims were walking testaments of the handiwork.

Waseem felt safe despite awaiting the arrival of two business associates he had yet to meet in the flesh. His abhorrence for direct interactions with outsiders in his illegal businesses had meant that the two men had dealt with his son Imran.

The partnership had been a successful one with a steady supply of quality ecstasy, MDMA and weed coming his way for eleven months now.

Imran had gotten himself locked up after being caught in a drug deal that he had no business being directly involved in.

Nevertheless, the two men — one white and one black — had made it known to him that not only did they wish for the relationship to continue, but they wanted to increase the trade.

Lights of a vehicle of this year's model of a light blue Audi TT illuminated the area. They dimmed before hitting the Jaguar. Waseem saw his two guards stiffen.

The Audi came into the bowling alley's carpark a distance away. It slowed to a glide before halting. After a few moments two men alighted. Waseem's eyes snapped to the driver; around the same height and build; this black man's physicality seemed to have an effect on the bodybuilders' posture.

Waseem could sense their unease from within his car.

Waseem knew the driver's name to be Louis Allen — the leader of The Southwark Union Gang. The SUG stood as an amalgamation of several Peckham gangs under Allen's leadership. The UK underground had been suitably impressed with the feat. Impressed and disconcerted at the gang's power.

He wore a dark blue Puffa jacket with black pants stretching over a pair of bulky legs before concertinaing at the trainers. Two or three days of bristle covered his strong jaw, with his hair not being much longer.

Waseem turned his attention to his companion, a Northerner by the name of Reed. He was of medium height, short sandy brown hair, with a face of symmetrical features. The blue eyes seemed full of wry amusement. He wore a dark green, thin leather jacket with a black t-shirt, dark blue jeans with brown boots.

Waseem observed Rashid and Varun beginning to fidget and then gesticulate. The newcomers remained still and staring. When his curiosity overcame him, he got out of the Jaguar and walked over.

"What's the problem gentlemen?" asked Waseem, directing his question towards Rashid.

"They refused to be searched"

"Gentlemen?"

Louis answered with his voice riveted with South-East London street, "I'll open my jacket so you can check for burners an' blades, but you buzzin' if you think anyone is putting their hands on me"

"But ya see why a man in my position would prefer it if you were searched given what we are here to discuss?"

The faintly coarse but well-clipped voice of Connor answered, "Of course we do. If you insist then you insist, but we'll have to insist on searching all three of you in turn. It's entirely up to you?"

Waseem allowed his Birmingham accent to become stronger, he found it disarmed people, "I fink we can dispense with that. There's naaa need ter get upset"

"This white man would be nothing without this gorilla," sneered Rashid in Punjabi, while looking at Connor.

"Calm yourself," replied Waseem in the same tongue, before addressing Connor and Louis, "ter business gentlemen"

"We gotta a case. In it is some Malcoms, white lady, and crow," said Louis.

"Alright?"

"You're going to take it and sell it"

Waseem glanced at his henchmen before answering, "I didn't bring any testing equipment. I am not paying for a product before I know its value."

"We didn't ask for money Mr Khan—at least not yet. After the feedback you'll receive from your fiends, astro-travellers and psychonauts, you'll ask for more. That's when we'll discuss payment for this and further packages"

There was silence before Waseem answered, "What's ter stop me from taken this an' never dealing with you again?"

Connor raised his jaw a little, "Then you will have lost a supply of the best product you'll ever come across. You are too shrewd a businessman to let that happen. That's why we have given you first refusal and not to your friends down at the snooker club"

Waseem pursed his lips at the Yorkshireman's reference to his main rivals for the city's drug trade. Their base of operations was one of Birmingham's biggest snooker clubs.

"OK, it is a deal —where is the case?"

Connor walked back to the Audi before opening up the boot and returning with the case. He set it down beside his foot.

"Now Mr Khan. We were going to give you this case for free," said Connor, "but that was before your man there said something along the lines of, 'that white bastard wouldn't be anything without that gorilla here' —there or there abouts —and I am sure a man of honour such as yourself can see that I can't allow that to pass. So him and I are going to fight. If he wins then you'll never have to pay for this case. Understand?"

There was tension-laced silence.

Waseem's mind whirled trying to look for any deception—any downside for him. He had never known a white man to understand Punjabi to that extent. Rashid dwarfed this man by four stone easily; surely he would not lose.

Still, there was not a hint of fear in the Northerner's voice.

"What if you win?" Waseem asked.

"Then I'll have had the pleasure of correcting his frankly rude manner," he replied, "just one condition, the fight is over when the winner says it is."

There were a few moments silence before Waseem nodded his head, "Seems reasonable," before looking towards Rashid.

He found his enforcer's wide eyes burrowing into the smaller man's, before he said, "You're fookin' dead gora."

ABOUT THE AUTHOR

+ Follow

Follow me on Amazon to be informed of new releases and my latest updates.

Quentin Black is a former Royal Marine corporal with a decade of service in the Corps. This includes an operational tour of Afghanistan and an advisory mission in Iraq.

AUTHOR'S NOTE

Join my exclusive readers clubs for information on new books, deals, and free content in addition my sporadic reviews on certain books, films and TV series I might have enjoyed.

Plus, you'll be immediately sent a **FREE** copy of the novella *An Outlaw's Reprieve.*

Remember, before you groan 'Why do I always have to give my e-mail with these things?!', you can always unsubscribe, and you'll still have a free book. So, just click below on the following link.

Free Book

Any written reviews would be greatly appreciated. If you have spotted a mistake, I would like you to let me know so I can improve reader experience. Either way, contact me on my e-mail below.

Email me

Or you can follow me on social media here:

The Bootneck

How far would you go for a man who gave you a second chance in life?

Bruce McQuillan leads a black operations unit only known to a handful of men.

A sinister plot involving the Russian Bratva and one of the most powerful men within the British security services threatens to engulf the Isles.

Could a criminal with an impulse for sadism be the only man McQuillan can trust?

Lessons In Blood

When the ruling class commoditise the organs of the desperate, who will stop them?

When Darren O'Reilly's daughter is found murdered with her kidney extracted, he refuses to believe the police's explanation. His quest for the truth reaches the ears of Bruce McQuillan, the leader of the shadowy Chameleon Project.

As a conspiracy of seismic proportions begins to reveal itself, Bruce realizes he needs a man of exceptional skill and ruthlessness.

He needs Connor Reed.

Ares' Thirst

Can one man stop World War Three?

When a British aid worker disappears in the Crimea, the UK Government wants her back—quickly and quietly.

And Machiavellian figures are fuelling the flames of Islamic hatred towards Russia. With 'the dark edge of the world' controlled by some of the most cunning, ruthless and powerful criminals on earth, McQuillan knows he needs to send a wolf amongst the wolves before the match of global war is struck across the rough land of Ukraine.

Northern Wars

The Ryder crime family are now at war...on three fronts.

After ruthlessly dethroning his Uncle, Connor Reed must now defend the family against the circling sharks of rival criminal enterprises.

Meanwhile, Bruce McQuillan, leader of a black operations unit named The Chameleon Project, has learnt that one of the world's most brutal and influential Mafias are targeting the UK pre-BREXIT.

Can Connor Reed survive his deadliest mission yet?

Bruce McQuillan's plan to light the torch of war between two of the world's most powerful and ruthless Mafias has been ignited.

Can his favoured agent, Connor Reed, fan the flames without being engulfed by them?

Especially as a man every bit his equal stands on the other side.

An Outlaw's Reprieve

"When there is no enemy within, the enemies outside cannot hurt you."

Reed, a leader within his own outlaw family, delights in an opportunity to punish a thug preying on the vulnerable.

However, with his target high within a rival criminal organisation, can Reed exact retribution without dragging his relatives into a bloody war.

The Puppet Master

For the first time in history, humanity has the capacity to destroy the world.

When a British scientist leads a highly proficient Japanese engineering team in unlocking the secrets to the biosphere's survival, some will stop at nothing to see the fledging technology disappear.

In the Land of the Rising Sun, can Bruce McQuillan protect the new scientific applications from the most powerful entities on earth?

And can his favoured agent Connor Reed defeat the deadliest adversary he has ever faced?

A King's Gambit

Can the Ryder clan defeat a more ruthless organization that dwarfs them in size and finance?

When the **dark hands of a blood feud** between Irish criminal organizations begin to choke civilians, and strategies to halt the evil fail, fear grips law enforcement in the United Kingdom, the Republic of Ireland and continental Europe.

When this war ensnares the Ryder clan, Connor finds with the choice between trusting the skill and mental fortitude of untested family members, along with the motives of his enemy's enemy.

Or the complete **annihilation of his family.**

Printed in Great Britain
by Amazon

31886513R00212